Praise for t

"The most heartwarming ... ...cu, literally explosive space opera I've enjoyed in a long time. Martha Wells is the best writer of lovable snarky gender-subversive killing machines out there!" —N. K. Jemisin

"We are all a little bit Murderbot." —NPR

"If you need something light, a little violent, and laugh-out-loud hilarious, dive into this series: You may find that you have more in common with Murderbot than you think." —Liz Braswell, *The Wall Street Journal*

"Readers won't miss the wall-to-wall action that defined the series from its beginning. The characters and the world-building remain engrossing and rewarding." —*Booklist* (starred review)

"I might have a little bit of a thing for a robot. Its name is Murderbot.... *Network Effect* [is] great." —*Wired*

"I can think of no better company than this paranoid android." —*New Scientist*

"Murderbot, with its on-point observations and addictive interior monologues, is easily one of my favorite characters in SF.... Highly recommended." —Charles de Lint, *The Magazine of Fantasy & Science Fiction*

"I could read about Murderbot all *week*." —*Locus*

ALSO BY MARTHA WELLS

THE MURDERBOT DIARIES

VOL. 3

FUGITIVE TELEMETRY

SYSTEM COLLAPSE

MARTHA WELLS

TOR PUBLISHING GROUP

NEW YORK

THE MURDERBOT DIARIES VOL. 3

Fugitive Telemetry copyright © 2021 by Martha Wells
System Collapse copyright © 2023 by Martha Wells

A Tordotcom Book
Published by Tom Doherty Associates / Tor Publishing Group
120 Broadway
New York, NY 10271

www.torpublishinggroup.com

Tor® is a registered trademark of Macmillan Publishing Group, LLC.

ISBN 978-1-250-38984-8 (trade paperback)

Our books may be purchased in bulk for promotional, educational, or business use. Please contact your local bookseller or the Macmillan Corporate and Premium Sales Department at 1-800-221-7945, extension 5442, or by email at MacmillanSpecialMarkets@macmillan.com.

First Edition: 2025

Printed in the United States of America

0   9   8   7   6   5   4   3   2   1

Fugitive Telemetry

Chapter One

THE DEAD HUMAN WAS lying on the deck, on their side, half curled around. A broken feed interface was scattered under the right hand. I've seen a lot of dead humans (I mean, a lot) so I did an initial scan and compared the results to archived data sets, like human body temperatures vs. ambient temperature, lividity, and various other really disgusting things involving fluids that happen when humans die. This was all data I still had in longterm storage. The comparison let me estimate a time of death. I said, "Four hours, approximately."

Dr. Mensah exchanged a look with Senior Officer Indah. Dr. Mensah's expression was dry. Senior Indah looked annoyed, but then she always looked like that when I was around. She said, "How do you know?"

I converted my scan data, my query, and the comparison results into a report that humans could read and sent it to her feed address, with a copy to Mensah. Indah blinked, her gaze turning preoccupied as she read it. Mensah acknowledged the report as received, but kept watching Indah, one eyebrow raised. (I was still using scan and visual to examine the scene, but I had a task group of my new intel drones circling above my head, supplying me with video.)

We were in a junction in the Preservation Station mall, a circular space where three small corridors met, one a short passage that led through to a large secondary main corridor: the Trans Lateral Bypass. (All the corridors here had names, a Preservation tradition that was only mildly annoying.) This was not a well-traveled junction, whatever its name was; it was mostly a shortcut to get from a residential area to a work area. (On this station there was no separation between transient spaces and longterm station housing like on stations in the Corporation Rim, but that wasn't even close to being the weirdest thing about Preservation.)

This junction, and Preservation Station in general, were also weird places for humans to get killed; the threat assessment for both transients and station residents was low anyway, and mostly involved accidents and cases of intoxication-related stupidity/aggression in the port area. In this specific junction, threat assessment for accidental death was even lower, close to null. There was nothing here except the lights in the high ceiling and the standard silver-blue textured wall panels, marked with some old graffiti and drawings that were actually being preserved as part of a station-wide history exhibit. I guess if you were really determined, you could find a way to get yourself killed by exposing the power connectors under the panels and shielding and, I don't know, licking them or something, but this dead human clearly hadn't.

The full station threat assessment for murder was sitting at a baseline 7 percent. (To make it drop lower than that we'd have to be on an uninhabited planet.) (I've never been on a contract on an uninhabited planet because if I was on the planet on a contract then we'd be inhabiting it.) You never found dead humans lying around on the floor like this.

"Well," Indah began, having finally finished reading the report. (I know, it takes humans forever.) "I don't know how accurate this is—"

Another security person walked in, one of the techs who normally worked on checking cargo shipments for biohazards, feed ID Tural. They said, "Our scan analysis says the victim's been dead for about four hours."

Indah sighed. Tech Tural, who had obviously expected this information to be greeted a little more enthusiastically, was confused.

"ID?" I said. The dead human's interface was broken so I couldn't pull anything off it. If whoever did it had been trying to conceal the dead human's identity, were they naively optimistic? Preservation Station kept an identity record and body scan for permanent residents and every disembarking transient passenger, so it shouldn't be that hard to run an identity check. "Known associates?"

Tural glanced at Indah and she nodded for them to answer. They said, "There was no subcutaneous marker or clip or augment or anything else with ID. We've done an initial search on recent arrival passenger lists using physical details, but couldn't come up with anything." At Indah's dissatisfied expression, Tural added, "Without an interface, we have to wait until Medical gets here to do the body scan so we can try to match it with the visitor entry logs."

Indah said, "And Medical isn't here yet because . . . ?"

Tural's face formed an anticipatory wince. "It's preventative health check day at the school and the bot who normally does the mobile body scan is busy with that? It has to move the mobile medical suite they use?"

Humans do the "make it a question so it doesn't sound so bad" thing and it still sounds bad.

Indah did not look pleased. Mensah's mouth twitched in an "I would like to say things but I am not going to" way. Indah said, "Did you tell them this was an emergency?"

Tural said, "Yes, but they said it was an emergency until the onsite medic pronounced the person dead/unrevivable, after that it went to the end of the list of non-emergency things they have to do."

Preservation has to make everything complicated. And that's not a metaphor for my experience here. Okay, yes, it is a metaphor.

Indah's jaw went tight. "This is a murder. If whoever did this kills someone else—"

Mensah cut her off. "I'll call them and explain that it's not an accidental death, and yes, it is an emergency and we need them here now." She looked toward the body again, her brow furrowed. "The council closed the port and deployed the responder as soon as we got the alert, but are you certain this person is—was—a visitor and not a resident?"

The responder was the armed ship currently on picket duty, discouraging raiders from approaching the station and rendering assistance as needed to local and transient shipping. With the port closed, it would be out there keeping any docked or undocked transports from leaving until the council ordered otherwise.

Tural admitted, "Actually no, Councilor. We're just guessing that they're a visitor."

"I see." Mensah's expression was not critical, but I can tell you the face she was making did not indicate that she thought Tural or Indah or anybody in the immediate area was doing a great job. It was obvious Station Security was out of its collective depth here. (At least it was obvious to me.)

Indah must have known that too because she rubbed the bridge of her nose like her head hurt. She was short for a Preservation human, a little lighter brown than Mensah and maybe a little older, but with a solid square build that looked like she could punch someone pretty effectively. That probably wasn't why she was senior security officer, which was more of an admin job. She told Tural, "Just keep trying to make an ID."

Tural left with the air of escaping before things got worse. Mensah's eyebrow was still aimed at Indah and it was getting pointed. (Not really. It's hard to describe, you had to see it.) Indah made a hands-flung-in-the-air gesture and said, "Fine, let's go talk about this."

Mensah led us away from the incident scene and out to the Trans Lateral Bypass. It was wide, with a high arched ceiling that projected a series of holo views of the planet's surface as if you were looking up through a transparent port. It was an offshoot of the main station mall, a thoroughfare to a section of service offices, with branches into supply areas. Traffic was minimal here right now, but a bot that worked for the station was out with a glowing baton, directing humans, augmented humans, and drone delivery floaters away from the junction entrance and Station Security's equipment. The group of security officers standing there tried to pretend they weren't watching us. Mensah's two council assistants who had walked down with us were watching the security officers critically.

The bot could have engaged a privacy shield but Mensah and Indah just stepped behind a large plant biome with giant paddle-shaped leaves that was screening the entrance to a food service place. (A feed marker in multiple languages and a colorful sign in Preservation Standard Nomenclature indicated it was called "Starchy Foods!!!" and noted that it was closed for its cycle rest period.)

It was relatively private, but I had my drones scan for any attempt to focus a listening device on us. Indah faced me and asked, "You have experience at this?"

Watching her via the drones, I kept my gaze on the Starchy Foods!!! sign, which had little dancing figures around it which I guess were supposed to be starchy foods. I said, "With dead humans? Sure."

Mensah's pointed eyebrow was now aimed at me. She tapped my feed for a private connection. I secured it and she sent, *Do you think this is GrayCris?*

Ugh, maybe? Right now all we had was an anomalous death with no indication of a connection to Mensah or any of my other humans that GrayCris might want to target. I told her, *I don't have enough data to make an assessment yet.*

Understood. Then she added, *I want you to work on this with Station Security. Even if it isn't anything to do with our corporate problems, it's a good opportunity for you.*

Double ugh. I told her, *They don't want me.* (Hey, I don't want me, either, but I'm stuck with me.) And it would be easier for me to investigate on my own, particularly if my investigations led to me having to do things like disposing of abruptly dead GrayCris agents.

(No, I didn't kill the dead human. If I had, I wouldn't dump the body in the station mall, for fuck's sake.)

She said, *If you want to stay in the Preservation Alliance, improving your relationship with Station Security will help immeasurably. This might lead to them hiring you as a consultant.*

Mensah didn't usually take the "this is for your own good, you idiot" tone, so the fact that she had meant she really thought it was a good idea. Also, I'm not an idiot, I knew she was right. But it wasn't like I could leave Preservation yet, anyway, even if I didn't like it and it didn't like me. My threat assessments were still rising steadily. (I had an input on my threat assessment module continuously now so I could get real-time updates instead of just checking it periodically, and yes, it was a constant source of irritation because it reacted to everything. No, it was not helping my anxiety. But it was necessary.)

Station Security had been briefed on the danger from GrayCris but I trusted them as much as they trusted me. (Surprise, it was not very much.) And they had no experience with corporate attacks. Their job was mostly accident first response and maintaining safety equipment and scanning for illegal hazardous cargo, not repelling assassination attempts. They didn't even patrol outside the port.

Indah watched us with an acerbic expression that indicated she knew we were talking privately on the feed. Mensah was still eyebrow-glaring at me so I answered Indah's question. "Yes, I've had experience with investigating suspicious fatalities in controlled circumstances."

Indah's gaze wasn't exactly skeptical. "What controlled circumstances?"

I said, "Isolated work installations."

Her expression turned even more grim. "Corporate slave labor camps."

I said, "Yes, but if we call them that, Marketing and Branding gets angry and we get a power surge through our brains that fries little pieces of our neural tissue."

Indah winced. Mensah folded her arms, her expression a combo of "are you satisfied now" and "get on with it." Indah narrowed her eyes at me. "I know Dr. Mensah wants you involved in this investigation. Are you willing to work with us?"

Okay, I'm not lying about having investigated this kind of thing in the past. It turns out the big danger to humans on any isolated corporate project, whether it's mining or—okay, it's mostly mining. Whatever—the big danger to humans is not raiders, angry human-eating fauna, or rogue SecUnits; it's other humans. They kill each other either accidentally or on purpose and you have to clear that up fast because it jeopardizes the bond and determines whether the company has to pay out damages on it or not. SecUnits are ordered by the HubSystem to gather video and audio evidence because nobody trusts the human supervisors, including the other human supervisors.

I had dealt with some instances of humans killing each other surreptitiously instead of, for example, in front of the entire mess hall during food service, but most had been pre–memory wipe(s) so the details were fuzzy. It was better to prevent them from murdering each other in the first place, by keeping watch for aggressive or destructive behaviors, things like trying to sabotage another human's life support pack or poison their water supply. Then you put in a notice to MedSystem to call them in for an evaluation, or reported to the supervisor who moved them to a different section so it would be someone else's problem if MedSystem couldn't convince them to stop. But whatever, the idea was to keep it from getting that far.

(And I know it sounds like they were all just running around trying to murder each other on these contracts but really, it was more like it had been with the poor humans on the transport I used to get to HaveRatton, who thought I was an augmented human security consultant. They had been complaining and fighting out of frustration and fear about going into contract labor. Actually being in contract labor just made it that much worse.)

I had archives of everything that had happened since I hacked my governor module, but I hadn't had as much relevant experience in that time. But what I did have were thousands of hours of category mystery media, so I had a lot of theoretical knowledge that was possibly anywhere from 60 to 70 percent inaccurate shit.

But Mensah was right, butting in on the investigation was the best way to find out if the anomalous death was a sign of GrayCris-related activity on station. I said, "Yes. Will you increase security around Dr. Mensah to the specifications I stipulated?" Yeah, that had been an ongoing argument.

Indah's jaw tightened again (she was going to hurt herself) but she said, "Of course, with a murderer running loose on the station, I am upping every security level, including those around the council and Dr. Mensah. I actually don't need you to tell me my job."

Oh good, maybe the security level would go from barely adequate to mostly adequate. I didn't make an expression because I knew Indah would be more annoyed by me not reacting than by me reacting.

Mensah cleared her throat in a "you are trying to annoy each other but are mostly annoying me" way. She said, "I assume an employment contract will be forthcoming."

Indah's voice was dry. "It will, no need to send the terrifying solicitor after me."

She meant Pin-Lee because she said "terrifying." Being the top Preservation expert in dealing with contract law in the Corporation Rim apparently made Pin-Lee like the CombatUnit version of a lawyer.

The employment contracts for Preservation citizens were pretty simple, because their planetary legal code had so many in-built protections already. (For example, humans and augmented humans can't sign away their rights to their labor or bodily autonomy in perpetuity; that's like, straight-up illegal.)

But I wasn't a citizen and also technically not actually a person, which made it more difficult. But Pin-Lee's contract would make sure that they couldn't make me do anything I didn't want to do and I would get a hard currency card out of it. (When we had first discussed the idea of me getting jobs as a way to encourage the Preservation Council to grant me permanent refugee status, I didn't know very much about the kind of contract in which I was actually an active participant. (My previous contracts were rental contracts with the company, where I was just a piece of equipment.) Pin-Lee had promised, "Don't worry, I'll preserve your right to wander off like an asshole anytime you like.")

(I said, "It takes one to know one.")

(Mensah said, "People, please. I'm scheduled to mediate arguments between teenagers on my next commcall home and I need all my patience for that.")

If I was going to do this, I wanted to get started so I could make sure this anomalous murder wasn't an indication of a threat to Mensah. Plus I had a lot of downloaded shows to get through. I said, "Can I examine the dead human now?"

Indah just looked tired. "Can you humor me and please refer to the victim as 'the deceased' or 'the victim' during the course of the investigation?" She turned to go, not waiting for an answer.

She missed Mensah mouthing the words *stop it* at me. (I guess the feed isn't adequate for all forms of communication, particularly those that involve a lot of glaring.)

Chapter Two

AT FIRST, PRESERVATION STATION Security had objected to my presence on the station. Correction, at first they were fine with it because they didn't know anything about me except that I was a security consultant who had retrieved Dr. Mensah from TranRollinHyfa Station, was injured, and was getting refugee status. Most humans, unless they get stuck working in an isolated corporate installation, never see SecUnits except in the media where we're always in armor. But Dr. Mensah had told the Preservation Council the truth (no, I don't know why, either) and then she had to brief Station Security.

(Senior Indah had been with the rest of the upper level security staff for the "hey, there's a rogue SecUnit here" meeting. You should have seen their expressions.)

There was a big huge deal about it, and Security was all "but what if it takes over the station's systems and kills everybody" and Pin-Lee told them "if it wanted to do that it would have done it by now," which in hindsight was probably not the best response. And then Mensah, Pin-Lee, and I had a private meeting with Senior Indah.

After some preliminary polite arguing between the humans, it became really obvious that Senior Indah was determined to get rid of me. She was trying to get Mensah to send me away somewhere, like a particularly isolated part of the planet, while the situation was being "evaluated."

I didn't even know how to react to that. For one thing, it was a terrible idea. Threat assessment for potential Gray-Cris retaliation suggested a steady increase, and I needed to stay with Mensah. I hate planets, but if she went to the planet, I'd go with her. (I really hate planets.) I wasn't going to the fucking planet alone and leave her here to get killed and let GrayCris rampage around the station.

Pin-Lee wasn't reacting, either, except to flick a glance at Mensah and send me a feed message that said, *Could you at least try to look pathetic.*

Yeah, I'm not going to respond to that.

Mensah didn't even blink. She said, calmly, "No, that's unacceptable."

Senior Indah's mouth went tight. I think she was angry Mensah hadn't told her about me as soon as we arrived from the Corporation Rim. (It had to be that, I hadn't done anything else yet to make her angry.) She said, "Just because you're accustomed to using a dangerous weapon doesn't mean it can't turn on you. Or harm others."

Okay, wow. But it wasn't like it hurt my feelings or anything. Not at all. I was used to this. Completely used to it.

Mensah was not used to it. Her eyes narrowed, her head tilted slightly, and her mouth made a minute movement that turned her polite planetary leader "I am listening and receptive to your ideas" smile into something else. (If she had looked at me like that I would have created a distraction and run out of the room.) (Okay, not really, but I would have at least stopped talking.) In a voice that should have caused an ambient temperature drop, she replied, "We're talking about a person."

Mensah can be so calm under pressure that it's easy to forget she can also get angry. From the minute changes in Indah's expression, she was realizing she had fucked up, big time.

Pin-Lee had a tiny little smile at one corner of her mouth. I checked her feed activity and saw she had accessed a station database and was pulling documents into her feed storage. Since she was human she was doing it slowly (it was like watching algae grow) but I could see the information she was assembling had to do with Preservation's original charter and its list of basic human rights. Also the regulations for holding public office. Public offices like Senior Station Security Officer.

Oh, maybe Indah had literally fucked up big time. Pin-Lee was planning a case for Mensah to take to the rest of the council to recommend Indah be dismissed.

(I knew by this time that on Preservation, dismissal isn't

as bad as it is in the Corporation Rim, so it's not like she would get killed or starve or anything.)

Indah took a breath to speak and Mensah said evenly, "Don't make it worse."

Indah let the breath out.

Mensah continued, "I'll agree to forget what you just said—" Pin-Lee made a sort of hissing noise of protest here, and Mensah paused to give her an opaque look that Pin-Lee apparently understood. Pin-Lee sighed and discontinued her document search. Mensah turned back to Indah and continued, "And I want to preserve our working relationship. To do that, we will both be reasonable about this and set our knee-jerk emotional responses aside."

Indah kept her expression reserved, but I could tell she was relieved. "I apologize." She also wasn't a coward. "But I have concerns."

So there was a lot of negotiation about me (always a fun time) and it ended up with me having to agree to two restrictions. The first one was to promise not to access any non-public systems or hack any other bots, drones, etc., a solution both I and Station Security were very unhappy with but for completely different reasons.

It's not like the private station systems were all that great; Preservation didn't use surveillance except on essential engineering and safety entry points. So it's not like I wanted to have access to their stupid boring systems anyway. If GrayCris shows up and blows the station all to hell, it won't be my fault.

Right, so it probably will be my fault. There just won't be that much I can do about it.

———————

So that's where I was, figuratively in an uneasy truce with Station Security, when Mensah had gotten the call that a dead human had been found in the station mall.

(She had pressed her hands down on her desk and said, "Could this be it?"

She meant the GrayCris attack we had been waiting for. Without access to surveillance I felt so useless. "Maybe."

Her face made a complicated grimace. "I almost hope it is. Then at least we could get it over with.")

And now I was literally standing over a dead human.

Tech Tural was back, and two other techs were lurking out in the Trans Lateral Bypass, running analysis via the feed and ineffectively poking databases. Mensah headed back to her council office, with her two assistants and the task group of drones I had assigned to her. Since there were no station cameras in the corridors (which, if there were, I have to point out, we'd know who had killed the dead human—excuse me, the deceased) I had sort of built my own surveillance network using my intel drones.

(I had promised not to hack Station systems. Nobody had said anything about not setting up my own systems.)

"No ID report yet," Tural was telling Indah.

Indah wasn't pleased. "We need that ID."

Tural said, "We tried a DNA check but it didn't match anyone in the database, so the victim isn't related to approximately 85 percent of Preservation planetary residents."

Indah stared at Tural. So did I, with my drones. Was that supposed to be a result?

Tural cleared their throat and forged on, "So we're going to have to wait for the body scan."

DNA sampling in the Preservation Alliance was voluntary and no samples were taken from arriving travelers. There were too many ways to spoof DNA-related ID checks so most places I knew of, at least in the Corporation Rim, didn't use it as a form of verifiable ID. Full body scans were more accurate, not that they couldn't be fooled, too. Example A: me.

Indah stared at me in a challenging "let's see what all you've got" way. Indah did not actually want to see what all I got so I just asked Tural, "Have you done a forensic sweep?"

"Yes." Tural didn't look like I'd asked anything strange, so I must have used the right words. Note to self: forensic sweep is not just a media term for it. "I'll send you the report when it's ready."

It was too bad they'd already done it, I wanted to see what it looked like for real instead of just in my shows. "Do you have the raw data files? I can read those."

Tural looked at Senior Officer Indah, who shrugged. Tural sent me the data files via the feed and I ran them through a quick analysis routine. There was a lot of stray contact DNA in the junction, caused by so many humans coming through here and touching stuff. (Humans touch stuff all the time, I wish they wouldn't.) But the presences and absences of contact DNA on the body told an odd story. I said, "The perpetrator used some kind of cleaning field after the attack."

Indah had just turned away to say something to one of the other officers. She turned back, and Tural looked startled. "You can tell that from the data?"

Well, yeah. Processing raw data and pulling out the relevant bits was a company specialty and I still had the code. "There's an unusual lack of contact DNA on the deceased's clothes." Samples from the deceased, the two humans who had found the deceased, and the first responder medical team had been included in the comparison file; the latter two groups of samples were present on the deceased's clothes, just like you would expect. But the deceased's own sample was not present. The clothes were as clean as if they had just popped out of the recycler or a sterilization unit. So therefore . . . Right, you get it. I turned my analysis into a human-readable form and sent it back to Tural and Indah.

Tural blinked and Indah's gaze went abstract as they both read it. That was going to take a while so I crouched down to look at the body's obvious wound. (There could be others, and this wasn't necessarily the cause of death; we wouldn't know that until they took the deceased to a MedSystem with a pathology suite.)

It was in the back of the human's head, near the base of the skull. All I could tell from a visual was that it was a deep wound, with no exit point. No sign of cauterization. And there should be more blood and brain matter on the floor plates. "If this was the cause of death, the deceased wasn't killed here."

"That we knew," Indah said, her voice dry. She glanced at Tural and said, "We need a search for what kind of cleaning tools could remove contact DNA and which ones are available on station. Particularly the ones that are small enough to conceal in a pocket or bag."

It's too bad we don't trust the SecUnit who is an expert at running those kinds of searches. Just to be an asshole, I said, "The tool could have been brought in from off-station."

She ignored me.

Tural made notes in their feed, then said, "Even without the contact DNA, the clothes should tell us something. They're distinctive."

You might think that. The deceased was wearing a knee-length open coat over wide pants and a knee-length shirt, which wasn't an uncommon combination as human clothing goes, but the colors and patterns were eye-catching. It might have been a clue leading to planetary or system origin, or at least suggest a place that the deceased had visited recently. But the chances were that it wasn't. I said, "Not necessarily. You can get clothes like this in the automated shops in some station malls in the Corporation Rim. If you pay extra, you can get whatever color you want and design a pattern." I knew this because my dark-colored pants, shirt, jacket, and boots had come from a place like that and I'd found it really annoying that the Preservation Station mall didn't have one. Most of the station's clothing supply came from the planet, where human-hand-made clothing and textiles were so popular there was hardly any recycler-produced fabric. (I told you Preservation is weird.)

Tural said, "I didn't know that." They leaned in with the scanner and took a tiny sample from the deceased's coat.

Indah's frown had deepened. She said, "So the clothes could indicate cultural origin, or have been chosen to blend in on some other station or system. Or just be a fashion whim."

Don't look at me like that's my fault. I'm just telling you shit I know.

Tural studied the fabric analysis report. "You're right, this is recycler fabric. It could have come from a store like that."

"Or a transport." They both stared at me. I said, "Some transports have very sophisticated onboard recyclers."

Indah pressed her lips together. Look, I know I wasn't narrowing it down, but you have to consider all possibilities. She said, "Can the clothes tell us anything?"

Well, sure. "The deceased wasn't afraid of being noticed. Or they wanted to look like they weren't afraid of being noticed. They wanted to look like a visitor." Humans from the planet wore all kinds of things, but on the station the most common were the work/casual pants, short jacket, and a short or long shirt or tunic, and the more formal long robes or caftans in solid colors with patterned trim. Bright multicolored patterns like this were unusual enough to stand out. "There are two ways to move through station transit rings if you're afraid someone's watching for you. You can try to fade into the background, which is much easier to do if there's a crowd. You can also make yourself look distinctive, like someone who isn't worried about being seen." I would never have been able to pull it off. But an actual human with actual human body language who didn't have to worry about the energy weapons in their arms pinging weapons scanners might. "You have to be ready to change out your clothes and appearance. You would always need to look like you came from somewhere else." Which was easy enough to do on big stations with lots of automated shops.

Tural's expression had gone from frustrated to thoughtful and even Indah looked speculative. Tural said, "Medical should check to see if this person's skin or hair color was altered recently."

Indah looked down at the body. "Hmm. If I saw this person swinging along the walkway, I'd think they were a legitimate visitor and not give them a second thought."

Uh-huh, and that's why I needed to oversee Mensah's security. I said, "You need a travel bag, too." It sounded facetious, but it really was important. If this human's distinctness had been a disguise, they needed a bag. A bag implied you had somewhere to go, it helped you fit in. I checked the images my drones had collected of the area surrounding this junction, but there was no stray discarded bag. "If the idea was to look like a visitor, there should be a bag."

"Can't hurt to look." Indah stepped back and said into her comm, "I need a check of the immediate area, and a station-wide check at lost-and-found depots. We're looking for anything resembling a travel bag." She paused to listen to her feed and added, "Pathology is here. We need to get out of the way."

Tural asked, "Can I take the broken interface for analysis? The scene's been scanned and position-mapped."

Indah nodded. "Take it."

Tural hesitated, glanced at me, but Indah told me, "That's enough for now. We'll call you if we need you."

I know a "fuck off" when I hear one. So I fucked off.

Chapter Three

MY FIRST JOB AS a consultant for Station Security had turned into a non-event, which was completely unsurprising. They really didn't want me here and whatever Mensah said, they weren't going to suddenly change their minds.

No access to private station systems was just the first restriction. The second was that I had to not conceal my identity. Not that I had been actively concealing it. Mensah's staff, family, and the council had been told what I was; it was just the rest of the station who either hadn't noticed me or thought I was Mensah's security consultant. Station Security had wanted me to implement a public feed ID and they had wanted to put out a public safety warning notifying Station personnel and residents that there was a SecUnit running around loose. Mensah had refused to consider the public safety notice, but in one of the stupid meetings with Indah she had asked, "What exactly would this feed ID say?"

It gave me a 1.2 percent performance reliability drop. I tapped Pin-Lee's feed and sent to her, *Make a legal thing so I don't have to do that.*

She sent back, *Mensah has to give them something,* but she sent to Mensah, *It doesn't want the feed ID.*

Humans and augmented humans can have null feed IDs. I knew from my shows that it meant different things depending on what polity, station, area, etc., they lived in. Here on Preservation it meant "please don't interact with me." It was perfect. And I'd already agreed not to hack their systems, what the fuck else could they want?

Senior Indah said, "The feed ID doesn't need to say anything other than what everyone else's says, just name, gender, and . . ." She trailed off. She was looking at me and I was looking at her.

Pin-Lee pointed out, "Everyone else who has a feed ID has one voluntarily. Consensually, one might say."

Senior Indah stopped looking at me to glare at Pin-Lee. "All we're asking for is a name."

I have a name, but it's private.

On their secure feed connection, Pin-Lee sent to Mensah, *Oh, that's going to go over well. When station residents are running into "Murderbot"*—

That's one of the reasons why it's private.

Mensah said to Indah, "I'm not sure we can agree to that."

"Frankly, I don't understand the problem." Indah made a helpless gesture toward me. "I don't even know what it wants to be called."

29

Senior Indah was acting like she didn't think she had made an unreasonable request. But the reason she was making it was that she didn't trust me and she wanted any humans or augmented humans who came into contact with me to be warned, in case I decided to go on a murder rampage. Because being warned by my feed ID would, somehow, mitigate being shot, or something.

Mensah pressed her lips together and looked at me. She sent, *Can you explain to her why it's a problem for you?*

I'm not sure I could. And I got why from their perspective it seemed like such a small thing. Maybe it was worth it to get this meeting over with and not have to listen to humans talk about how they didn't want me anywhere near their precious station.

For a name, I could use the local feed address that was hard coded into my neural interfaces. It wasn't my real name, but it was what the systems I interfaced with called me. If I used it, the humans and augmented humans I encountered would think of me as a bot. Or I could use the name Rin. I liked it, and there were some humans outside the Corporation Rim who thought it was actually my name. I could use it, and the humans on the Station wouldn't have to think about what I was, a construct made of cloned human tissue, augments, anxiety, depression, and unfocused rage, a killing machine for whichever humans rented me, until I made a mistake and got my brain destroyed by my governor module.

I posted a feed ID with the name *SecUnit,* gender = *not applicable,* and no other information.

Indah had blinked, then said, "Well, I suppose that will have to do."

That was the end of the meeting. Pin-Lee and Mensah hadn't talked about it, but Pin-Lee had stomped off to have intoxicants with some of her friend humans. And Mensah had called her marital partners Farai and Tano on the planet, and said she thought the future of humanity was pretty dismal, and they should take all the kids, siblings, their kids, and assorted relatives and move to a shack in the terraforming sector on the unsettled continent and start working in soil reclamation, whatever that was.

(I wouldn't enjoy it, but I could work with it. It would be a lot easier to guard her from GrayCris there. But Farai and Tano hadn't gone for the idea.)

Then two cycles later, someone had sent a photo of me to the Station newsstream identifying me as the rogue SecUnit mentioned in all those Corporation Rim newsfeed rumors.

There was little surveillance in the station but, at least before the agreement not to hack station systems, I had still been redacting myself from it. This photo had come from another source, maybe an augmented human's feed camera. It had clearly been taken after I had completed my memory repair, after a public inquiry about GrayCris that had been held in the large Preservation Council meeting chamber. Mensah was walking down the steps away from the council offices and I was standing behind her between Pin-Lee and Dr. Bharadwaj. We were all looking to the side, with various what-the-fuck expressions. (One of the journalists had just asked the council spokesperson if GrayCris reps would be allowed at the meeting.) (It had been such a stupid question, I had forgotten not to have an expression.)

Supposedly it wasn't Senior Indah or anyone else from Station Security who had sent the photo to the newsstream. Right, sure.

After that, Mensah, who was very angry but pretending not to be, gave me two boxes of intel drones, the tiny ones. (Indah had objected and Mensah had told her that it was a medical issue, that I needed them to fully interact with my environment and communicate.)

I think Mensah had already ordered the drones, as a sort-of bribe for me not continuing to point out that she hadn't had any trauma treatment or retrieved client protocol after what had happened to her on TranRollinHyfa. Indah didn't know that, right, so she thought Mensah getting the drones for me (giving intel drones to a rogue SecUnit nobody wanted around anyway) was Mensah's way of telling her to fuck off.

She wasn't wrong. Mensah's really smart, she can sort-of bribe me and tell Indah to fuck off simultaneously.

I did have other things to do besides watch for GrayCris

assassination agents and keep track of Station Security's attempts to shove me out of the Preservation Alliance. Dr. Bharadwaj had started the preliminary research for her documentary on constructs, so I had been to her office five times to talk to her about it, and she wanted to set up a regular schedule of meetings with me.

(Dr. Bharadwaj was easy to talk to, for a human. On the first visit, after the photo of me was in the newsstream, we had talked about why humans and augmented humans are afraid of constructs, which I hadn't meant to talk about and somehow ended up talking about anyway. She said she understood the fear because she had felt that way to a certain extent herself before I had stopped her from being eaten to death by a giant alien hostile. And she was trying to think how other humans could come to this understanding without the shared experience of almost being chewed up together in an alien fauna's mouth. (Obviously she didn't use those exact words but that's what she meant.)

The second time we had talked I had somehow just come out and told her that I thought being here on Preservation Station as myself, and not pretending to be an augmented human or a robot, was disturbing and complicated and I didn't know if I could keep doing it. She had said that it would be strange if I didn't find it disturbing and complicated, because my whole situation was objectively disturbing and complicated. For some reason that made me feel better.)

I had also been helping Ratthi with the data analysis for his survey reports, and he was trying to convince me that could be a job I could do for other researchers. Which, sure, I mean, it could. If I wanted to be almost as bored as when a lot of my job had been standing in one place unable to move and staring at a wall. It wasn't boring with Ratthi, but not all researchers were going to be so happy about the reports we constructed, or get me to go with them to live performances in the Station's theater.

But whatever, now I just needed intel for threat assessment so I could figure out if GrayCris had killed the dead human or not and go back to my happy boring life on Preservation Fucking Station.

I knew from my drones that Mensah was back in the council offices (I had a routine in place to check my various task groups of drone sentries every seventeen seconds). If the station had better surveillance, or if I had access to what little surveillance was installed in the transit ring, I could start an image search for the dead human, get a timestamp of when they arrived, and match it to the Port Authority's record of entry. Probably before Station Security managed to get the body scan from Medical.

It did seem unlikely that the dead human had been a GrayCris agent, because somebody had killed him. As far as I knew, I was the only one currently on the station looking for GrayCris agents to kill.

I just realized I don't like the phrase "as far as I knew" because it implies how much you actually don't know. I'm not going to stop using it, but. I don't like it as much anymore.

And speaking of not knowing things, I couldn't be sure the dead human wasn't tangentially involved in a GrayCris operation. He could have been sent by a rival corporate, even by the company, to shadow GrayCris activity, and been killed by an actual GrayCris operative.

Right, so while the corporate-operative-killed-by-GrayCris-agent thing was a scenario that made sense, there was zero data to indicate that it was actually connected in any way to reality. But the fact was, looking for anomalous activity is how you detect security breaches. A murder in a very non-murdery station like Preservation was definitely anomalous.

Unless the dead human had been here to visit other humans, they would have needed a place to sleep and put their stuff. Humans need stuff, I had never seen one travel without at least something.

Near the port was a large housing block for short-term residents, transients who were usually waiting for something: for a transport to arrive, for permission to continue to the planet or another in-system destination, for approval to become a longterm resident, other reasons.

Preservation Station didn't get nearly as many transients as the major hubs I'd passed through in the Corporation Rim.

Most humans who came here were going to one of the planets in the Preservation Alliance for a long stay, either permanently or for a term of work. The others were from outside the Rim, using Preservation as a waystation heading somewhere else, or they were traders or independent merchants with cargo transports. Occasionally there were humans from sites that were not part of the transit network, "lost" colonies, independents who had not maintained contact with transit stations, "lost" stations, whatever. There were no Corporation Rim corporations here, so no reason for corporates to come on business. Some came as visitors sometimes, but most were afraid to travel outside the Rim. (They thought everywhere outside the Rim was all raiders killing everybody and cannibalism.)

There were places to stay other than the housing block, like the hotel for longterm residents where Ratthi and the others who didn't have permanent quarters on the station had rooms. Where I sort-of lived now. Again, surveillance was stupidly minimal and without access to their systems . . . permission to access their systems.

But there was another way to get the data I needed.

———

I went to the transient housing block first because it was statistically more likely, if the initial theory was correct and the dead human had been a recent visitor.

I stopped outside the entrance, near a seating area with chairs and tables, surrounded by large round plant biomes that were partly decorative and partly an information exhibit about what not to touch if you went to the planet's surface. (Yeah, good luck with that. Trying to get humans not to touch dangerous things was a full-time job.) I stood in a spot where I could pretend to be reading the hostel's feed instructions and sent a ping.

After 1.2 seconds (I'm guessing the pause was due to astonishment) I got an answer, and I went through the entrance into the lobby.

It was a round high-ceilinged space, with registration kiosks, lots of corridors leading off toward the room sections, and an archway into another room with shelves and cold cases where food products were stored for the humans staying in the hostel. (Or really, for any humans or augmented humans who wandered by. The Preservation Alliance has a weird thing about food and medical care and other things humans need to survive being free and available anywhere.) The bot was in there, restocking items from a floating cart.

It was sort of humanform, but more functional, with six arms and a flat disk for a "head" that it could rotate and extend for scanning. It had rotated it to "watch" me walk through the lobby, a behavior designed to make humans comfortable (its actual eyes were sensors that were all over its body.) (I don't know why bot behaviors that are useless except to comfort humans annoy me so much.) (Okay, maybe I do. They built us, right? So didn't they know how this type of bot took in visual data? It's not like sensors and scanners just popped up randomly on its body without humans putting them there.)

This is one of the Preservation "free bots" you hear so much about. They have "guardians" (owners) who are responsible for them, but they get to pick their own jobs. (Are there any who don't have jobs and just sit around watching media? I don't know. I could have asked, but the whole thing was so boring it might send me into an involuntary shutdown.)

It said, "Hello, SecUnit. What brings you here?"

Yeah, whatever. I said, "You don't have to pretend I'm a human."

The data in the ping had told me that this bot had different protocols from the ones in the Corporation Rim, probably because it had been constructed somewhere else. I identified its language module, pulled it out of archive storage, loaded it, and established a feed connection. I sent it a salutation and it sent back, *query?*

It was asking me why I was here. I replied *query: identify,* and attached an image of the dead human.

A non-dead human walked into the lobby, one of the hostel supervisors. He stopped, stared at us, and said, "Is everything all right, Tellus?"

(The bot's name is Tellus. They name themselves and hearing about it is exhausting.)

Tellus replied, "We are speaking."

The supervisor frowned. "Do you need any help?"

Since the bot was still unloading the cart with three of its arms, obviously he was talking about me. The bot said, "No help needed."

The supervisor hesitated, nodded, and then continued on down a corridor. I don't know what they think I'm going to do to their bots. Teach them to hack? Bots don't have governor modules like constructs and it's not like the Preservation bots weren't supposedly able to do whatever they wanted.

It's also not like I didn't know what the real problem was. I'm not a bot, I'm not a human, so I don't fit into any neat category. Also, I hate being patronized. (The whole bot-guardian system is like an attraction field for humans who like to be patronizing.)

Resuming the conversation with me, the bot said, *query?*

Because I could tell it was already running a search against its visual archives, I answered with a copy of the alert Mensah had gotten from Station Security.

It hummed aloud, surprise and dismay, another imitation human reaction. I would have been more annoyed if it hadn't also just produced a query result: an image of the dead human in mid-stride, passing through the door into one of the hostel corridors.

Hah, got you. *Query: room?*

The bot said, *query: ID?* It couldn't find the room assignment without the dead human's ID. Or at least the ID the dead human had been using.

I said, *ID unknown.* We were going to have to do this a different way. *Query: rooms plus target corridor = engaged plus without resident plus target time.*

The bot ran another search and delivered thirty-six results, all assigned rooms where the occupant was not currently present and was known to have exited the hostel before the dead human's estimated time of death. The bot added, *entry re: unoccupied maintenance inspection authorized. Concern: privacy. Query: item examine?*

The bot was authorized to make inspections of unoccupied rooms to check for maintenance issues and was implying I could come along, if I told it what I wanted to see, and if it didn't think it was a privacy violation.

It would be nice to look for memory clips or other data storage devices, especially if they were concealed data storage devices. But to make an ID I thought I only needed to see one thing. I told it, *clothing.*

Acknowledge, the bot said. It pulled its arms in and led the way toward the target corridor.

We checked seventeen of the currently empty rooms, and while the bot didn't let me touch anything, it did open the clothing storage cubbies so I could see the contents in the rooms where the humans hadn't left their stuff strewn all over the bed and desk. It didn't need to do that in the eighteenth room. It was fairly neat but the scarf draped over the chair was the same style of pattern as the dead human's shirt, but in a different color combination.

It could easily have been a coincidence, the style and pattern could have been popular and cheap at some transit station hub. And even with the image it wasn't actually a positive ID. But Station Security could make it a positive ID with a thorough search of the room and a DNA match.

I created a quick report with images of the scarf, the location of the room, and the feed ID associated with it (name: Lutran, gender: male), and the room-use record, which indicated that Lutran had been registered here for two station cycles. I included the bot's authorization to view the rooms, and sent it off to Station Security tagged for Senior Indah and Tech Tural. (Station Security was used to getting messages from me about their completely inadequate arrangements for Mensah's security.) I sent a copy to the hostel bot so it would know what was going on if they came to ask it questions. Then I signaled that I was leaving.

It followed me back through the corridors to the lobby, where a few new humans had arrived and were standing in front of a kiosk like they had never seen anything like it before. It went to help them, but sent me *query: next action?*

I still didn't have enough for a real threat assessment. I should go back to monitoring Mensah's security arrangements while lurking in the hotel near the admin offices and watching media. I didn't think I'd hear from Station Security again. (Or at least not about this; I figured they would come up with other ways to try to get rid of me.) I'd have to get intel on their investigation through Mensah's council channels. To get the bot to leave me alone, I answered, *task complete.*

I was already out the door when the bot said, *query: arrivals data,* meaning I should look for the dead human in the transit ring and its traveler records.

I didn't respond because I don't need a critique from a "free" bot and I couldn't access the arrivals data without Station Security's permission anyway, and fuck that.

Huh, I just thought of another way to do it.

It was annoying that the "free" bot was right, but I needed to go to the transit ring.

———

Preservation's transit ring wasn't that big compared to the major Corporation Rim hubs. Or even to the nonmajor Corporation Rim hubs. It had only one entry/exit point for passengers, near the booking kiosks where you could search for berths on the docked transports offering passage. There was another entry/exit point for crews of private ships and cargo-only transports in the Merchant Docks, and Dead Lutran might have come in through that section, but it made more sense statistically to start at the public entrance.

This being Preservation, there was a nice waiting area to one side of the transit ring's entry hall for humans to sit and figure out what they were doing, with couches and chairs and a mosaic floor with tiled images of the planet's flora and fauna, all tagged in the feed with detailed descriptions. Wooden conical structures that were duplicates of the first shelters used on the planet sat around, most of them holding information kiosks or displays for visitors.

I found a chair behind yet another plant biome (a big one, with reedy plants in a simulated stream) and sat down.

I had an ID that Dead Lutran must have used on entry in order to get a room assignment for transient housing. Finding the ship he had come in on could be an important data point. Based on the tech used to create his clothes, I was betting he had come here from the Corporation Rim and not another non-corporate political entity, station or whatever, but it would be nice to be sure.

I could hack the port's transient arrivals system but I had said I wouldn't, so I wouldn't. Also, it seemed pointless to do it just to run a search that Tural and the other Station Security techs could run as soon as they bothered to read my report. But just asking for information had worked really well the first time so I decided to try it again.

I leaned back in the chair, told my drones to form a sensor perimeter, and verified that my inputs for the constant cycle of checks for Dr. Mensah's sentry task group were all still open. Then I closed my eyes and slipped into the feed.

Transports don't hang out on the feed constantly downloading (not that there's anything wrong with constantly downloading) but they do access it to keep in contact with the transit ring's scheduling and alerts channels, and also to allow local feed access to any humans on board.

I had to sort through the hundreds of different connections currently attached to the station feed in the transit ring, humans, augmented humans, bots, bot pilots, small and large scale port systems, all interlinked and busy doing their jobs. Or in most of the humans' cases, wandering around. I was looking for the distinctive profiles of transports, which were different from any of the other connections. I could have done this a lot more easily by walking around from hatch to hatch and using the comm to contact each transport directly, but it would have been ridiculously obvious that I was doing something, even if the humans couldn't tell what it was.

(The humans not being able to tell what I was doing just guaranteed that whatever they assumed I was doing would be way, way worse than me having a brief comm interaction with each transport in dock, trying to get info for stupid Station Security.)

I found a transport connection and pinged it. It pinged back readily, with enough identifying information to class it as a passenger transport whose home destination was a small hub station outside the Corporation Rim. It visited Preservation on a regular route, carrying cargo and passengers, continuing on to five other non–Corporation Rim polities and then looping back home. Transports don't communicate in words (most transports don't; ART did, but ART was ART) so I wasn't really asking it questions so much as sending images and code back and forth. It had no record of Lutran as one of its passengers, and I moved on to the next.

This got boring very quickly. And it was the tedious kind of boring where I couldn't run media in the background. I couldn't code this process, each transport needed an individual approach based on its capabilities, and finding their connections to the station feed out of the confusing mass of inputs and outputs took more finesse than I was used to needing. I couldn't use a data range to exclude transports, since Lutran could have come in on any of them; some transports didn't require passengers to disembark immediately and Lutran could have stayed in his quarters on board for some time before applying for transient housing.

I also couldn't pull the transport's date of arrival until after I made contact with it.

And this whole exercise could be totally useless, if his transport was one of the three that had left before the body was found and the council had closed the port.

If I didn't find anything, this was going to be a huge waste of my time.

Possibly I should just stop complaining like a human and get on with it.

I had checked 57 percent of the transports in dock, when I hit an anomaly. I pulled a transport connection and pinged it with a salutation. It pinged me back with a salutation. (This is not how it's supposed to work, there's usually an answer protocol, even if it's in a different language.) But maybe the transport had missed part of the ping or had a different kind of protocol. (Unlikely. Ships from outside the Corporation Rim, particularly on the routes intersecting Preservation, had a variety of different protocols, some of them horrifyingly jury-rigged by humans. But by the registry signifiers in its feed connection, this transport was from a Corporation Rim origin.) I pinged it again. It pinged me back, still a salutation. Okay, I'm just going to start talking to it.

By poking around in its open feed, I found out the transport was a lower level automated crewless cargo hauler with booked passengers on the side. Preservation was self-sufficient and didn't import or export raw materials from the Corporation Rim, but did act as a cargo transfer point for other non-corporate polities that did. Talking to it was reminiscent of dealing with Ship, the cargo hauler I had taken to Milu and back, which had not abandoned me to die in space even though I wasn't entirely sure it had understood it was saving me, but whatever; it made me more inclined to be patient.

On my initial query, Transport tentatively identified Lutran as a passenger but I honestly couldn't tell if it was just doing that because it thought that was what I wanted to hear and it was trying to be polite. I backtracked and tried to get some more baseline data. What was its route? How many passengers, where had they boarded, and what were their destinations?

It sent me a garbled cargo manifest.

Uh. That was . . . not normal, not a lower level transport failing to communicate.

I asked it to perform a diagnostic and after five seconds got a stream of error codes.

I opened my eyes and pushed out of my chair, startling the group of humans at the opposite end of the waiting area who hadn't known I was there. My drones dropped down from their perimeter positions and followed me through the entry gates to the transit ring.

The weapons scanner (which I was not allowed to hack,

and which I wasn't hacking) alerted on me, but it had my body scan ID on the weapons-allowed list so it didn't set off an alarm. (I have energy weapons in my arms and it's not like I can leave them behind in the hotel room.) (I mean, my arms are detachable so theoretically I could leave them behind if I had a little help but as a longterm solution it was really inconvenient.) I was sure the weapons scanner would alert Station Security that I was in the area.

I took the wide ramp down to the embarkation floor, which was much less busy than usual. There were still humans and augmented humans wandering around, plus some hauler bots and maintenance bots, catching up on cargo transfers that had been ordered before the port closure. Some humans glanced at me but obviously didn't know what I was; the Station Security officer posted in the help area at the base of the ramp did, and watched me walk down the floor toward the transport docks.

(I hate being identified like that. I had gone to a lot of effort to not be immediately identified as a SecUnit, and now it all felt like a waste.) (I grew longer hair and everything.)

I had gotten enough info from the confused transport to figure out what dock it was attached to, and I confirmed it in the public access port directory. Nine minutes later I was standing in front of its closed lock where it was attached to the transit ring. I touched the hatch and pinged again. The direct connection gave me a sense of the transport's urgency that I hadn't been able to detect through the Station feed.

Instead of a ping I got a different garbled manifest file back; it knew the first file had somehow communicated to me that it needed help and it was sending the second to reinforce the message. Something aboard was terribly wrong, something that had left it with no way of notifying the Port Authority that it needed help. I don't think it had any idea what I was, but I thought it was relieved that I was here.

I needed to get onboard.

I also needed not to give Station Security any opportunity to fuck me over. There was surveillance on the embarkation floor, and I can tell when I'm on camera, even when I'm not supposed to access the system.

From my drone sentries I knew Mensah was in a council meeting now. I tapped Pin-Lee's feed to check on her but she was in a different meeting. I knew the others were on planet: Dr. Bharadwaj on a family visit and Arada and Overse at the FirstLanding university working on preparation for the survey they wanted to do, and Volescu was retired.

That left me with the human most likely to want to drop

everything and come watch me break into a damaged transport and the human also most likely to come watch me break into a damaged transport but only so he could argue with me about it.

So I called both of them.

Chapter Four

WATCHING ME TRY TO get the transport's lock open, Ratthi said, "You don't think we should call Station Security?"

I had my hand on the entry panel. The transport wanted to let me in but couldn't get the lock open. I was trying to force an emergency open through the transport's feed but the connections were inactive and it was like groping around in a giant bin of tiny broken drones for the one that was still intact. I said, "No. They told me they didn't need my help."

"Did they tell you that?" Ratthi said. His expression was doubtful. "What exactly did they say?"

I pulled it from memory. "They said, 'We'll call you if we need you.'"

Gurathin said, "I can't tell if that's you being passive aggressive or you being willfully obtuse."

I would be more pissed off about him saying that except a) he was right about the passive aggressive thing and b) he was standing where I had told him to stand, blocking the nearest port camera view of what I was doing.

Ratthi was on a rest break after finishing his work for the

last survey and getting ready for the next. I had been lucky to catch him on the way back after a meal appointment with his human friends. Gurathin didn't have any other human friends from what I could tell but he had been taking a cycle rest period, reading in one of the lounge areas with lots of plant biomes.

"It's definitely not willfully obtuse," Ratthi told him. He told me, "I do think we should call Station Security."

"The transport said I could come in," I said. "But it's too damaged to open the door."

"So we should tell Station Security—"

"It might be just a maintenance issue, which would fall under the Port Authority's remit," I said. I almost had it. "We won't know until we get inside."

Gurathin sighed. "You sound like Pin-Lee."

"No, Pin-Lee is much worse than this. And if it was her, she would be swearing at us by now," Ratthi said. He asked me, "I've always wondered, did you learn to swear from her or did you already know how? Because you two use a lot of the same—"

I finally managed to get the transport's mangled feed to trigger the hatch to open. I stepped back and pulled Gurathin out of the way of the port camera view, so whoever was watching could see the hatch wasn't damaged, that it had been opened from the inside. I'd managed to keep the transport from automatically triggering any station alerts, too. So even though it was me, we should have a few minutes to take a look around and pull info from the transport's systems before a human from either Station Security or the Port Authority showed up.

Ratthi craned his neck to see inside the hatch, but let me walk in first. "Are you sure no one's aboard?" he asked as he followed me through the lock.

I was not. There shouldn't be, but I hadn't been able to get a confirmation on that from the transport. I sent my drones ahead and said, "Stay behind me."

"This is ill-advised," Gurathin muttered, but he clomped along after Ratthi.

On visual and via drone cam I was looking at small low-ceilinged corridors, dingy and scuffed but mostly clean, worn gray and brown upholstery on the seats along the bulkhead in the small lounge we passed through. Lights were up, life support set for humans, but the transport was clearly designed mostly for cargo shipping with passengers as an afterthought. Ahead off the main corridor, my drones encountered a transport maintenance drone, wobbling in the air with its spidery arms drooping, beeping pathetically.

"Do you smell something bad?" Ratthi frowned.

Gurathin said, "Something's happened to the waste recycling."

The air cleaners were working but the filters needed

maintenance the transport couldn't perform. Or maybe it had stopped deliberately, hoping to try to alert someone.

The limping ship's drone swerved away from my drones and led them through a short upward passage and into the main crew lounge. Right, so this wasn't a recycler problem.

I followed the drones but stopped in the hatchway to the lounge compartment. Ratthi and Gurathin halted behind me in confusion. I had trained them too well to step past me in a situation like this, walking into a strange place, but Ratthi peered around my side and Gurathin stood on his tiptoes to see over my shoulder.

It was a fairly standard lounge with padded seats along the walls and quiescent display surfaces floating in the air. In the far wall, a set of steps wound up to the cabin area just above. On the floor in the middle were dried stains of various disgusting fluids that tend to come out of human bodies when they die. (I also have fluids that come out of me when I'm injured; they aren't any less disgusting, just different.) (But I also have fewer places for fluids to come out of, unless you count open wounds.) (Right, this is completely irrelevant.)

And sitting on the curved couch along the bulkhead was a utilitarian blue bag with a shoulder strap.

"That's blood, and—" Ratthi stopped as the realization hit him. "Oh no."

"Was someone ill there?" Gurathin asked, still trying to

see. (Note to self: tell someone to tell Gurathin his vision augments need adjusting.)

"Someone was dead there," Ratthi told him. He stepped back, worried and clearly upset. "Now can we call Station Security?"

My drones had just completed a fast scan/search of the transport and I knew it was unoccupied; whoever had killed Lutran—hopefully it was Lutran who had been killed here and not some other human we hadn't found yet—was long gone. The damage to the transport's systems meant there was no chance of retrieving video or audio without some extensive memory repair. There was nothing else here we could do.

I said, "Now you can call Station Security."

Station Security swooped in like they were a big deal and not hours too late to catch anybody, and made us wait outside the transport's hatch in the embarkation hall. It had taken seven minutes for them to arrive, and I had been able to collect a lot of visual and scan data in that time, including the download of the bio scan filters that Ratthi had suggested. I felt we had done a complete job, even with Gurathin distracting us by standing in the hatchway yelling at us to get out of the ship.

A bot that worked for the Port Authority had shown up before Station Security, pinged me, and then it just stood there. I'd seen it in the embarkation area a lot, and I'd never seen it do anything but just stand there.

(I had considered leaving a few drones hidden strategically around the transport to keep track of the investigation. But I had seen the thorough imaging scans they had done of the area where Lutran was found, and if the drones were discovered it would have been humiliating. I felt like I was at least one if not two points up on Station Security at this moment and I wanted to keep it that way.)

The initial response team was three Station Security officers and a Port Authority supervisor. They had taken a verbal report from Gurathin while eyeing me like they expected him to turn me in for whatever I had probably done. The first officer, feed ID Doran, said, "How do you know there's no one on the transport?"

Ratthi and Gurathin looked at me, and I said, "I checked the transport for possible fatalities and injured crew or passengers in need of assistance, as well as potential hostiles. It's clear."

The expression range was dubious to skeptical.

Gurathin made an exasperated noise and said, "That's what SecUnits do, that's their job. Why don't you do your jobs?"

"That's what we're here for," Officer Doran said, beginning to fluster.

I said, "Station Security Initial Incident Assessment procedures require one of you to view and verify the scene before calling additional assistance from the Major Incident Team, if the surroundings are safe." Not long after I'd first gotten here, I'd downloaded all the Station Security procedures so I'd know what I was dealing with. I added, "The surroundings are safe."

Ratthi had to fold his lips almost completely inside his mouth to keep from reacting.

"We know that." Officer Doran said to the Port Authority supervisor, "We'll go in. You wait out here." The Port Authority supervisor rolled her eyes and went to go stand with the Port Authority bot.

They had gone in, and after three minutes, came out again and stood around talking on their feeds. The PA supervisor started to set up a feed marker perimeter to warn off the hauler bots. The PA bot followed her around, which while not exactly helping, at least was better than just standing there.

Then Indah showed up with the same group of techs and officers who had been at the Lutran site. A second response team from the Port Authority, this one with more bots and different techs, showed up to mill around. Ratthi said they were here to assess the damage to the transport and try to repair it. (Apparently on Preservation this would be free? Gurathin said it fell under what they called a traveler's aid rule. In the Corporation Rim, the transport would have had to sit there damaged and racking up fines until its owner or an owner's rep arrived.) Station Security told the PA team to hold off, since the damage to the transport was evidence and would have to be documented before it could be repaired.

Gurathin kept saying we should leave, but I didn't and Ratthi didn't, so he stayed too, shifting around uneasily and occasionally pacing. "You don't think this is related to GrayCris, do you?" Ratthi had asked me after he had called Station Security.

"It's a possibility," I said. I explained my idea about Lutran being another corporate agent who had been killed by a GrayCris agent. "But without corroborating evidence, the threat assessment is undetermined." I could come up with scenarios where a GrayCris agent would have reason to kill another passenger on their transport, but without evidence I was just making up shit. (If I'm going to make up shit I'd rather do it about something else besides how a human got murdered by another human.)

"Then why was this Lutran killed?" Gurathin asked, his big brow creased.

"We don't have enough data to make a guess yet," I said, not as patiently as would have been required by my gover-

58

nor module. "There are too many factors involved, like did Lutran and the killer know each other before they boarded the transport. We don't even know yet if the killer was another passenger or someone who was invited aboard, or who managed to trick or force the transport into letting them aboard. We don't know how they moved the body from the transport to the station mall junction. We don't know the motive, if it was corporate espionage, theft, a fight, or even a random opportunity killing." We didn't know shit, basically.

Because this is Preservation, Ratthi said, "What is a random opportunity killing?"

"When a human kills another human just because they can." It's also the kind of thing that's much more common on media than it was in real life, but still.

Neither one of them seemed happy with that answer. I actually wasn't either. From everything I'd seen in the media, assholes who just like to kill other humans are hard to catch. But without more info, I thought it was more likely there was a reason that Lutran had been killed, and that it would have to do with who Lutran was and why he was traveling. Threat assessment agreed.

Besides, as soon as Station Security got off their collective ass, we'd—they'd have the surveillance video from the transit ring cameras.

Indah stepped out of the hatch, speaking to another

officer I hadn't seen before, with a private feed ID. Then she walked over toward us, trailed by the officer and Tural, the tech who had been trying and failing to identify Lutran.

Something in their body language made Ratthi step up beside me. It occurred to me Gurathin was maybe right for once and we should have left. It would have possibly been another point up for me, to send the report about the incident to Station Security and then be back in the hotel or Mensah's office acting like it was just another day by the time Station Security arrived at the transport. But it was too late now.

Indah stopped just out of what humans would consider comfortable conversational distance, looking at me. Then she hesitated, glanced with some annoyance at Gurathin and Ratthi, then back at me, with more annoyance. Tural was looking at Indah, and a little agitated like they wanted to talk and were just waiting for permission. The other officer was trying to do a stony stare at me but good luck with that, you need an opaque helmet to really make that work. Indah said, "Officer Aylen, this is . . . SecUnit." She didn't quite stumble over it. "And Survey Academics Ratthi and Gurathin, our other two witnesses."

Gurathin said, "We didn't really witness anything. I don't think we have much to tell you." Gurathin seems to hate talking to strange humans almost as much as I do. And he wasn't wrong, he and Ratthi hadn't seen anything that

I didn't have video of. But him talking gave me a chance to work around the privacy seal on Aylen's feed ID and see she was listed as a Special Investigator. I didn't know what that meant, but it was a good job title and honestly it made me a little jealous.

Indah was looking at me again. I hadn't said anything because what was I supposed to say at this point? Oh, I guess I could have said "hello." Well, it was too late now. Indah said, "I saw the report and I know how you identified Lutran as our deceased. We got verification from Medical on the body scan right after that. But how did you know Lutran was a passenger on this transport?"

Ratthi had shifted from acting defensive to acting like this was a meeting we were all having. He said, "So it was him who was killed in there, then? The person who was found?"

Tural said, "Unless it was spoofed, there was a DNA match. Spoofing isn't unlikely, but in this case—" Indah glared at Tural and they shut up.

I answered, "The transport identified him when I asked it. With its systems damaged it was unable to report the on-board incident to the Port Authority."

Tural was nodding. "The transport's giving us nothing but error codes. The analysts are going to try to do a restart but they'll copy the memory core so they can get the latest passenger manifest, and restore if anything—"

Indah gave Tural a "not now" eyebrow scrunch and they

shut up again. She asked me, "But how did you know it was this particular transport?"

"I didn't, I was checking all the transports." Then I added, "That's why it took so long." Yes, I was rubbing it in.

Indah squinted one eye. Aylen looked me over again in that way humans do when they're trying to intimidate you and they fail to understand you've spent the entire length of your previous existence being treated like a thing and so one more impersonal once-over is not exactly going to impress you. Then Aylen said, "One point I'd like to get out of the way. Did you have anything to do with this?"

Wow, really? I'm better at keeping my expression neutral after so much practice, but I was surprised at how pissed off it made me. Compared to a lot of things that had happened to me, you'd think it wouldn't matter. But here, now, for some reason, it mattered.

Ratthi made an angry snorty noise. Gurathin was grimly staring up at the arch of the transit ring's ceiling; they had both suspected this was coming, that's why Gurathin had wanted us to leave and then had stayed around himself when we wouldn't. I said, "No, I didn't. Why would I?"

Aylen was watching me intently. "I don't like having private security with its own agenda aboard this station."

Oh wait, she thought it was GrayCris. That maybe I had found out Lutran was a GrayCris agent and killed him, and now I was trying to lead the investigation along a specific path, using my two oblivious human friends as cover.

So, the problem was, that wasn't an unlikely idea at all. It was something I might have to do if I did find a GrayCris operative on the station. Which meant I had to answer very carefully.

There were a lot of humans lying to each other on *The Rise and Fall of Sanctuary Moon*, and I knew outright angry denials tended to sound incredibly guilty, even though they were often an innocent human's first impulse. You wouldn't think lying would be a problem for me, after 35,000 plus hours lying about not being a rogue SecUnit while on company contracts, then the whole lying about not being an augmented human and lying about being a non-rogue SecUnit with a fake human supervisor. But the last two hadn't exactly been failure-free; what worked best was misdirection and not letting myself get caught in the wrong place at the right time, and making sure no humans ever thought about asking the wrong questions.

Misdirection, let's try that. "I would have either disposed of the body so it was never found, or made it look like an accident."

Indah frowned, and Aylen's brow creased, and they exchanged a look. Eyeing me, Indah said, "How would you dispose of a body so it wouldn't be found?"

I'm not the public library feed, Senior Officer, go do your

own research. I said, "If I told you, then you might find all the bodies I've already disposed of."

"It's joking." Ratthi managed to sound like he completely believed that. "That's how it looks when it's joking." He sent me on the feed, *Stop joking.*

Gurathin sighed and rubbed his face and looked off into the distance, like he regretted all his life choices that had led to him standing here right now. On our private feed connection, he sent, *Or you could just show them where you were when this person was being killed.*

(Yeah, on reflection I think I misdirected in the wrong direction. It was the kind of thing a human or augmented human could get away with saying, not a rogue SecUnit. Even if they knew I was just being an asshole, I'd made them wonder, I'd put the idea in their heads.)

(And now if I did have to kill some GrayCris agents, I'd have to be really careful about what I did with the bodies.)

(It was probably better to make it look like an accident.)

I hated to admit it but Gurathin had a point. I pulled the right section of video from my drone archive. (I don't keep all my drone video because it would take up storage space that could be used for media, but I run an analysis of it for relevant stuff before I delete it. I was behind and still had the last 72 hours stored.) I clipped it around the relevant section and sent it to Indah and Aylen.

The clip was from one of Mensah's sentry drones parked

up on the ceiling of her council office. I was sitting on a corner of her desk and she was pacing. I'd muted the audio; her complaining that Councilor Sonje was an ass was proprietary data. I let the clip run, showing I'd had an alert from another sentry drone, warned Mensah, and got off her desk in time to be standing by the wall when Councilor Ephraim walked in. Then I stopped the clip.

So that was one planetary leader plus one councilor who had seen me at the council offices across the station when Lutran was being killed.

Indah sighed (yes, she did that a lot around me) and said, "Continue, Officer Aylen."

Aylen said, "The reason I had to ask was this," and via the feed she sent me a video clip.

It was the video from the transit ring surveillance camera. The clip had been processed already but the timestamp was intact. It showed the transport's lock, and Lutran walking up to it, asking for entrance, and being admitted. The hatch closed after him. I fast-forwarded through the video, but there was nothing else. No one else approached the transport's hatch, no one had entered the transport after Lutran. I said, "There was someone already in there?"

My drones showed me Aylen's grim expression. "No. No one other than Lutran ever entered or exited that transport."

It had to be a hack. It wasn't like the way I removed myself from video surveillance—I did that from inside the system, removing the images of me and substituting images taken before or after I walked into view. It was nearly seamless, but it was easier to spot than this. The person who had done this had known the video might be checked by humans, not just a monitoring system.

If it was a person. Could GrayCris have sent another SecUnit? Or a CombatUnit?

My organic skin actually had a prickling reaction like from sudden exposure to cold air. Could they afford that kind of firepower just for revenge? I checked Mensah's drones, and tightened the drone sentry perimeter around the admin office block anyway. I didn't want to scare her with something that might just be me being nervous.

(Ratthi was asking Indah, "Can I see too?"

"No," she told him.)

I pulled the clip apart to look at its underlying code, but it didn't tell me anything. Aylen said, "From the report on how you rescued Dr. Mensah from the corporate station, you can do something similar?"

I said, "I can, but only under certain circumstances." Circumstances which I am not going to explain to you, Special Investigator. "Is your security system compromised?" It was kind of an urgent question.

Indah was watching me closely. "Our analysts say the PA's system hasn't been hacked. They think it could be a jamming device."

Which was good, because that meant it wasn't a construct. A construct would use a hack, not a tool. "I don't know of anything that could do that." I started a search against my own archives, which included the tech catalogs I'd used to pick out the new drones Dr. Mensah had bought for me. "And the Corporation Rim runs on surveillance, there's no way a tool like this wouldn't be banned there. At least, banned for commercial sale." My search wasn't finding any results. The only jamming devices I'd seen like this were in the media, secret weapons or magical artifacts. "It might come from outside the Rim."

"So it would be an espionage tool." Aylen glanced at Indah, who looked grim.

I started to say that they never used SecUnits for espionage, and then realized I didn't actually know that for sure. Take away our armor and alter our appearance and give us the right module . . .

There was a lot I didn't know for sure.

I am going to have to stop scaring the shit out of myself.

I asked, "Did they use this when they removed the body from the transport?"

"No." Aylen sent me another clip. "A simpler method."

On this video there was no attempt to hide what was happening. A floating delivery cart arrived, and the transport's hatch opened to let it in. Seven minutes later, the hatch opened again and the cart floated out. Well, that sucked because it was so obvious. It looked like a standard large cart, a three-meter square box used for deliveries around the port. I said, "The subject is in the cart with the body. Who called for the cart?"

Aylen said, "We're looking for the cart now. But it's likely the perpetrator would have cleaned it. We already know they have access to a sterilizer to remove contact DNA. And it's unlikely they used their own ID to request it."

This sucks more. All you needed to get a cart was an address, and the subject could have used the transport's lock ID.

Gurathin said, "Then why didn't this person clean the transport? If they had, we wouldn't have known this was where what's his name was killed. We'd know the transport was damaged, that was all."

It was a good question and I had a good answer. "They meant to. They thought they had more time to come back."

Indah made a thoughtful noise. Aylen was still eyeing me like she suspected something. Then Indah shook her head and said, "Forensics and Medical are going to need this scene for a while. Investigator, what's your next step?"

Aylen wasn't caught unprepared. "We can't locate this transport's contractor yet, but we have the ID of the outsystem ship that was supposed to deliver its next cargo. I'm going to the private dock to speak to them."

"Outsystem" on Preservation meant the same thing as

what the Corporation Rim called "non-corporate political entities," which were basically planetary settlements, stations, moons, floating rocks, whatever that were not under corporate ownership. They might be nice like Preservation or total shitshows, you never knew.

Indah said, "Good. Take SecUnit."

Yeah, I was surprised too.

Chapter Five

AYLEN MADE IT CLEAR Ratthi and Gurathin were not invited, which was fine, since Gurathin didn't want to go and Ratthi was glad because he thought this meant that Station Security knew I didn't have anything to do with Lutran's death. Aylen did not make it clear that she didn't like the fact that I was invited. It would have been easier if she had, because then I would have known where I stood, and if I should be an asshole or not.

Followed by two Station Security officers (feed IDs Farid and Tifany), the Port Authority supervisor (feed ID Gamila), and the Port Authority bot, we walked over to the end of the public docks, through the gates into the cargo section. I did a quick search on Preservation's local (public) newsstream archive, and found out that Aylen's title meant she was called on by Preservation authorities to investigate stuff they couldn't figure out, both on the station and down on the planet. She also did family and workplace arbitration, which meant a lot of talking to upset humans. So, not as cool a job as the title implied.

PA Supervisor Gamila had been pulling info into her

feed, and now said, "This cargo transfer has been on hold for two cycles. We were waiting for an authorization but it hadn't shown up yet when the order to close the port came through."

Aylen asked her, "Do you know why?"

"No idea. The ship, the *Lalow,* isn't responding to messages." Gamila sounded annoyed. "It doesn't use modules, and there's no record of the cargo being offloaded, so we assume it's still aboard."

Aylen didn't react but my drones saw Farid and Tifany exchange significant looks. They weren't wrong; we already had one dead human associated with this ship, there was a 42 percent chance the *Lalow*'s failure to respond meant something more suspicious than ignoring their Port Authority feed messages.

The cargo section of the Merchant Docks wasn't that different from the Public Docks. There was the big space of the embarkation hall with a line of sealed docking hatches against the far bulkhead. Big cargo bots (the configuration that usually only lived on the outside hulls of stations and hauled transport-sized modules) were sitting around or hanging, dormant, from the curve of the high ceiling. The low-level specialized lifters were parked and only a scatter of humans and augmented humans wandered the stacks of pressurized containers. Large modules were pushed back against the bulkhead, waiting to be loaded and shoved out the module drop so they could be attached to transports. Most of the ships currently in dock didn't use modules, they had cargo compartments that had to be unloaded through inconvenient specialized hatches. That wasn't unusual for an outsystem/non-corporate political entity ship.

Preservation has high safety standards so we passed through two air walls before we got to the cargo ship's hatch. (High safety standards are great when they're designed to protect humans against dangerous stuff like hatch failures and hull breaches; when they're designed to protect humans against rogue SecUnits, not so much.)

I tried a ping but only got a response from the ship's transit ring–assigned marker, which had its docking number and the *Lalow* registry name. This meant no bot pilot that I could get information from. That was depressing. I had no idea what else I was supposed to do as a member of this group and just following humans around listening to them talk felt a lot like just being a SecUnit again. I mean, I am a SecUnit, but . . . You know what I mean.

Aylen tapped the ship's comm for attention and sent her feed ID, and added, "I'm a Special Investigator for Station Security. I'm here with a Port Authority supervisor. We need to speak to you about the transport contracted to your trading concern, the one currently in dock in the public transport ring. It's urgent."

I'd stopped out of view of the hatch cam, standing to one side, because that's what SecUnits do. The PA bot came over and stood next to me. Great, that's great. I wondered if it did anything that wasn't related to standing around.

The comm acknowledgment pinged and a voice, echoing with the feed-assisted translation, replied, "Just you and the PA. Leave the port heels outside."

I wonder what the original word choice was that the feed's translation algorithm had decided "heels" was a good equivalent in Preservation Standard.

(I wasn't the only one wondering. Tifany's eyes narrowed and Farid mouthed the word "heels" slowly.)

Aylen glanced at Gamila, and told the officers, and me and the bot I guess, "Wait here."

The hatch slid open and as they stepped toward it, my threat assessment module spiked.

I checked my drone inputs from Mensah's task group first, even though they had reported in on schedule, eleven seconds ago, but they were all nominal. Mensah was still in the council offices, the big meeting having broken up into little meetings. She was sitting with four other councilors going over feed documents while they had cups of one of the hot liquids humans like.

Aylen and Gamila had just walked through the hatch, which was now sliding shut. I had the impulse to lunge

something was jamming me, something that had been activated since the hatch had closed.

Fuck not hacking systems. I hit the port admin feed and connected to SafetyMonitor, the PA system that kept up a constant connection with all ships and transports in dock. I used it to find and break the ship's secure connection to the feed, and tried to pull camera views from inside, but I couldn't find any video connections except the stupid hatch camera. I caught an audio source but all I could hear was humans yelling some distance away; they must be in another part of the ship, away from the audio pick-up. I found Aylen's connection to the port feed and upped it, trying to get through to her.

I upped it enough that I caught a burst of static from her and relayed it to the Station Security feed. Both Tifany and Farid looked startled and Balin the bot expanded a sensor net from the back of its neck. I stripped out the static; it was Aylen's ID, and she was sending a Station Security urgent assistance code.

For fuck's sake, I knew this was a bad idea and I stood here like an idiot and let it happen. I turned to Tifany and Farid. "I need to get in there."

Farid had a hand on his interface, sending another urgent-assistance-needed code to the Station Security comm. Tifany was more direct. She drew her baton and said, "Balin, get us inside."

The PA bot stood up to twice my height (I honestly hadn't realized it had been crouching until that point), extended an arm, shoved spidery fingers into the control interface in the bulkhead next to the hatch, and sent a complex ping I realized was a decoder. The hatch slid open.

Okay, so that was what the PA bot did when it wasn't just standing around.

My drones zipped past me and I dove through the hatch after them. This is what I do when I'm not standing around.

Past the airlock, I had a drone view of a shabby corridor, an open hatch at the end, and a shabby human/Target One standing there with a big energy weapon. Audio picked up angry human shouting. Past the target and the hatch was a large compartment with three corridors leading off it. Aylen and Gamila were backed into a corner, Aylen in front with her arms out, trying to shield Gamila. Four additional targets, two armed, faced them. Target Two was the closest, aiming a projectile weapon at them and yelling. Target Three: initial assessment = most likely to fire. She was further away from the hostages, also yelling, and waving her projectile weapon.

Warned by the hatch opening, Target One had time to turn toward me and lift the weapon. I had two humans trying to come in behind me so I didn't dodge, but I didn't want to block the energy burst with my head, either. I fired from my right arm and hit the Target's weapon. (I could

have aimed for his face but I didn't consider him that much
of a threat.) He yelped and spun sideways as I reached him.
I bonked his head against the edge of the hatch and yanked
the damaged weapon away.

I flung him through the hatch in front of me to draw fire,
and then stepped through to throw the broken weapon at
Armed Target Two. It bounced off her head as I fired my
left arm weapon at Armed Target Three and hit her in the
chest and shoulder. I was still moving across the compartment and I slammed into Unarmed Target Four along the
way and threw him into Target Two who had stumbled
back and dropped her weapon. They both went down in a
heap and I slid to a stop with my back to Aylen and Gamila.
I had my drone task group do a fast circuit of the compartment then break into small squads. Three squads took up
sentry positions and the rest shot out of the hatches to
search the ship for more targets.

Not an ideal intervention/retrieval; my speed had been
a little low. Trying to keep Tifany and Farid from getting
shot had thrown me off. Also, I wasn't sure yet if the Targets
were hostiles or just really stupid, so I had held back a little.
Target Three had crumpled to the floor, still conscious and
trying to grope for her weapon. Before I had to shoot her
again, Tifany and Farid barreled in and Farid scooped up
the weapon. Targets One and Four were dazed and not attempting to move, Target Five had dropped to the floor and

was screaming for no reason. Target Two sprawled on the floor, pretending to be unconscious.

I would have worried about an as yet unknown Target trying to lock us inside (it wouldn't have worked, but it would have been annoying to deal with) (nobody wants to be locked in a ship with an annoyed SecUnit) (nobody) but my sentry drones had a camera view of Balin planting itself in the hatchway and extending four bracing limbs to keep it open. (I'm guessing the Port Authority has dealt with problem crews before.)

Tifany moved further into the room, taking up a guard position to my left as Farid said, "We've called for assistance, and uh, I'll alert Medical."

I was getting drone video telling me that the ship was a stripped-down cargo hauler, with a small livable space. The drones hadn't found any other occupants. From inside, the jamming was easy to take down, and I pulled a manifest from the ship's feed to double-check the complement. I said, "Ship is clear, listed crew is accounted for." Because I was tired of Target Two's shit, I turned around to ask Aylen and Gamila, "Are you injured?"

Target Two made a wild grab for her fallen projectile weapon. I kicked the weapon over to Tifany, who snatched it up and secured it. (Yes, it was unnecessary and showing off.)

Aylen said, "We're unhurt." She sounded calm, a dry

edge to her voice, but her forehead was damp with sweat and her heart rate was still elevated. Her jacket and shirt had been disarranged, like someone had grabbed her and pushed her. "Thank you for intervening."

Gamila leaned against the wall, a hand pressed to her chest. "I'm not even sure what happened! They threatened us, wouldn't even listen to why we were here."

"You're here to take our ship!" Target Two snarled, the feed translating. "You pussing corporates! You sent a Sec-Unit after us!"

I turned to look down at her. "You didn't know they had a SecUnit until we broke in. Try again."

Target Two's brow knit as she looked up at me and her mouth hung open.

Target Five moaned, "Shut up, Fenn. They're going to take our ship."

Aylen shook her head wearily and Gamila said, "You should have thought of that before you attacked us!"

My drone sentries saw the Station Security Response Team thunder up to the outer hatch. Balin unwedged itself from its guard position, strode down the corridor, and folded itself down to get into the compartment. It extended a limb across to Gamila, she took it, and it led her out of the ship.

Nobody moved until they were out of the way. Then the response team crowded in and Aylen said, "Arrest everyone associated with this ship. They obviously don't want to talk to us here, so we'll do it at the station."

———

Putting it mildly, it was weird to voluntarily walk into a Station Security office.

I had never been to one before on any station. (If I had, I'd be parts and recycler trash and you wouldn't be reading this.) SecUnits weren't normally used in stations in the Corporation Rim, and we sure weren't used in normal station regulation enforcement. We were only deployed on a station as an extreme measure, like repelling a raider attack. (And stations with deployment centers weren't likely to be attacked anyway, unless there were an absolute shit-ton of raiders or they were really stupid or both.) Palisade Security, working for GrayCris, had used a SecUnit as part of their hostage security team on TranRollinHyfa because they were worried about me showing up. And they had used two SecUnits and a CombatUnit as fugitive pursuit when I escaped with Mensah. And look how that had turned out for them.

But anyway, for most of my career as an escaped rogue SecUnit, staying away from Station Security had been kind of important.

Preservation's Station Security office was next to the Port Authority, part of the barrier that separated the port's embarkation area from the rest of the station. Both offices had entrances into the admin section of the mall and the transit ring.

Not long after I had first gotten here I had accessed a map of the security office interior from the station archives. The first level was a public area, where humans came in to complain about each other and to pay fines for cargo and docking violations. (Preservation had two economies, one a complicated barter system for planetary residents and one currency-based for visitors and for dealing with other polities. Most of the humans here didn't really understand how important hard currency was in the Corporation Rim but the council did, and Mensah said the port took in enough in various fees to keep the station from being a drain on the planet's resources.) The second level was much bigger and had work spaces, conference rooms, and accident/safety equipment storage. There was also a separate attached space for holding cells, and a larger separate section for storing and analyzing samples from potentially hazardous cargo, and a small medical treatment area that seemed to be mostly used for intoxicated detainees.

The response team brought in the detainees through the transit ring entrance. Targets Two and Three had already come in on gurneys headed for the medical area but the others were mostly ambulatory.

The weapons scanners on the station's entrance went off on me, of course.

It caused some confusion, because the response team thought someone had screwed up and not searched the detainees properly. I stood there for two minutes and twelve seconds wondering if anyone would figure it out while they searched the detainees again, looking for the weapon the scanner was alerting on. In their defense, they had actually done the weapons search right the first time (I had verified it with scan and visual), and they had confiscated the detainees' interfaces. (None of them were augmented humans—apparently it wasn't common to be feed augmented in the polities outside the Corporation Rim that used Preservation as a waystation.) But not so much in their defense, they had forgotten a SecUnit was standing behind them.

Finally I pulled up my sleeve (using my onboard energy weapons made holes in fabric, so I'd have to get my shirt fixed) and held my arm up. "Hey, it's me."

They all stared. Still woozy, Target Four said, "It's a slitting SecUnit, you pussers, how stupid are you?"

Yeah, these Targets are going to be fun to chat with, I can tell already. I told him, "You're the one who got yourself bodyslammed into station detention, so let's talk about how dumb you are."

Target Four seemed shocked. "SecUnits aren't supposed to talk back," Target Five said weakly.

Tell me about it. "Cargo ship crews aren't supposed to take Port Authority supervisors as hostages, but here we all are."

From the front of the group, Aylen snapped, "Get them inside!"

The officers hurriedly milled into a more efficient configuration for taking the Targets in through the foyer. As I was rolling my sleeve down, Aylen stepped over to me. I don't know what I was expecting; nothing good, basically. But keeping her voice low, she said, "I've just had a preliminary report from the Port Authority inspectors. They did an initial scan of the *Lalow's* storage, and the cargo containers are empty. And there's no record of anything leaving that ship."

Empty? What the fuck? I actually locked up for a second, still rolling down my sleeve. Threat assessment had just spiked and even risk assessment (which really needed to be purged and reloaded) tried to deliver a report.

I was thinking a lot of different things but the one that came out was, "So what was the transport waiting for?" I knew from my drone search that the transport Lutran had been killed in didn't have a cargo module attached. At the time, this hadn't seemed a big deal, since if the transport was sitting in dock it was probably waiting for modules to be loaded.

"A good question," Aylen said. Her expression was still in the neutral range but I could tell she was intrigued by the report, just like my threat assessment module.

I wasn't sure why she had told me this. Unless it was because she had just gotten the news and after the weapons scan fuck-up I was the only one involved with the investigation who she wasn't currently pissed off at. It would be nice if she had recognized me as the only other one here who actually knew how to investigate a suspicious incident that wasn't a cargo safety violation, but I doubted that. I said, "They know a lot about SecUnits for a ship with a non-corporate registry. We're usually only deployed as rentals on mining or other isolated contract labor installations, or by licensed security companies. They could have seen SecUnits in the media, but . . ." I couldn't finish that sentence. The fear and hatred had felt different from the fear and hatred generated by shows like *Valorous Defenders*, which sometimes featured rogue SecUnits as scary villains. The crew's reaction had felt like there was personal experience behind it, but I had no data to back that up.

"Hmm." Aylen lifted her brows. "According to their

ship's circuit report, they've never even visited a corporate dock."

"There could be an explanation," I said, because there could be, and I'm used to having to be as accurate as possible or get my neural tissue fried and old habits, etc.

"Let's ask them," she said, and went on into the station.

There was a delay, because there was documentation on the arrests that needed to be completed and the Targets all needed medical checks because that was a regulation and blah blah blah. Also more relevantly, a tech team was searching the ship for anything that looked like 1) a contact DNA cleaner and 2) something that could cause the visual jamming effect with the transit ring's surveillance camera or 3) a suspiciously fluid-stained floater cart. It also gave the Port Authority more time to pull corroborating documentation about the ship and the missing/nonexistent cargo.

I had feed messages; one from Ratthi asking if everything was okay and had I caught the murderer yet, one from Gurathin which was the same except he didn't ask if I was okay, and one from Pin-Lee saying she wanted me to contact her now, no she meant right now, it was important.

I had followed the others into the main office space on

level two, which had a large holo map of the whole station in the center, with a running status display on all station locks, air walls, and other safety systems, plus a scroll of data on cargo regulation checks throughout the port. It was surrounded by work areas and floating display surfaces. Also way too many containers with food residue, ugh. Several humans were sitting around working in their feeds and none of them looked up when I came in.

I found an unoccupied corner to stand in and sent acknowledgments/reply-laters to Ratthi and Gurathin, and tapped Pin-Lee's feed.

The first thing she sent was *I saw the update Indah sent to Mensah about an incident in the cargo dock. Is it GrayCris?*

I told her, *I don't know.* I just didn't have enough data yet for my percentages to be meaningful as anything other than theoretical shit-talking, even with the info Aylen had given me. I added, *It might be.*

Her feed voice sounded weary. *Are we ever going to be at a point where we can forget about those assholes?*

I didn't want to just say "eventually" so I told her, *I can't give you a timeline. But GrayCris can't get the currency to buy the company off, and even if they could, it's too late for that.* GrayCris had ordered a security firm to attack a company gunship, and worse, almost succeeded. There was no going back from that, at least as far as the company was concerned.

Farid came into the room, spotted me, and came over to say, "Uh, we're making tea. Do you—"

I paused my feed and told him, "I don't eat."

"Oh, right." He wandered off.

Pin-Lee sent, *There's been a Station Security request for documents from the General Counsel's office relating to cargo brokering between the Corporation Rim and outsystem polities and trading concerns. It sounds like they're looking at a possible fraud or smuggling investigation to go along with the murder. Do you want a copy of the report when we send it?*

Yes. Farid was back, this time waving at me to follow him. *I have to go.*

Find out what the hell is going on, Pin-Lee sent back, and cut the connection.

I followed Farid out of the work space and around into a conference room. Indah and Tural were seated at a table facing a large floating display. It was divided into three separate sections, each showing a different much smaller conference room. In each room was a response team officer, sitting across from a Target. Aylen was in the room with Target Five (yeah, I had picked Target Five as the one who probably knew the most about whatever it was they were doing) and the other two officers were with Targets Two and Four. One and Three were probably still in Medical.

I pulled the individual feeds so I could put them into separate inputs, in case I wanted to review them later. Right now

Aylen and the other officers were explaining to their individual Targets what rights they had as detainees in Preservation Alliance territory. (It was a lot of rights. I was pretty sure it was more rights than a human who hadn't been detained by Station Security had in the Corporation Rim.)

Chairs were scattered around and Indah waved me toward one, so I sat down. Again, it was a little, more than a little, weird. I was in a Station Security office, sitting down. (Non-rogue SecUnits aren't allowed to sit down on duty, or off duty, if there's any chance of being caught.)

Farid, Tifany, and three other officers stood back in the doorway to watch. (I will never figure out how humans decide who gets to sit where and do what, it's never the same.) (There were more cups and small plates with food residue on the table. They're always eating.)

On the three feeds, Aylen and the other two officers started the initial questions, basically "who are you," "why are you here on Preservation Station," and "what the hell were you thinking?"

The Targets' stories were fairly consistent: they were traders originating in what they called an indie station designated WayBrogatan (a quick search on the Preservation public library feed confirmed its existence) and they shipped small cargos on a regular route that never, ever, at any point intersected the Corporation Rim. And they never took on passengers, no, no way no how, never! Way-

Brogatan had special regulations and they weren't licensed for it. (That was Target Five's earnest contribution.)

Tural muttered, "Because crews who take station staff hostage are going to be sticklers for licensing regulations."

Indah agreed. "Whatever they're afraid of, it's about passengers and cargo." She tapped the investigators' private feed, which I had not been given access to and did not hack, because apparently I get to sit in a chair but not participate.

The other two officers, Soire with Target Two and Matif with Target Four, started in with questions about the ship's cargo definitely-not-passenger route, making the Targets go over what the ship had been carrying and what it had dropped off and picked up in exhaustive detail.

Aylen worked on that with Target Five, then smiled, not in a friendly way, and said, "Now. Care to explain why you tried to abduct a Station Security officer and the Port Authority supervisor?"

"Too soon?" Farid asked Indah.

She shook her head slightly. "Maybe not."

Target Five vibrated with dismay. "I didn't—We didn't do that—It was a misunderstanding—"

Weirdly, I got the sense that was true. It had been a misunderstanding.

Aylen said, "Before you argue with me about it, please recall that I was the Station Security officer you abducted."

"But—It was—" Target Five subsided and looked glum.

"Attempted abduction is the charge my senior is at this moment bringing to the Preservation Station judge-advocate." Since Aylen's senior was at this moment sitting with her arms folded intently watching the display, I guess this was a tactic. It seemed really transparent to me, but then I wasn't the one who'd landed myself in detention for what I was beginning to think was not monumental stupidity, but just a monumentally stupid mistake.

Aylen listened to Target Five sputter and protest. She said finally, "Unless you have an explanation?"

"We're just shipping cargo," Target Five said, too desperately. "It was a mistake. We overreacted. Fenn and Miro would never hurt anybody."

"It didn't look that way from the other side of the guns they had aimed at my face." Aylen was still calm and pointed.

I said, "They were expecting someone else. Someone they didn't know. They thought Aylen was lying about being Station Security."

All the humans in the room turned to look at me. I always hate that, but Tifany was nodding, and Indah said, "I'm leaning that way myself."

Targets Two and Four had been giving very convincing descriptions of their cargo route. Clearly they had taken some effort to get their stories straight. But Target Four had gotten the too-detailed story confused after the third stop and was now winging it very badly. It could have just been that Target Four had a bad memory. (I was always having to remember that humans didn't have full access to the archives stored in their neural tissue, which explained a lot about their behavior.)

Indah was subvocalizing on her feed. Aylen paused to listen, then said, "Who did you think we were?"

Target Five flustered, then leaned forward, confiding now. "The rings we go to aren't nice like this one, you can get your ship raided by the people who work there. That's what we thought it was."

Aylen nodded, like there was some tiny chance in the realm of possibility that she was buying that. "These rings are in the Corporation Rim?"

"No, no, no." Target Five did an agitated shaking movement that was apparently emphatic denial. "We've never been there. Too many permits, we can't afford it. And it's dangerous."

Aylen eyed her. Then she said, "Do you recognize this person?" and used her feed to throw an image of Lutran up on the room's display surface.

The image wasn't one of the good close-ups of Dead Lutran but the one of him alive, from the hostel. Scanners had been activated in the conference room and the real-time reports were running alongside the video display. As part of the rights thing, Aylen had told Target Five the scanner would be on, which I thought was playing way too fair, but maybe not, because Target Five didn't show an elevated heart rate or any other neural cues indicating recognition.

Target Five frowned, a clearly "why the fuck is she asking me this" expression. She said, "Uh . . . No."

Matif and Soire were getting similar reactions: Target Two clearly thought it was a trick and Target Four demanded to know who "that picker" was.

The humans all looked at the scan results and I said, "Chances that they're lying are below 20 percent." I had tapped the scanner's raw feed so I could process the data faster. (Tapping a feed that's being displayed in front of me is not hacking.)

Everybody looked at me again, then at Indah, who nodded, her gaze not leaving the display of Target Five's face. It looked like she knew what she was doing. It would be interesting to compare her data to mine. Then I remembered the main reason I was doing this was to make sure there was no connection to GrayCris and I wasn't going to refine my methods, such as they were. (What they were being mostly: crap I made up on the spot as I needed it that sort of worked, and leftover company code analysis.)

Aylen tilted her head, an unconscious gesture while she was receiving feed reports from Matif and Soire. She said, "Here's a better view of his face."

This time Lutran was dead in the image, lying where he had been dumped in the corridor junction. Target Five shook her head slowly, eyes narrowing. "No. I don't know this person. Why are you asking me about them?"

Similar reactions from Targets Two and Four. (Well, Four wanted to know if it was the same person in the two images. Matif looked like someone who was desperately repressing the urge to sigh.)

From Aylen's briefly preoccupied expression, I thought Indah had delivered another instruction via the feed. Then Aylen said, "His name was Lutran. He was found—"

She stopped abruptly because the scanner spiked. Target Five had had a reaction, a controlled flinch, and her skin was flushing as her internal fluids moved around. Target Two blinked rapidly, also flushing. Four said, "Fuck no."

Indah said softly, "Oh, now, here we go."

Aylen asked Target Five, "So you do know him?"

Target Five forced her expression back to blankness. "No."

Target Two folded her arms and pushed back in her chair. "I'm finished talking. You go ahead and throw us in detent."

Target Four said worriedly, "What about the others?"

Matif's expression of borderline frustration snapped to calm and neutral, but he was probably lucky the scanner wasn't pointed at him. He said, "I'll check. Can you tell me their names? Describe them?"

Aylen and Soire both stopped to listen as Target Four described ten humans, three of them adolescents. Apparently his memory was terrible for lies but great for the truth, and I didn't (and the scanner didn't) think he was making any of it up.

Matif leaned forward, making sure his feed recording was getting all the details. "You're saying these people should be with Lutran?"

"He was taking them home, to a home." Target Four tapped the table earnestly. "We never saw him, you know, compartmentalize to make it hard for them to catch everybody."

"Them?" Matif asked. "Who is them?"

Target Four said, "The Brehars. It's Brehar something."

I ran a quick public library query while the humans were fumbling to access their interfaces. "Possibly BreharWall-Han. It's a mining corporate . . ." I pulled more results, looking for connections. Oh, there was a big one. "It owns a system only one direct twenty-eight cycle wormhole jump from WayBrogatan."

Indah's whole face was scrunched in concentration. Tural whispered, "People. The *Lalow* was smuggling people."

Soire was having Target Two taken to the holding cell, but Aylen's face had gone preoccupied as she listened to Matif's feed. Target Five watched her, frowning in growing consternation. "Miro's talking, isn't he?" she said in despair.

Indah relayed my info to Matif, who asked Target Four, "These people came from BreharWallHan?"

"Yeah, they were slaves," Target Four told him. "They call it something else, but it's slaves, right, dah? That's what it is. Out in the rocks."

Putting together Target Four's story with what my library searches were turning up, BreharWallHan had a mining operation in an asteroid belt. The type of mining meant the contract labor had the ability to move around, to go from one asteroid to another, but they had no way to get anywhere else in the system, or out of it, and BreharWallHan controlled all access to supplies. But someone (Target Four either wouldn't or couldn't supply a name) had started an operation where contract laborers would make their way to the edge of the asteroid field, where a ship would slip in, pick them up, and take them away via the wormhole, to a point where the Targets aboard the *Lalow* would meet them and take them to a station where they would find the next step in their escape route.

"The corporates don't notice?" Matif was fascinated but skeptical. "You taking out so many people at one time?"

Target Four was unfazed. "Cause we're taking out their kids, dah. These people been out in those rocks so long they got kids older than me."

Behind me, Tifany said, "What the fuck?"

"Wait, wait." Matif was having a moment. "Are you

saying these people were shipped to this belt as contract labor, but they've been there so long they've had families—children—and those children are being born into slavery? They aren't allowed to leave?"

"I know." Target Four spread his big hands on the table. "Penis move, right? That's why we're doing this, dah. Our grandperson was contract labor, like back in the back of time, before they got away and bought the ship."

Aylen told Target Five, "Oh yes, he's telling us everything."

Target Five tried, "He has a head injury."

Aylen was unimpressed. "He seems perfectly lucid." Indah was subvocalizing again, talking to Aylen on her feed. "Even if you took payment to bring those people here, it's not illegal, and it's not illegal to be a contract labor refugee on Preservation. You can tell us where they are, we'll get them proper help. But you need to tell us how Lutran fits in to this."

Matif had just said, "But what did this have to do with Lutran?"

"He was the one, the plan person, right?" Target Four said. "He was supposed to handle what happened next."

"What happened next?" Matif asked.

Target Four put his hands in the air. "I don't know, that's what I was asking you."

Target Five slumped back in her chair, telling Aylen,

"Lutran was our contact, he always meets us at the station, whichever one it is." She added miserably, "If somebody killed him, they know about us."

I said, "The perpetrator is a BreharWallHan agent." I mean, probably. The chances were running over 85 percent.

Indah flicked her fingers at the display surfaces, and Aylen and Matif stopped talking. She said, "Not necessarily. We need to find out what happened aboard that transport. We know Lutran used it to get here, that it was involved in a cargo transfer contract with the *Lalow,* and that Lutran was killed aboard it. What does that tell us?"

Tural said, "I bet the refugees were meant to go aboard the transport, to be taken to its next destination." They made a vague gesture. "The refugees either never made it to the transport, or they were killed as well, and . . . we just haven't found their bodies yet."

Indah was frowning. "Or the refugees killed Lutran? Because he demanded something from them, like payment?"

I said, "What did the review of the Merchant Docks surveillance video show?"

Yeah, it was a trick question. I knew from my drones still out in the main office area that the video had just been transferred from PortAuthSys to StationSecSys, and none of the humans working on the case had had a chance to download the files yet.

Indah looked at me, and I realized that she knew exactly what I was doing. She said, "If that's your way of asking if you can review the video, then yes." She nodded to Tural.

On reflection, I could have handled that better.

Tural got into their feed and gave my feed ID permission to download the video. I pulled the files while they were explaining how to access and play the material, and got to work.

Indah signaled for the questioning to continue, but there wasn't much left to find out. Target Five gave in and supported Target Four's version of the story, and they both insisted that they didn't know what was supposed to happen after the refugees disembarked. All they knew was that Lutran would take care of getting them off the station to safety.

We needed to find out where the refugees were now, if they were either a) murderees or b) murderers. Concentrating on the video taken in the area around the *Lalow*'s dock, within 1.3 minutes I had isolated the moments when the refugees had left the ship. That gave us more to work with than just the descriptions Target Five had provided to Matif, though the camera's estimates weren't as good as full body scans.

The refugees were dressed in work clothes, and a few had small shoulder bags. They looked lost, stopping to check the feed markers frequently and moving slowly, as if they had never seen a station like this before. (Trapped in a contract labor camp spread out over an asteroid field, they probably hadn't.) It didn't catch any attention in this section of the docks, where ships from a wide range of places disembarked a lot of humans who had no clue what they were doing. And one of the regular-route merchants had just set a large noisy crew loose, plus there were three cargos being unloaded with varying degrees of efficiency and confusion. The *Lalow* had probably waited until the docks had gotten busy, to let the refugees mix with the crowd. The Port Authority personnel were obviously too worried about humans causing hauler bot accidents to notice the quiet group hesitantly crossing the embarkation floor.

I spotted Lutran entering the Merchant Docks one minute after the refugees left the *Lalow*. Seventeen minutes later, he left again. He had managed to avoid any cameras while inside the docks, so there was no indication of what he had done while there. It was too bad he was dead; for a human, he had been pretty good at this.

I sent the images of the refugees to Indah and Tural, then checked the video near the Merchant Dock exits to see if we could get some idea of where the refugees had headed next.

Then it got weird.

It got so weird I took extra time running the video back and forth, checking for anomalies and edits.

The Targets had been sent to detention cells to wait, and Aylen, Matif, and Soire had joined Indah and Tural to make exclamations over what they had found out instead of anything more useful. I said, "They never left the Merchant Docks."

"What?" Indah turned toward me.

I threw the video onto one of the display surfaces. I accelerated the speed, pausing it for two seconds when any human, augmented human, or bot left either of the two exits. "There's no sign of any member of the refugee party leaving the Merchant Docks. They disappear somewhere between the dockside cameras and the exit cameras' fields of view."

The humans stared at the video, Aylen moving so she could see better. "They've changed their appearances—" Soire began.

"Body types don't match." Since the security cameras used the same calibration standards, it had been easy to include a comparison check in the search. The security system noted feed IDs of known humans and augmented humans (Security officers, Port Authority staff, the merchant crews who did regular runs to Preservation) and I'd used them to annotate my sped-up video. There were only seven unidentified humans who had wandered out of the dock exits during our time frame, none matching the body type estimates the system had taken from the refugees, and all seven unidentified humans had returned via the dock entrance. I matched them on the dockside camera returning to their ships.

Aylen shook her head and reached for a jacket slung over a chair. She had the expression of someone who wanted to curse a lot but wasn't going to. "We need to get over there and find them."

Because obviously, if they hadn't left, they were still there.

Whatever, the chance that it was GrayCris activity that had caused Lutran's death was dropping rapidly. I could leave Station Security to finish up. Go back and catch up on my media while I kept watch over Mensah. I should do that. The rest of this was Station Security's job, I could leave. I could pretend to be the enigmatic SecUnit and just get up and walk out. Pin-Lee had written my employment contract that way, so I could just leave.

I wasn't leaving.

I didn't think I'd have a better time to push for this. I waited until Indah finished ordering all response teams into the Merchant Docks for a search, then said, "Has there been a diagnostic analysis of StationSec and PortAuth and all associated systems?"

Aylen, Matif, and Soire were already on the way out to get their gear and Tural was in the feed mobilizing the tech crew. Aylen stopped but Indah waved her on to keep moving.

As the door slid shut behind them, Indah said impatiently, "No, not since you asked the first time and I told you the analysts had checked for hacks and there was nothing, no alerts had been tripped."

Alerts? She hadn't said that the first time. "They relied on alerts?"

Tural was listening now, their face turned guarded in that very familiar "someone else is getting in trouble" way. Indah said flatly, "I don't know. The report they sent said that in their opinion, there had been no hack."

I said, "With the safety of the station depending on it, are you sure you don't want a second opinion?"

There was a moment, slightly fraught. Indah said, "You want access to our systems."

I could go into all my reasoning and my threat assessment module's indicator that there was only a 35 percent chance there was a jamming device present on this station. (I was 86 percent certain that type of device actually existed somewhere, but I just didn't think it would be easily available, even to a security company. Mainly because, if something like that was easy to obtain, the company would have countermeasures for its SecSystems, and I would know about it. Obviously, it could have been a casualty of one of my memory wipes, or it could be something only available outside the Corporation Rim, but still.) If someone had gotten far enough into the port's system to tamper with the camera video, they might have done/do anything.

I could have also said that Indah had me, the best resource Station Security could have for this situation, and she was too afraid to use me. I said, "To check for hacking, yes."

Tural shifted uneasily, but they were brave, and said, "We should make sure. If there has been interference with our camera video, we could be looking for the refugees in the wrong place."

Indah didn't reply. It occurred to me if she turned me down, I was going to feel . . . something, probably general humiliation, and basically like an idiot. Which sucked, because I had set myself up yet again. But what she said was, "How much access would you need? And how long would it take?"

Okay, huh. "Admin access, under five minutes." I know, five minutes was a hilariously long time, but I wanted a good long look around while I was in there.

Indah didn't reply. I figured it was about 40/60 between "it will take over the station and kill us all" and "this isn't the worst idea I ever heard." Then she said, "Only five minutes?"

"I'm fast," I said. "If the dock surveillance system is hacked, then everything on the Port Authority systems could be compromised."

Indah said, "You don't have to spell it out quite so pointedly, I understand the consequences. But we have data protection on the security systems—"

Data protection, right. Guess what provides your data protection—another security system. I had to make her understand. "And that's what everybody says. When I walked onto TranRollinHyfa and walked out with Dr. Mensah, that's exactly what they said."

(I know, very dramatic and also inaccurate. Dr. Mensah walked out barefoot and I limped out leaning on Ratthi and Gurathin. But you see my point.)

Indah's mouth twisted in skepticism. Okay, fine then. I said, "Are the systems in the Security Station offices monitored for breach attempts?"

Her brow furrowed. "Yes."

I'd chosen the StationSec office because it had a nested set of high security systems not connected to the Port Authority, so a demonstration there was unlikely to alert our hostile. I had several options to go with, having been in the systems and rummaged around a little when Mensah had first brought me here, before I stupidly promised not to touch anything. I decided on something showy.

I took control of the visual and audio displays in the main work space. Through the open door, we heard the humans in there make startled noises. Indah glared at me. "What did you—"

I put a camera view up on a display surface. In the main office area, the three-dimensional station safety map was now showing episode 256 of *The Rise and Fall of Sanctuary Moon,* the scene 32.3 minutes in when the solicitor, her bodyguard, and the personnel supervisor are having a relationship argument that is abruptly cut off when a raider ship crashes into the shuttle bay.

Tifany, Aylen, and the others getting ready for the search stared at it in bafflement. "What the balls?" somebody said.

Indah's face was . . . interesting. She gestured to the display surface. "How are you getting this view of the room? There's no camera in there."

I could have used a drone's camera, but this way made for a better demonstration. "It's Farid's vest cam," I told her.

Indah grimaced. "You've made your point. Fix the screen," she said. "And check the systems for hacking."

Chapter Six

AFTER ALL THAT, IT took me six minutes to find out the dock surveillance system had not been hacked.

I didn't find anything. No aberrations in the logs, no anomalous deletions, no foreign code, no traces at all.

So, that's just great.

There had to be something I was missing. Or maybe I'm just a robot with enough human neural tissue jammed in my head to make me stupid who should have stayed with the company, guarding contract labor and staring at walls.

Fortunately Indah and Tural had followed the others out to the main office to get their gear for the search, and I could have an emotion on my face in relative private.

I'd decided to stay, but I really wanted to leave.

I'd been so sure I was right.

I went out into the main office and told Indah, "There's no hack. The surveillance system was clear."

I was braced for something, I had no idea what. But the fleeting look of disappointment that crossed Indah's face wasn't it. She grimaced, and used the feed to revoke my system access.

Aylen came in from the other room, pulling on a deflection vest. "The off shift volunteered to come in early," she said. "And Supervisor Gamila is helping with coordination."

"Good, take all of them." Indah glanced at me. "And Sec-Unit."

Well, fine.

An evidence team was still searching the *Lalow* and Indah sent them an order via the feed that they might be looking for "signs of body disposal." One theory was that the refugees had been killed in the docks by the *Lalow*'s crew and the remains somehow smuggled back into their ship.

(I know, if they could do that to ten refugees why didn't they do that to Lutran? But sometimes you have to look into every possibility, even the dumb ones.)

The *Lalow* search team had already found evidence that the refugees really had been aboard long enough to get here from a point near the BreharWallHan mining field: the ship's recycler stats showed waste and water conversion from at least fifteen humans for the duration of the trip, and the ship's stores had a suspiciously large amount of bedding and food, plus games for pre-adolescents.

(Yes, again, I know. Why bring them all the way here

alive and in relative comfort, let them disembark, then kill them? Theoretically the *Lalow* crew could have been paid to do that, but if there had been a hard currency transfer it wouldn't have occurred on station so there was no way we could find that out.)

Station Security was only allowed to keep the *Lalow* for one Preservation day-cycle before they either had to charge the crew with something or let them go. Indah could charge them with the threatening and imprisoning or whatever else they had done to Aylen and Supervisor Gamila any-time she wanted to give us more time to investigate, but she was holding off. Before we had left for the Merchant Docks again, Indah told the special investigation team, "If this circus act is telling the truth and they're the only lifeline those people trapped at BreharWallHan have, then we'll release them without charge. Until then I don't want to risk any information about any of this getting into outsystem news-feeds. Normally this isn't a problem but—" She pointed her eyebrows at me. "We seem to be getting a lot of attention from the Corporation Rim lately."

Like that's my fault.

She continued, "I think we all realize by now that be-tween the murder and the missing individuals, this is un-likely to be a single local actor. Our most likely perpetrators will be agents of the corporate entity BreharWallHan, who came here specifically to stop this refugee operation. With the port closed, they're trapped here."

I was with her right up until the "they're trapped here" part. I wasn't willing to count on that because it involved depending on humans and bots and systems I didn't have access to.

Aylen had formed up two more teams to search the ships in dock, though Station Security was starting to run short of personnel. There were ships not attached to the docks, in holding positions around the station, who had either been stopped in the middle of approach or departure by the closure of the port. If we didn't find anything in the port, the ships stopped in departure were going to have to be searched next. Even with the responder patrolling out there to keep everybody from leaving, that was going to be a mess.

From what I could hear over the team feed channel, the ships in dock were cooperating with the search so far. The teams were going with the story that they were looking for "adults and adolescents who might be in the company of individuals who had committed violent acts on station," which was probably true.

No, I was not helping with the ship-to-ship search because the humans thought there would be "panic and resistance" if any of the search teams tried to board with a

SecUnit. (Yeah, let's revisit that the next time you get held hostage.)

So I was searching the dock utility areas with the hazardous materials safety techs and the cargo bots. The modules had drives but they weren't the kind you could turn on inside the station, so the cargo bots lifted and moved them for us so the techs could check the interiors.

Since this was the oldest part of the transit ring, we were moving along the stationside of the dock area, climbing in and out of outdated cargo storage chambers, safety equipment deployment corrals, office spaces that were long abandoned to storage. One of the techs muttered, "We can take our video and make a historical documentary."

Another tech walked up to me. "Um, SecUnit, we need someone to help move this cabinet—"

"Then you should find someone to do that for you." I was not in the mood.

"Well, it's in a small space and JollyBaby can't fit." They gestured to the cargo bot looming over us.

"Its name is not JollyBaby." Tell me its name is not Jolly-Baby. It was five meters tall sitting in a crouch and looked like the mobile version of something you used to dig mining shafts.

JollyBaby broadcast to the feed: *ID=JollyBaby*. The other cargo bots and everything in the bay with a processing capability larger than a drone all immediately pinged it back, and added amusement sigils, like it was a stupid private joke.

I said, "You have to be shitting me." I already wanted to walk out an airlock and this didn't help. (The only thing worse than humans infantilizing bots was bots infantilizing themselves.)

JollyBaby secured a private connection with me and sent: *Re: previous message=joke.* And it added its actual ID, which was its hard feed address. So it was a stupid private joke. I don't think that made it any better.

The human was still looking at me helplessly and I said, "Where the fuck is the Port Authority bot? Isn't this its job?" All those arms had to be good for something besides holding hatches open.

The human shrugged vaguely. "I think it's with the Port Authority supervisor. It doesn't work in these docks." Jolly-Baby sent me another private message: *Balin not equal cargo hauler Balin equal cargo management.*

Balin didn't lift heavy things? Well, fuck Balin then. I said, "All right, where's the fucking cabinet?"

On the team channel, Matif was saying to Indah, *But would these refugees have a device that let them jam the port cameras?* He didn't think the refugees were responsible for killing Lutran, either. He added, *And know they could call a cart to the transport to dump the body? That seems like it has to be someone who was already here on station.*

The other conversation was Tural and Aylen, with Tural saying, *Why didn't the refugees just stop here? Why take the transport somewhere else?*

Aylen replied, *Maybe another group, or groups did. But they couldn't bring all the groups here without the risk that someone would find out about the scheme and expose it.*

No shuttles had left for the planet or any other insystem destination in the incident time frame, and I guess we were all just assuming the refugees hadn't been spaced, though the exterior station scan results hadn't come back yet.

The refugees couldn't have gotten off this dock, and Lutran's killer couldn't have entered his transport without the cameras' data on the PA systems being hacked. And I had of course proved that it hadn't.

Which . . . was a massive fuck-up on my part.

Because this was the kind of hacking a SecUnit could do, specifically a CombatUnit. If this was a BreharWallHan operation to stop the escapes, they might have brought in a security company with a CombatUnit doing exactly the kind of thing I had pretended to do on Milu: operating almost independently with a human supervisor planted somewhere on station. I just hadn't been good enough to find that Unit's trail in the PA's system.

I didn't know what I was going to do. I could call Mensah and ask for advice, which would actually be a cover for asking her to fix my fuck-up. Except I had no evidence of the hack; I couldn't even prove it to myself, so I didn't know how Mensah could fix it.

On the comm, one of the techs said, "Officer Aylen." It was the one who had made the comment about a historical documentary on the crap stored in the private docks. "I've got a problem with the empty modules."

Sounding frustrated, Aylen answered, "What problem?"

The tech explained, "According to the inventory, we're missing one. I'm guessing it's outside for transfer, so we need it brought in so we can verify—"

I cut into the channel and said, "A module is missing?" at the same time as Indah, Aylen, and Soire. Matif was already on the feed telling the Port Authority that we needed the spare-module use records and could they confirm an empty module outside the station?

"Ask them who authorized that transfer," Soire told Matif at the same time Aylen said, "Those modules can be pressurized, correct?"

I said, "Correct." I was already walking out of the ancient storage compartment back toward the embarkation area. They could finish the historical documentary without my help. If I was going to be useless, I could at least be useless where stuff was going on.

Indah said, "Find that fucking module."

I reached what the humans were calling the "mobile

command center," which was actually just one of the portable Port Authority terminal and display surfaces for accessing all the transit ring's traffic data. Indah stood next to it with PA Supervisor Gamila. Aylen, Tural, and other officers and techs sprinted in from different directions. Gamila controlled the terminal via her feed, the display surface floating above her head and flicking through sensor views of the outside hull of the station. I picked up a live feed from the station responder on picket duty, supplying alternate sensor views. Gamila was talking to someone on the responder, saying, "No, those modules are for the *Walks Silent Shores,* that's a scheduled transfer, they're all accounted for. We're looking for a single unregistered module—"

No authorized transfer, Matif reported via the Station Security feed. *It's just missing.*

Soire added, *Somebody must have deleted its records.*

(If it seems like they twigged to this faster than they had anything else, it was because cargo safety/smuggling and hazardous material prevention was actually most of their job. I'm sure they were great at talking down aggressively intoxicated humans, too.)

Still breathing hard from running down the dock, Aylen said to Tural, "Could someone install longterm life support in one of those things?"

"Theoretically, I guess." Tural's face scrunched with worry. "Not in a hurry. These are just transfer modules.

They're pressurized and they hold air, but . . . They're not meant for . . ."

They're not meant for anything that needs to breathe, not for longer than a cycle or so, Tural meant. If the refugees were in there, they didn't have much time left.

As a means to quickly move humans from the private Merchant Docks to a transport, it would have been fine, especially on a small transit ring like this one where the trip would have taken no more than half an hour at most. It was the ideal means of getting them from one end of the station to the other with no one noticing, especially if you were desperate to cover your tracks and throw off any corporate pursuit.

"Was this a trick all along?" Tifany said, low-voiced. She and Farid were standing next to me, for some reason. "Bring those people here, then put them on the module to kill them?"

"No, that's way too elaborate, if they just want to murder whoever tries to escape," Farid told her.

Well, yeah. The *Lalow* had thought it was delivering the group of refugees to the next step in their route to safety. The crew had sent the refugees out to meet their contact, who they knew was called Lutran, though they didn't know what he looked like. There had been no reported disruptions on the embarkation floor, no fight, no struggle picked up by the cameras, so the refugees had had no idea they were in danger.

So, working theory: Lutran meets the refugees and gets them to board the module that is due to be transferred from the Merchant Docks to his transport waiting in the Public Docks. (The transfers were all done by bot; haulers moved the recently loaded modules to the lock and pushed them out. If it was an inert module, the cargo bots would take it and attach it to its transport. If it was a powered module, the cargo bots would place it on one of the set paths around the station where it would get a go-signal and then head toward its destination. When it arrived, another cargo bot, or the transport itself if it had the right configuration, would attach the module.) With the refugees safe aboard the module, Lutran then goes back to his transport to make sure the module attaches correctly when it arrives and that the refugees get aboard. But it's not there, the module has been diverted to an unknown destination. Someone else is aboard the transport, and that person kills Lutran. Then that person, who somehow has hacked the PA's systems, deletes the record of Lutran's module transfer.

This scenario was the most likely one, the probability was 86 percent, easily. But it was impossible unless the perpetrator could 1) hack Lutran's transport, 2) hack the PortAuth surveillance cameras, and 3) hack the Port-Auth transfer records.

So where was the module? It couldn't just be floating around out there. The responder would have found it by now. Wherever it had gone, it must have looked like it was headed toward a legitimate destination, so the systems that did nothing but scan and monitor all station traffic wouldn't alert on it.

It had to be attached to a ship.

And that ship, and the BreharWallHan agents, was still out there. It had been unable to leave before Lutran was discovered and the port closed. Most stations wouldn't close their transit rings because someone found a dead body, but most stations weren't as short on random dead bodies as this one.

The BreharWallHan ship hadn't run, or tried to fight the responder, because Indah was right, they wanted to keep it quiet. They wanted the *Lalow* to continue its part of the operation until the BreharWallHan agents could trace all the routes, all the stations where refugees had been transferred, maybe until they could figure out where the pick-up point was inside the mining field.

All of this was leading to the conclusion . . . Oh, shit.

Which meant . . . I had to stop the search.

I could call Mensah and get her to make Indah listen to me. I could do that, but I still thought it would sound a lot like the time Mensah's youngest child had got hold of the comm and demanded that Mensah tell an older sibling to stop taking all the squash dumplings. Mensah could make Indah listen to me, but it would waste time, and Indah being made to listen to me against her will was step one of a failure scenario. (I don't know much about human interactions, but even I knew that.) I had to get Indah to trust me.

I could start by talking to her, I guess, I had actually not tried that yet, really.

I secured a protected feed connection with her and sent, *Senior Officer Indah, you have to stop the search. The module must be attached to a ship still holding position off the station. If the BreharWallHan agents know we've found the module, they'll kill the refugees and run. Everything on the Port Authority systems has to be treated as compromised. Whoever is on that ship could be using the dock cameras and Supervisor Gamila's comm to listen to you and your officers right now. If you find the module while they're listening—*

She objected, *You said that system wasn't hacked.*

I said, *I'm wrong. Whoever did this is good enough not to leave any indication they were in the system. They are as good at this or better than I am.* (Oh yeah, it hurt to say that.)

Aylen was trying to say something to her and Indah held up a hand to show she was on her feed. Her eyes were narrow and her mouth was thin. I had no idea what that meant. She said, *How do you know this hacker isn't listening to you right now?*

Because that's how fuckers get permanently deleted, is what I wanted to say. What I actually said was, *I can secure my own internal system. I can't secure the Port Authority's systems or yours.*

Indah hesitated, then switched to her all-team comm, "Aylen, come with me, we've got to reorganize this. I think we're wrong about that module." She told Matif, "Tell the search parties to resume, and we're extending the search to the Public Docks."

Matif glanced at Soire, clearly dubious. "Uh, all right. I mean, yes, Senior."

Indah and Aylen were already walking away and I followed them. Keeping her voice low, Indah said, "Comms off." Aylen immediately complied and my drone video showed a visible shift in her attitude, from confused protest to still confused but no longer protesting.

Indah added, "SecUnit, I assume you can get me a secure connection to the station responder?"

"Yes. This way." I secured a connection with Dr. Mensah's feed. *Hi. I have a request.*

I knew from her guard drones that she was still in the council offices on the other side of the station mall, working in her feed. *What's up?*

Senior Indah and I need to borrow your private office.

Mensah's private office was close by, in the admin block with the Port Authority. But the important part was that her comm and security monitoring wasn't connected to either StationSec or any of the PortAuth systems, it was a separate secure system used by the council.

And it was really secure, because one of the first jobs Mensah had got for me was to make sure it was "up to date and resistant to corporate or other incursion."

It was such a relief to step into a place where I had control of the security. As we crossed the tiled floor of the lobby I felt the tension in the organic parts of my back ease. Mensah had notified her staff to let us through, and I removed us from the surveillance camera, just in case.

One of her assistants opened the inner office for us. He had already closed and opaqued the transparent doors on the balcony that looked out over the admin plaza. He was used to me and used to confidential council stuff, so he didn't even glance up at my drones, just nodded to us and slipped out as we stepped in. He said, "I'll be in the reception area, just message me when you're finished," and engaged the privacy seal on the door.

Indah had been here before but Aylen clearly hadn't, and looked around at the family images and the plants. (It was a nice office, I had spent a lot of time on the couch.) I used the feed to open the secure terminal, and the big display surface formed in the air above the desk. I opened the secure channel for Indah and for Mensah, who had been holding on her secure feed in the council offices. Then I sent a hail for the responder. When it answered, I opened the connection.

Indah ordered the responder to scan the ships in holding positions off the station and sent the module's specifications. She told them there was a possibility the Port Authority systems had been compromised and they needed to communicate only with her or Aylen, and via the council system and not Station Security's system. The responder asked for a confirmation order from the council and Mensah supplied it. Mensah then signed off, telling Indah to contact her immediately if she needed any other assistance, and Indah thanked her.

Then me, Aylen, and Indah were standing in the office looking at each other. Or they were looking at me and my drones were looking at them.

"You really think our systems are compromised?" Aylen asked.

Indah had her arms folded, her expression grim. It had occurred to me she was maybe worried about feeling stupid too, if we were wrong about this. She said, "Yes. It's the only thing that makes sense."

I had control of all inputs to this room's comm and feed, and I caught and bounced a comm call for Indah with Balin the Port Authority bot's feed ID. It was probably an important call from Gamila but if something had blown up the council's system would notify us and everything else could wait five minutes. It was time to be honest. I told Indah, "You were wrong when you said it was unlikely to be a local actor. But I think you know that now."

Indah glared at me, but it was more wry than angry. "Is that what you think? Because you keep insisting it's a mysterious ultra-hacker."

Okay, that one stung. "I didn't use the words 'mysterious' or 'ultra.'"

Aylen watched like it was one of those human games where they threw balls at each other. (I'd had to stop a lot of those while on company contracts; they violated the company personal injury safety bonds.) (Yeah, it was super fun telling the humans they couldn't do it because SecUnits always like giving their clients more reasons to hate them.) But Aylen also looked relieved. Like she was beginning to wonder if we were stupid or what. She muttered, "Thank the divine, can we talk about it like adults now?"

Indah pointed the glare at her. "If the Port Authority systems weren't hacked, then the files and camera data were altered by someone on station who has legitimate access, who knew how to cover their tracks." She made an impatient gesture. "It even fits with the tool that was used to remove contact DNA from the body. The PA uses sterilizers for hazardous material safety, they're all over the port offices."

Aylen nodded. "But who? Everyone's worked here for years, grew up here."

I told Indah, "You thought it was me."

She snorted in exasperation. "We thought it was you when we thought Lutran was a GrayCris agent. But we dis-proved that—I forget how many hours ago that was, this has been a long damn day."

Aylen was annoyed. "If it was you, why would you tell us where the original crime scene was, which led to finding the *Lalow* and the refugees?"

Indah added, "You are the most paranoid person I've ever met, and I've worked in criminal reform for twenty-six years."

I don't even know how to react to that. She's not wrong but hey, I need my paranoia. Speaking of which, I asked Aylen, "Where were you when Lutran was killed?"

She didn't blink. "I was on a shuttle, coming back from an assignment in FirstLanding."

"She was docking when the body was found." Indah huffed impatiently. "Give me a little credit."

The responder had kept its channel open and we could hear the crew talking in the background. "SatAmratEye5 is in the best position . . . That one's clear . . . If they aren't local they probably don't know our satellite placement . . . There we go. Senior Indah, we've got it. There's a ship with a module attached hiding in station section zero, in the shadow of the Pressy's upper hull." They were sending data and I transferred it to the big display above our heads.

It was a sensor schematic of a long shot view of the station, the curve of the ring tucked below the main structure and the shape of the giant colony ship it had been built out from. The view turned into a scan schematic and focused in on a shape huddled not far from the colony ship's starboard hull.

It wasn't a modular transport, it was a ship more like the *Lalow*. A bulky tube with round parts sticking out, and the module clamped onto its hull stood out in the sensor view like a . . . like a weird thing that shouldn't be there. Aylen swore in relief and Indah told the responder to hold position and wait for orders.

Indah said, "The priority right now is to get to those people and if they're alive, to get them out of there."

Aylen looked grim. "That's not going to be easy. It's close enough to the colony ship that we could reach it with a team in EVAC suits, but we can't arrange that from here. If the BreharWallHan agents have someone in the Port Authority who can listen in on our comms and feed, they're going to know what we're doing."

Yeah, not we, me. I said, "This is the part that's my job."

Chapter Seven

I'D BEEN BROUGHT TO Preservation on one of their older ships, which had been refitted over and over again. This section of the colony ship had never been refitted. The corridors were dingy, the paint on the dark metal patchy where it had been rubbed off by hands and shoulders.

The colony ship hadn't just been left to rot; the humans liked it too much for that. It smelled of clean emptiness in a way human places never do. Pieces of clear protective material had been placed over the occasional drawings on the bulkheads, and on the pieces of paper stuck to them and covered with scribbled handwriting and faded print. Feed markers had been installed by Station Historical/Environment Management with translations into Preservation Standard Nomenclature. My drones picked up whispers of lost-and-found notices, messhall schedules, and the rules for games I didn't recognize.

It should have been creepy. I had been in places like this that were really creepy. But this wasn't. Maybe because I knew where the humans and augmented humans who had last used this ship had gone, that their descendants were running around all over this system, and that one of them was in my secure feed right now, demanding an update.

I'm almost there, I told Aylen. *Just give me a fucking minute.*

Indah had gone back to the mobile command center to be visible, but she wanted me to have backup. Aylen was waiting at the entrance to this section of the colony ship, making sure nobody followed me up here. If she had to call in a team for help, she was going to hold off as long as possible, to keep our local actor from knowing what we were doing until hopefully it was too late.

Aylen said, *You know, swearing during operations doesn't meet the professional conduct standards of Station Security.*

By this point I knew that was Aylen's idea of a joke. I replied, *Because Senior Indah has never told anybody to fuck off.*

You have me there.

I reached the lock corridor and sent, *I'm going offline now.*

Understood, she sent back. *Good luck.*

I understand why humans say that, but luck sucks. I found the lock and dropped the EVAC suit container on the deck to expand and unpack it.

Once I had it out, I started to pull the tab to activate it. Then I processed the instructions it was loading into the feed . . . *this emergency device alerts the Port Authority emergency notification network and the transponder will send your location to . . .* Ugh, of course the EVAC suit had a transponder, this was a stripped-down emergency version for stations, not the full ship corporate-brand EVAC suits I'd used before.

The local actor, if not the hostile ship itself, was sure to be monitoring the station's search and rescue channel. They would know someone was trying to approach surreptitiously.

I was going to have to turn the transponder off. There was no way to do that via the feed so I needed to find the physical switch. I pulled the schematic from the instructions and found the transponder was buried in the sealed drive unit.

Oh, you have to be kidding me. I'd be pissed off at the humans but I had brought this thing up here without checking. Seconds were ticking away while I wasted time. I couldn't take the drive unit apart without breaking it, I had no idea how. I didn't have the ability to disguise the signal. I could jam it, but at such close range any static leakage, any hint of activity on the otherwise silent search and rescue channel, might alert the hostile ship. It would sure as hell alert me if I was in their position. There was no time to go back for another EVAC suit or . . .

Or Murderbot, you dummy, you're on a giant spaceship that has been meticulously preserved as a historical artifact. If they still had intact lunch menus from however many years ago, the chances were good they still had the safety equipment.

Big green arrows scrawled along the bulkhead pointed me toward the nearest emergency lockers and I opened the first one. The inside was neatly packed with safety supplies, all of it tagged with explanatory labels and scrawled symbols on the containers, all of it simple and easily readable for any panicky untrained human. Except I didn't have this language loaded.

So I had to go back online for a minute. I secured a connection with Ratthi and Gurathin and said, *I need help.*

They were eating together in one of the station mall's food places; Ratthi stood up and knocked his chair over and Gurathin spilled the liquid in the cup he was lifting. Ratthi said, *SecUnit, what's wrong?*

I understood the reaction. I didn't ask for help that often. I sent them my drone video: *Which one of these things is most like an EVAC suit?*

Uh, are you up in the Pressy? Ratthi asked, baffled. *The closest thing I see to an EVAC suit in there is a life-tender. But—*

There, third shelf down, with the red tags, Gurathin added. I yanked one out of the rack and he said, *Wait, why do you need it? What are you doing?*

It's a Station Security thing, I'll tell you later, I said, and cut the connection. Now that I had the name, I used the station feed to hit the public library, where I pulled a description and operating instructions from the historical records.

The life-tender wasn't so much an EVAC suit as it was a small vehicle. It opened into a kind of diamond-shaped bag with rudimentary navigation, propulsion, and life support. According to the library record, it was designed to get several humans off one ship and onto a new one, usually because the first ship was about to have a catastrophic failure. This one also had a transponder but it was set to the colony ship's comm ID, which had been delisted as an active channel and turned into an audio monument, broadcasting historical facts and stories about the colony ship's first arrival in the system. It was unlikely the hostiles would be monitoring it and the chatty broadcasts would provide cover for my comm and the life-tender's location transmissions. The library entry also said life-tenders weren't used anymore because without their transponders, they were difficult to locate and didn't meet Preservation's current safety standards. Difficult to locate sounded good, though, like the hostile ship wouldn't know it was out there unless it specifically scanned for it, which was what I needed.

The historical story currently playing on the colony ship's comm sounded interesting, so I set one of my inputs to record it as I carried the life-tender to the airlock. Following the instructions, I pulled the tabs, set the safety to active, tossed it into the lock, and cycled it through. It was old, but its sealed storage was designed to keep equipment functioning for long periods of time, just like everything else on this ship; it was how these old colony ships worked. (You couldn't be on Preservation for more than five minutes without being forced to listen to a documentary about it.)

I just hoped all the documentaries were right.

The life-tender signaled the ship's comm that it was ready and I stepped into the airlock and let it cycle shut. I could see the life-tender on the lock's camera, where it had clamped itself around the outer hatch. Wow, that is just a bag, is what that is.

I didn't need as much air as humans did, but I needed some, and it was really cold out there, in the colony ship's shadow. This meant that if the life-tender failed it would take me longer to die so I'd have longer to feel dumb about it than a human would.

So here goes. I told my drones to get in my pockets and go dormant. Then I opened the hatch and leaned out to sort of float/fall into the tender. Okay, new problem. It's really fucking dark.

The huge hull of the colony ship blocked any light from the primary, the station, the planet, whatever, which was probably why the hostile ship had picked this spot to hide.

It's cold, it's dark, whatever was generating the air smelled terrible, I'm in a bag in space. I thought about going back for the EVAC suit, but the chance that the hostiles were scanning for transponders on the station search and rescue channel was still hitting 96 percent. If what I was doing in this stupid bag was dumb, going out here with a beacon I couldn't turn off or disguise was much more dumb.

Okay, fine, let's just get it over with.

I sealed the bag's entrance and let the ship's hatch close. The tender was controlled via a local connection to its drive and navigation, so it could still be used if, say, your ship blew up and you couldn't access its comm or feed. I had the location for the hostile ship and I fed it into the simple system, and my little bag headed off through the dark.

I carefully explored the control options, and wow, I now knew why the bag was described as "difficult to locate in a combat situation" because its power supply was so minimal it was almost nonexistent. Even my body heat was already causing condensation. I found the menu for monitoring life support, such as it was. The bag had lights but turning them on would just be stupid plus I didn't really want to see what was happening.

Then the bag bumped (it wasn't really a bump, it was more like a blorp) into something solid and stopped. I checked navigation and holy shit, we're here.

The bag's sensor system was primitive but it knew it had blorped itself up against the curving hull of a ship. I detected the ship's feed connection but it was silent. Not locked down, just quiet as whoever was aboard tried to minimize contact.

Modules didn't have an airlock, they relied on attaching
to the transport or station cargo lock; I wouldn't have been
able to open the module's hatch for the EVAC suit without
killing everyone inside, so the plan had been to get into the
hostile ship through its lock and then run around getting
shot and murdering my way through whoever was aboard
until I could get control. (I hadn't used those exact words
during the planning process with Indah and Aylen, but
we all knew what we were talking about.) But my maybe-
not-so-dumb bag made its own airlock, that was the whole
point of it.

If I could get the refugees out of the module and over to
the colony ship's lock without the hostiles even realizing I
was there, then the responder would be free to take over
the hostile ship.

That plan was easier plus 100 percent less murder. And
I liked it better.

Huh. I liked it better because it wasn't a CombatUnit
plan, or actually a plan that humans would come up with
for CombatUnits. Sneaking the endangered humans off
the ship to safety and then leaving the hostiles for someone
else to deal with, that was a SecUnit plan, that was what we
were really designed for, despite how the company and every other corporate used us. The point was to retrieve the
clients alive and fuck everything else.

Maybe I'd been waiting too long for GrayCris to show

up and try to kill us all. I was thinking like a CombatUnit, or, for fuck's sake, like a CombatBot.

I got the bag to blorp along the hull over to where the module should be, then along its side to where scan detected the outline of the module's access hatch. Once the bag was in place, its automatic functions took over and it enlarged itself to completely cover the hatch. The bag assured me it had made a secure seal. Okay, it hadn't lied to me so far.

Now this part might be tricky. I carefully felt around in the empty feed, looking for the ship's bot pilot. Oh, there it was. It was a limited bot pilot, just there to steer and dock the ship and guide it through wormholes. It was startled to be accessed, even though I was spoofing a Port Authority ID. It's usually easy to make friends with low-level bot pilots, but this one had been coded to be adversarial, directed to operate in stealth mode, and was wary of incursion attempts. It tried to alert its onboard SecSystem, but as the old saying (which I just made up) goes, if you can ping the SecUnit, it's way too late.

I took control, disabled the SecSystem, and put the bot pilot in sleep mode. Having to keep it dormant was annoying, because it limited my ability to use the ship's functions, but it meant the hostiles wouldn't be able to fly off toward the wormhole or fire weapons at the responder or whatever else they felt like shooting at.

Next I accessed the module's hatch control. I didn't want to risk trying to use the comm or feed to check if anybody was inside, because not alerting the hostiles was the whole point of going in this way.

I checked the bag's airlock seal again, then told the module to open its access hatch.

Oh, shit, my stupid, stupid feed ID that identified me as a SecUnit. Just as the hatch slid up, I switched it to the last one in my buffer, the Kiran ID I'd used on TranRollinHyfa.

The lighted interior would have blinded me if my eyes worked that way. I meant to say something before I went inside but the bag had no grav function and the module did, so let's put it this way, my entrance was abrupt and not graceful.

The module was a big oblong container with ribbed supports and racks folded into the bulkheads and no padding anywhere, making it clear it was designed for cargo, not passengers. It was colder than the bag and the air smelled wrong. The bunch of humans inside screamed and threw themselves away from the hatch that from their perspective had apparently just opened into empty space. Then they realized I was standing there and they screamed again.

Fortunately I had a lot of experience being screamed at and stared at by terrified humans. It was never comfortable, and I couldn't let my drones deploy so I had to look at them with my actual eyes, but I was sort of used to that by now. Also, I'd spent a whole trip through a wormhole pretending to be an augmented human security consultant for humans who badly needed one, so I had coping mechanisms in place. Sort of.

I held up my hands and said, "Please calm down. I'm from Preservation Station Security and I'm here to get you to safety." They huddled at the other end of the module, still staring, but I thought that was shock and surprise. I added, "You've been abducted by whoever is aboard this ship, they were not sent by your contact Lutran."

"We know that," one of the humans said. They started to unfold from defensive positions as they realized I wasn't here to shoot them. I didn't see any signs of serious injury but from the disarray of their clothes and some visible bruises, they had been knocked around in the module at some point. I wasn't picking up any augments or interfaces. Which made sense; only the non-augmented contract labor would be able to leave BreharWallHan without being traced, and the escapees would know to leave their interfaces behind. Their captors would have confiscated any comms or interfaces the *Lalow* crew had given them. Human One continued, "They're bounty-catchers, sent by the supervisors." She pointed up.

It could have been a trick but I looked up anyway. Oh shit, the module is attached to a lock. An appallingly jury-rigged lock, way too small.

The module's other hatch, the large one meant to load and unload bulk cargo, was open, sealed directly against the hull of the ship. For fuck's sake, I could see part of the ship's registration number.

The ship's lock, roughly in the center of the opening, was only about two meters square and had no transparent panel, just a camera, and no controls to open it from this side. It was terrifying, both from a safety standpoint and an "oh shit" standpoint. It's a good thing I can have a horrified emotional reaction while also simultaneously pulling the latest video out of the ship's SecSystem, deleting myself and the open hatch, and starting a loop so if any hostiles checked their module camera, everything would look normal. Was there even an air wall behind that lock? Holy shit, who does this?

The hostiles up in the ship might have heard the screaming. I lowered my voice. "We need to get you out of here now." I hadn't meant to say that next but it just came out, because this could be such a disaster. All the hostiles had to do was disengage the seal on the module and I'd lose every one of the humans. With the bot pilot down, they couldn't disengage via the ship's feed, but the chance that the seal had a manual release was high.

My bag, blorping quietly to itself on the access hatch, was starting to look really friendly in comparison.

I connected to the hostile ship's hamstrung SecSystem

again and started to feel for more cameras. There wasn't a full set; obviously this crew didn't like the idea of a video record of all the fun they were having while hunting contract labor refugees. But I needed to get a view of the compartment on the other side of the hatch of jury-rigged terror.

"So your station can send us back to the supervisors and get the bounty?" Human One said. The humans were all shivering and showing various signs of physical and emotional distress. I didn't know what the air quality rating was in here but I could guess it wasn't good. This was no time to explain Preservation's attitude toward forced labor and the fact that the council would be unlikely to allow corporate bounty-collecting as an alternative income for the station. (A bounty probably wouldn't pay for even a week of Jolly-Baby's annual maintenance, anyway.)

I said, "Contract slavery is illegal on Preservation. You have refugee status here and no one can send you back or make you do anything you don't want to do. If I can get you back to the station." I pointed at the bag. I know, I felt like an idiot. "This is a life-tender. You're going to need to get in it."

The three humans in front, the brave ones, came forward, still afraid but desperately willing to be convinced. Human One stepped close enough to peer through the hatch, where the module's light was not being kind to my giant bag. "In that?" she said, as if honestly baffled. The others recoiled a little.

"It's not as bad as it looks," I told her. The bag had already set itself to return to the colony ship's lock and was just waiting for a go code. I wanted to pile all the humans in but the instructions insisted there was a per trip limit. I could override it, but . . . Yeah, no, better not. On the ship's feed I found cameras in engineering, the passage into the bridge, and finally, a camera pointed at the other side of the lock where the module was attached. There was no air wall, no full lock, just that round hatch. Oh, huh, I think this is a modified raider ship and that hatch is designed for ship-to-ship boarding. And there was a box attached to it that looked suspiciously like a manual release. Yikes.

(I mean, there had been an 80-plus percent chance it existed, but seeing it drove home the whole oh shit aspect of everything.)

I needed to keep telling the humans to get in the bag. "It'll hold six of you and you need to get in, now." I pointed up at the obviously rigged-for-rapid-decompression-hole in the roof of the module. "It's better than that." Was I going to have to make them get in the stupid bag? I really hoped not, because if they realized I was a SecUnit, this situation was going to go from awkward to . . . really fucking awkward. "It's self-guiding, it's a short trip, all you have to do is go through the station airlock when it opens for you."

Then Human One, still looking out at the bag, made her decision. She turned back to the others. "Come on, the youngs go first."

She picked out the three adolescents and three of the adults. There was some muffled crying and protests as she shoved them into the bag. They were afraid, they didn't want to leave the others, etc.

The bridge passage camera picked up a human in tactical gear moving past. I said, "How many aboard?"

Human One said, "We only saw two, but there has to be more. They opened the hatch once after we were locked on to look at us."

Human Two said, "They said they wanted us alive for the bounty."

Then Human Three added, "They got a SecUnit."

"They do?" Did they? I hadn't caught any pings and there's no way a SecUnit wouldn't have noticed when I took control of the ship's SecSystem. I'd had the theory that PortAuth system had been hacked by a SecUnit or CombatUnit, but that didn't fit with our current working theory that there was a local actor who had legitimate PortAuth access. "Did you see it?"

"Behind the others, in the armor," Three said. Two and Four nodded.

One made a noise under her breath and I said, "You don't think it's a SecUnit." I should have been more careful there, but I was trying to get into the ship's memory archives without waking the bot pilot, and with my drones hidden, I was mostly looking at the hatch or the bag. I wanted schematics, controls for the jury-rigged lock. No, they could still use the manual release, I couldn't jam that from here. Another hostile in tactical gear left the bridge. Yeah, I think they've alerted on me, somehow.

Human One said, "They use SecUnits up in the processing centers, not in the backrocks where we were most of the time."

When the sixth human tumbled into the bag, it signaled that it was at capacity and ready to leave. I let the module's hatch close. Then I wished I'd left a drone in the bag so I could monitor it directly. Whatever, I was just going to have to trust the damn bag.

At least I had its channel as an input and could tell it had sealed itself and scooted off to take the most direct route back to its "home" airlock. "How long will it take?" Human Three asked.

"Not long, just a few minutes," I said. If we were lucky, there would be time for a second trip and I wouldn't have to do this the hard way.

A vibration traveled through the hull and the humans flinched. "What was that?" Human Two demanded.

"They're trying to dump us!" Human Four's voice was shrill. He was right, someone in the bridge had tried (and failed, because I had control of SecSystem and it was preventing the command from going through) to release the clamps on the module. Something had spooked the hostiles and they were trying to dump the incriminating module and leave. Well, crap. Time to shift to Plan B. I connected to the station's feed and used it to send the "proceed" code to the responder. Since there was no point in hiding anymore, I also sent a feed message to Aylen and told her refugees were incoming to the colony ship.

Human One took a sharp breath. "Thanks for trying, Station Security."

Above us the ship's camera picked up a hostile in an armored suit, the one that the refugees had mistaken for a SecUnit, stepping into view of the hold camera near the jury-rigged lock above us. Oh, I get it. The hostile wasn't strong enough to activate the manual release without the armor. But I'd finally found the code they used for the jury-rigged hatch.

In one of my shows, this would have been a great time to say something brave and encouraging. I suck at that, so I said, "Get to the back of the module, on the floor, and cover your heads."

I checked my input for the life-tender; it had reached the colony ship's hull and was blorping along toward the airlock. In my peripheral vision, Human One jerked her head at the others and they scrambled toward the far end of the module. I said, "When I yell clear, I need you to follow me up into the ship."

Skeptically, Human One said, "How are you gonna—"

I pulled my explosive projectile weapon off its strap, then climbed the folded cargo rack nearest the module lock, braced my feet against the bulkhead, and held on with my free arm. As the armored hostile leaned down to reach the release, I triggered the ship's system to open the jury-rigged hatch.

It rotated open with a hiss of released air, and the module immediately smelled better.

I didn't move. The camera showed the armored hostile jerking back in surprise. A panicky yell from a hostile on the bridge came over the comm; they must have realized the bot pilot was unresponsive. But the armored hostile couldn't pull the release now, while the lock was open, without depressurizing the ship. (I'd also frozen open all the interior hatches, which, from the additional yelling over the comm, was something the bridge crew had just discovered.)

The armored hostile hesitated. Come on, look down here, you know you want to. There was going to be an orientation change between the ship's gravity field and the module's gravity field, and I'd have to take it into account. The humans huddled at the far end of the module, frozen, waiting.

The armored hostile leaned down and cautiously extended a weapon through the lock.

(I already knew it wasn't another SecUnit inside that suit, but this was another giveaway. A SecUnit would have moved fast, propelling itself into the module. There's no point in being cautious when your job is to draw fire, right?)

I woke my drones as I grabbed the armored arm and yanked it down. Twisting the hostile's weapon free and dropping it, I swung myself over to clamp my body around the armor's helmet and upper body.

I have a file of access codes I could have used to take control of the armor, but that would take time, and this was an expensive brand and might be newer than my code list. Another reason this wasn't a SecUnit—our armor was never this nice.

With my chest clamped to its helmet, Armored Hostile couldn't see and events were moving a little too fast for it to take advantage of the armor's scan, cameras, or defensive functions. I jammed the nozzle of my projectile weapon into the back neck joint where the important parts were, switched it to full power, and fired. The armor spasmed (an explosive projectile in your motor control functions will do that) and went limp.

My drones shot up through the lock and the hold, and straight into the faces of the two hostiles in tactical gear running toward us down the corridor. They screamed and flailed backward.

I climbed around the dead weight of the armored hostile and up into the ship. Then I dragged the body out of the way and yelled, "Clear!"

I took a guard position at the inner hatch and watched my drones zip through the ship. Behind me the humans scrambled to climb up through the hatch, exhausted and struggling, trying to help each other. When the last one collapsed on the deck, gasping at the fresh air, I let the lock close. That was a relief. Now that there was no more danger of everybody getting sucked into space, I checked my other inputs.

I had confirmation from the bag that it had delivered its humans to the colony ship, where the airlock had accepted its safety code and cycled them through. The responder had sent a confirmation code, and, according to the hostile ship's SecSystem, had just hailed the hostiles and informed them that they were about to be apprehended.

The armored hostile was still alive, just stunned and trapped in the immobile suit. The other hostiles were confused, panicking about the drones, and there was every chance of getting them to surrender, or at least violently encouraging them to surrender without having to kill them. To the humans, I said, "I'm going after the others, just stay here—"

I felt a hard thump from behind. It was low and to one side, where a fairly important part would be, if I was human.

I turned. Human One had the armored hostile's weapon, the one I had taken away and dropped down into the module. And she had shot me with it.

I reached her before she could fire again, twisted it out of her grip. Then I walked out of the hold and let the hatch shut behind me.

By the time the responder locked on and its armed intervention team boarded, I had the other hostiles disarmed, restrained with cuffs I'd found in a locker, and sitting on the deck near the main airlock. I'd found their medical unit (it was an off-brand model, and installed in the galley, but whatever) and was letting it seal up the hole in my back. (Just a regular projectile, not an explosive one, so most of my back was still there. I just didn't feel like walking around leaking in front of humans right now.) I'd gotten Aylen on comm and confirmed she had called in her team for support and was now trying to coax the six refugees out of the colony ship's airlock corridor. Apparently they weren't believing the whole "we're Station Security and we're here to help" story. Whatever, it wasn't my problem.

I'd switched my feed ID back to SecUnit.

Senior Indah walked in. I knew from listening to the responder's comm that she had taken a shuttle out to it, but I hadn't expected her to come looking for me. She frowned at the galley. The surfaces were smeared with dried food, and it smelled bad, even worse than human food prep areas usually smell. She looked at me and said, "You were hurt?"

I told the MedUnit to stop and pulled my shirt back down. "What gave it away?"

She folded her arms and leaned against the side of the hatch. My drones showed her expression was sour. "The refugees told me they shot you. They realized you were a SecUnit and thought . . ." She scratched her head, leaving her short hair sticking up unevenly. "I don't know what they thought, I'm too tired to sort that out. Do you want to make a criminal complaint against them?"

Uh-huh, very funny. "No." I didn't want to talk about it, so I stared at the wall. I just wanted to get off this ship, back to the station, back to my regular job making sure no one killed Mensah. "My short-term contract is completed."

"Is it?" Indah lifted her brows. "Do you know who killed Lutran?"

With everything else, I'd forgotten about the original objective of this whole mess. "No, who?"

Now she rolled her eyes. "I was asking you."

Oh, right. "But the hostiles will know who they were working with in the Port Authority."

"We questioned them briefly and they say they don't. They were given some instructions to send to a scramble-coded feed address, and they have no idea who was on the other end. We checked and the address has been deleted. I don't know if I believe they really didn't know who they were talking to, but it's going to take time to get them to realize that they can help themselves more by telling us everything." Her mouth set in a grim line. "I don't want to wait. I want to find that traitor before they do any more damage."

Did I want that too? Yes, yes I did. And the parameters of the problem had changed, drastically, in a way that made it solvable. Our suspect pool had been a bunch of humans and augmented humans wandering around in the Merchant Docks mostly unobserved and not interacting with station systems, as we tried to identify an actor who could remove themselves from the few surveillance cameras at will. Now we knew it was a local, someone with legitimate access to Port Authority systems. Locals living on the station do stuff that leaves a trail, that generates records in log files. "You need a surveillance audit."

Her frown turned confused. "A what?"

"You take all the data available during the time frame when the incidents occurred, not just from the Port

Authority systems, but from StationSec, StationComm-
Central, TransportLocal, the distribution kiosks, the door
systems that allow people to enter their private quarters,
anything that saves an ID that tells you what someone
was doing at the specific moment when we know the
perpetrator was active, and you compare it to the list of
potential operators to start eliminating them. It's going
to be harder because your surveillance is crap, but it can
still drastically reduce the suspect pool." She didn't react
and I added, "If we know someone is in the station mall
accessing a food kiosk at the exact time the transport
suffered the catastrophic failure, then they can be eliminated as a suspect."

Her gaze turned intrigued. "Some of those systems are
under privacy lock, we'd need a judge-advocate to release
their access records, but the others . . ." Then she shook her
head. "We narrowed down the time of death, but it's not
exact. And the theory was that some of those actions, like
using the cart to dump Lutran's body in the mall, were pre-
arranged. The actor could have been eating in the station
mall when it happened."

I explained, "But not when the transport was hacked.
That can't be done over the feed. When the transport went
down, the actor was there, on board."

Indah's face did something complicated, which I think

was an attempt not to show enthusiasm. "How long would this take you?"

"A few hours. And I'd need outside processing and storage space." I'd have to pull a bunch of old company code out of archive storage, build the database, and write the queries.

She pushed off the hatch. "Then let's get out of here and get started."

Chapter Eight

WE GOT ON THE responder, which had collected the refugees and the hostiles, and was now ready to leave. A station tug had already arrived and was maneuvering into position to haul the hostile ship and the module to the impound bay so they could be checked for evidence. In light of the whole traitor in the Port Authority thing, Indah had ordered the tug to keep the ship and the module in isolation until Station Security cleared it. She hadn't exactly lied, but she had implied that the ship might be contaminated with something. (Anybody who saw the galley wouldn't have any trouble believing that.)

On the quick trip back to the transit ring, I checked my feed messages. Mensah wanted me to report when I had a chance, Ratthi wanted to know if I was all right, and Gurathin wanted to know if I'd used the life-tender and if it had worked okay. I also had a report from Tural, the combined forensic/medical report, which among other things identified the cause of Lutran's death as a long "needle-like device" that had stabbed into his head, leaving no identifiable fragments behind. Tural also said the transport was being repaired, but the team hadn't managed to pull any usable data off it. And Pin-Lee's General Counsel report had arrived, which showed Lutran's name came up multiple times in regard to cargo transfer on Preservation Station and on three other allied polities. Which meant Lutran had been funneling refugees for years, through multiple stations, as we'd theorized. And he wouldn't be doing that anymore, so who the hell knew what would happen to all the other parts of the organization and the humans trapped at BreharWall-Han. I sent acknowledgments/reply laters to all of them so they'd know I was still alive, because what I really needed to do was stand here and watch the beginning of episode 132 of *Sanctuary Moon*.

I'd followed Indah to the responder's bridge, where she and the responder's captain lied to the Port Authority about what the responder was doing. (They told them that a trader ship had had an onboard emergency that caused a comm and drive failure, and that the responder had alerted because it looked like the ship was trying to break port lockdown and leave. The misunderstanding had been cleared up now and the responder was arranging to bring the ship in for repair.) (I thought it was too complicated for a good lie, but whatever.) As we docked I followed Indah down to the airlock foyer to disembark. She stopped abruptly at the top of the corridor and I didn't run into her because unlike the humans who are usually following me I pay attention. Audio picked up movement ahead; I sent a drone around the corner for a look. Oh, right, they were leading the refugees off the ship and she didn't want them to see me. Which, fine.

But standing there, I thought of something. Whoever the actor was in the Port Authority, it was a human or augmented human who thought they were pretty clever and able to manipulate systems to their advantage.

Maybe we could get them to try again. I secured a connection with Indah's feed: *I have an idea.*

She replied, *Well, your last idea didn't work out so badly. Let's hear it.*

The hard part had been deciding who/what was going to be the bait. It couldn't be me; the important part (the thesis? I guess?) of our theory was that the actor was a local, with access to Port Authority if not Station Security systems. This person would know what I was and that attempting to attack me was not a good idea. (I wasn't in a great mood right now, so it was an even worse idea than it usually was.) And there had to be some explanation of how/why the bait human knew who the actor was, so it couldn't be a Station Security officer or a random station resident. I suggested Target Four from the *Lalow,* who had all the characteristics of a human who could be talked into doing anything.

Indah disagreed, on the grounds that Target Four had been talking to anybody who got within range while he was on detention in the station, and there was too high a chance that the actor would realize he didn't know anything he hadn't already told us. She thought it had to be one of the refugees, who had all had an opportunity to over-hear/get information from the bounty-catchers. Which meant that even though it was my plan I couldn't be in the middle of it. Which, whatever, I didn't want to be in the middle of it where the excitement was, I wanted to be in an office working on a giant database in case the stupid plan didn't work.

For the refugee/bait, Indah chose Human Three, the one who had been convinced the armored hostile was a SecUnit. She went to talk to him with the new special in-vestigation team she had conscripted from the responder's crew. (They had all been in the responder, which had been undocked on picket, so they couldn't have been in the transport to kill Lutran.) (The other special investigation team was still potentially compromised, except for Aylen and Indah.) (And me, I guess.)

Human Three was in the responder's medical compart-ment because he or someone else (I was betting it was him) had forcibly removed an interface from the skin of his fore-head before leaving BreharWallHan and it had become infected. (Either the *Lalow* crew hadn't offered the use of their MedUnit or with his curly head hair flopping over the wound, they hadn't noticed.)

He was sitting on the med platform listening to Indah explain what we wanted him to do, with the other members of the new team gathered around. (I wasn't there because I'm an evil SecUnit. I was out in the responder's secure bay waiting for Indah's request for system processing space for our database to be approved, checking my inputs, pulling and sorting code out of my archive, and watching the conversation via drone.)

Human Three, hair pulled back with a big patch of new skin on his forehead, said, "I'll help you, but you got a SecUnit here. It's probably passing tales to BreharWallHan."

This would bother me more if it wasn't so fucking typical.

So it surprised me when one of Indah's conscripted responder team members said, "It was the SecUnit got you out of that module. You wanted to stay in it? It's coming with the tug, you can hop back in."

"No, no, we're not corporates, we have laws. One of which is it's illegal to put people in transfer modules so he couldn't get in it again even if he wanted to," Indah said, leaning against the bulkhead with her arms folded, as if none of this was urgent. "What we should do is charge his friend for shooting a Station Security consultant."

Human Three (whose actual name was Mish) looked uneasy. "Are you going to do that?"

Indah said, "No, because I understand she's experienced extreme trauma and because the consultant refused to make a complaint. Now are you going to work with us so we can find our killer and I can clear the *Lalow* crew and send them back to their ship? Or is this just how your whole group treats people who get hurt trying to help you?"

"I didn't say I wouldn't do it," Mish grumbled. "I just want to know why you have a SecUnit if—"

So that's how that was going.

It was the end of the day cycle and the station agencies were shutting down for their rest period, but I had asked Mensah to push through Station Security's requests. By the time Indah came out into the bay, I'd gotten a feed message that Station Resource Allotment had approved the temporary processing and storage space we'd asked for. I'd already received a notice that I now had access to StationSec and provisional access to PortAuth. We still needed to arrange data dumps from the station mall systems we could get without needing permission from the judge-advocate, but even without those I thought we had enough to get started. If I was lucky, I could at least get the original special investigation team uncompromised with the data I had so far, once I could get it into a usable form. Their help would make the bait operation easier.

Indah walked up to me, saying, "So that part's done. I just got a feed message from Aylen, she wants you over in the Security Office. The responder team will be bringing Mish with them, and I'll meet you there."

Threat assessment spiked. Huh.

I said, "So you're staying here?"

Her expression turned hard. "Not that you have any right to ask, consultant, but I need to go to the Merchant Docks and try to stand down the search teams in a way that won't alert our traitor."

"Because wandering off alone across the transit ring when we're trying to bait a murderer to act sounds like a good idea to you."

Indah glared at me. "You talk to Dr. Mensah like that?"

"Yes. That's why she's still alive."

She kept glaring. I was glaring at the air next to her head. She rubbed a spot between her eyes. "Fine. I'll bring a couple of the responder crew with me."

I waited around long enough to make sure she did. I left with them through the secure entrance and the air wall, past the access for the responder's dispatch station where I split off to cross the Public Docks toward the Security Office.

It was quiet except for the whisper of the air flow and the low hum of active energy fields. Not anomalous since the last cargo transfer had been completed hours ago and there wasn't any reason for anybody to hang around in here now. The transport crews were either on board their ships or in the station mall. It was perfectly normal and not creepy at all.

I was poking at threat assessment, trying to get a breakdown of the factors that had caused that spike. I had a lot of drone inputs sending me video and other data, but the reaction had been to what Indah said, not anything to do with Mensah's security or anything else I was monitoring. And it had spiked before I had seen how empty the Public Docks were, with the cargo bots all gone to the Merchant Docks to help with the search. Though on a normal work cycle, the cargo bots would be outside, launching and attaching modules.

Huh. We knew Lutran had arranged for his module to be launched from the Merchant Docks and directed toward the Public Docks and his transport. We knew somebody, the actor inside the Port Authority, had redirected it toward the bounty-chasers' ship. The bounty-chasers' bot pilot had picked up the module just like a raider locked onto an unarmed ship, no cargo bot needed, but Lutran's transport should have had a cargo bot assigned to help attach the module. The module's transfer records had been deleted, but the cargo bots might have a record of the request for attachment and its cancellation. Indah had gotten me provisional access, and the cargo bots' movements outside the station weren't under any kind of privacy lock, so I ran a query.

I was distracted, so it was a good thing I'd had my drones form an extra-large spherical perimeter.

The three at the sphere's apex picked up the sound of

snapping metal and gave me a .5-second warning to move. The two further out on the sphere's curve gave me an estimate of the dimensions of the falling object so I knew what direction to go in.

I threw myself out of the way and hit the metal floor in the gap between the crane's second and third arms. Nothing hit me but the sound of a heavy thing striking the floor all around and the vibration rattled the shit out of me. I'm hard to kill, but an entire hover crane landing on me would sure do it.

My drones reported no additional falling objects and I scrambled away from the crane. I used my StationSec access to kill all surveillance on the embarkation floor so whoever it was couldn't take a second shot.

I sent an alert code to the responder team and directed my drones to form a perimeter again. With nothing else heavy about to fall on me, I did what I should have done before I left the secure bay, and used the comm to call Aylen.

Farid answered, "Special Investigator Aylen can't take your call, can I help—"

"Farid, this is SecUnit, did Aylen send a feed message to Indah telling me to meet her in the Security Station Office?"

"I don't know." He sounded startled. "Maybe? She's not here yet and she's off feed for a quick break. It took forever to talk the refugees out of the colony ship's nav control and I think she just needed some personal time—"

"Find her. Make sure she's all right." Hopefully Aylen was in a restroom and not dead somewhere in a corridor. Then I signed off because my query had returned results. The cargo bot scheduled to attach Lutran's module to his transport had been cancelled by the Port Authority and directed to the opposite end of the Public Docks. Which wasn't helpful because we knew our actor was in the Port Authority so . . .

Oh. For fuck's sake, you have to be kidding me.

Pin-Lee tells me I have to make everything complicated, and wow, is she right this time.

I established a secure feed connection with Indah and said, *A crane almost fell on me in the Public Docks. Aylen didn't send you a message, someone spoofed her ID. Did you tell Supervisor Gamila about the trap?*

No! She was startled. *Of course not, I—Damn it, I told her we needed a Port Authority data dump. I had to, she had to authorize the transfer to the temp storage—It can't be her. We grew up together—*

It's not her, I said. *But I know who it is.*

I had never been in a Port Authority office before, for the same reasons I had never been in a Station Security office. But there had been a lot of firsts for me on this contract.

It was a multilevel structure, mostly private work spaces,

with the public entrance on the second level opening inward to stationside, for humans who couldn't/didn't want to do their business over the feed. There were secure entrances I could have used, but I took the public one, sending my drones zipping ahead as the transparent doors slid open. I didn't bother to remove myself from the surveillance camera at the doorway.

I did remove the responder team and the special investigation team, who were coming in through the secure dock entrance on the lower level and evacuating Port Authority workers in case a big structural-integrity-imperiling fight started.

I passed through a large open room with only two humans working with display surfaces. They looked up, startled, but I didn't stop. I walked into Supervisor Gamila's office, which had a wide curving window looking down into the Public Docks. The transparent material was interior port grade but not hatch grade. (I'd looked it up on the walk over here, along with the structure's schematic.)

Gamila sat at her desk, a half dozen documents and database results open in her feed and floating on the display surfaces around her. She was surprised to see me. Then her expression turned frightened when she saw the large projectile weapon I was holding. I said, "Run."

Balin stood beside the window, pretending to be dormant.

Gamila shoved to her feet, bumped into the desk, and bolted out the door behind me. My drone video saw her run into Aylen, who caught her and hurried her out of the office after the other workers.

I said to Balin, "The humans think you're hacked, but we both know that's not true."

Balin stood up and expanded its limbs, the top of its carapace almost brushing the curve of the high ceiling. It sent into the feed, *query: would it make a difference if I was hacked?* Then it launched a code attack to slam through my wall and hit my feed and comm connections and disrupt my processing. At the same instant it extended a limb at high speed right toward my chest.

Nice try. I deflected the code attack and stepped to the side. The limb shot through the empty air where I had been standing and punched a hole in the office partition.

My turn. I lifted my weapon and put three explosive projectiles into the center of Balin's carapace. I was hoping that would do the trick but I had a bad feeling it wouldn't. But it would still confirm my working theory.

I had run a quick check of Balin's records on the way here. It had been on Preservation Station for 43.7 local planetary years, and its original "guardian" had been the Port Authority supervisor at that time, who had taken it on when Balin jumped ship from a corporate cargo transport and asked for refuge. It had been the first and only bot to do that, which, you know, should have told the humans something.

The projectiles broke through Balin's carapace but barely dented the underlying shell. Yeah, I figured. In all its years on station, it had never requested maintenance. It couldn't, because a maintenance scan would have revealed its interior structure. Even a Preservation human would have wondered why a general-purpose bot had been fitted with military-grade armor under its outer body.

Balin dodged sideways and extended two more limbs to trap me in the corner. I ducked and rolled before another limb could pin me and fired three more bolts at its lower undercarriage. A non-standard configuration meant design flaws and gaps in its armor, and I only needed to find one.

Whatever reason Balin had originally been sent here for, nothing had ever come of it as far as I could tell from the historical search. The corporation that deployed Balin had been killed off in a takeover 27.6 years ago; its second function must have remained dormant. Until somehow BreharWallHan had ended up with its command codes and, looking for a way to plug up the pipeline of escaping contract labor running through Preservation and the other non-corporate independent polities along these trade routes, they had decided to activate it.

Possibly there had been two distinct bots in there, and Balin the general purpose bot had been erased once its secondary function had been activated by BreharWallHan. But this was why I didn't want Station Security officers in here with me: Balin's secondary function allowed it to kill humans and there is only one kind of bot made in the Corporation Rim with that function.

Under Balin's general purpose carapace, it was a Com-batBot.

My second hit on its undercarriage caused it to lurch erratically. I pushed up into a better firing position and oh, that had been a trick. It pounced forward to land on me but slammed into the floor when I rolled out of the way.

It shot another limb at me and I went up the wall, fired at its extended limb joints and flipped down to land on my feet. The impacts shattered three joints before Balin slung itself around and jettisoned the broken limbs. It had more where they came from, though, and this was going to take a while. I sent, *Are you trying another code attack on me? Because I'd think a CombatBot would know the difference between a helpless transport and a SecUnit.*

I wanted to provoke it into reacting and of course it did, because it was a bot and it made mistakes, like trying to kill me when it realized the database we were building was going to show an anomalous exit and reentry through one of the outer station airlocks.

(Okay, so a human or augmented human might have made those same mistakes. Maybe exploring every possible outcome of each action in an inescapable loop of paranoia and anxiety wasn't the most normal reaction-state but hey, if it was, there would be a lot fewer stupid murders. I don't know what I'm trying to get at with this. I'd make a better corporate spy? Probably? Except not being a corporate spy left a lot more time for media so that was just never going to be an option.)

(And also, I'd rather be disassembled while conscious, again.)

I needed to get close if I was ever going to finish this, and I feinted toward the right. But Balin knew I needed to get close and decided to shift locations where it would have more room to run me down. It swung and dove for the window into the Public Docks. I'd told Station Security to keep the area clear but I had no eyes down there to make sure. So as Balin slung itself past me I grabbed a trailing limb.

I hadn't expected Balin to be able to smash through that window so fast but wow I was wrong. Falling with the shattered transparent material through the air wall and toward the transit ring floor, I jammed the projectile weapon right up against the undercarriage where Balin's lower limbs connected and fired over and over again. Then we hit the floor.

The impact knocked me off Balin and I landed two meters away. SecUnits don't stun easily and I managed to hang on to the weapon, but I'd damaged an ankle joint and struggled to get upright. Then a giant scoop thing slammed down in front of me.

For .05 of a second I had no clue what it was, then I picked up my drone inputs. JollyBaby the cargo bot had just put its hand down between me and Balin. This whole section of the ring was suddenly full of cargo bots. My drones picked up a dozen emergency medical bots, general purpose bots, even Tellus from the hostel, gathered at the public entrance on the other side of the Port Authority.

They weren't sending pings, they weren't making any noise. I had JollyBaby's hard address and sent it: *query?*

JollyBaby sent back: *Balin off network. Intruder destroyed Balin.*

For another .05 second I thought by intruder it meant me. Before the "oh shit" moment could sink in, I realized what it was actually saying.

At some point during the fight Balin had dropped its wall and its designation as a CombatBot was now open on the feed. To the other bots it looked like one moment Balin was there, and the next its body was occupied by the CombatBot. They thought the CombatBot had killed Balin. I wasn't sure they were wrong.

Balin stood there, carapace broken open, armor dented and cracked from repeated close-range projectiles, broken limbs trailing, as the other bots waited. There were no threats, no communication on the feed or comm, but the message was clear: we know what you are. None of these bots knew how to fight, but they were high functioning and would move to protect humans and each other from a violent intruder. Balin could try to fight; a CombatBot could destroy a cargo bot, no problem. But it couldn't destroy this many cargo bots plus one slightly banged up SecUnit, not all at once.

Balin's mission had depended on stealth. Now its mission was over. Its presence in the feed faded as it dropped into a resting configuration and shut itself down.

I was sitting on the platform of the Security Station's MedUnit, getting my ankle adjusted, when Senior Indah came in.

(I'd already talked to Dr. Mensah on our secure feed. She had asked if I was all right and I said yes, which was sort of true but sort of not. Mensah and Dr. Bharadwaj had been trying to think up ways to make humans less afraid of SecUnits and here was Balin, or Balin's secondary function, running around murdering humans, or a human. And Lutran's elaborate refugee escape network was cut off, leaving the current group safe on Preservation but with no idea where the rest of their people had ended up. The *Lalow* crew might try to continue their part of it, but with BreharWall-Han already on to them, they wouldn't last long. As usual Mensah didn't believe that I was all right but pretended to and said, *Why don't you come to the hotel when you're done and we'll do something fun.*

All I wanted to do was watch media and not exist. I said, *You know I don't like fun.*

Well, Ratthi has a reservation for the opening night of that new musical theater thing in Makeba Hall and he wants us all to go.

That . . . was actually really tempting. Also, guarding her in the hall would be easier if I was sitting with her. Still trying to resist, I said, *You know you don't like musical theater.*

Yes, but I like to watch other people enjoy it. Are you coming?

I gave in, said yes, and cut the connection.)

Indah said, "Good to see you in one piece."

Yeah, whatever. "You read my report?"

"I did." She added dryly, "I'm glad you documented the whole process. It's good to have a reminder that we actually didn't do too badly, except for that one basic wrong assumption."

The assumption that the perpetrator had entered the transport from inside the station instead of outside, she meant.

Balin had redirected the cargo bot in that area to the other end of the docks, then it had gone outside, walked across the station's hull, and come in through the transport's module lock and waited for Lutran. It had used the narrow rods in its hand, the rods that were part of its sealed hatch decoder, to stab him. Balin didn't have any DNA to conceal, but part of its onboard PA equipment included a hazardous materials sterilizer. It had used that on Lutran's body, to make it look like a human had killed him and had needed to remove contact DNA and any other traces left behind.

It had attacked the transport's bot pilot to cover its tracks, then it had used Lutran's ID to call the delivery cart, put the body in it, and sent it to dump it in the station mall, meaning to direct attention away from the port. Then it had returned to the station via the outside lock.

But it was a PA bot/CombatBot, not a SecUnit or a human. Its orders had been to kill Lutran, conceal its involvement, and deliver the refugees to the bounty-chasers, and that's what it had done. It could anticipate some countermeasures to its actions but didn't have the capacity to evaluate all the possible responses. And the bounty-chasers who were giving it orders hadn't anticipated the fact that Preservation Station, unused to casual or any other kind of murder, would put the port into lockdown.

Unlike Indah, I wasn't happy with our performance. Especially since I'd been the one to confuse everything by insisting the surveillance video on the transport dock had been altered. I just said, "I didn't want anything to be left to the imagination."

"Probably for the best." Then Indah sighed, and said, "I wasn't the one who sent that photo of you to the newsstreams."

It was unexpected and it made me drop some inputs. I picked them back up again. I didn't know what to say, because obviously what I should say was *I didn't think it was you* except that was absolutely not true, I had been 96 percent sure it was her.

She continued, "I wouldn't use the newsstreams like that. If we have to fight about Mensah's security, we'll fight, but I won't undermine you. Since we are actually both on the same side."

I hate being in this situation, not knowing what to say, and I couldn't even figure out a query for a search of my media archive for similar conversations because I didn't even know what kind of conversation we were having. But I didn't want to look like it had thrown me as much as it had because . . . I have no idea. The MedUnit was finished so I rolled my pants leg down and said, "I have to meet Dr. Mensah now."

Indah stepped aside as I climbed off the platform. She wasn't making an expression anymore, as if maybe she had noticed how uncomfortable I was with the conversation. Which made me more uncomfortable. She said,

"I'll authorize the hard currency card payment for you. And I assume you're open to another contract the next time something weird happens."

I paused in the doorway. The expected wave of depression at the idea of ever doing this again had somehow not happened. Huh. I said, "Only if it's really weird."

She said, "Understood."

System Collapse

Chapter One

DR. BHARADWAJ TOLD ME once that she thought I hated planets because of the whole thing with being considered expendable and the possibility of being abandoned. I told her it was because planets were boring.

Yeah, that was a lie. Objectively, planets are less boring than staring at walls and guarding equipment in a mining installation. But planets tend to be less boring in the bad way.

Planets where you have to investigate the probably-not-empty, possibly-alien-contaminated Pre–Corporation Rim occupation site while wearing an environmental suit instead of armor are especially not boring in the bad way, maybe the worst way.

Especially when you could have been wearing armor, but you decided to be weird about it instead.

I should back up.

File access 47.43 hours earlier

So the next time I get optimistic about something, I want one of you to punch me in the face. Okay, not really, because let's be real, that would end badly. Maybe remind me to punch myself in the face.

On the team feed, ART said, *SecUnit, status report.*

Or punch ART in the face. I sent back, *I wish I could punch you in the face.*

ART said, *I wish you could try.*

Yes, I know it was just humoring me. And yes, we were still on the stupid alien-contaminated lost colony planet despite the fact that we (me, ART, our humans, but mostly me) really wanted out of this system.

ART added, *I still need a status report.*

I said, *Status: in progress.* I'd been sending it drone video plus it had access to my visual data, so it knew I was still currently moving through tumbled rockfall at the foot of a low plateau, with an agricultural planting area to my right. Whatever was planted there was green and taller than me, and providing adequate cover from our currently designated Hostile One.

It was midmorning planetary time and the cloud cover, which was a by-product of the terraforming, was patchy enough for the sun to come through. ScoutDrone1 was overhead giving me a vantage point of the ongoing situation, so I could see the router installation on another rise past the far end of the planted field. The building itself was smallish, about the size of one of ART's shuttles, but it was enclosed in a much bigger protective shell made of artificial stone. It looked like a big cylindrical boulder, placed at the foot of the low plateau, which had crumbled into a slope of slabs of rock and actual boulders. (Why artificial stone?

Because the dead people from Adamantine Explorations had meant for everything to look pretty once the colony build was complete. I don't know why that's more depressing than them doing a shitty job and intending to abandon their colonists, but it just was.)

The thick green flora waved in the slight breeze under the colony's air bubble, and despite my scan and the drone's scan, it was making me nervous. At least it was making me nervous for a survival-based reason instead of . . . *redacted*.

The front of the installation had an indentation artistically carved to look like a natural curve in the rock, but it was actually shelter for the metal hatch that was currently open. At the moment, it would have been better for the hatch to be closed, but when Ratthi and ART's humans Iris and Tarik ran in there, they hadn't had time to close it behind them before Hostile One had jammed one of its long metal limbs through.

Remember those agricultural bots that I said looked scary but were actually harmless? Yes, I was hilariously wrong about that at the time and I hadn't gotten any less wrong since then.

This ag-bot was only nine meters tall but still covered with spike-like feelers for planting or tilling or whatever. Its lower body had twelve long jointed limbs for moving through thick foliage without crushing plants, and its upper body was a weirdly long curved neck with a small head on top where its main sensors were. It was also batshit out of control, its feed locked, and, according to what Iris had been able to observe before she needed to run like hell, chock-full of alien contamination.

ART said, *I need your status, not the mission status.*

Ugh, my status.

I wasn't supposed to come down to the planet again. Me, ART, Mensah, Seth, and Martyn had all made that decision, because of *redacted*. I had even had an assignment during this day-cycle, sort of. It wasn't really busywork, but it wasn't not busywork, either. Karime had an in-person meeting planned with a faction of colonists at the main site habitation, and Three was going with her for security while pretending to be a human (always a fun time) and I was supposed to monitor Three and make sure it knew what to do and to not let ART give it anxiety. (Or more anxiety than it already had on its own.) I had been lying on the bunk in one of ART's cabins watching *The Rise and Fall of Sanctuary Moon* (episode 121, on repeat) while waiting for Karime and Three's shuttle to arrive at the meeting site, when ART had slammed into my feed and said, *I need you.*

ART couldn't use one of its remaining weaponized pathfinders to take out the agricultural bot. I mean, it could, but that was problematic for a couple of reasons, one being that the pathfinders are jury-rigged bombs—they detonate on command but there's no way to regulate their impact area. The bot was too close to the router installation and more importantly to the open hatch where the humans were taking shelter.

On the feed, Ratthi said, *SecUnit, how are you doing?*

I couldn't get a drone into the router installation without alerting the ag-bot that I was there, but according to the humans they were in the far end of the housing, in a recessed maintenance bay, about three meters from what is apparently the maximum reach of the ag-bot's . . . tentacle, poking limb, whatever it's called. *I'm fine, Ratthi. Don't get any closer to the tentacle.*

It's a growth stimulator, Ratthi said. *You don't have to rush, we're fine.*

You're not fine, Ratthi, for fuck's sake. (For however many corporate standard years, all I got from humans was "Run in there now no matter how likely you are to get blown to tiny pieces when a quiet tactical approach has a higher percentage of success" and now it's "Oh no we're fine, we can hang out in this objectively terrifying immediately hazardous situation for however long.")

(I'm just saying that it would be nice for the humans to give me a realistic situation report for once.)

(Dr. Bharadwaj says even good change is stressful.)

ScoutDrone1 hadn't found a decent vantage point yet for me to get close enough to take a shot. Sort of a shot. The weapon I had was not actually a weapon, it was a recall beacon. (I know. It sounds like the whole retrieval is jacked from the beginning. "The weapon is a recall beacon." They wouldn't even pull this off on *Sanctuary Moon*.)

I had an actual gun, one of ART's projectile weapons, but we knew from experience how many shots it took to down an enraged ag-bot, and getting up right on its processor for a point-blank impact was not something anybody wanted me to try to attempt, especially me. And shooting it with my onboard energy weapons was not going to work. (ART had altered an environmental suit for me so the sleeves locked in to my weapon ports and I could fire without burning holes through the fabric, but I just didn't have the capacity to take out this thing.)

I needed something that would work from a distance, and the recall beacon was similar to certain models that the company used, though not nearly as powerful. It was designed to allow a human to hold it during operation and not be exploded into bits, so it could be operated by a landing party in distress. The idea was to get a payload with a transponder high enough in atmosphere that the signal pulse it would broadcast could easily be picked up by a ship in orbit. But you know, if you hit something with that payload at closer range, it'll knock a really big hole in it.

Back aboard ART, while I was getting into my environmental suit, ART had chosen the recall beacon out of its inventory as the tool most likely to be used in a way it had never been designed to in order to stop a contaminated ag-bot.

This was all just great, since I'd already gotten the shit kicked out of me by an ag-bot before, though that one had been controlled by a higher level of sentient virus. This one was probably just a leftover fragment with a few commands left twining through the bot's code, like "chase and kill moving human-shaped things." Iris thought it must have been dormant up to this point, and maybe restoring the routers in this area had woken it up again. (During the intra-colony fighting, one colonist faction had destroyed the feed routers, which we knew now had not been a source of contamination transmission. Not exactly helpful, but of all the weird shit these people had done to each other during the worst of the incident, sabotaging their own routers was low on the list, maybe all the way down into the vaguely rational category.)

By the time I had reached the storage locker where the transponder/bot-buster was kept, Seth was already there. He handed it to me and said, "We've only had to use it a couple of times, once on a planet where atmospheric conditions had blocked our comm, and once in an asteroid mining belt where Matteo— It's a long story." He scratched the back of his head and added reluctantly, "I know we said you wouldn't have to go back . . ."

I didn't have time for this. I told him, "It's fine."

So I'm here now and it's fine, everyone shut up about it, okay.

ScoutDrone2 had found a good line of sight with cover, approximately twenty meters to my left through the boulders and up onto the ridge a little. I started making my way toward it, but my plan was not giving me great numbers in threat assessment or in the potential for a successful retrieval, which is usually not a metric I look at while in progress. (I don't want to jinx myself.) But I still felt radically off my game and I was hoping for reassurance rather than statistics that confirmed that I was correct in thinking that everything sucked right now.

ART was right, a hit from the launcher would stop the ag-bot. (It wouldn't stop a CombatBot, but it might make one reconsider for .03 seconds before it came at you again. A CombatUnit would be unlikely to let you get into position to use a slow-loading tool like this in the first place, but you could definitely kill the shit out of a normal SecUnit with it. Note to self: don't let the ag-bot take it away from you and shoot you with it. Talk about adding insult to injury.) But I knew how fast the ag-bots could move. I had skimmed through the transponder's instructional feed module on the shuttle ride down and the launcher was not meant to be used in a hurry, and it only had two reloads.

Yeah, this plan was . . . not going to work.

(I could see my mistake now. I'd let ART and the humans come up with this idea. They had the right weapon, just the wrong way to use it. I should have been more proactive, but, ugh, *redacted*.)

I recalled ScoutDrone2 and started back the way I'd come, toward the field and the tall plants. *What's wrong?* ART said.

This isn't going to work. I stuck my calculations of the ag-bot's speed vs. my speed vs. the launcher's speed and capacity into a chart and sent it to ART so it wouldn't keep asking me questions. This was where I could have really used Three for backup, but it was arriving at the main colony site with Karime now and diverting it would mean canceling her meeting, and that was important, and honestly, there was no reason—no nonstupid reason—I shouldn't be able to handle this. And I already had a new terrible plan. The transponder's instruction module had helpfully explained that the launcher could also be triggered remotely via a secure feed connection.

This plan was going to look more stupid, but threat assessment liked it better: it got the explosive devices farther away from the trapped humans.

I entered the field, the tall stalks of green plants well above my head, the wind making the little lumpy seed-looking things knock together. This field was actually growing out of the ground, not out of growth-medium racks, so it was easier to get through it. The breeze covered the sound of my environmental suit brushing against the plants. The ground was wet and smelled like the inside of a biome display, even through the environmental suit mask. (Yes, I was wearing it despite the fact that we were in an air bubble so I didn't need it. It wasn't like I thought it could protect me from alien contamination, it just felt nice, okay.)

The air movement also made the plants sway, covering my progress as I worked my way through. ScoutDrone1 fed me overhead video so I could make sure my motion wasn't obvious. I came up on the edge of the field, my vision still blocked by the last few heavy rows of stalks, but Scout-Drone1's vid and scan showed I had about thirty meters of open sandy ground between me and where the ag-bot was patiently jammed into the router housing, waiting for prey.

I checked the one transponder in the launcher, made sure the other two were primed for remote detonation. Then I ran forward.

I dropped the first charge fifteen meters out and the

second five meters later. (No, they did not go off on impact, I did check that.) I slid to a stop and shouted, "Hey! Over here!" (Yes, I could have been more quippy like in a show, but an ag-bot that's meant to be controlled via code delivered through a local feed and doesn't understand more than a limited range of vocal commands is not exactly going to be impressed or intimidated by sarcasm.)

It didn't react, at least from what I could tell on visual. For 2.3 seconds I thought it would ignore me. Which, having to walk up to it and actually put the transponder on its carapace was not the worst thing that could happen.

Then it ripped its limbs out of the doorway and flung itself at me. Okay, that was not the worst thing that could have happened, either, but it was high on the list.

Bots like this don't have to turn around—it didn't have any apertures or sensors in its body that it needed to point at the annoying thing it wanted to kill, it just reversed right out of the installation and lunged. It was really fast, is what I'm saying.

But I'm fast, too, and I was moving back even as it surged at me. Running toward the field, I had ScoutDrone1's video in one input so I saw the ag-bot's first three legs hit the ground two meters from the first transponder. I only had an estimate of its speed (really fast) so I couldn't do a precise calculation, but it looked right. I triggered the first transponder.

The fucker jumped. It was cut off from the feed, it shouldn't have been able to pick up my detonation command. It also shouldn't have been able to take in the visual data of what I had done and interpret it as a trap, but that had to be the alien contamination augmenting its processing capacity. It went ten meters up in the air (ScoutDrone1 almost bought the farm but shot out of the way just in time) and it only lost the tips of two legs instead of taking a disabling blast to its joints. And it became obvious it was aiming to land on me, and there was no way I could get away in time.

Two things happened at once: (1) I threw myself down and rolled to face upward, aiming the launcher with the last transponder at the approximate trajectory the ag-bot was arriving at; and (2) I caught a ping from another SecUnit.

My first thought was *What the hell is Three doing here?* but less accusatory and more relieved. It would be embarrassing to be rescued by Three, but it wasn't anything that hadn't happened before. The next thought was: *That can't be Three.* I knew its location as of 5.4 minutes ago, there was no time for it to get here.

Then: *Oh shit, it's Barish-Estranza.*

That was why Karime's meeting was too important to put off, why she needed Three with her, why ART couldn't/shouldn't use its weaponized pathfinders or try to arm a shuttle or anything else that might seem out of capacity for a university's deep-space mapping transport.

Four corporate standard day cycles after the Preservation responder had shown up with Dr. Mensah to look for us, another Barish-Estranza explorer had arrived, complete with a new complement of at least three SecUnits that we knew of. Since then the B-E task group had been much more active, sending teams to the planet to "evaluate" the situation and talk to the colonists. There was no legal way to keep them from doing it and killing them all was problematic, though don't think ART hadn't run those numbers a few times.

The ag-bot plummeted toward me in a controlled fall, and I was about to hit the triggering sequence. Then a quick scatter of large explosive projectiles from off toward the right hit the central part of the bot's body. Right where its processor would be.

The bot made a clunking noise. Metal shrapnel sprayed out and a couple of limbs flew off. I scrambled out of the way as the torso broke loose and slammed into the ground. Oh, great save, B-E SecUnit, most humans wouldn't have been able to evade that. What the hell kind of retrieval was that supposed to be?

ART, watching my visual data, said, *That was .2 degrees away from a murder attempt.*

Important question you might have: Did this SecUnit know I was a SecUnit?

Answer: I fucking hope not.

On the secure team feed, I said, *Use the feed for anything you don't want them to know. Their SecUnit can pick you up on audible from over there.* ScoutDrone1 was already in stealth mode and I told it and ScoutDrone2 to head for the nearest shuttle, which was the one the router team had left up on the plateau. The shuttle ART had landed for me was farther out, past the field, out of the ex-ag-bot's sensor range. I had one backup drone in the pocket of my environmental suit and I told it to go dormant. I had already let go of the launcher and made sure it rolled out of my reach. I was running all my move-like-a-human code, and I had improved it substantially from the first version I'd written. My feed, the team feed, and my connection with ART were all locked down tight, though SecUnits with intact governor modules aren't free to detect and hack systems like I am. They have to receive a specific order to do it, and most employers are too paranoid to allow that. But this SecUnit (designate: B-E Unit1) was only about four meters away; it might just look at me, know what I was, and report it.

The only thing I could do was confuse it as much as possible. I rolled over and groaned like a human (potentially not a great idea, it sounded embarrassingly fake) and pulled a few clips from *Sanctuary Moon* of the various scenes where the colony solicitor's bodyguard had been injured and had to stand up again. On the team feed, ART was talking to Iris. She leaned out of the installation and called out, "Can you ask your SecUnit to fall back, please."

Without drones, I couldn't see what it was doing. ART had switched over to Iris's feed, using her enviro suit camera, and the resolution at this distance wasn't good. ART needed a field equipment upgrade. Wait, a human would look at it, right?

ART said, *Look at it. It's obvious you're avoiding it.*

Maybe I'm a nervous human who's afraid of bots, I told ART, but I looked at it anyway.

The SecUnit was walking away, and five humans in the red-brown Barish-Estranza-branded environmental suits were coming toward me/us. They would have a shuttle nearby somewhere, with probably two more humans and possibly one additional SecUnit inside. They weren't obviously armed, but intel suggested that at least some members of the B-E scout teams regularly carried sidearms while on planet. The Targets/infected colonists had taken weapons off the previous/posthumous B-E explorer scout team.

And they had brought a SecUnit armed with a nonstandard medium-distance bot-busting weapon, better than anything ART currently had on board.

Ratthi ran to me and on our secured team feed I told him, *Pretend to help me up.*

"Are you okay?" he demanded. I'd restricted my camera views to ART to keep the humans from getting more agitated, but once it was clear I had survived, ART had shared a clip of my close call. Probably so it had someone to be angry about it with. I let Ratthi grab my arm and made it look like he was taking most of my weight as I pushed upright. "That was too close!" He threw a glare toward the Barish-Estranza party. He added on the feed, *Was that intentional, do you think?*

Maybe. Maybe it's just a shitty SecUnit, I replied. I was not in a good mood.

Okay, I'm not perfect, I think we all know that by now, but B-E Unit1 should have understood the trajectory situation and used the explosive bolts a beat earlier and then accelerated in to roll me away and shield me from shrapnel. That was what I would have done. Tried to do. There was no way a client-supervisor would have had time to countermand that save. Fucking assholes.

(Obviously this is not actually what I'm upset about, it's just easier to be angry about B-E Unit1's fuckup and/or disregard for minimum client safety.)

Safer to be angry about it, ART said on our private connection.

I was not even going to respond to that. ART had told Mensah it wouldn't push me. Just because its MedSystem was certified for emotional support and trauma recovery it thought it knew everything.

I was on my feet, pretending to have an injured ankle and leaning on Ratthi. Iris had come out and moved forward to meet the lead Barish-Estranza human, and Tarik had stayed with her, which was good. He had also dropped his enviro suit helmet visor before he came out, so it wouldn't look strange that I still had mine down, which was also good. Just us humans here, some of us like to wear our visors down when we don't need them to breathe and some don't, we just like to mix it up.

The B-E humans had their visors up, and we'd seen the lead human before. He was Sub-Supervisor Dellcourt (male/demi) and he was one of the smart ones, which was just how this day was going.

"Thank you for your help," Iris said, in a way that could be mistaken for politeness by a bot but a human would definitely know there was an undercurrent of *fuck you.* "Are you going to bill us later?"

Martyn told me that Iris and ART have been interacting since Iris was a new human baby and ART was a new whatever the hell it is and sometimes that is not surprising at all.

Dellcourt said, "We'll put it on your creditor's statement," and chuckled. Iris smiled with a tension in her jaw that indicated gritting teeth.

The billing thing is not actually a joke; Pin-Lee and Turi, who does the accounting for ART, were preparing a counterbill to present to Barish-Estranza after this was over. (If this was ever over.) These money fights between/with corporations were very common and incredibly boring.

(According to Martyn, ART is of course capable of doing its own accounting, but it always ends up with extra numbers that no one can trace. So now Turi does it and has to keep a hardcopy ledger because otherwise ART would alter their data. No one knew if ART was making up numbers for the hell of it or if these numbers represented actual credit balances that ART was hiding somewhere.)

Still smiling, Dellcourt said, "Can I ask what you are doing here? Besides antagonizing the local inventory?"

Inventory = the ag-bot. The explosive had destroyed its processor, so it was no longer a contamination hazard to humans, which was not a coincidence.

Iris said, "Only if I can ask you what you're doing here."

This was some kind of human posturing thing. It was pretty obvious Iris's task group had been fixing the routers; if the B-E humans had been oblivious, their SecUnit would have called their attention to it. It was also pretty obvious that, considering the specific explosive bolts their SecUnit had been armed with, they had been out looking for contaminated bots.

That's not encouraging, ART said, which was understating the case dramatically. We were collecting depressing datapoints indicating Barish-Estranza's intentions all the time.

The first thing the new Barish-Estranza explorer had done was power up to ART and try to intimidate it/us. (I know. I was below 66 percent operating capacity at the time and I thought it was a bad idea.

ART had dropped its main weapon port and transmitted, *Targeting lock acquired.*

The explorer had replied something to the effect that they didn't mean to be intimidating and was the widdle academic transport crew scared, but in corporate speak, and ART had replied, *It's so easy for ships to disappear out here.*

There was a pause, indicating a scramble to adjust operational parameters, then they made the mistake of trying to intimidate back with something like *Oh yeah well you'll get damaged, too,* and I am not exactly an expert on nonfictional human interactions but that just obviously wasn't going to cut it.

ART transmitted, *You can make this complicated situation simple for me.* Which I can tell you was not any kind of posturing, it 100 percent meant that.

Barish-Estranza must have picked up on that subtext because they backed down and now they think ART is a human commanding officer who's a giant asshole.)

(ART is a secret from everyone except for the upper level departments at the University of Mihira and New Tideland. Barish-Estranza had no idea what it was dealing with.)

The rest of the B-E group was staring at me and the humans. Overse had said that the B-E corporates always look like they're trying to figure out how much to sell you for, and she wasn't wrong. I was glad I had refined my move-like-a-human code because if I had to wing it on my own, I wouldn't have known what to do with my hands. Iris was doing a good job of trying to keep most of the B-E humans' attention, but I could tell the SecUnit was looking at me.

I don't know if Iris had noticed this or not, but she turned in the SecUnit's direction and said, "Thank you for your help."

Dellcourt's expression was startled. "It's a SecUnit."

Iris ignored him, and we collected our remaining transponder and the launcher and left.

Chapter Two

ONCE WE WERE OUT of sight behind an outcrop, I did a quick scan for stealth drones, then took my weight off Ratthi and straightened up. He said, "Are you all right?"

I said, "Sure."

Iris was watching me worriedly and pretending not to. She said, "Why don't you stay with us? We've only got one more router to do."

I said, "Sure."

We climbed a rough trail back up to their shuttle, which was set down on the small flat plateau above the router site. Since I was staying with the humans, ART recalled my shuttle. It would hopefully make the lurking B-E team think we had left.

The original Barish-Estranza task force had told us the new arrivals were a scheduled reinforcement, not a response to the distress beacon they had sent. But Seth had said they were probably lying about that. And if they were lying, it meant B-E had more backup waiting at a wormhole somewhere relatively close to this system. Which made sense, if they had been sending multiple explorer groups to systems in this general area.

But the real problem was that now B-E had a supply ship and an armed explorer, and there was still no sign of a support ship from the University of Mihira and New Tideland. And we really needed one.

Phase I of Plan A: Get the Hell Out of Here had involved trying to get a specialized decontamination update to the colonists' MedUnits so they could run the alien decontamination protocol on each other. That took longer than it should have because all the medical equipment in the colony was proprietary-branded corporate designs from thirty-seven-plus corporate standard years ago.

Thiago and Karime had talked one faction of the colonists into sending us a copy of the software on their main medical unit, and ART had removed any traces of contaminated code and modified its own decontam package to run on old shitty equipment. Then each unit had to be individually accessed and reloaded with the cleaned and enhanced operating systems via elaborately overcautious procedures to eliminate cross contamination or recontamination. Mostly in case we had fucked up massively and there were dormant virus fragments in play somewhere in the medical systems whose behavior didn't match the human-machine-human transmission pattern we had previously noted.

Fortunately, between ART, me, our humans, and the colonists, the level of paranoia about virus contamination on this planet was more than adequate, even by my standards.

Phase II of Plan A was the legal case to keep Barish-Estranza from asserting salvage-right ownership of the colony's humans, which Pin-Lee was still working on. ART's crew had also started a planetary alien contamination assessment, and things were looking iffy. There was a lot of technical detail I didn't care about, but basically if they couldn't make a good case to certify the contaminated site as sealable, then the planet would be placed under interdict and the colonists would have to leave anyway and Barish-Estranza could make yet another case for claiming them as salvage.

The first subsection of Phase II involved asking the colonists what they wanted to do. I know, it seemed simple. (And I am aware of the irony, since I know exactly how hard the question "what do you want" can be when you don't have a fucking clue what you want. But we weren't talking existential questions of existence here, just the basic: Do you want to be salvaged by Barish-Estranza as corporate contract labor for the rest of your lives? Select (1) yes (2) no.)

The problem was who to ask.

("They're split into even more factions than they were when we arrived," Thiago had said, after collating early intelligence received via survey drones deployed by ART and by some comm conversations with different colonists. "They've divided their compound up into at least two different areas, and other groups have scattered out to camps on the far side of the inhabited plateau."

Karime, who was the primary negotiator on ART's crew, said, "They've done things to each other that can't be easily forgiven. We know—and they know—it was caused by the alien contamination, but I think it's going to take time for them to come to terms with that."

"Time we're running out of," Mensah said.

Which, it's not like I don't understand the whole idea of not forgiving stuff that happens to you. But it seems like they could not-hate each other long enough to avoid getting turned into corporate slave labor, and then start hating each other again after the threat assessment percentage went down.)

We took the shuttle over to the next router, which was on a small rocky hill west of the main colony site, surrounded by sparse clumps of gray-greenish spindly tree-fern things.

By the time we got there the other current operation, the one I was supposed to be monitoring security for before *redacted,* was already in progress. I was bored, so I reversed Three's video to watch from the beginning.

Karime had come down in a shuttle with Three, and they had disembarked on the secondary colony site's landing pad. The primary colony had been near the Pre–Corporation Rim site and had been abandoned after the first encounter with alien contamination. The colonists had put this one on the lower terrace of a plateau, using heavy equipment to carve out chambers and passages before building their habitats on top, so the colony had both open-air structures and belowground shelters to retreat to and to protect supplies and vital systems. Below the habitat, they had carved vehicle landing areas and ramps down to another agricultural installation and water production plant.

Karime had to greet the colonists waiting for her. That took a while, so long I had time to catch up to real time where they had started up the rock-cut steps. The weather was clear over there, visibility good. We could replace me with an automated weather drone, that would work, too.

Iris and Tarik started on the router, which looked like another big rock and was surrounded by a ferny-tree grove. Past it was a plain with reddish vegetation and some rocky outcrops. There was no way for the humans to get lost out here. There was ART, and the human colony wasn't far away, and the comm was working, and the lift tower for the drop box shaft was visible in the distance, stretching up until it finally disappeared into the upper atmosphere. So even if the shuttle broke down, even if the comm and our feed stopped working, all they would have to do was walk toward the tower until one of ART's patrolling pathfinders came to look for them and called for another shuttle.

I could walk in the opposite direction, just walk until— Yeah, I'm going to tag this section for delete.

I accessed Three's drone feed so I had a better view of it and Karime. It was out of its armor, wearing an enviro suit, pretending to be a human. I tapped Three's feed and said, *More casual. Are you running your walk-like-a-human code?*

Three replied, *I am running the walk-like-a-human code.* But it slowed down, made its joints looser. After two seconds, it added, *This is unexpectedly difficult.*

Tell me about it. *You're doing fine,* I said.

We didn't want the colonists to know Three was a SecUnit, mostly to fend off conversations about how much the giant angry planet-bombing transport likes this SecUnit and will it lose its mind if a rock falls on it or something. The colonists thought Three was just a really awkward augmented human. It's not like there aren't a lot of those around.

Karime and Three followed the colonists through the main part of the secondary colony and it looked way more like a human habitation than what was left of the original Pre–Corporation Rim site. (Which before coming here is not something I would have thought was a positive, but right now anything that didn't say "major alien contamination incident in progress" was a plus.) This colony's occasional bits of exposed piping, recycling storage, decorative planting, and interrupted partial constructions all looked messy and human and very not hostile-alien-virus-intending-to-take-over-your-brain.

Because that had happened. Almost happened.

ART was all over this feed, because it was not exactly thrilled with any of its humans going down to the planet at all.

(Transcript of the conversation during the initial mission briefing:

ART: *If Karime is present at the colony and the colonists or corporates attempt to harm her, a threat to bomb this site may be ineffective.*

Seth: *Peri, can I speak to you in private for a moment?*

Iris: *It's just joking.*

Ratthi: *Is it.*

Me: *You can bomb the terraforming engines on the other continent, it's a better target anyway.*

Thiago: *I suppose SecUnit is joking, too.*)

(ART actually was joking. Mostly. Iris told Thiago that it had undergone a traumatic experience and would verbally act out until it had fully processed what had happened. Thiago said he knew that but he also thought it enjoyed terrifying people. Iris was pissed off and just smiled in an "I'm going to pretend you aren't serious so I don't have to fight you right here in this corridor" way.)

(I've realized that Iris is ART's Ratthi.)

(Thiago is incorrect: ART doesn't enjoy terrifying people, it enjoys getting its own way and it has a variety of techniques it finds effective for that and vaguely or not-so-vaguely threatening statements are sure one of them. Iris is also correct that ART is still processing its traumatic experience and the fact that it had such a great result with arming its pathfinders and making the colonists think it was about to bomb the crap out of them is maybe something we should worry about, but I just have a lot to do right now, okay.)

(I was not joking. The terraforming engines are a perfect target: zero casualties if we evacuate the colony site immediately afterward and irreparable damage to infrastructure.)

(I'm just saying.)

Even with Three shadowing her, it wasn't easy to watch Karime follow her colonist guide through a doorway and down another set of steps into the depths of the habitation. From ART's personnel file, she was older than Mensah and she didn't look like an intrepid space explorer, either, even in the protective environmental suit.

Martha Wells

They led her into a room where she took a seat on a cushion on a stone floor, Three taking up a position behind her. It tried to stay standing, but Karime looked back, smiled, and motioned for it to sit down. It did. It reminded me of the feed vids of very young and very awkward baby fauna with limbs they apparently can't fully control yet.

I guess at some point I was that awkward, but seriously.

Three's intel drone went to the ceiling where it had a 360-degree view. The room was round and carved out of the rock, with a couple of lights attached to the high domed ceiling. The colonists took seats on the floor cushions to face Karime.

One was an older female human named Bellagaia, who had been the first colonist to try to initiate contact again after the explosion of the Pre–Corporation Rim site. ART's human Kaede thought Bellagaia had probably been instrumental in bringing Faction One around to the idea of actually talking to us. She was here with the leaders of Faction Two, Danis and Variset, the "we're too confused to know what we want and trust no one" faction. Bellagaia had managed to talk them into this meeting and we had sent Karime because she was not only ART's lead negotiator but also looked nonthreatening.

ART wasn't happy, but Three was sharing its threat assessment, which was running acceptably low. The colonists had put out cups and a flask of hot liquid, and some pieces of food on a plate. Instead of their surface work clothes, the three participants in the meeting wore softer clothing in brighter colors. Body language and other signs indicated

they really did want to talk. When all the humans had settled into place, Karime said, "Thank you for allowing me
to come here and speak to you." There was a few seconds'
delay on the feed, as Thiago's language module translated
for her.

Karime was clearly prepared to be all reasonable and calm
and persuasive about how banding together temporarily
with the other factions in order to get the whole population off the planet would be the best solution if the legal
case couldn't stop Barish-Estranza. Danis and Variset were
looking at her like she was going to suggest they all set
themselves on fire for fun. More colonists had gathered in
the doorways to listen or pretend to listen and then inevita-
bly interject stupid comments. So, situation totally normal.

On my mission (make that "mission" because I was actually just standing there) the humans were already finishing up. Tarik was carrying the tool cases back to the
shuttle, which was parked on the flat ground past the trees.
Iris had finished the router diagnostics and had tuned in
to the team feed to watch Karime's conference. Ratthi had
stopped looking at his data and was watching Tarik walk.

Then Bellagaia said, "First, before we get started with
our questions— Some of us don't want to tell you this. But
there's another colony site on this planet."

Uh, yeah, we know that. The primary, and the other fac-
tional sites.

It took Karime three seconds to process the abrupt statement. (She was almost as good at not looking annoyed as
Mensah was.) She kept her expression neutral and patient.

"I'm sure we can accommodate their needs." She gestured to Danis and Variset. "If there are other members of the different groups who should be present—"

"No, not one of our groups." Bellagaia cut her off. Danis and Variset gave Bellagaia "what the hell" expressions. They didn't like that she was saying this, whatever it was about. "Another site entirely. They split off nearly thirty years ago. They're at the pole, near the terraforming."

On the team feed, ART said, *For fuck's sake.*

I said, aloud, "You have to be kidding me."

The last thing we needed was more colonists. It was going to throw off all the contingency planning and resource-estimating and calculating that the humans had been doing.

It was going to keep us here longer.

Onboard ART, Martyn, who was monitoring from ART's lounge, almost spilled his cup of hot liquid and said, "What?"

Sitting next to him, Kaede tapped the ship-wide comm and said, "Seth, come in here, please."

On our router hill, Iris muttered, "What?" Ratthi turned to stare at me, worried. He hadn't been monitoring that feed, just our separate mission group. Tarik, on his way back from the shuttle, saw that there was agitation and jogged to reach us faster. I added Ratthi and Tarik to Karime's mission feed, which was quicker than explaining.

In the underground colony room, Karime lifted her brows. "Another occupied site?" I thought she was being careful not to show too much reaction. It was the way Mensah would have played it. On the feed, she said, *The terra-forming stations on the other continents are all supposed to be uninhabited auxiliaries, correct?*

Correct, ART said. *Perhaps they are intoxicated.*

Karime replied, *You know, I'll believe anything right now.*

Bellagaia explained, "They left when the contamination reports first started. In the beginning, we would hear from them on the comm, sometimes they'd fly in for holidays. Less over the years. We grew apart. We can't call them directly, they have to call us."

When she said that, I had a moment of hope. Maybe these other humans were imaginary. Humans are great at imagining stuff. That's why their media is so good.

Possibly Karime also had a moment of hope because she said in a very even voice, "Why do they have to call you?"

Bellagaia explained, "The comm won't work up there. It's interference from the terraforming batteries."

On the team feed, Iris said, *Peri, would that kind of inter-ference block your initial scan for signals?*

ART answered, *Yes, it did. But there was no priority for further scanning after the active colony site was located.*

Sounding resigned, Seth said, *So there could be another colony site.*

Kaede said, *There's nothing about that in the mapping data we found in the drop box station.*

Martyn added, *Didn't we get visual images of the engines at the pole?*

Reconstructed scan images of the engines themselves, not the terrain around them, ART said.

"If we want to talk to them, we have to go there," Bellagaia was saying. "But when this last outbreak started, we
were afraid to send anybody up there, that we'd just be
spreading the contamination. So they were never infected."

Danis muttered, "We think they were never infected."
Impatient to get back to refusing to be convinced to not be
stupid, she added, "They're probably dead."

One of the others, standing back in the doorway, said,
"We survived. Until now."

There was a murmur of "Despite you" from someone in
the back, but the other humans pretended to ignore it.

"I see." Lines formed on Karime's forehead. She was distracted, listening to the chatter in the feed. Before I could
put up a filter for her, ART said, *Please stop excessive speaking on the mission feed* and they all shut up. I know what humans are like, so I had only given Ratthi and Tarik read
access. Karime said, "You said they were at the pole?"

Bellagaia nodded. "Yes, near the service base for the
terraforming engines. They were mostly the original tech-
nicians who serviced the engines before they went on full
automatic. They said they had found a good site up there to
build in."

Karime was thinking fast. "We can speak to them, warn
them. Does Barish-Estranza know about them?"

Bellagaia shook her head and looked pointedly at Danis.
"I don't know."

Danis's expression was militant. "Our group wouldn't
tell them."

Variset added, "We think our group wouldn't tell them."

Danis conceded, "The others might. Some of them are still confused."

That caused a lot more muttered commentary from the audience in the doorway. Apparently they also thought Danis's group was confused. Three sent me a report saying the movement and activity in the surrounding humans was still non-hostile. Yeah, I fucking know. (I didn't say that, I just sent *Acknowledge.*)

Another human wriggled into the doorway and said, "That site, it was never meant to be a secondary site. It won't be on the original colony charter."

In ART's lounge, Seth pressed his hands to his face and groaned. For a second I didn't get it. I mean, I want to press my hands to my face and groan, too, but I pretty much always do.

Oh, right, I get it. The University's legal case stipulating that this planet was a sovereign political entity and not salvage was based on the re-creation of the original colony's charter that Pin-Lee and other humans had been working on. This was going to trigger another revamp. And with the new Barish-Estranza explorer here, we were running out of time.

Planets are big, and we could have missed other landing and habitation sites. ART must have scanned for other air bubbles at some point (I didn't know what it did in its spare time), but when we first got here it mostly hadn't given a crap about anything except finding its crew. The kind of mapping scans that would turn up low-impact habitations were usually done by satellite. (Or pathfinders, most of which ART had weaponized.) The planet had no intact satellites, just orbital debris from dead ones, too fragmentary to be identified as Corporation Rim or Pre–Corporation Rim.

ART said, *The terraforming site would create signal interference that would disrupt both communication and feed traffic.* Yeah, that's what I thought. ART added, *It would also interfere with a colony-sized air bubble installation.*

Seth was frowning as he flicked through reports. He said, *Right, right. That initial pathfinder scan was looking for air bubbles.*

Karime nodded to herself. "Okay, that makes— Can you tell me anything else about this other colony site?"

Bellagaia gestured to the doorway behind her and said, "This is Corian." She used a pronoun that our translator rendered as vi. "Vi's the historian."

Corian elbowed someone out of the way to get into the room. Vi dropped to the floor and curled vir legs up, facing Karime. Three didn't alert, which was good. Threat assessment was reading Corian as a non-hostile anxious to communicate. Vi patted vir chest. "I keep the records, understood? This is not personal knowledge."

Karime nodded. "Understood."

Corian had an intent expression, like vi had been waiting for a long time to talk about this. "Contact stopped twenty years ago. There have been reports of connections, from maintenance taking up birds to check on terraforming progress, but none verified. The engines are too noisy."

Somebody else countered, "Auntie said the connections had the right signatures—"

Bellagaia was watching Karime carefully and must have gotten some sense of the turmoil that was going on. To the others, she said, "Shush. Let Corian speak." Amazingly, they shut up.

Corian continued, "It wasn't just the contamination, see. I read the journals from the time they left, and they were separatist. Multiple disagreements on multiple levels. That's why the lack of communication. We can't tell you where they are exactly, because we don't know. They wouldn't tell us."

I thought Karime was having the same "oh shit" moment as the rest of the crew but hiding it very well. She looked around at the colonists. "Thank you for trusting us with this. We won't share it with Barish-Estranza." She hesitated, clearly trying to say the next part without sounding like she was giving them orders. "I understand you haven't made a decision about what you want to do yet. It's in your best interest not to share it with them, either, until you're certain."

They may already be aware of it, ART sent.

"Important, yes, but that isn't my primary concern," Corian said, still focused on Karime. "The journals talk about a rumor that they had settled underground, in a cave system."

Three's drone saw Karime's face sink and her shoulders tighten. Me too, Karime, me too. She echoed, "A cave system."

Danis tossed her head. "With the geology of that region? A cave system big enough for a colony? Not likely."

Ugh, you are kidding me. I had (a) visual input, which was Ratthi shaking his fist at the sky and Tarik making hair-tearing-out gestures and Iris sitting there with her face set in a wince; (b) the video feed from ART's lounge, where Seth was gently banging his head against the table while Martyn patted him on the back. Karime said, "You think it's another Pre–Corporation Rim site. Or an alien remnant site?"

"More likely to be Pre–Corporation Rim, but—" Corian made an openhanded gesture. "You see the problem."

Yeah, we saw the problem.

Mensah tapped my feed from the Preservation responder. *Seth just messaged me that we have an unexpected development. Is Karime all right?*

Yes. She's busy getting some fantastic news right now. I forwarded the last section of the conversation.

Some of the other colonists were protesting that there was no evidence of any other Pre-CR site and certainly not any alien remnant site, how could you even think that, etc., while Bellagaia looked at them like she was exhausted. Karime stayed focused on Corian, listening intently as vi talked. After vi finished, Karime asked, "Can you give me any more information where this site might be?" No, it turned out, vi could not, and nobody else had a clue, either, just that it was near enough to the terraforming engines to disrupt attempts to reach them by comm. Corian had been checking the records vi had access to, trying to locate anyone still alive who might have talked to the separatists at some point in the last twenty years, but with no success.

Mensah had had time to review the feed video. She muttered, "Oh, you have to be kidding me."

Yeah.

Chapter Three

SO THERE WAS A fight at that point. Not a fight, a discussion. Whatever, agitated humans figuring out what to do.

Karime still had to continue with the original purpose of her meeting, trying to get the colonists to at least agree in principle to the idea of letting the University evacuate them to keep them from getting dumped into Barish-Estranza labor camps. Seth, Martyn, and Kaede were part of the argument/discussion—call it the argucussion—with Mensah and Pin-Lee on the comm from the Preservation responder. So Thiago and Turi and Overse had stopped working on what they were doing and tagged in to Mission One to give Karime advice and look things up if she needed it. Matteo and Arada were still working on medical upgrades. I backburnered all those feeds, though I kept a channel open with Three, who was still doing a good job of sitting there with Karime and not screwing anything up.

I wasn't doing a good job of standing here, because my current three humans had just volunteered to go check out the new probably-not-apocryphal colony site. "We're in a good position to get there without Barish-Estranza noticing," Tarik said. Ratthi and Iris had already pulled the shuttle's supply and equipment manifest into our team sub-feed and were going over it.

On the comm, Mensah said, "It's not a bad idea." I couldn't pull video from the responder right now, but ART was supplying camera views from its galley, and I could see Mensah on the floating display surface there. Someone had pulled up the operation timetable in the general team feed, where Iris had just updated the completion of her team's task with the routers. Mensah added, "And they've finished the last router. They have time for it, if they're willing to go."

"We can't comm the colonists first and ask for a visit," Martyn said again from ART's lounge. "I don't like that."

"I don't like that, either," Kaede agreed. "We all know how dangerous cold contacts can be. But it's not as if they're refusing to answer. They may have no idea what the situation is here."

ART was rotating through displays of all its data on the terraforming engines. It could "see" the engines by assembling a picture using the raw data from its scans, and it actually looked enough like a visual image to fool human vision, except that the topography around it was mostly extrapolated and sketched in. The amount of signal noise the engines were emitting blocked everything else out, so they were the only things the scan could pick up—this was the blackout zone the colonists had talked about. We could send in pathfinders but they wouldn't be able to use their scans, either, so they would have to visually record and then return to a point where they could send ART their data. Barish-Estranza was trying to keep an eye on everything we did, obviously, but planets being large, that was impossible, just like it was impossible for us to know everything they were doing. If they did spot ART's pathfinders entering the blackout zone, we could say we were gathering data on the status of the terraforming engines. But if we sent pathfinders into the blackout zone that then came out and delivered reports, and then we sent a shuttle in, that would tell B-E that we had found something worth looking at in person. Better to send a shuttle with the pathfinders, and log it as an evaluation of the terraforming engines.

I could have said all that, but ART was already doing it. Seth, who had been pacing the lounge with the heel of one hand pressed to his forehead in a way that seemed to indicate that he was having almost as great a time as I was, said, "Iris, see if they're actually out there, make contact at your discretion, agreed?"

"Agreed." Iris looked from Tarik to Ratthi, getting various signals of agreement. She said, "SecUnit?" and I realized she was looking at me, too.

I said, "Sure." Because they were going anyway. It was a bad idea to let them go alone.

Iris and Tarik turned to Ratthi, who did a good job of pretending this didn't worry him, and said, "Great! Let's go."

I caught a private message Seth sent to Iris, a quick *Be careful, honey.* And from Martyn, *And keep us updated as best you can! And watch out for the weather up there!*

She replied to both, *Yes, Dad. Of course, Dad* and added a smile image.

I called in ScoutDrones 1, 2, and 3 from where they were patrolling our perimeter as we headed down the rocky hillside and back through the tree-flora to the shuttle.

(Okay, the drones. Another thing I hate about this planet is that I lost all but five of my drones. I was already operating with a reduced number because they got left behind when ART kidnapped me and Amena, and everything that happened here had left me with only five. One I had sent to keep an eye on Three before I knew I needed to come down here, one I had left onboard ART because I needed to keep one safe, I didn't want to lose them all. So I only had three drones with me, and try making a perimeter with that, that's why the stupid Barish-Estranza team and their stupid SecUnit had walked right up on me and I had no fucking idea.)

Mensah tapped my private feed and said, *If you're not all right with this, you don't have to go. Tarik has a security specialty, or we could send Three if you think it's ready.*

Tarik is a human, and a first contact with isolated colonists is not the way I want to find out that Three is not ready to interact unsupervised with humans I give a shit about. I replied, *I'm fine.*

Because privacy is just a hypothetical concept to ART, it broke in and said, *I'm downloading to my ops drone stored in the shuttle.*

Good, Mensah said, *thank you,* Perihelion. And it was good. If the mission turned out to be boring, we could watch media together.

I saw I had four private messages waiting from Arada, Amena, Overse, and Pin-Lee. I can't do that right now. Pretending I'm fine for Mensah was hard enough. I forwarded the messages to her and said, *Can you tell them I'm fine?* I hate this. It's not like I permanently lost an appendage or something.

There was a pause while she checked her queue. *I'll tell them you're fine and that you just need a little space. Good luck.*

In the team feed, ART said, *ETA is 1.03 minutes. Comm/ feed blackout point approaching.*

I stopped the episode and sat up. I had been watching a lot of *Sanctuary Moon* lately, but ART had wanted to go back to a show that we had watched that was popular with the humans on Mihira. It was semi-historical, about early humans leaving their original system for the first time. I'd seen documentary-style series about this before, but this one mixed parts that were realistic with fun stuff like space battles and rescuing people and space monsters and throwing asteroids at planets. (That last part is actually realistic, too, but if you try they will send a bunch of gunships to fuck you up.) Anyway, it was a good show, though I hadn't told ART that.

We had been flying over a mountain range with lots of craggy peaks and cliffs and it would be a relief to get past it. Even though this was one of ART's long-range shuttles, not a company hopper constructed and maintained by the lowest bidder. It had actual working safety/emergency equipment (besides me) and behind the seating compartment were tiny secondary cabins with bunks, a small MedUnit, a small galley, plus cargo and lab sample storage space. It also had an actual shower in the restroom unit. But still, a small metal container filled with mushy humans hurtling over spiky rocks for long periods agitates my threat assessment module. There were so many ways to crash and die in mountain ranges, it was also making my stupid risk assessment randomly alert.

"Acknowledged, Peri," Tarik said. He and Iris were up in the cockpit, which could be sealed off from the rest of the compartment by a hatch, but it was open now so they could talk to Ratthi, who was sitting up in the front row. They still had their environmental suits on as per safety protocol but had let the helmets fold back. Iris had her curly puff of hair tied up in a headband/scarf thing.

Tarik was in the pilot's seat even though ART had a bot pilot active in the guidance system right now. Even under bot pilot control, there should always be a human or SecUnit at the controls. Preferably a human or SecUnit who actually knows how to use the controls. (Considering how many contracts I had been on where this was not the case, it's amazing I'm still here in (mostly) one piece.)

I don't have a module for flying a shuttle, so it's not like I could do anything if the humans and ART suddenly lost control or there was a catastrophic mechanical failure. (And that just pissed me off. I should have a fucking shuttle piloting module for emergencies. What if all the humans are incapacitated and the SecUnit is the only one who can get them back to the baseship/station/whatever in a shuttle? It's a more likely scenario than a rogue SecUnit using one to crash into a transport or a mining installation. Believe me, there are a lot more efficient ways of taking out both.)

Iris had gotten up and was looking out the port next to Ratthi's seat. They were chatting and pointing out evidence of groundwater and vegetation, signs that the terraforming was working. It was one of the things that really sucked about the alien contamination.

From the previous assessments that ART's crew had done via pathfinder, Adamantine had at least paid for a process that wouldn't leave the planet trashed if the terraforming engines had to be shut down, unlike GrayCris at Milu. Back on Preservation, the last newsfeed report I had seen about that clusterfuck said that GoodNightLander Independent had taken the planet over as salvage and was trying to untrash it.

Of course I hadn't seen any newsfeeds since we left for our survey. Huh, I wonder if there had been a news report about our kidnapping. Mensah hadn't been as interesting to journalists since she ended her term as planetary leader, but Amena was one of her kids and having a kid be dramatically kidnapped during a space battle was probably a big deal, at least on Preservation. (It wasn't infrequent in my media, but it was one of those things where real life didn't live up to expectations raised by fiction.) Especially if the journalists realized Mensah's rogue SecUnit had been involved. If the newsfeeds got interested, was there a way for them to find out that ART was the kidnapper? If they started investigating the University's lost colony operations, that could be really bad in a lot of really bad ways for a lot of humans, augmented humans, bots, heavily armed judgmental machine intelligences pretending to be ordinary transports, and whatever and whoever else the University had working for it.

Great, something else to worry about. Getting attached to an additional group of humans was always going to be complicated, but. Ugh, I wish I felt like I was prepared for complication. Or prepared for anything.

Redacted

Mensah and the responder had left Preservation Station within an hour of the attack on our survey vessel, as soon as they had found the location data buoy ART had deployed on the way into the wormhole, so she and the crew wouldn't have any updated newsfeed data. Depending on where the newly arrived Barish-Estranza explorer had embarked from, they might have missed any recent news, too. (The as-yet-hypothetical report would originate from Preservation and take multiple cycles to circulate from station to station, planet to planet—unless we were lucky and Senior Indah had been able to keep it quiet under the Ongoing Investigations rule. Which I absolutely was not counting on.)

(Right, okay, Preservation Station Security is not as shitty at what they do as I originally thought when I first ended up there, but what they do is still mostly accident first response and maintaining safety systems and checking for hazardous cargo violations, and I could think of at least five of them who would blab to everyone in range about the kidnapping with no clue it might make things worse before Senior Indah had a chance to tell them to shut the fuck up. No, six.)

Whatever, we wouldn't have hard data until the University sent their response vessel, if then. I would just factor the possibility into the projected long-term threat assessment and increase my anxiety levels by the commensurate amount. *ART, define commensurate.*

It's a synonym of proportionate. ART's drone rose up out of the back row behind me and unfolded a lot of spiny arm extensions. The handoff hadn't occurred yet, but we were almost to the blackout point, forty-two seconds to go.

The drone was a thin oval platform fifteen centimeters in width with a lot of folded-up armatures tucked up against it that were supposed to be helpful in planetary exploration or contact missions and, knowing ART, who knew what they actually did. It added, *That was a mission-critical query?*

That wasn't actually a question, so I didn't answer it. Yes, that's ART in the drone, and ART flying the shuttle as a bot pilot, and ART monitoring operations with Three back at the colony site, and ART working on repairing its drive, and ART maintaining standard transport functions, and ART following the Barish-Estranza ships with its sensors hoping they'll do something to justify fucking with them (they started it, as it would point out), and ART currently arguing with Seth about his selection of a high-carb protein for his meal break and threatening to inform Martyn and Iris about it. Most transport bots have to be able to distribute their awareness to some extent, but ART is more complicated than that.

(I had uploaded myself into a bot pilot's control interface once during a viral attack, and had consequently hard-crashed myself and had to rebuild my memory table from scratch. If I didn't have human neural tissue also storing archival data, I would have been fucked. (So it did one thing right for once.) If I were uploaded to the entirety of ART's architecture, I would probably last a few painful seconds at most.)

(That's why we had to code 2.0 for the viral attack on the contaminated Barish-Estranza explorer.)

(If 2.0 were still here, I probably wouldn't *redacted*.)

Each one of ART's partitions is a little different, depending on its function. For example, ART-drone is not currently protecting a shipful of its important humans, so it's less likely to blow things up and ask questions later.

Tarik was counting aloud to the blackout point. On the team feed, ART said, *Handoff initiated. Good luck.*

"Acknowledged. Thanks, Peri," Iris said, smiling. "Be careful up there. See you soon."

On my private feed, ART said, *Take care of them. And yourself.* Before I could come up with a reply, my awareness of ART, its cameras, its feed and comm, the humans working and talking to each other on ART, or using the comm to talk to Mensah and the other humans on the Preservation responder, dropped away. I had expected it to be immediate, but the voices and signals gradually lost volume, fading into an echo, then into nothing.

Threat assessment spiked hard, then dropped back, and for once risk assessment was actually right. Even though it was planned and expected and we had resources like the pathfinders, losing comm and feed contact with your base-ship is never going to be a zero-consequence operation.

I still had our shuttle feed, but even with three humans and my three whole drones and our pathfinder escort, it was weirdly isolated. ART-drone was already active, but the sense of it in the feed was much smaller. It said, *This process is unnecessarily dramatic.*

Absently poking the planetary data in her feed, Iris said, "Honey, you're the one who comes up with the processes."

"Is that . . . weird, that *Perihelion* does this?" Ratthi asked. He had turned around in his seat to look at ART-drone.

"Everything about this job is weird," Tarik told him from the cockpit.

Especially Perihelion's *high tolerance for certain members of its crew,* ART-drone said. It added, *Iris, put your safety restraint on, no one wants to scrape you off the interior port.*

Yes, ART-drone is still ART, even though it's talking about itself in the third person.

Its download was up to date so I didn't have to restart the episode we had been watching. I restarted where we left off as the shuttle flew farther into the blackout zone.

When the terraforming engines came into visual range, the shuttle started a slow descent. I pulled the camera views. I caught pings from ART's pathfinders that had followed us in. These weren't the armed ones, these were the ones that had actually been doing their real jobs, wandering around making terrain and signal maps of various parts of the planet, concentrating on the areas around the colony sites, until now. They had been dropping on and off the feed since we entered the blackout zone, but were close enough to the shuttle at this point to resume limited contact. That was good, since we knew the terraforming engines were interfering with comm into and out of the blackout zone, but had speculated that at close enough range, our team comm and feed traffic would still work. Unfortunately, from what I was picking up from the shuttle, its scans and the pathfinders' scans were still borked.

ART-drone told the pathfinders to drop into formation behind us, since they couldn't do any mapping at the moment.

As the mountains fell away, we flew over a plain that might have been tundra, but without the terrain scans there was no annotated map data showing up in the feed. The shuttle's forward cameras were focused on the terraforming engines, which were a pretty big thing to focus on.

The structure was partially buried in the plain and formed a giant mound with skeletal metal towers, round things, and big tubes and whatever along its top ridge. And when I say it was big, I mean really big. Like the size of the Preservation colony ship big, if it had a lot more pointy parts and tubes and was embedded in the dirt on a planet.

The terraforming engines would have been built by the initial Adamantine team, long before the colonists arrived. The individual parts would be sort of like a transport module, with each one capable of subspace propulsion. They had been towed here through the wormhole, then released into the system where they would have flown the rest of the way to the planet and landed under their own power. Traveling with the engine modules would be a human and bot crew that specialized in terraforming assembly and installation, who would have connected everything up and gotten it started. At least, that's what the Adamantine brochure I'd downloaded from the drop box control station had said.

(That's how it's supposed to work, anyway. You can imagine what happens when you get your terraforming engines built and assembled by the lowest bidder.)

The shuttle slowed and moved into a circular pattern around the engine mound, keeping out of the danger zone, which was cordoned off by floating marker buoys beeping staticky warnings to our comm and feed. There were a lot of blank spots in their cordon where they must have broken down over the years. Or been hit by meteors, taken out by extreme weather incidents, or accidentally winged by aircraft. There's a lot of things that can happen in forty planetary years.

I didn't know what any of the terraforming equipment did, except it affected the atmosphere, so it would have to be a safe distance from any air bubble the colonists might have established for habitation in this area. Except that the pathfinders still couldn't find any sign of an air bubble on visual search.

The humans had noticed that, too. Ratthi was saying,

"What are we thinking? That they really did find, or build, an underground habitat in a Pre-CR artificial cave system?"

Iris flicked through the reports the mission teams had assembled so far on the colony's development. "We know they had the construction equipment. It may have seemed like a better option than a surface settlement, considering how close they are to the terraformer and the weather up here."

Ratthi was dubious. "Even knowing about the alien contamination at the main site?"

Iris's brow was furrowed, like the conclusions she was drawing troubled her. She said, "I was hoping the part about finding a Pre-CR dig was apocryphal, something the colonists came up with to make the stories about the splinter group who went off to live at the pole more interesting."

Ratthi thought that over. "It would make sense, with an elaborate Pre-CR structure always within sight of the main colony, to make up legends about another even stranger one somewhere else. And the rugged band of adventurers, or alternately, the scary weird people, who went to live in it."

Iris's mouth made a tighter line. "It's better than being honest about the fact that you had a split within your community bad enough to send a group looking for another home as far away as possible." She shook her head and sighed a little. "It would be nice to know why it happened. It might help the colonists become more cohesive about moving toward an evacuation if we had a better understanding of their history."

"You can't do therapy on a whole colony," Tarik said, "no matter how much they need it."

"But if the story is true and they did find a Pre-CR site up here," Ratthi added, "it makes the whole thing that much more mystifying."

It should be reassuring that humans don't get what other humans are thinking, either, but it just highlights how fucked up human neural tissue can be.

Ratthi waved a hand beside his head, like he was shooing away the idea. "We should stop speculating with no data. It's much more likely that they're living in an Adamantine-era structure created by the original terraforming crew, or that they built one themselves with the digging equipment that was left behind."

Tarik was impatiently cycling through the long-range camera displays. "Speaking of data, I'm not seeing any indications of any kind of habitation—no roads, no structures, nothing. Peri, I don't suppose a miracle happened and the terraformer stopped interfering with your pathfinder scan?"

Miracles are unlikely. ART-drone put the annotated pre-mission chart we had made into the team feed and on visual on the shuttle's floating display surfaces. The chart basically said there were three probable reasons why we hadn't noticed a secondary colony/habitation site on this continent earlier during ART's initial scans of the planet: (1) the colonists here had deliberately meant for their power output and signal activity to be concealed by the massive interference broadcast by the terraforming engines' normal operation; (2) the colonists put their site where they wanted to put it and didn't consider the fact that they would be concealed by the terraforming interference because the other colonists knew where they were so the subject had just never come up; (3) they were all dead, due to the alien contamination or some other cause, and there was no power output or signal activity to detect. ART-drone added, *As noted previously, limited signal traffic from pathfinders and the warning buoys is still possible. The humans here should be able to detect our comm pings at this close range. So they may be dead, their equipment may be damaged, or they may be deliberately ignoring us in an effort to stay concealed.*

Ratthi frowned at the big patchy blanks in the incoming survey data. "We have no idea how much they know about what happened in the main colony area, either. They could be ignoring us because they're too afraid to answer."

ART-drone said, *That would demonstrate a more developed sense of survival than we have previously encountered here.*

"Benefit of the doubt, Peri," Iris said. "I'm going to record an explanation of who we are and why we're attempting to contact them and put it on broadcast."

Since shuttle and pathfinder scans were useless, a search for human habitation would have to be visual. Video recording wasn't affected by the terraforming interference, but since this was a shuttle and not a specialized survey vehicle, there was no search-and-interpretation package for visual data, only for scan data, because no one thought they'd ever need it.

ART-drone had already given me full access to all the feeds off the shuttle and had opened a new joint processing space for us. I pulled all the visual terrain data from the shuttle cameras and got it formatted for queries. ART-drone saw what I was filling our shared space with and sent me a list of topographical features and disruptions that might indicate human surface or subsurface activity. That saved a lot of time. I started running the comparison in ART-drone's processing space.

Tarik curved the shuttle away from the terraforming engines and put it into a holding pattern while Iris got her broadcast recorded and sent. The humans talked about what to do next while Iris and Ratthi pulled up the original survey data to look at again. Or what we had left of it, since the original Adamantine files had been intentionally corrupted in what was possibly an attempt to protect the colony from the hostile corporate takeover that had destroyed the corporation. While they were scrolling through the data, Tarik said, "Does SecUnit want to weigh in on this?"

I had ScoutDrone3 up on the ceiling of the compartment, and it watched Ratthi glance back at me. I don't know what he saw; my face felt normal. But Ratthi has watched me work on a lot of stuff, and I guess there was something about me that told him I was busy. (It was a big search, not something I could have done without ART-drone's input and extra space. Plus it generated a shit-ton of false positives that I had to pull and study individually before I could dismiss them. (Example 243602–639a: no, that's not a human-built structure, it's just a weird rock.)

This was not the kind of process I could do in background, even with ART's help.) Ratthi said, "It's working on something now."

Three seconds later I hit a result. I still needed to finish the rest of the search to look for other indications, but the timing on this was too perfect to resist. I paused the process, said, "I've got a possible landing area on visual," and sent it into the team feed and to the display surface.

To the northwest of the terraforming engines' mound, a couple of kilometers out of the danger zone, was a section of ground, dust-covered but clearly too flat to be natural. Dirt had drifted up to disguise the edges, but what was visible indicated an octagonal shape. Also, it was about the right size for a couple of the colony aircraft to land and sit next to each other without pushing safety requirements. (The main colony had three left of the original set of air vehicles, and a few built-from-scratch models. The originals looked like early, half-assed versions of the company's hoppers, with scratched and fading paint in the Adamantine brand colors. I could see why there wouldn't be a lot of visiting back and forth, even if the two groups had been friendly; I wouldn't have wanted to fly across a planet in one of those things, either.)

Ratthi expanded the display surface across the upper portion of the front port. Iris studied the image, nodding. "Okay, that's got to be it. Good job, SecUnit."

Tarik said, "Huh." Ratthi sent me a glyph of a Preservation party sparkler exploding.

I didn't say anything. (I know I get pissed off when

humans don't acknowledge my work, but why is too much acknowledgment also upsetting? Sentience sucks.)

On our private feed connection, Ratthi said, *How are you doing back there?*

I am absolutely fine, I told him.

Tarik took the shuttle out of its holding pattern and brought it around for a better visual sweep of the target area. I restarted the visual search process and ART-drone narrowed our query to the area around the rocky hills near the landing pad. I eliminated more false positives as Ratthi and Iris studied the live camera view of the potential landing site. Tarik pointed out, "It's about equidistant from the hills and the terraformer."

Ratthi was biting his lip, which meant he was thinking. "If there was any kind of a road, we'd be able to see it from above. Of course, a very light ground vehicle wouldn't make much impact."

"They had to bring heavy supplies in here at some point." Iris squinted and used her feed to magnify the images of the ground around the pad.

Tarik was frowning. "Digging equipment, because even if they had a tunnel network to start with, they must have had to modify it. And you can tell this place has been changed by intense weather patterns. A bad storm could have wiped out any aboveground equipment, roads, quarries, maybe even the whole colony site." His eyebrows were doing things that made him look angry, but from his tone and the read that threat assessment was getting off his body language, he was just concentrating. I knew from media that humans sometimes had the same problem with lack of control of their faces that I did. Like, obviously it wasn't my unique problem or a unique problem for constructs in general, and possibly paranoia made me worry about it a lot more than necessary. But it was still weird to see it in action. Tarik added, "Uh, why is there a drone in my face?"

"Ignore it," Ratthi said. "There would be pitting and warping on the barrier around the terraforming engines if there had been a colony-eating storm here at any point, even with the structure's heavy shielding. Also a close look at the weathering on the surrounding rock formations would tell us a lot if the sensors were operational." He waved his hands. "This is very frustrating! And all our geological evaluation software is back at home in Preservation space on our survey vessel."

"There should be some in our archive, but I doubt it would work without functioning scanners. We need to get down there and do some surface exploration." Iris glanced back at ART-drone. "What do you say, Peri?"

I say without functioning sensors you can't determine whether the ground is stable enough to land the shuttle, ART-drone said. *Also, the flat area may not be a landing pad, but the roof of an underground habitat.*

Ratthi winced at the thought. "Not the most diplomatic of introductions to this group, landing on their habitat without permission."

"So we land on flat ground somewhere, the area looks

stable," Tarik said. He's not stupid. I think he was trying to annoy ART-drone, but I poked Ratthi on our private feed connection with a video file.

"What?" Ratthi said aloud, distracted by the autoplay images. "Oh, SecUnit wants me to mention the time I was almost eaten by fauna that came up underneath our aircraft on an inadequately mapped ground survey."

"Point taken," Iris said, though she hadn't given any sign that she had ever actually considered doing what Tarik suggested and I thought that might be her way of indicating that Tarik and Ratthi should both shut up while she was thinking. She rummaged in the equipment bag on the seat next to her. "A ground sensor might do it, if we can get it close to the surface so the interference won't—"

"I'll do it." I released my safety restraint and stood up. My drone had caught Tarik and Ratthi both taking a breath to say something and I knew what it was going to be. They were going to volunteer to go down to the surface and check for landing stability. And right after I had made Ratthi talk about almost being eaten, too. Iris must have agreed because she handed me the portable ground sensor as I crossed the compartment. I stepped over to the main cabin hatch and said, "You can let me out now."

Now Tarik looked alarmed. "Whoa, whoa, hold on! We're still more than twenty meters above the ground. Let me get us just a little closer."

On our private feed, ART-drone said, *If you open that hatch now I will turn this thing around and go home.*

I pulled archival footage from a recent documentary

about a failed planetary survey from a non-corporate polity. (Back on Preservation Station, Pin-Lee and I had discovered a shared interest in disaster evaluation via watching "true life" documentaries where terrible shit happens, and she had sent me this clip.) In this sequence a subsurface hostile fauna takes down an aircraft at forty meters. I sent it into the team feed.

Tarik yelled, "What the— What the fuck was that?"

Raising his voice to talk over Tarik, Ratthi said, "I understand your concern, SecUnit, but you are not jumping out at this height!"

Iris yelled over both of them, "People! Calm down! We have soft-drop packs in the emergency locker. SecUnit can use one." She had large yelling capacity for a human her size. I had the feeling it came in handy.

The locker was right next to the hatch. I opened it and ART-drone had already told the inventory system to rotate the soft-drop packs to the front. I pulled one out and said, "I knew that."

I did not know that. But whatever, I was fine either way.

I pulled up the hood of my environmental suit and let it secure the face mask. The temperature and air quality outside were impossible for humans without environmental suits and it wouldn't have been much fun for me, either. I ordered ScoutDrones 1 and 2 to get in my side pockets. The wind might be too high for them to be much use, but it would be stupid not to bring them just in case. Ratthi said, "Just be careful, all right? You can get eaten, too!"

I have guns in my arms, Ratthi, I said on our private

connection. That is literally the whole point of me. Plus I still had the projectile weapon, clamped to my environmental suit's harness in the back. It didn't have the capacity to handle an ag-bot, but there shouldn't be any large roaming alien-contaminated bots here. There really shouldn't be. If there were . . . yeah, don't think about that.

The soft-drop pack's instructional feed told me how to fasten it to my environmental suit. I got it attached and ART-drone finally cycled the lock for me.

I stepped in and let the inner hatch close. Inside the cabin, Iris asked, "So what is it with worrying about humans getting eaten all the time?" While Ratthi tried to explain, the outer hatch slid open and I gripped the safety handle and leaned out for a look.

Tarik had put the shuttle into hover mode, activating an air barrier over the lock to protect against the high winds. (ART has such nice equipment; in a company shuttle I would probably have fallen out already.) The wind would interfere with the soft-drop a little but not enough to fling me into any rocks, and the terraforming engines were too far away to be a factor. I aimed for the pad and stepped out into the air.

The soft-drop controlled my fall and I landed lightly on my feet. I didn't even have to mitigate the impact with a fall and roll. I set the ground sensor down on the pad. It detected natural terrain, switched out of dormant mode, and booted itself.

The cloud cover was thicker here, obscuring the sun and

making the daylight gray. Dust blew across the site from the south, toward the line of rocky hills approximately two kilometers away. My scan was just as fucked as the shuttle's and the pathfinders', but visual was good, and the faceplate kept the fine dust from obscuring my vision. There was just nothing to see.

In the other direction, the plain was open and mostly flat, except for some low mounds closer to the high metal shields around the base of the terraforming engines. Those mounds looked human-made, but were so close to the shield that they were probably only artifacts from the initial construction. It would be stupid to build a habitat so close to the engines. I'm not even sure putting one here under a roof that looked like a landing pad was a great idea. Any Pre–Corporation Rim structure that had already been here, buried or not, this close to the build site would have been discovered by Adamantine during the initial engine installation. Not that they would put it on the survey or anything.

Could Adamantine have found a Pre-CR underground structure that it had intended to repurpose, that only some of the colonists knew about? Maybe just the ones who had been involved with the initial installation? One of the things Corian had told Karime was that colony history/lore said at least some of the separatists had been part of the terraforming crew. Vi had also told her that census records for that point in the colony's development were currently inaccessible due to the alien virus issue. (A lot of older data had been locked out of the active system to hopefully keep it safe, which was useless, since that wasn't how the virus was transferred, which they didn't know then, but anyway. Their systems colony-wide were completely shit-creeked and I don't know who was going to fix it except it sure as hell wasn't me.) So there was no way to know how many humans had actually left the main colony to come here.

Adamantine had leaned toward new permanent structures that could be repurposed as the colony grew, like the surface dock for the drop shaft, which could have been just a rough utilitarian cargo off-loader, and instead was a nice building with lots of space for storage and workshops and offices, designed to eventually become a commercial entry point for the colony, built solid enough to shelter a large portion of the population in a bad weather event. The drop box's arrival and departure even had its own theme music. It was a great design. Except for the whole alien contamination thing.

If Adamantine had wanted a habitat up here, they would have made it a nice structure that could be expanded later for education or tourism or something. Which meant it would have been in the foothills, not down here close to the engines. Except why would Adamantine want a structure here at all, in a blackout zone?

Unless they had a compelling reason to need a more secure colony site. Like if they had some kind of warning of the hostile corporate takeover that had eventually destroyed them. Maybe these separatists had been following secret Adamantine directives to look for a new site near the engines to build a habitat.

That made sense, actually, on a lot of different levels. (Mark save-for-later: Did Adamantine direct a select group of colonists to build an emergency habitat up here? Because the blackout zone would hide them from scanners and/or because the terraforming engines were an expensive asset too essential for an invading corporation to bomb? Or both? Then the colonists had lost contact with Adamantine and changed their mission parameters.)

(If you think it sounds like I'm trying to talk myself out of the idea that there's another buried Pre-CR structure up here, you're right.)

ART-drone said, *Your performance reliability level had a .05 percent spike.*

ART has been monitoring me due to *redacted*. Which is a whole thing, I don't know, I don't want to talk about it.

The ground sensor had started to send readings into my feed, and I told ART-drone, *I had an idea,* and sent it the save-for-later tagged info.

ART-drone said, *Interesting.*

It was humoring me again.

Sensor results = a large volume of solid material with the chemical composition matching the dirt and rocks in this area. So no hidden underground habitat here, at least, not that I was really expecting one. But we were right about the pad. It was the same composition as the artificial stone in the surface dock and the other Adamantine-constructed structures at the main colony site. Which meant this landing zone was definitely Adamantine-era, not Pre–Corporation Rim. Which we probably knew anyway, but you know, science.

Also it was a relief. If there was a hidden Pre-CR structure up here, I wasn't standing on it.

I'd given ART-drone access to my eyes so it had been looking at the terrain with me, and it said, *There was only a twenty-two percent chance that the separatist colonists would construct an underground installation this close to the terraforming engines.*

They might want to, if they were very, very stupid, I told it. *But they wouldn't be able to get a company bond on it.* We didn't know if Adamantine had contracted for safety bonds on its colony. That info would have been in the destroyed records that we only had fragments of. And I wasn't sure how common safety bonds had been forty-plus corporate standard years ago, or how the presence of Pre-CR structures would affect the price. ART could probably find it in its historical data if I could construct a good query.

Or, you know, if there were safety bonds, or any kind of guarantor bond, it would be a reason to conceal the existence of additional Pre-CR structures that might be associated with past alien contamination incidents.

I don't know, I'm kind of all over the place right now.

You're stalling, ART-drone said.

I am not. I can stand here and be useless without any ulterior motives, thanks.

My drone on the shuttle heard Tarik say, "Are we going to get a report anytime soon?"

The drone watched as Ratthi's face did a thing and his voice went a little tight. He said, "When there's something to report."

"Since when did you become a micromanager, Tarik," Iris added, in what definitely wasn't a question. She was smiling a little, and I'm pretty sure she was bantering at him, but it could also be a hint for him to leave me alone.

Tarik held up one hand. "I was just asking."

ART-drone said, *And I am asking if you are critiquing my administration of this mission?*

Yes, because ART loves to be critiqued.

Tarik obviously knew that, too. "Hey, hey, I was just curious about what was happening, that's all! I am absolutely not critiquing anybody!"

The thing about Tarik was that he was new and had only been with the crew for the previous three hundred and eighty-seven corporate standard day cycles. So everybody fucked with him constantly.

At least while they were fucking with Tarik nobody was noticing that I actually hadn't made a report yet and was in fact just standing there. Well, obviously, ART-drone had noticed. And Ratthi had noticed or he wouldn't have shut Tarik down in an un-Ratthi-like way. Iris had probably noticed, too.

Get it together, Murderbot.

I sent the ground sensor's report into the team feed. While the humans read it and also came to the conclusion that there was nothing under the pad, I tried to think what to do next.

Okay, even if you're using low-gravity movers to transport your heavy digging equipment or building supplies, there should still be some sign of a road between here and the habitat, wherever it was. As far as we knew, the separatist colonists weren't hiding when they came up here; the other colonists knew where they went. They would have built a road, or a walkway or something. It was here somewhere, even if it was buried under the dust.

Or something.

I pulled some video of the digging equipment I had seen stored in the deep excavation under the Pre–Corporation Rim colony structure when the Targets had stuck me down there to get contaminated. I had been more occupied with leaving than with taking archival footage of aging construction equipment, but while there had been some wheeled vehicles, most had been the kind that can float a little distance above the ground. Which made sense in a developing colony where you would need to build your infrastructure as you went along. But it would also use a lot of power. There were more efficient ways to move those vehicles.

I picked up the ground sensor, which beeped angrily because I wasn't supposed to move it without switching it to dormant mode, but it was too late now. I went to the buried edge of the pad and set it down again. It went through its cycle, found rock again, and I moved it two meters around the edge of the pad to scan the next section. My limited range scan for metal or energy sources would be really helpful, but every time I tried I still got static. In our private feed, I could tell a lot of ART-drone's attention was on the shuttle scanners, still trying to get a clear scan of the hills where the buried habitat probably was, hoping the closer range would give us some workable data.

On the team feed, Ratthi asked, *Can we come down and help you, SecUnit?*

No, I told him. He hadn't asked me what I was doing, probably because he was afraid I didn't know. Which, valid, but this time I actually did know. I continued around the edge, because if I was right, the first one would be directly attached to the pad. If it wasn't here, I was going to look incredibly fucking stupid and the humans were going to assume because of *redacted* I—

Oh, here it is. Metal composition, buried under accumulated dust, dirt, and rock fragments. On the team feed, I said, *There's a rail here.* The kind of powered rail that floating equipment pads will attach to so they can be moved more efficiently. It wasn't powered up now, just so much inert metal. Up in the shuttle, the humans were excited, thinking we could follow it all the way to the hidden habitat.

Then with the ground sensor, I followed it for ten meters before it hit the rim of a buried hatchway.

Chapter Four

HATCHWAYS DOWN INTO HIDDEN underground tunnels = not generally a great situation, on a survey. But this was attached to our Adamantine-era landing pad, and still way too close to the terraforming engines. I was pretty sure what we had here was a construction delivery access for the original engine build.

The humans were disappointed. I was . . . not.

Once Tarik and ART-drone used an air-blowing excavation tool to clear the surface dust away, we saw this was a large hatch, the size that would accommodate the kind of cargo bots and load haulers that might be used to supply terraforming engines. When I got the control pad open, there was also an Adamantine logo on the inside of the case. So this definitely wasn't another Pre–Corporation Rim ruin, which I already knew, because the materials and assembly matched what we had seen of the other Adamantine installations, and because all indications said it wasn't.

That didn't mean it wasn't connected to a Pre-CR structure.

Murderbot, you have got to stop this. Do your fucking job.

"You'd think if they were down there, they'd have heard

us by now." Tarik sat on the ground trying to get power into the controls. There was no feed or comm associated with the hatch, and banging on it and yelling "hello" had done nothing.

Yes, the humans had wanted to come down here and poke around. I had let Iris and Tarik secure their environmental suits and get out to look at the hatch, but made Ratthi stay at the controls. It was hard keeping him in there because he really likes to walk around on planets and he is also great at finding dangerous shit. The original planetary survey data that still existed was corrupted and incomplete, but so far the colonists hadn't said anything about dangerous flora or fauna. Which meant I assumed there was some because humans have a bad habit of assuming that if they know a thing, all the other humans in the vicinity know it, too. Either that or they believe none of the other humans know anything that they don't know. It's either one or the other and both are potentially catastrophic and really fucking annoying.

What this planet did have was at least one contingent of isolated colonists who might still be alive out here and if so, might react badly to unexpected visitors. Ratthi had asked how exactly he was supposed to fight off an attack on the shuttle and I told him he could just not open the door. ART-drone was outside with us, but bot pilot could fly the shuttle and follow Ratthi's commands, one of which should be to take the shuttle out of the blackout zone where ART-prime would reestablish contact. Ratthi wasn't happy, but he stayed in the shuttle. (I'm off my game, obviously, but I'm not dead.)

Iris shook her head, her expression pinched in a worried way. "This is still too close to the terraforming engines. They couldn't be living here."

From the shuttle comm, Ratthi said, "I don't know, people have done weirder things. We think they left the main colony at least partly because of the first contamination incident. The way the engines disrupt scans and communications, maybe they thought this was a safer environment."

If I was a human trapped on this planet, I'd go live inside the terraforming engines.

Something under the controls thunked and the small dusty interface lit up. Tarik sat back with a woof of breath and said, "Ready?"

On our private connection, ART-drone said, *SecUnit.*

Shit, I'm just standing here watching. "Tarik," I said, "Get back. Toward the shuttle."

He looked up at me, frowning through the suit visor. Then he said, "Right, right." He stood up and moved back.

Iris was already out of the danger zone, walking backward so she could watch. "Be safe, SecUnit," she said.

I don't know how to respond when humans say that. It was always my job to get hurt.

There was still no feed connection for the controls, so I leaned down and hit the switch for manual access. The hatch creaked and started to slide open, and a small avalanche of the dust and rock chips piled up along the sides started to fall. The space below was a lightless void.

I sent my two drones down into the darkness.

Okay, anticlimactic news first, it was a big bare cargo receiving area. The drones circled, catching video of discolored stone walls with metal scaffolding to support the hatch mechanicals and various cables. No feed markers, but a few signs I translated via Thiago's language module; all were cautions about the proximity to the engines and possible damage to unshielded sensor equipment. There were two dark openings leading off somewhere, probably access tunnels. Also more heavy equipment rails built onto the natural rock floor, as well as a big lift platform stored vertically up against one wall. Cargo transportation using permanently installed rails was usually cheaper, more power efficient, common for systems you'd only need while the engines were being constructed.

The drones weren't picking up any sign of current habitation—no trash, no belongings, no humans standing around wondering why the hatch had suddenly opened. But I needed to verify those two tunnels were just for equipment access to the terraforming engines.

The hatch opening was wide enough now to reveal a space that a shuttle could land in, and it was still going. A lot of dirt was sliding in. Iris said, "We need to stop it. SecUnit, you okay with that?"

Sure, whatever. I sent her an affirmative through the feed. Tarik hurried over and cut the power. Then we all kind of stood there for a second.

Iris looked at me and I saw her hesitate, because her hesitation looked a lot like Dr. Mensah's hesitation.

And I realized I really didn't want to go down there. Even though what we could see of it was clearly unused, and the hatch probably hadn't been open since the terraforming installation had been completed however many years ago. But I wanted to let the drones do it.

I had to go down there. It was stupid not to go down there. This was just a construction access point on a planet that would have a general risk assessment in the low 30s if not for the alien contamination. That's not helping. All right, come on. If I couldn't do this, I couldn't do my job. I said, "Wait here until I check it out."

Iris smiled and did a good job pretending that she didn't know anything was wrong. Tarik looked uncomfortable but stood up from the controls and stepped out of the way. Yeah, uh-huh, this is great.

The lift platform controls were down at the bottom of the well and probably too much of a pain in the ass to make work anyway, but there was a manual access tube with a stairway thing to one side. It was covered with sandy dirt and dust but not blocked. I climbed down into it and then forced my right boot onto the first step of the stair.

Okay, it was easier once I got started. I climbed down to the bottom of the well.

The daylight coming down from the hatch above helped. I could see the two tunnel entrances, both big enough for folded construction cranes and bots and haulers. This time I remembered to send my camera view into the team feed.

On the comm, Ratthi said what everyone was thinking: "This looks fairly normal. I wonder what the second tunnel is for?"

Yeah, I wonder, too. The rail system led into the tunnel that headed west toward the base of the terraforming installation. I sent ScoutDrone1 down it to verify and kept Scout-Drone2 hovering over my head to watch my back. The other tunnel went off toward the northeast at an angle that was odd, considering the orientation of the rest of the space. I couldn't see into it from here so I started across the floor, my boots losing traction in the soft dirt we'd just let in.

"Storage, maybe," Tarik said. He was at the access tube, leaning down as far as he could to see the space without violating my implicit instruction not to follow me. "If there are any admin offices down there with intact devices, do you think . . ."

He trailed off, because ScoutDrone2 was getting video that I was still sending to the team feed.

Yeah, that's weird.

I was picking up faint light, not much for an industrial-sized corridor, but still. If the terraformers had left emergency lighting on . . . There was an obstruction.

I told myself it was unlikely to be an alien-contaminated bot. Really unlikely. Maybe a little likely. I made myself keep walking.

Okay, it was a vehicle. A flat one with wide wheels designed for rough terrain, with benches instead of seats and the steering apparatus in front. It wasn't for the surface, unless the humans were wearing protective suits, or unless whoever was transporting the humans didn't give a crap whether they got hit by ground debris. So yeah, probably the latter. It was for the surface and the workers had used it down here where they were less likely to get injured. (And it being here wasn't the weird thing; this had been a work site, there could be all kinds of equipment abandoned down here.)

The weird thing was that just past it the mostly smooth curving sides of the tunnel stopped in a pile of rubble where there was another opening.

The building crew for the terraforming cargo installation had encountered an existing tunnel, larger, square, made of smooth gray artificial stone that was mottled just a little for what had to be aesthetic reasons. I could see that, because there was active emergency lighting, little blue flat squares of it about three meters up the tunnel walls. My risk assessment finally caught up to what was happening and hit the roof.

We were looking at a Pre–Corporation Rim site. A Pre–Corporation Rim site that was drawing power.

We didn't know what had happened to the Pre–Corporation Rim colony that was on this planet long before Adamantine arrived. We just knew that at some point the Pre-CR group had encountered alien contamination, that it had been severe enough to result in "compulsive construction" of a structure over their original mostly underground habitation, and that nobody was here when Adamantine arrived however many years later to start terraforming. The fact that the Pre-CR group had left equipment, including an active central system, behind in that original habitation, indicated that they had left in what Arada had euphemistically described as "disarray." If they *had* left, if they hadn't all died or killed each other, their remains weathered to dust.

And no, we couldn't do a systematic archaeological survey of the Pre-CR site to discover what had happened to the Pre-CR colonists because the compulsive structure and the original habitation under it got blown up and buried in a whole big thing that happened. And the alien contamination was, you know, still under there. Waiting for more humans to forget or lose the records of it, and come back, and excavate the strange colony site to see what had happened there.

Redacted

Okay, alien contamination. The thing about it is that a large percentage of alien remnant materials are harmless and inert. The commonly identifiable ones are classified as strange synthetics, and you can get licenses in the Corporation Rim and multiple other independent polities to mine them and research them and work with them.

But even for the ones that aren't harmless and inert, a contamination incident is not an attack or a trap. It's not actually considered hostile in the same way as someone shooting you or telling a CombatBot to shoot you or something trying to eat you or melt you or smash you or whatever. There's no intentionality, as Ratthi explained once.

It's like if there was a hostile that killed us all and then a rockslide fell on us and buried us and then a couple of thousand corporate or Preservation standard years went by and then aliens showed up and dug us up, and they, I don't know, touched the human food, or pulled apart the shuttle's power source, and stuck their hands or fungus-tentacles or whatever in it, it might poison them. It might just kill them, it might make them very sick, it might affect their neural tissue, or do weird things to their cells and cause their bodies to change, or all of those things.

Not all Pre–Corporation Rim sites are alien-contaminated, obviously. A lot of them became long-term occupation sites, the nucleus of what are now independent polities or Corporation Rim–owned planets (page 57, paragraph 6, *Introduction to the History of Human Expansion, Volume I*, eds. Bartheme, de la Vega, Shanmugam, et al, Cloud Sun Harbor University Press). But abandoned sites are sometimes abandoned for a good reason, and humans didn't understand back then how careful they needed to be with alien remnants. (Or maybe they did and they just didn't care. I mean, let's be honest, which one is more likely? I'm just making an observation here.)

Back on ART, during one of our strategy sessions for Plan A: Get the Hell Out of Here, Thiago had pulled some research about how so many of the known alien contamination sites were underground, were uncovered via construction or mining or exploratory digging. The idea was that maybe the contaminants were hazardous material the aliens had been disposing of, and they hadn't expected anybody to come poking into the ground in those places. So that was even less intentionality and even more bad luck. I don't know why that's objectively better than ancient aliens out to get us. (How would that work? "We're dead, but we're taking you hapless fuckers who might wander by thousands of years later with us, ha!" Yeah, I don't think so, either.) But it is better, weirdly enough. Shit happens, basically.

On our private feed, ART-drone said, *What the hell are you doing? Your stats are dropping.*

I was just thinking about alien contamination, I told it.

Stop that immediately, ART-drone said.

Right, good luck with that. I was thinking about it because I am currently standing in front of what is clearly a Pre–Corporation Rim site. A lot like the one where I *redacted.*

Yeah, this was where we'd started, back at the beginning of the file.

"So it looks like the other colonists were right about this place," Iris said, deeply reluctant. She had been held prisoner by colonists under the influence and direction of viral alien contamination that had given them a violent drive to get off the planet. She had escaped with only half her crew and one of her parents, and had to leave the other behind. She didn't want to do this any more than I did, except somehow she had a lot more control over her neural tissue. "We have to check it out."

"Yeah." Tarik had been with her for that whole thing and he didn't look happy, either. He reached up like he was going to rub his face, then remembered his helmet and put his hand down again. He sighed. "Yeah."

I had already sent ScoutDrone2 ahead. It was able to go at nearly its top speed down the wide corridor, the lighting and width and breadth of the tunnel allowing it to take the turns without running into walls, though its flaky navigation scan was getting a little better the farther it got away from the terraforming engines. The Pre-CR corridor was continuing to head northeast, toward the foothills.

I said, "Ratthi needs to stay in the shuttle."

Iris nodded. "Follow us from the air. Just not too close."

Ratthi's sigh was audible over the comm. On Scout-Drone3's camera view I could see him leaning back, wincing with worry. He said, "Ah, we don't have a choice, do we."

Tarik kicked the tire of the vehicle. "Should we take this? If they are still alive down here somewhere, moving it might upset them."

Ratthi said, "But you'd be driving it toward them, not away. And we can put it back if this is where they want to keep it."

Humans from Preservation have no concept about what happens in the Corporation Rim to humans who borrow corporate property, even if they put it back when they're done.

You could make a case that I should have done this alone. (In the company, or any other corporate context where I still had a governor module, I would definitely be doing this alone.) But in this context the humans expected to go, and I wasn't going to argue about it. If the colonists were still alive and I found them, I needed Iris and Tarik to talk to them, since Ratthi would be in the shuttle. Isolated as they were, the chances of them recognizing me as a Sec-Unit were low. But I just couldn't talk to strange humans about important shit right now while pretending to be a human, I'd fuck it up. And fucking it up could mean Barish-Estranza hauling everybody off to be slave labor.

Tarik got the vehicle running while Iris recorded a brief report for ART-drone to send to its bot pilot iteration. Bot pilot would upload it to a pathfinder that would then take the report out of the blackout zone for ART-prime to find. "The battery still has juice in it," Tarik reported. He had climbed into the driver's seat and was scrolling through the controls. "Either it's a really good battery, or someone charged it within the past ten years or so."

Iris took the bench seat behind and to his left, looking around optimistically for safety restraints. "It doesn't look like it's been moved in a while."

I took a fold-out jump seat within arm's reach of Iris so I could catch her if she fell out. It would be hard to get Tarik, too, from this angle, but ART-drone floated up and attached itself to the opposite side, within easy grabbing distance of him. (This was a gesture of trust from ART, I know that. Iris is its favorite and it was trusting me with her.)

On the comm, Ratthi said, "This is killing me. Just be careful."

Tarik got the vehicle moving, slowly at first and then

increasing the speed gradually as he got used to the controls and the traction. And we headed into the dark.

41.32 minutes later, I said, "Stop."

Tarik hit the brake control on the steering device, not abruptly enough to throw us out. He and Iris didn't slide forward because I grabbed the safety harness of Iris's environmental suit and ART-drone grabbed Tarik. (Not so much grabbed as leisurely lifted an arm and extended it across his chest .02 of a second before the jolt as the vehicle stopped.) Iris glanced back at me, startled, and then smiled. "I forgot how fast you are."

(For a human, I was fast. For a SecUnit, I felt like I was moving in slow motion.)

(The only reason I wasn't panicking more about that is that ART-drone is slower than ART-prime but that is still really fucking fast.)

On the comm, Ratthi said, "What is it? Are you all right?"

He and Tarik had been having a rambling conversation about Pre-CR history and ruins; neither one of them had certifications in it, but they knew a lot about it, or at least they thought they did. Iris had been talking to ART-drone on their private feed; I couldn't listen in but I could tell the connection was active. I was too tense to even think about media, let alone watch anything, or even run it in the background.

Ratthi had access to the team video feed I was sharing, he had just forgotten about it because for the past forty minutes it had been so boring. I pulled it to the front of his interface and he said, "Oh!"

ScoutDrone2, approximately three hundred meters ahead of us, had encountered an even larger space. It was still at the same depth as this tunnel. There had to be an opening to the surface somewhere in it because it looked like a hangar for aircraft and vehicles larger than our shuttle.

I counted six landing platforms extending out from the walls or on pylons, fanned out to allow access from above. The light was inadequate, which suggested the light we had in the tunnel was an emergency backup system. The hatchway must be up in the ceiling somewhere, probably not unlike the one for the terraforming construction access, except maybe nicer and not made by the lowest bidder. But ScoutDrone2 couldn't see the upper part of the chamber without going up there, and I wanted it to stay where it was in the tunnel entrance. If anything in this chamber came rushing out toward us, it would be nice to know what was coming our way.

And something might come rushing out, because one of the platforms was occupied.

The vehicle looked like an aircraft, sort of like the ones the main site colonists had built for themselves. A little like a hopper, if a hopper was bigger and had more things sticking up off it and more windows.

All three humans were watching the video now in the team feed, as ScoutDrone2 turned slowly to get the best view, its stupid borked scan picking up sporadic metallurgy readings that ART-drone identified as being associated with Pre-CR builds. In case there was any doubt, which there pretty much wasn't.

Tarik did a little annoyed sigh. "Why in the name of everything holy did those colonists think coming up here was a good idea? After they'd already had a contamination incident?"

"Maybe they didn't understand how dangerous it was." Iris sounded calm but she had both hands pressed to the chin plate of her helmet like she was willing something to happen, like maybe for the whole Pre-CR installation to just disappear. (I could have been projecting, there.) "If they'd had any idea . . . Surely they would have at least warned the other colonists, and not just described this place as a cave system."

On my shuttle drone-cam, I could see Ratthi's face was worried, though he didn't sound like it over the comm. "Even if they didn't understand all the implications, so much of their trouble has stemmed from that bunker excavation under the first Pre-CR structure. They must have known."

So I wasn't alone in my reaction, and they hadn't even seen the horror show in the original Pre-CR structure except for the very end, via Three's mission recording.

Ugh.

Okay, right, this whole thing might be a nonevent. There was still a 78 percent chance that the splinter group of colonists who had decided to live here were dead. They might have died long before the more serious contamination incident that produced the Targets.

But we were going to have to find out. If they were still alive and needed medical intervention and decontam. If this was a clean site and they had managed to avoid the viral attacks. If they needed to evacuate before Barish-Estranza found them. If this was just a mass grave.

I said, "You both should wait here with the vehicle. I'll go ahead on foot." Uh, should they wait? Or just take the vehicle back to the construction access and have the shuttle pick them up? I should know this. I used to be good at this, what the fuck happened to me. Oh right, that happened.

They both turned in their seats to look at me. Even through the environmental suit faceplates, I could see objections coming in as big as cargo drop modules. Tarik said, "You know we're all certified by the University in hazardous exploration, right?"

Ratthi, maybe not unexpectedly, came in on my side. Through the comm, he said, "I have a specialist survey certificate from Preservation's FirstLanding and seven years of on-planet experience, but it didn't stop me from nearly being murdered on a survey. SecUnit stopped me from nearly being murdered." He added, "If these people are still alive in there, we don't know anything about them. If they were attacked by some of the other colonists under the influence of the contamination, or if they were in contact with the contamination and were affected themselves."

"We've done this kind of thing before," Tarik said, not quite arguing, but not not arguing. And great, I know ART wants this to work out, but even if I were still capable of doing my fucking job, if they don't listen to me, I'm useless.

Then Iris said, "Tarik used to be in a corporate combat squad."

Wow. Okay. That was unexpected, and it caused a reaction in my organic parts. I had been staring forward down the tunnel while ScoutDrone1 circled my head, keeping watch. Now I and my drone turned to look at Tarik. Even ScoutDrone2 far ahead in the hangar entrance did a pivot.

I still couldn't read any expression through his face plate and I was pretty sure he couldn't read mine, if I was making one, but he immediately held up his hands, palm out. He said, "I don't want to fight you under any circumstances, period, end of story."

I wasn't the only one who had reacted. On the shuttle's comm, Ratthi had made a startled but somehow not startled noise, like an "ah." Tarik's head made a minute jerk, like he wanted to respond but didn't let himself.

ART-drone hadn't reacted at all, so obviously it knew. It just hadn't told me.

His voice deliberately ironic, Tarik added, "And thanks, Iris, anything else you want to tell the new people about me?"

"Yes." Iris was looking at me. As far as I could tell, she was the only one not having a moment right now. "He hates corporates more than any of us. They made him kill."

It hadn't seemed quiet before, even down here underground, with the hum of the vehicle's motor and the humans talking and ART-drone. Now it was quiet.

Iris added, "Sorry, Tarik, but I wanted to get that out in the open. I don't like surprises and I'm assuming ex-SecUnits don't like them either." I remembered to tell ScoutDrone1 to go back on watch. She continued, "So Tarik does have some experience in these kind of situations, where we're making contact with a group that might be perfectly friendly, might be hostile, or might have good reason to be terrified of strangers. You two should work together, but Dad and Peri were agreed that SecUnit would take point on all issues dealing with mission security."

(*You were?* I asked ART-drone on our private feed.

Of course we fucking were, it said.)

I needed to respond to Iris. I said, "Okay."

"It's not an ex-SecUnit," Ratthi corrected gently, before the quiet could get too quiet again. "You can't be an ex-SecUnit until you're dead. But thank you for your honesty."

So it was still my decision, and I needed to make it. At least the talking had given me time to process and check threat assessment. Did I want to go on alone, without ART-drone? Fuck no. Did I want to send Iris and Tarik back alone, without ART-drone? Fuck no. Fine, okay, fine. "We'll go on to the entrance to the hanger."

Iris nodded. "Thank you for listening to us."

On the team feed, ART-drone said, *You can have your emotional reactions and phatic communication after you restart the vehicle.*

Yes, it's just as rude to its humans as it is to everybody else.

Tarik lowered his hands, still looking at me. "Right. We should talk about this later."

We probably should but we absolutely are not going to, not if I can help it. Wait, had Tarik been ART's mission security before me? Had I taken a human's job?

Under normal circumstances that would be kind of hilarious.

He got the vehicle started again and we proceeded down the stupid tunnel, into the stupid danger. I sent Scout-Drone1 flying ahead at its highest speed, so it could at least scout the hangar a little before we arrived. I still didn't want to move ScoutDrone2 from its watch position at the tunnel opening.

ART-drone let go of the vehicle and flew a little ahead of it. It looked like the ominous, scary-looking bot from a horror drama that ends up trying to kill everybody in the deserted space station/deserted planetary installation/deserted generic underground habitation.

Without good scan data I had to pay more attention to visual input, even though currently the tunnel was boring. The humans had stopped talking. (It should have been a relief, but it wasn't. Weirdly, I'd gotten used to humans talking in background, like music that isn't your favorite but is still vaguely nice to listen to.)

ART-drone and I might be having our own awkward silence. On our private feed, I said, *You knew that about Tarik.*

Yes. It's been a complex situation. Seth registered an objection when Tarik was first assigned to me, and I seconded it. Seth thought he would be too rash, and that having been required and often compelled to display aggression toward humans in the same situations as those we were trying to help would be a habitual behavior that might recur under pressure, even for a human who was actively trying to suppress it. The faculty director persuaded us to give him a chance. They were correct, it has worked out. So far.

The "so far" was interesting. The thing with ART is that it isn't a construct, it has no human neural tissue, and the way it processes its emotions and impulses is completely different from the way I do it, let alone the way the humans do it. That's why it prefers to watch media with me, because it can understand the emotional context better with me as a filter.

Did I understand how it processed its emotions? No. But I don't understand how I process my emotions, either.

So with everything that was going on right now, it was particularly stupid that what I felt was, you know, whatever it was. Not jealousy. Sort of like jealousy. If Tarik after all the time he had been on the crew was still a "so far," what was I? I said, *If you already have a security consultant—*

ART-drone interrupted, *He's not a security consultant, he's a mission specialist. He has a good knowledge of the tactics that corporates like Barish-Estranza employ. You are a security consultant.*

That would have been encouraging, before *redacted*.

Chapter Five

FINALLY, WE WERE CLOSE enough to see the dark opening into the hangar at the end of the corridor. Without me having to say anything, Tarik slowed down almost to a halt, then stopped when we were about ten meters away.

ScoutDrone1 had already reached it and started a search pattern, and I sent ScoutDrone2 in after it. A shaft of dim daylight and a sand drift on the floor had led it immediately up to a big seam in the ceiling that should be part of the hatch system that allowed the ships in and out. A small section had been cut open at some point, large enough to allow in the aircraft that was parked on the landing platform. The shuttle, following our progress from the air, had already gotten there and found the opening. ART-drone was building a map using ScoutDrone1's movements.

Ratthi and Iris and Tarik were examining the video views from the drones inside and the shuttle's cameras outside. The hanger area was darker than they expected, since they had been viewing it through the drone camera's dark vision filters. They were speculating about whatever equipment failure or natural disaster had buckled the hatch so somebody had to cut a hole in it or something, I didn't really care.

Because ScoutDrone1 had also found the entrance to the Pre-CR installation the hangar had been built to access.

It was on the farthest wall, where the shadow was deeper, directly opposite this tunnel. When completely open, it would be big enough to fly our shuttle through. (Which was something we absolutely would not be doing, because holy shit no, what a bad idea.) It was set between two giant rounded half-pillars carved out of the rock wall, angled back as if to brace the sloped stone slab above it. I guess that was the pillars' purpose; if they were supposed to be making the place pretty, they weren't doing their job.

My drones had skimmed over the hangar's floor panels, which were a stone/metal combination that Ratthi said were common in Pre-CR structures, and which were coated with layers of dust. No signs of recent traffic so far, but that wasn't convincing evidence that this place was uninhabited. The hole in the overhead hatch meant there was a lot of dust in the air and it would settle frequently, covering tracks and signs of movement.

I got out of the vehicle and said, "Iris, you and Tarik should return to the shuttle. ART-drone can get you up through the broken hatch to the surface. You can locate a landing spot for a retrieval with the ground sensor."

Iris looked toward the far side of the hangar, in the direction of the interior hatch which she wouldn't be able to see in the dark at this distance. (Iris had augments for extra feed connectivity and storage, but nothing for vision or anything else helpful under the circumstances.) There was a frown in her voice. "Are you sure you're going to be all right?"

Well, no. Obviously.

She continued, "Remember pulling out of this mission and going back to Peri to report and regroup is always an option."

She had a point, but we were close. If the separatist colony had failed and there weren't any survivors here, we could be done by the time the humans needed to eat again and we wouldn't have to plan a follow-up mission. "It's fine. I'll notify you immediately if I encounter any not-dead humans."

I was trying to lighten the mood but that one absolutely did not stick its landing.

Then Ratthi tried to help and made it worse. "You mean not dead, of course, as opposed to un— Ah, never mind, I'm going to stop talking now."

Tarik did a body language thing that started as an aborted clap on my shoulder and ended with an awkward shrug as he remembered I wouldn't like it. He said, "Just remember you've got backup." I suddenly got why Iris had brought up his past in sanctioned corporate murder; she wanted him to think about his current job vs. my job, about who would make the security decisions. How we had something in common, I guess.

ART-drone didn't say anything but I knew it was happy that I was sending the humans back to the shuttle.

As ART-drone gave first Iris and then Tarik a ride up through the hatch opening, I crossed the expanse of the dark hangar and stood in front of the installation hatch. It was partially open, a long dark line down the center, a very very dark line, indicating the emergency lighting from the tunnel was not active in there, either. I called ScoutDrone1 and 2, and sent them inside.

Humans. For fuck's sake, why would the separatists want to live here? Because they were afraid? If the theory in my save-for-later tags was right, and Adamantine had had an early warning about the hostile takeover of its headquarters and assets, and told some of the colonists that another corporation might want to come along and eliminate any evidence of alien contamination so the planet wouldn't lose value . . . This place might look like a potential shelter.

And it was doable with the resources at hand. The Adamantine main colony site had some underground bunkers for food production that they had mostly stopped using once they got their oxygenating crops started under the air bubble; there would have been spare hydroponic equipment and growth supplies available. Even if this place hadn't had its own still-functioning power source, the terraforming engines were right there to tap, and the terraforming techs among the colonists would know how.

I was getting drone video of the installation, sort of, kind of. It was so dark, the drones' filters weren't working well, which meant mine wouldn't, either. With my scans still borked and barely any visual, there could be a hundred alien contaminated humans standing around and I wouldn't know they were there until I bumped into one.

I'm not actually stalling, okay, I'm doing stuff. The drones, I'm waiting on the drones.

I could have been wearing armor for this part.

(So earlier, after *redacted,* Three had told me that I could wear its armor, if I wanted. Well, it hadn't used those words. It hadn't gotten the idea yet that it might have personal possessions that belonged to it and no one else, so it had gotten me to follow it to ART's secure storage where the armor was being kept and just stood there pointing at the door with a confused expression.) (Yes, it had taken 2.3 minutes of questioning by both me and ART and Overse and Turi to figure out what it was trying to tell us.) (The armor was equipment and Three didn't understand why I didn't just take it.) (Because I didn't fucking want it, that's why.) (And I left this out when it happened earlier, but while we were still at the router site and Ratthi and Tarik and Iris were volunteering for this mission, Three had asked me again. The armor was still in secure storage, but someone could have put it in a drop case and a pathfinder could have brought it to our position. And I said no again.)

(Yes, I know now it was a mistake. Three had offered me its drones, too; it had a lot more left than I did, after all the shooting and using them to bore holes in hostiles' skulls and getting stepped on by Targets. And I had said no. Murderbot, why are you like this?)

From the shuttle, watching through my feed, Ratthi said, "Why are round hatches more frightening than square ones?"

Iris and Tarik were up on the surface with ART-drone, on a flat stretch of rocky ground at the base of a plateau.

They had just located a safe landing spot with the ground sensor and signaled the shuttle to come down. From the shuttle's camera, the plateau looked natural, the same dark rock streaked with red mineral deposits, as the rest of the area. But the extrapolated map ART-drone had constructed said the installation had to be under it. Confused, Tarik said, "What?"

"This is a well-known fact," Ratthi said, from the copilot's seat. He had my camera view up on a display surface. "Round hatches are terrifying."

"This is fact where?" Tarik demanded as the shuttle landed in a whirl of dust. "Why are any hatches terrifying?"

Two drones were not enough for this job, but there was nothing I could do about that. Shielded from the terraforming interference by all the rock, their scans had started to function again, but only at extreme close range. I had clearer camera feeds and actual movement checks and that was a fucking relief, let me tell you. Even if right now all I was getting was darkness and the occasional too-close view of a wall as the drones' guidance system detected one just in time to keep from smashing into it. This was going to be the slowest scouting run these drones had ever done, but at least it was happening.

Also, while I could understand Tarik's confusion, Ratthi wasn't wrong. I ran a quick query on hatch shape in my media storage, focusing on popular adventure and suspense/horror dramas and the high incidence of hazardous fauna, raiders, human and/or bot murderers, and/or magical fauna, unidentified but terrifying dark presences, and straight up monsters associated with round hatches. I sent the results into the team feed.

ART-drone said, *You wasted processing space on that?*

"Eighty percent," Ratthi said, genuinely shocked. "I thought I was making a joke."

As the ramp lowered, Iris swung up onto it. "It's not the shape of the hatch," she said, "it's the symmetry of the columns to either side."

I said, "I'm not running the query again." My two pitiful drones were still getting nothing on visual but they were giving me some data indicating relative positions of walls, ceiling, and floors, and their limited close-range scan picked up something that was probably dormant power conduit under stone veneer. But there just weren't enough of them to build a real sensor map of a space as large as this appeared to be, even with their full scanning capacity. It was even larger than the hangar, and mostly open.

Iris and Tarik were through the airlock and inside the shuttle now. They let their helmets disengage and fold back. Tarik dropped into a seat and Iris leaned on the back of Ratthi's headrest, watching the display screen.

ART-drone floated back down through the hangar hatch to return to my position. I should have told it to get into the shuttle and stay with the humans, but. I hadn't.

"Let's wait and let the evidence stand for itself," Ratthi said. He meant the hatch evidence. Yes, we were still on that.

Iris is correct, ART-drone said, *it's the symmetry of the*

hatch's placement between the two columns and the equal size
of the space to either side. To individuals subject to suggestion,
it implies that something is about to cross the line of sight.

By "individuals subject to suggestion" it meant "idiots."

Tarik said, "You know if this place is empty, all this monster talk is going to sound ridiculous."

Iris's tone was dry. "I hate to tell you, but it already sounds ridiculous." She added, "SecUnit, do you have a plan to proceed?"

ScoutDrone1 alerted and I told it to halt. Its camera had just detected artificial light, and it didn't match the emergency lighting in the tunnel corridor. It was identical to the battery lighting used in the Adamantine main site. Well, here we go. "Contact," I said. Space monsters and dark presences weren't going to need battery light. Alien-contaminated humans, however, would. Probably.

"What? Where?" Tarik frowned at the feed display.

"The drones are reporting in," Ratthi explained. He opened a private feed connection to me and said, *SecUnit, you're not telling us what you're doing.*

Shit, he's right. I am fucking this up again. On the comm, I said, "A drone encountered artificial lighting in a corridor."

Trying to cover for me, Ratthi was telling Tarik, "Just always assume there are drones doing something."

ART-drone said, *Before contact was made, all findings were preliminary and inconclusive.*

Yeah, that's ART-drone covering for me, too.

I shared my drone video with the team feed, which I

should have done earlier, but the results were so minimal . . . I just hadn't shared it. What, it hadn't occurred to me? I was ashamed of it? I don't know, I need to snap out of this.

Iris frowned. "If you find anything that might be a sign of compulsive construction, get out of there immediately."

Ratthi made a thoughtful "mmph" noise, which I translated as him not considering the presence or lack of compulsive construction as indicative as we hoped, but not wanting to say it aloud and bring the group down.

On the drone video, the outline of a corridor was taking shape as the light grew brighter. It was a lot like the tunnel but the material was lighter in color, the floor darker. There was no decoration, like there had been in the other Pre-CR site. But if this place had been built by the same Pre-CR group, it probably wasn't intended to be a major occupation site. I guess. I have no idea, don't listen to me.

There was also no sign of graffiti, but it was hard to tell if the graffiti in the Pre-CR site had been another sign of alien contamination affecting the humans or not. We hadn't seen any so far in the Adamantine colonists' habitation. (Ugh, tag this bullshit piece of data for delete. There was graffiti in Preservation Station, for fuck's sake, sometimes humans want pretty pictures on the walls. It could mean anything or nothing.)

ScoutDrone1 followed the light into a larger passage, turning a corner . . . It was another hatch, smaller, sized for humans and not large cargo containers. The battery light was stuck or mounted to the wall to one side of it.

Ugh.

This is supposed to be my job/reason for existing, right, doing the dangerous thing so the humans don't have to. And I need to do it, right now. I said, "I'm going in. ART-drone will stay at the entrance."

I should accompany you, ART-drone said.

Iris said, "Peri, it's SecUnit's call."

I didn't want to argue in front of the humans (I know, right? Like we've never done that before. But I didn't want to do it now) so on our private feed, I told ART-drone, *You need to not undermine Iris's authority right now. And you need to stay at the entrance so if anything chases me out you can slow it down so the shuttle will have time to take off.*

ART-drone said, *Your attempts at emotional manipulation need work. But your point is taken.*

I kept my camera feed on the shuttle's larger display surface and crossed the last bit of hangar floor to the hatch. The open gap between the huge doors was more than wide enough for me to walk inside.

With the data the drones had sent me, I had a sensor map (a half-assed sensor map) that I could use to enhance my dark vision filters. So I could see to a certain extent, enough not to run into a wall. Though everything was in grayscale, and details were fuzzy. I was in an entrance foyer, large enough for heavy cargo bots or hauler bots to wander around in. The forward wall was open to the giant space that ScoutDrone2 was currently attempting to map singlehandedly. (Intel drones are supposed to do this kind of thing in swarms, which did not make me feel super competent right now.) The righthand wall had an opening that was probably the entrance to a large lift shaft, possibly where the cargo was meant to get shunted as soon as it came in through the hatch. I checked my scan and for once it was good news. With the thick layer of rock overhead shielding us from interference, I had limited function back, though not as much as the drones had right now. But I could tell the lift wasn't powered up, at least. And the percentage chance of being surrounded by silent alien-contaminated humans dropped to fluctuate in the low 80s. Oh, and there was a metal safety screen that had been pulled across the shaft entrance to keep anyone from falling in. That might be an indication that an orderly shutdown of this site, or at least of this entrance, had occurred at some point.

On the feed, Ratthi checked my scan of the metal's composition. He said, *That screen doesn't look Pre-CR.*

Right, and that, too. Big clue there, Murderbot, you might want to notice things like that.

Could have been the terraforming crew, Tarik said. *They must have explored this place.*

On the other wall of the foyer, my scan found some metal plates with inscribed writing. It didn't match anything in the language module Thiago had written to communicate with the Targets and colonists, so it was likely yet another Pre-CR language. I made sure I got good images and sent stills to Ratthi to tag for later, once we got out of blackout. Without access to ART's enormous archive storage and Thiago's translation abilities, we weren't going to be able to read it.

I walked to the front of the foyer. (In the shuttle, Ratthi whispered, "I hate this part." He and Tarik and Iris watched the display surface intently, frozen except for the way Tarik kept pinching his lip compulsively.) I could just see the ramp that stretched out and down. Three stories down, according to ScoutDrone2. It was like the ramp at a transit ring, cutting back and forth down the wall to keep its angle gentle. There was nothing else I could really see from this point; the space was too big and dark. (I could turn on my helmet light, but it would make me a great target, if a hostile had detected my entrance. Which, if I were a human hiding up here in isolation and a stranger walked in suddenly in an unfamiliar brand of environmental suit, I'd shoot at me.) (Okay I wouldn't, but then I'm not a human who was panicking about getting murdered or whatever.)

(I'm a SecUnit who was panicking about getting murdered or whatever by panicking humans.)

I started down the ramp. It helped that ScoutDrone2 was down there bumping into walls. I let it continue to wander; it had found five other corridor entrances by this point, but hadn't picked up any traces of artificial light like ScoutDrone1.

From what I could tell, this space was a lot like that central area of the other Pre-CR site: a large multilevel space with corridors leading off it, though it wasn't as tall. (And yes, I know that's not a wildly unusual design for the majority of human cultures.) I wasn't picking up any sense of air movement, except what was being caused by my own drones, and audio was null. (I'd backburnered the shuttle comm channel, which at the moment was three humans breathing tensely, plus the occasional creak of seat upholstery.)

I found little domed bumps on the floor, my scan picking up the dormant tech inside each one. They were simple beacons, probably marking vehicle parking/landing zones. The hangar had been intended for larger craft; this area could be meant for small aircraft or cargo lifters or vehicles that would travel the tunnel, hopefully with more safety features than the jury-rigged one we had found. ScoutDrone2 had just encountered a foyer leading to a small set of rooms with plumbing attachments and drains, probably a restroom.

This place wasn't as creepy as it had been at first. It was also, weirdly, way easier to walk around in here than it had been to step through the hatch. I tapped my private feed connection with Ratthi and said, *Can you burn out your ability to feel that a place is creepy?*

Ratthi answered, *I think that's called being in shock.*

Thanks, Ratthi. If I wanted someone to ruin my fun, I'd have asked ART-drone.

I reached the bottom of the ramp and headed toward the corridor ScoutDrone1 had found. The floor was smooth underfoot and I could see just well enough not to trip on anything.

Then ART-drone said, *I'm picking up a nonstandard transmission.*

I froze.

So here is the thing. The redacted thing. I should tell you about it, or this isn't going to make sense.

Twelve plus hours after the new Barish-Estranza explorer arrived in the system, something happened. I don't have a memory of what triggered it, except maybe in my organic neural tissue which is no fucking help at all.

I was in the control area below ART's bridge with the humans, going over plans for dealing with Barish-Estranza since our strategic situation had just blown up in our faces. I can access that moment and see what I was paying 87 percent of my attention to: Iris explaining how the University normally handled evacuating colonists and how those options might work or need to change in this situation. Mensah and Ratthi were sitting in chairs listening to her, Pin-Lee was standing, staring at nothing while she scrolled through legal documents in her feed. The rest of ART's crew were scattered around the compartment, quiet because they were listening or hurriedly pulling information from their feeds and ART's archives so they could present potential solutions. Arada, Overse, Amena, and Thiago were on the Preservation responder, listening in on comm with some of the other crew. I had my drones in standby, and Three had just been coaxed by Matteo to sit on a couch.

My next functional memory was a forced restart in ART's medical bay.

ART had to get into my archive and processes to see

what had knocked me offline. Apparently, I'd had what appeared to be a visual memory of what happened under the Pre-CR habitat, with the infected human corpse and all that. When ART showed it to me after restart, I could tell some of it was inaccurate. (Really inaccurate. The human corpse did not catch me and eat my right leg. For one thing, there's not a lot of organic tissue on there to eat, for the other, we had video confirmation that I still had it after the escape.)

The original memory wasn't corrupted, it was still intact for comparison, and there were other anomalies in the new memory once ART ran an analysis of both. There was no indication of where the inaccurate memory had come from or what had caused it to show up in my archive. I hadn't been hacked, ART hadn't been hacked, the Preservation Responder hadn't been hacked, our feed networks hadn't been hacked. We ran a check of my media storage to make sure that the memory wasn't a corrupted clip from a show. It turned out there was a (not surprisingly) large percentage of my media that included scenes of humans, augmented humans, bots, humans and/or bots pretending to be aliens, and animated and/or machine-generated images of aliens, being chased by scary things. But none of the files were corrupted and none included the accurate details present both in my original memory and the false version.

Whatever caused the false memory to spontaneously appear out of fucking nowhere, it had made my performance reliability drop so quickly that I shut down, variously upsetting and freaking the humans out. Their hypothesis, as delivered by Dr. Mensah in Medical after I was online again, was that it was like what happened when a human had a flashback. And because no one had any information at all on the effects of trauma on a construct's machine/ organic neural combo, the MedSystem hadn't recognized it for what it was until ART got into my activity logs and rummaged around.

Mensah was upset that it had happened though she was pretending not to be. (And we both straight up lied to Amena, over the comm to the Preservation responder, and told her I was still having functional issues due to the repairs necessitated by the viral contamination, and it was nothing to worry about, nothing at all, ha-ha. Yeah, I don't know if she believed us or not, our consensus was that we made a shit job of it.)

But it happened in front of eleven humans, Three, and ART, and by the time they and ART figured out it was not some kind of viral attack, or a new contamination outbreak, there was no chance to keep it private and everybody who had been present knew I'd borked myself over a weird anomalous faulty memory that I had apparently created myself, somehow. Not exactly a confidence builder.

(They were all so nice about it. The whole thing made me understand the human expression "it made me want to vomit." Why would you ever want to do something that was so objectively disgusting and looked so painful. Oh, this was why, I get it now.)

I unfroze to the scene from *Rise and Fall of Sanctuary Moon* when the solicitor is waking up in the medical bay and her bodyguard is there. It's from episode 206, one of my favorites. Time check: offline = .06 seconds. If this had happened during an attack by hostile(s), I'd be dead now and the hostiles would have probably destroyed ART-drone and attacked the shuttle and killed all the humans.

ART-drone had not ratted me out and Iris was in the middle of saying, "—possible contamination hazard?" on the comm. ART-drone had already taken our feed down in case it was a contamination hazard, which was good. I could see on my shuttle drone's camera that Ratthi had pulled his interface out of his ear.

ART-drone said, *Viral contamination cannot be delivered to me or SecUnit via this method. I have already blocked the shuttle's feed and comm from receiving the potentially hostile channel.* On our private feed, it said, *Are you back?*

Yes, I told it. Sort of, mostly. *Was it that memory again?*

You showed the same performance reliability drop and error codes, but the duration was comparatively short, and you didn't go into shutdown. So it's more likely to be a variation on the same issue. We can't verify that until I have time to check your active logs.

Iris asked, "Can you show us the transmission?"

ART-drone converted the transmission into visual data that the humans could understand and put an image of it on the shuttle's display surface.

Begin session acknowledge greeting
Begin session acknowledge hello

Begin session acknowledge salutation

Ratthi's brow was doing things to show simultaneous intense worry and intense interest. "It's an automated system, do you think?"

"No, it's an active system trying to initiate a connection with either Peri or SecUnit." Iris bit her lower lip in a way that looked like it hurt.

Correct, ART-drone said. *It knows we're here. It must be continuously scanning for activity and picked up our comm and feed signal.*

Tarik said, "You think this is like that Pre-CR central system?"

I could talk now, so I answered, "Yes, like that." Like the other central system we had found, this one was using LanguageBasic, which is still common in the Corporation Rim for connection protocol between different architectures using different and often proprietary codes. It was invented in the Pre-CR times, I guess. I have no idea.

"Is it a distress call?" Ratthi was really concerned. So was I. Because it wasn't a distress call.

Begin session acknowledge hand-clasp
Begin session acknowledge wave
Begin session acknowledge bow

ART-drone said, *No, this is not a distress call. It is cycling through alternate data transfer protocols until it finds one we will accept.*

The other Pre-CR central system had not infected me with the alien contamination. The other Pre-CR central system had, with 2.0's help, in fact saved my ass. It had been

sitting in that place, contaminated and cut off from its network, calling into the dark for someone, anyone, to help its
humans, until we found it.

I did not want to answer this one. I also did not want
my stupid neural tissue or whatever was causing my stupid repeating false memory error to win. Win what? That's
a good fucking question, I wish I could answer it. I said,
"Iris, I want to answer it. Do I have a go to proceed?" Because if this turns out to be a really bad idea, it wasn't going
to be just me in the shit. I was really glad I'd made them
stay in the shuttle, with one of ART's iterations piloting,
far enough away to get in the air before, say, a running contaminated human or bot could reach them. But that wasn't
me being especially smart, it was just me not being especially stupid.

Ratthi was clearly not happy. Tarik's face set in a wince,
anticipating disaster. Iris bit her lip again, then said, "Go, at
your discretion."

ART-drone said, *We will be out of contact briefly. Confirm.*

Iris has that same thing as Dr. Mensah, the thing where
she's able to look and sound calm under circumstances
where shit is possibly about to go down. She said, "Confirm. See you on the other side."

ART-drone cut the comm and I missed them immediately. It wasn't like the humans could do a lot to help me
in this situation if everything went sideways, but not having them there was not . . . It was not great. (It was tempting to take this as another sign of possible performance

dysfunction, but objectively I knew it was probably the opposite.) (It was still annoying.)

ART-drone threw out an extra comm- and feed-block wall between us and the shuttle and I said, *Let's do full containment protocol.* Which was the protocol we'd come up with (we being ART, Martyn, and Matteo and me, before my incident when I effectively became useless) for dealing with potential contamination situations.

Let's, ART-drone said, which was its way of being nice and not letting me know that it didn't need my advice about which containment protocol to use. Then it made it worse by adding, *Be careful.*

The wall went up and I was alone in the dark except for my two drones, both on standby now, and the Pre-CR system.

Begin session acknowledge hail
Begin session acknowledge salute
Begin session acknowledge nod

I sent, *Acknowledge, session.*

There was no pause, like it had no concerns about contact with foreign systems. It sent, *Connection: ID: AdaCol2. Query: ID?*

Okay, this is going to be tricky. *ID: SecUnit.*

Function: query? Registration/organization: query?

The other central system had been altered to work for the Adamantine colonists who had found it in the Pre-CR structure. This one must have been altered, too, because of its designation. (Ada = Adamantine; Col = Colony.) (I'm guessing the other central system was AdaCol1, unless there was a whole other Pre-CR network still active on this planet.) (I really hope there isn't.) But this system didn't sound like it had been altered, and I can't describe that any better without copying in a lot of code. But that other system, AdaCol1, had sort of gotten what I was; this one had no clue. The concept of me was not in its archive, if it even had archives like I did.

I responded, *Function: survey. Organization ID: PSUMNT.*

Trying to explain what a SecUnit was in LanguageBasic was hard enough, and the Pansystem University of Mihira and New Tideland, since it hadn't existed back when this code was in common use, had no ID that AdaCol2 would even recognize as an ID, so I just made one up for it.

It didn't respond. Yeah, I think I fucked that up.

It sent, *ID: PSUMNT added to ContactBase.*

I guess machine intelligences of that era were too polite to say "that sounds fake but okay."

It added, *query: contact AdaCol1?*

It could be asking for something else, and not the other central system, the one that I'd destroyed along with 2.0 to stop the source of the alien contamination.

I hoped it was asking for something else.

I was taking too long, and it sent, *AdaCol1 contact lost. Query: contact AdaCol1?*

Yeah, there was a 95 percent chance that it was asking for the other central system. I sent, *AdaCol1 location?*

It sent me a string of numbers. Not active code . . . oh, right, probably map coordinates. It took me a second to figure it out but they matched the Adamantine mapping data. And the coordinates pointed to one side of the main colony site, where the Pre-CR structure was.

So it was a 100 percent chance. I made myself reply, *AdaCol1: offline.*

This time there was a pause. 2.3 seconds. It sent, *query?*

AdaCol1 saved me. It was half eaten by an alien contaminant transferable via organic DNA into machine code and vice versa. It was held a prisoner in the dark while the humans that had rescued it from the ruin it was abandoned in were infected and driven to do terrible things to each other. It let me kill it if I promised to save its humans. How did I put that into this stupid limited language?

I sent, *AdaCol1: contamination incident.*

Query?

I should be asking AdaCol2 if it was here alone, though I was 97 percent sure it wasn't. I had only interacted briefly with AdaCol1 but it had—*felt* is the wrong word but it makes sense in context—or not, whatever—it had felt alone. Its access had been cut off, none of its normal functions were in process, it had little to no data as to what was happening outside the limited network it had been trapped with.

AdaCol2 was an active system. It could even have been stalling me while its humans got their SecUnit-busting weapons out.

And if it was like AdaCol1, it was probably a lot smarter than this limited connection protocol made it sound. I pulled a report like I would for a SecSystem's or HubSystem's internal use, all data, no visuals or documentation for humans. No way to make what had happened sound better.

I hesitated. This was hard. It might try to kill me and then I'd have to kill it. Or try to kill it, it might be on ART's level and smash me like a bug, I didn't know.

I said, *query: accept data file?*

In response it sent me a hard address, different from the one it was using for our connection. It was probably the equivalent of a run box, a separate processing area it could view but that nothing could get out of. (Theoretically, anyway. I would have bet 2.0 could have gotten out of a Pre-CR run box.)

I sent the file, and the connection went quiet.

I didn't want to just stand here waiting, and watching media under these circumstances was clearly not a good idea no matter how much I really, really wanted to watch media. So I made a copy of the conversation and pinged ART-drone with it.

ART-drone dropped the wall between us, though not the one protecting the shuttle's systems. *Is that a good idea?* I asked it. *Is containment protocol for everybody but you?*

After it sees the file it will either attack us or ask for further contact, ART-drone said. *The wall will have to go down either way.*

Right, fine, whatever. Then AdaCol2 sent, *query: function, query: connection, query,* and followed it with a current timestamp.

It had just asked us why we were here.

On our private connection, ART-drone said, *It wouldn't question you like this if it was alone here. It has something to protect.*

ART in any format is absolute shit at talking to other bots, but in this case I knew it was right. I needed to reply in a way that would make sense to a Pre-CR central system jury-rigged to network with Corporate-era tech. The Targets, ART's crew being captured, Barish-Estranza, the hopefully dormant alien contamination site now lurking under the collapsed ruin of the Pre-CR colony site. But I kept seeing the memory of that last moment before AdaCol1 shut down. I put together a response and sent:

AdaCol1 request: assistance needed, PSUMNT response assistance in process then *ID: Barish-Estranza Explorer Task Group: threat condition high* and finally *PSUMNT request: client-to-client connection.*

Which meant, "AdaCol1 asked for help, we are trying to help, Barish-Estranza is dangerous, can you please let our humans speak to yours."

It sent back: *query: 'client'?*

This system didn't know what client meant. I tried not to take that as a sign of complete failure while ART-drone ran a quick query for alternatives and sent me the results. I picked the top one: *'client' = operator.*

It sent, *connection accepted, request accepted, assistance* and I had another camera view in my feed.

It was so sudden it startled me, and it took me .03 seconds to understand what I was looking at. ART-drone said, *Shit.*

AdaCol2 was showing me a view of a large room, built from the same artificial stone and either part of this installation or very near it, with at least twenty-two humans, two of them wearing patched Adamantine environmental

suits. At least twenty-two, there were small humans playing along one wall and the camera view didn't take in the
whole space. The humans had a normal range of skin tone,
dark brown through light tan, no visible signs of contamination effects. (It was impossible to tell about their hair;
most of them had it wrapped up in a cloth or covered by a
cap.) None of that was the "oh shit" part.

The "oh shit" part was that they were facing five humans
in Barish-Estranza enviro suits and gear, and one SecUnit.

Yeah, we were too late.

ART-drone had already ended our containment protocol and opened comm and feed to the shuttle. It said, *Iris,
we have a problem.*

Chapter Six

I DON'T KNOW WHAT the initial reaction was for the separatist colonists when they suddenly found a Barish-Estranza exploration team on their doorstep, but our little shuttle family was not happy, let me tell you.

It was early for our scheduled check-in, and the messenger pathfinder wasn't back yet from delivering our earlier report, but ART-drone pulled down another one so Iris could record and upload an updated status for it to carry outside the blackout zone. Hopefully both pathfinders would be back soon with instructions or some sort of insights as to what the hell to do next. But mostly it would let everybody else know our situation in case Barish-Estranza tried to attack us. Because keeping our presence secret from B-E was completely blown as soon as our humans made contact with the colonists.

(Threat assessment on the probability of an attack by Barish-Estranza was depressingly low. Depressing because the low figure was not because they had suddenly decided to be nice humans who would leave us alone on principle, but because we were so unlikely to be a threat to them that it wasn't worth the operating expenses to send their SecUnit over here to kill us.)

(Not that I liked its odds if they did. There was me, for

what that was currently worth, and ART-drone shared ART-prime's hit-them-before-they-know-they're-in-a-fight attitude toward hostile overtures.)

And yes, the humans were all over the place about that SecUnit. We had a conversation about it on the comm while waiting for AdaCol2 to brief its primary operator.

Ratthi had asked me, "So you could"—he waggled his fingers at the side of his head—"to this one, set it free?"

The humans were all watching my shuttle drone, like it was my face. That's not disturbing at all. I said, "They're not all going to be like Three."

What I didn't want to say was that even though Three had saved my life, I still wouldn't have left it alone with my humans, whatever threat assessment said, if ART-prime hadn't been there to keep an eye on it. We hadn't known Three very long, and we hadn't seen it under much stress. It was still learning that it could make choices. We wouldn't know to what extent it was trustworthy until it made some more choices and acted on them.

Iris had her arms folded, her expression deep in thought. She had grown up with ART, and probably knew a lot about bot relationships. (She probably knew more about bot relationships than ART did.) But SecUnits aren't bots, we're constructs, and we don't have relationships like that. Governor modules don't encourage that kind of thing.

(And I know Three had talked to Ratthi and Amena about the two other SecUnits in its task group, one of which the Targets had directly killed, and the other they had indirectly killed by forcing a human to order it to stay behind on the drop box station. (SecUnits have to stay within a certain range of our clients or the governor modules fry your brain and it is not pretty.) I know Three felt . . . whatever toward those two units, but I have lots of feelings toward the imaginary humans on my media, and I am perfectly clear on the fact that those relationships are one-sided. There is literally no way to tell if the feelings among those three SecUnits were reciprocal in that situation, even for Three, because governor module.)

(And frankly, the potential to blame all humans for killing its possibly apocryphal friends makes Three's threat assessment rise even higher.)

Tarik was slumped back in the pilot's seat with one knee hooked over the armrest (how can that be comfortable) and his expression was opaque, but I also got the feeling he wasn't unhappy to hear my reasons for why I wouldn't be doing the thing.

Ratthi was unhappy. He said, "Yes, but it seems . . . To not offer one the choice, given the opportunity . . ." He waved a hand. "I'm sorry, I believe you that it's a bad idea, but I can't help talking about it anyway. I'll try not to, I don't want you to feel like I'm pressing you to do something you don't think is safe."

Ratthi knows more about constructs than any human here.

The problem was, 2.0 had been in a unique position with Three. There was no way to replicate that here, even if I didn't know that just replicating conditions doesn't always give an identical or even similar result. I said, "We don't know if they have a SecSystem or HubSystem, or whatever their branded equivalent is, on their shuttle. If I was willing to do this I'd have to take the controlling system over first to make sure the governor module didn't trigger during the process. Then I'd have to kill its clients to cover up what I'd done."

Well, probably. And wiping out even a little part of the reinforced Barish-Estranza explorer group was not an option. Okay, it was an option, but it was not an option Seth or Iris or Mensah or any of the other humans seriously wanted to consider. Both Preservation and the University of Mihira and New Tideland would not be okay with it, for one thing. For the other, it was strategically iffy, now that their reinforcements had arrived. It led to a scenario where, at best, we wiped out the whole task group and then had to hide the evidence and just hoped none of the humans felt bad and reported it once we got out of the system.

Whatever, we're not doing it unless they try to do it to us first. Just to make sure everybody understood, I continued, "Even if I did free the SecUnit, I might have to kill it anyway, if it goes rogue and tries to murder all of you."

"I see," Iris said. She looked like she was thinking through about half a dozen scenarios at once and none of them were panning out the way she wanted. Or maybe I was projecting.

There are no easy answers, as Dr. Bharadwaj says. And this will never be an easy question.

While that was happening, AdaCol2 and I arranged a secure comm connection between Iris and its primary operator, a human called Trinh. Who was more than a little weirded out to be contacted by a second group of new humans so soon after the first contact after years of no contact whatsoever. I could sympathize: it would have freaked me out, too.

I listened to bits of the conversation, but it was just too painful, even though Iris was good at talking. After the introductions she opened with, "I know Barish-Estranza told you they're here to help you. But they're from a corporation that is trying to take possession of this planet to claim and exploit its assets, and right now those assets are you."

Through the translator module, Trinh said, "So you're saying the same thing as they did, that you're here to help us."

Ugh. They had no reason to trust us.

In the shuttle Tarik and Ratthi and ART-drone were strategizing, coming up with plans to try to convince the separatists and looking up stuff for Iris to show Trinh to better explain the situation, including vid clips of the fighting between the different factions at the main colony site. The humans had already sent a request via the pathfinder report to bring in a colonist who was willing to vouch for us and give an eyewitness account of the alien contamination incidents. But they knew that might not help, either, because the two groups hadn't communicated for however many years. (At least that's what historian Corian back at the main colony had thought. The separatists may have spied on the main group via AdaCol2's former connection with AdaCol1. Ratthi had been putting together a feed document on what they might know/what we were certain they did know. The concluding paragraph that he was still working on indicated that he agreed with the theory that there were specific reasons for the split between this faction and the main site that didn't have as much to do with the contamination incidents as previously indicated.) But basically the separatists had no reason to believe the main group's opinion of us. "Or to even believe anybody we bring up here is actually a colonist," Tarik had pointed out, "and not just one of us in a stolen environmental suit."

Tarik has trust issues, ART-drone told me on our private connection. Yeah, I guess that was related to the whole ex-corporate-death-squad thing.

Ratthi, still with the pinched expression that indicated he didn't think anything was going well, added, "Yes, and Barish-Estranza may be able to bring in a colonist to vouch for them, too. We know they're in contact with that group out to the south of the main colony."

It was a mess and it was getting more messy every second. I keep telling myself I'm security, my job is to protect my humans while they try to save these other humans. There wasn't anything I could do to help except stay out of it. But no one was attacking us right now and I felt useless.

I wasn't just standing around, at least. AdaCol2 had given me the location of the Barish-Estranza shuttle and told me the best way to get to it without alerting the separatists or the B-E team. I needed to know where it was in case threat assessment was wrong and they did attack us, and I wanted to take a look at it just to make sure . . . I don't know, that it didn't have a giant explosive device attached

System Collapse

to it I guess. I needed to do something and going to stare at their shuttle felt proactive.

AdaCol2 had directed me to a passage heading north, not the one ScoutDrone1 had found. AdaCol2 had confirmed the hatch with the functioning emergency light led into the inhabited portion of the installation. I had left ScoutDrone1 there in sentry mode just in case the Barish-Estranza team or the separatists tried to come through it to look for our shuttle. Due to the scanning blackout on the surface, they wouldn't know where we were unless they went out and looked, or B-E sent their SecUnit to look.

AdaCol2 told me it didn't have cameras through this section of the installation and that there were no exterior cameras on the surface near the opening above the hangar area. (I know, right? But until now there hadn't been anyone on the planet who (a) wanted to sneak up and attack them and (b) was even sure where they were.)

(Which just shows you, you should have the cameras installed, just in case.)

ART-drone had taken a position just inside the installation, as a line of defense if hostiles chose to come from that direction. It was also using the shuttle's cameras to look for approaches on the surface. ART-drone would have difficulty hacking a SecUnit in the blackout zone, but it would be relatively easy to direct one of its pathfinders to smash into one attempting to approach the shuttle from ground level. ART-drone also had more pathfinders in patrol pattern above us, watching for anything attempting to approach via air. It

291

wasn't nearly as efficient a defense without the pathfinders' scanners online, but then B-E wouldn't be able to scan, either.

The passage AdaCol2 had directed me toward was on the opposite side of the foyer space, in the section that ScoutDrone2 was still searching. I had to go down a ramp from the landing level, which led to a junction of three corridors, and take the one that led off to the west, deeper into the rock. Yes, I did this in a strange installation, on a strange system's say-so.

Because the thing was, Trinh and the other separatist colonists might not have any reason to believe us, but AdaCol2 seemed to.

You can get a long way with bots by just keeping things simple and knowing which requests for information or assistance are unlikely to trip the parameters they've been given to guard things and to tell humans "no you can't go in there/do that." Bots (normal bots, not combat or spybots, etc.) are usually programmed to default to being reasonable in response to reasonable human or other bot behavior.

I didn't know what AdaCol2 was programmed to do. Except, like AdaCol1, it put its function to protect its humans first. It had left the channel accessible with the camera view of where B-E was meeting with its humans, so ART-drone was monitoring. No sound, but ART-drone was enlarging it and using the facial and mouth movements it could pick up to interpret the human speech. Ratthi and Tarik were monitoring it and probably understanding more of what was going on than the B-E negotiator because Thiago's translation module was clearly better.

There was no power for lighting in this corridor, either, which was not super fun for me and made it slow going, even with ScoutDrone2 going ahead to look for things to bump into. AdaCol2 asked if I wanted the emergency lights turned on and I asked if it could do it without someone noticing the allocation of power to a supposedly shutdown area of the installation. It said no. So we were in the dark.

I knew AdaCol2 vouching for me, if in fact it was willing to vouch for me, was not going to change any human minds. (Let's face it, actual solid physical or visual evidence will often not change human minds.) It probably wasn't like ART-prime, who is considered to be in command of itself as an individual and second-in-command of missions after Seth, and also has the same title and position both in the teaching faculty and the freeing-former-corporate-colonies side business as Iris, though most of the students and lower-level personnel it interacts with don't know what its full capability is. (ART had shown me a personnel chart; it was complicated.) I wasn't sure what kind of relationship the humans here had with AdaCol2 but the chances were good it wasn't like that.

AdaCol2 could be walking me into a trap, because anything is possible and bad things may not be more statistically possible but it sure seems like they are.

AdaCol2 sent, *ID: B-E-SecUnit connection request negative acknowledgment repeat query.*

It was telling me that it had been asking the Barish-Estranza SecUnit for a connection but had been ignored, and wanted me to explain why. That was probably a good thing, though normal SecUnits can't hack, only Combat-Units. From the visual AdaCol2 had given me from its recording of the B-E team's initial approach, I was 87 percent sure that the unit wasn't a CombatUnit. It had the same basic armor style as Three and the dead B-E units we had encountered. Plus nobody had been shot yet. CombatUnits don't get deployed to stand around while humans talk.

But now I was going to have to explain the governor module to a system with no experience connecting to or interacting with SecUnits, except for me, just in the past hour. Here goes. *ID: B-E-SecUnit not autonomous.*

AdaCol2 responded, *query?*

Explaining the existential horror of the governor module in LanguageBasic took me through until the end of the corridor, which was at least long enough to circumvent what had to be a large installation. In the shuttle, Ratthi and Tarik were speculating that there were more sites, discovered and undiscovered, all over the planet. Ugh, I hope not.

I passed two sealed doors with transparent ports, one that AdaCol2 said was a maintenance storage chamber and another it said was a junction station for the now defunct life support/atmosphere control in this section. Which explained why the separatists weren't using this space. The whole place was so big they hadn't needed to put resources toward repairing this area yet.

Other doorways had been closed up with cut stone blocks and sealant. AdaCol2 said it had been done when it became clear this part of the installation would not be useful for habitation again without a major refit. I couldn't tell if it meant that had happened in its Pre-CR occupation or when the Adamantine colonists got here.

At the end of the corridor ScoutDrone2 bumped into a hatch similar to the one at the cargo entrance, but only about three meters high. We had gotten through the governor module conversation, which had ended this way:

AdaCol2: *query?* (translation: why? = why is this necessary and/or why is this considered functional and/or why is this permitted and/or why is this allowed)

Me: *answer null* (translation: I don't know and/or unknown and/or I don't want to talk about it)

With the power out in this area, the hatch was on manual and could be opened from this side with a mechanical wheel and lever, which was incredibly stupid if you didn't take into account the fact that this whole place had been designed to keep humans safe from a hostile environment, not other humans. AdaCol2 didn't have cameras out here, either, but the old landing areas scattered around the edges of the installation did have mostly functioning weight sensors, and it knew the shuttle was not in line of sight from the door. So as long as AdaCol2 hadn't been ordered to lie to me in order to walk me into a trap, I should be okay to open it.

The hatch was heavy and stiff with disuse, but I shoved it open just enough to let ScoutDrone2 out.

Gray daylight and a breath of wind and dust came in.

ScoutDrone2 lost its limited scan function as soon as it left the shelter of the emplacement around the hatch, but it still had its camera. It saw a large hangar space, this time with lights, and the far wall was open to a view of more red striated slopes and tumbled rocks. The B-E group must have spotted the opening on visual, though that didn't explain how they knew to search around here in the blackout zone. (Ratthi had said that they might have been checking out the terraforming engines to see if they could sell them for scrap, but that was mostly sarcastic.)

An angled stone wall, maybe designed to give the hatch a little protection from the weather, blocked off the rest of the hangar. ScoutDrone2 wasn't picking up anything on ambient audio but the wind and dust movement from outside was enough to obscure small noises like voices and human movement. ScoutDrone2 went low to the ground and edged around the wall. Uh-huh, there was the shuttle, sitting on one of the three intact landing platforms. It was bigger than ART's, longer, with the cockpit set higher. Through the bubble-shaped port, I could see a human or augmented human sitting inside. Outside, standing beside the ramp to the hatch, was a second SecUnit.

Before she had started speaking with Trinh, Iris had asked ART-drone if it thought the B-E shuttle had actually followed us when we entered the blackout zone. ART-drone did not; post-handoff it had retained ART's most recent pathfinder scan data from this area of the planet and also its estimated location of the Barish-Estranza ships and their shuttles that were currently deployed. It thought this shuttle could only have entered the zone earlier, maybe even by a day or so. Further analysis would have to be done by ART's primary iteration, but there must have been a gap in pathfinder scanning that B-E had exploited. ART-drone was miffed by this lapse and figured that ART-prime would be fucking furious.

Iris had said thoughtfully, "The timing is suspect, isn't it. I wonder if the historian decided to tell us about this place because Bellagaia got word that one of the colonists in the other factions had told B-E."

Tarik had groaned and rubbed his eyes. "A little heads-up would have been helpful."

No shit. There was at least a 65 percent chance that we were stuck in this situation because some asshole main site colonist had talked. Why they would do that, I had no idea. Trinh had told Iris that there had been no sign of any kind of alien remnants in or near this installation and, more important, no contamination incidents. So maybe it was jealousy? Except the main colony would have no way to know that after they lost contact. I don't know, not even humans know why humans do things.

I realized I'd just been standing here again when Ratthi, still monitoring my drone video from the shuttle, asked, "What's that other door for? Another section of the hangar?"

So I'd missed that, nice. It was a large hangar door, not unlike the one in the hangar we had entered from on the terraforming side, but less monumental. It was still big enough for a shuttle to fly through. To AdaCol2, I said, *query?*

It showed me a map, pretty limited, of just this part of the installation. This hangar was on the north side, and the corridor led across to another hangar on the east side, so you could fly a shuttle through it to the other side of the installation and were apparently supposed to.

I sent the map to the shuttle's display surface to show the humans. Iris, now on hold with separatist Trinh, said, "I wonder what this planet was like before the terraforming."

"Much worse than it is now, apparently," Ratthi said. "I wonder if the Pre-CR inhabitants also terraformed?"

"Huh," Tarik commented, and started pulling up geographical data.

Nothing was happening, I might as well stand here as anywhere else I guess. I leaned against the hatch, watching the SecUnit and the B-E shuttle through ScoutDrone2's camera. Both continued to do absolutely nothing, too. The wind was getting worse outside the shelter of the hangar. It suddenly made an unpleasant shrieking noise that was so loud threat assessment threw an "unidentified condition" alert. It would have been terrifying (I saw the human in the B-E's shuttle's cockpit make an abrupt motion, probably a flinch), but ART-drone's analysis of the sound said it was just violent air movement. I looped my ambient audio so I could filter the wind noise and turn it down a little. ART-drone said, *Pathfinders report that weather conditions are deteriorating. The possibility that I may lose contact with them is high.* That meant they'd go dormant and set down somewhere, or leave the storm area, depending on how bad it was.

AdaCol2 popped in to confirm that matched with the data from its surface weather stations.

That's great.

Iris's comm alerted as Trinh came back on to start talking again. I shifted them to a backburnered channel. I had run out of proactive things to do. I set some alerts and pulled up an episode of *Sanctuary Moon*. I didn't want to watch anything new without ART-drone, who couldn't split its attention to the same extent as ART-prime.

I had been watching for 2.45 minutes when AdaCol2 said, *query: activity?*

It could tell I was doing something but not what it was. There was no reason not to tell it and I didn't want it to think we were hiding things from it. Up until we actually needed to hide something from it, anyway. I replied, *monitoring media.* I didn't know if it had the kind of visual interpretation function that would let it "see" the show; there are bots that like visual media even though they can't interpret the images like a human would. Even ART had trouble with the emotional parts, things like how the music meant mood and tone changes, unless it was watching through my filter. (In its spare time, now that it has some data for comparison, it's writing an update for itself to fix that.) There are some parts of media that you really need human neural tissue to fully understand, but most higher-level bots could still take in the visual information and follow the story, the same as with a text-only or audio-only file. So I put the episode into our connection for AdaCol2 to access.

It said, *Type: entertainment* and gave me access to a partition loaded with media files.

Oh, hello.

The books and music section alone was huge. I checked the tags on the shows, running them through Thiago's translator module. It was 82 percent fiction, heavy on the pre-adult programming according to the category index. There was *Cruel Romance Personage,* which I had never watched (maybe it was good, I didn't know, I couldn't get past the title). It had been around for at least four decades in corporate standard years, longer even than *Medcenter Argala.* But there were so many others I had never seen or heard of before. Some words in the titles and descriptions weren't matching the versions in the language modules I had loaded. I checked the book and audio sections again and got similar results.

I hadn't pinged ART-drone because it was busy, and this hadn't seemed like a ping-worthy conversation at first, but the additional connection from AdaCol2 must have tripped an alert. ART-drone said, *It's linguistic drift. Many of these are Pre–Corporation Rim media.*

———

Okay, the thing I didn't tell anybody about my right leg getting eaten in the altered memory sequence: I'm 73 percent certain that never happened to me, but there's an 89 percent chance I did see that happen to a human at some point.

Before I hacked my governor module, I did an initial survey contract on a planet that had many types of extremely hostile fauna. (Initial surveys are the ones where you get all the data that gets written up in the documents that all the later surveys are furnished with so they don't get killed. Initials should ideally be bot- and drone-only but some surveys go cheap and use humans, sometimes conscripted humans.) The archive of that survey hadn't been wiped, but I may have deleted portions of it myself. Yeah, so.

Am I making it worse? I think I'm making it worse.

The other thing is, I did not handle the news that I had crashed myself with an altered memory fragment very well. Or at all well.

Can you tell?

"I've fucked everything up," I'd told ART. This was when I was in Medical after my "incident." Mensah and I had called Amena so she wouldn't worry (or at least so she would know that I was still alive, even I know that's important for human children). I told Mensah I wanted to watch media and she had left, and I'd blocked the humans' comm and feed access to the room.

ART had said, *That's nothing new.*

I ignored that because it was just trying to reassure me. If it started being sympathetic it would be terrifying. "Your crew isn't going to want me to do their security anymore."

Why is that?

That question was obviously a trap and I should ignore it. It wasn't as if I could put the answer into words. I was different. It wasn't just the alien contamination. What came out was, "Something in me broke."

My wormhole drive is broken.

"That can be fixed," I said, and knew immediately it was a mistake. ART had been hurt by the Targets' attack in a lot of different ways. It had been invaded by hostiles and taken over by another system, its memory archives altered. It hadn't been able to protect its crew. I knew what that had done to it. Wait, no, I didn't really know. I could only extrapolate based on things that had happened to me. Whatever, it was bad, right? Worse than what happened to me. But I kept talking. "This is happening in my organic nerve tissue."

Yes, which is why the humans diagnosed it so quickly, ART said. *When it happens to them, are they considered disposable?*

"That's what the corporations say." I should just shut myself down right now, I'm losing this conversation so badly.

Of course ART said, *I am not a corporation.*

"Stop, stop it. This isn't you talking, this is just your . . ." Yeah, I'd walked into that one, too.

My certification in advanced trauma protocol? it said. *Of course, that can't possibly be useful in this situation.*

I said, "That's for humans." Yes, conversational trap, snapping shut.

ART said, *This affects the part of you that is human.*

I said, "I'm not talking to you anymore."

My first impulse was that I needed copies of all AdaCol2's new-to-me shows and its text and audio libraries, and that it would want copies of mine in return.

Then I remembered that its humans weren't going to be

staying here, whatever they thought at the moment, cozy in their underground colony, choosing media off their Pre-CR central system's catalog.

The only good thing about the extent to which this situation sucks is that it's at least distracting me from how much I suck at the moment.

Wait, something had happened and I'd missed it.

I pulled our team feed and the camera view from my shuttle drone forward and ran my backburnered channel back to pick up on where Iris's conversation with Trinh had left off. Iris had been trying to negotiate an in-person meeting with the colonists, and Trinh had consulted some others and had indicated they might be amenable. Okay, that didn't sound like everything had gone to shit. I went forward, almost to real time. Oh, here it was.

Trinh had invited the humans to come into the installation for the night, because of the weather and so they could arrange the in-person meeting.

Ugh, I know, it did sound a lot like a trap. None of the humans looked happy, either. On mute with Trinh, Iris said reluctantly, "Barish-Estranza did it, and we need to show the same degree of trust. SecUnit, do you think we should?"

Right. Wind conditions were getting worse, it was getting dark, and the dust in the air was getting much heavier, obscuring visibility for the shuttle and making the pathfinders that were still responding useless. And me, with no working scan functions and drones relying on visual navigation and hardly any range. The shuttle could handle the storm as long as it was grounded and had power, but anything could come up on us. Like a Barish-Estranza SecUnit. The only other option was leaving the blackout zone, which meant giving up on the separatists. I caught up with current time and said, "Yes."

On our private feed connection, ART-drone said, *Thank you.*

I wasn't the only one imagining that other SecUnit walking silently up to our shuttle with our humans sleeping inside.

Trinh sent navigation coordinates, which we didn't need because AdaCol2 had already given me a map. It would put us at the opposite end of the complex from the B-E group, which was a nice gesture but the distance was only about a twenty-minute walk for a strolling human. It was a suite of rooms with two exits and two different approaches which would let me post the drones as sentries.

Bot pilot brought our shuttle around to the other open hangar on the map. It was the one on the east side, not too far from our original position, similar to the one the B-E shuttle was in but about half the size with only two landing platforms. I met the humans and ART-drone at the hatch.

Then AdaCol2 directed me through a sequence of passages and another hatchway into a corridor. All three humans took video as we walked, with ART-drone drifting along as rearguard. The lights and life support were on through this whole section, lighting up the large corridors. The humans had folded their hoods and helmets back, so I did it, too. (The most important part of pretending to be a human is not standing out from other humans.) They all looked sweaty and tired.

There was some decoration here, mainly painting on the corridor walls. There were little signs of habitation, like a box mounted beside a doorway and filled with extra air filters for the old-style enviro suits the colonists used. Weirdly, it felt far less safe than the dark creepy corridors because it was obviously a place that a human could wander into at any moment. I wasn't sure how much AdaCol2 had told its human operators about me and I was hesitant to ask, in case it took that as a sign that I wanted it to tell them about me. Which I really didn't. Not that I thought we could keep me a secret, but the less interaction I had with the colonists, the better.

("I don't know what's wrong with me," I had told Mensah.

"I think you might know," she had said. "You just don't want to talk about it.")

As we walked, Iris said on the team feed, *Trinh and the other leaders have refused requests to let the B-E reps speak to the whole colony, so far. That's a small mercy.*

I had told our humans that once they were inside the installation, not to say anything aloud they didn't want B-E to know about. If there was a SecUnit here, there could be drones, and with the scanning issues I couldn't count on detecting them and/or deploying countermeasures.

Ratthi glanced at Iris. *You think B-E will make some sort of... employment pitch to this group? Ask them if they want to sign themselves over into slavery?*

Tarik answered, *They dress it up nicer than that, but yes, they could try. They have an isolated group here that might be vulnerable to manipulation.*

Iris said, *From talking to Trinh, this group seems independent and not easily convinced about anything. I think the chance they would fall for something like that is low.* She rubbed her brow, wincing a little. *I don't even know if it's in their best interests to try to get them to leave with the others. If we can lock down the colony's charter to the colonists, then they'll have the option to stay here. They could change their minds later, or not, but at least that way it would be up to them.*

Especially if the University makes the deal to put a research group in the drop box station, Ratthi said thoughtfully. *They could come and go as they pleased, as long as everyone avoids the contamination.*

That was one option ART's crew had been discussing: using the drop box station not only as access for the colonists to board orbiting ships and receive cargo, but to get the University to use it as a place for a lab to study the alien contamination site. The colonists would have to agree to it, which, good luck with that, but it would be a source of income for their colony. If the planet didn't fail its alien contamination assessment, if the University won the legal case on the colonists' behalf, if B-E didn't just kidnap them all anyway. It was all up in the air still.

Tarik was not optimistic. *That "if" is carrying a lot of responsibility there.*

Ratthi made a palm-up gesture. *This planet is never going to be completely safe, not until someone discovers why the alien materials cause these reactions.*

The humans all sounded as tired as they looked. Oh, shit. I'd forgotten all about that. On our private channel, I asked ART-drone, *How long since they took a break to sleep?*

ART-drone said, *They were supposed to take short naps in rotation at some point during the flight into the blackout zone, but the overexcitement made that impossible to implement.*

I should have paid more attention. I'd fucked that up, too.

We both fucked that up, ART-drone said. No, it doesn't read my mind, it just knows me really well. *I should have banned refreshment items containing stimulants earlier in the day.*

When we were only two turns away from our destination, AdaCol2 signaled me that a human would be meeting us. I pulled my drones in and made sure my move-like-a-human code was active. *Is this a gesture of trust, do you think?* Ratthi asked on the team feed.

Tarik said, *They met the corporates in person, so maybe they just don't have much of a sense of survival.*

Ratthi said, *I meant on the central system's part, not the colonists'.*

Iris said, *That's an interesting thought. Peri, is that possible?*

Seriously, who the fuck knows?

ART-drone said, *We've talked about these assumptions before, Iris.*

Assumptions? Ratthi asked.

Attributing human characteristics to machine intelligences, ART-drone said. *That this is meant as a gesture of trust may be possible but not likely, and shouldn't be a factor in decision-making.*

Ah, but what do you consider human characteristics? Ratthi said.

Tarik said, *Oh please, don't start with it.*

Why not? Ratthi's voice in the feed was amused.

Tarik is confused by philosophical debate, ART-drone said.

Because it likes to win and it won't shut up until it does, Tarik said.

Tarik has an issue with projecting his emotions onto others, ART-drone said.

People, stop. I'm sorry I asked, Iris said, and added a laughing sigil.

I am so not in the mood to listen to banter. We turned the corner and the colonist was there. There was no feed ID, but AdaCol2 supplied the name Lucia and when I asked it for more info, the gender signifier bb (which didn't translate) and he/him pronouns. (I asked because the humans would bug me for the information; I was as indifferent to human gender as it was possible to be without being unconscious.) Iris said, "Hello. Thank you for inviting us in."

Lucia was small as humans go, about Iris's size, and pale compared to her and Ratthi and Tarik. His dark hair had been shaved into a geometric pattern. His clothes were loose pants and a long flowy shirt, different from what the main site colonists wore. But then this group didn't necessarily need to go out in environmental gear all the time so their clothing didn't need to be practical. "Ah, you're welcome," he said, and looked nervous.

Was it me? Was I looming? It was too late to shove Ratthi in front of me without looking even more weird.

Lucia led the way to the rooms we had been assigned. The walls were dark blue and textured in a way that looked like it would be rough but felt smooth to the touch. The artificial stone floor was a mottled gray with wispy streaks. Lucia showed the humans the attached restroom and how to make the beds fold down out of the walls while Iris tried to initiate three conversations (1. "How strange it must be to meet new people after so long"; 2. "It must have been fascinating to explore this place when it was first found"; 3. "Are you interested in research into Pre–Corporation Rim cultures?") and then gave up. I could tell that even with Ratthi and Tarik trying to help she was starting to look desperate.

Lucia did a little head-tilt goodbye thing and left. Iris stood in the middle of the main room and on the team feed said, *Shit.*

Ratthi plopped down on a bed. *I couldn't tell if he was awkward, afraid, or thought we'd contaminate him if he stayed any longer.*

Tarik leaned in the doorway of the other room. *You think Barish-Estranza has already poisoned the well.*

Iris rubbed her temples, then pulled off her scarf thing and let her hair pouf out. *Yeah. I just hope Trinh wasn't being overly optimistic about the other leaders wanting to meet. We're just going to have to wait for them to make a move.*

The humans had some food from one of the bags they had brought in, and everybody asked me if I was all right so I had to say yes, and Iris went to lie down on one of the beds in the other room. Ratthi and Tarik sat down together on the bed/couch thing in this room. There was a junction area between the two rooms where I had an adequate view of both doorways, so I sat there, ART-drone settled next to me. I had put ScoutDrone1 and 2 on sentry duty, but if B-E tried to sneak a drone or countermeasure in here, visually was the best way to detect it. ART-drone was cycling through shows for us to watch in background, but I was actually really in the mood for a good long stare at a wall.

Ratthi and Tarik were talking about the Thing Going on Between Them, which, ugh. His voice low and worried, Tarik said, "I wasn't leading you on."

"Ah, weren't you?" Ratthi said. He sounded like he wanted to sound unconcerned, but I thought he was actually pissed off. I did a quick voice tone comparison to archived recordings of Ratthi in various agitated discussions and arguments and oh yeah, he was pissed off. He continued, "I don't break up relationships."

(Four planetary days before the mission to fix the routers (I should say *ill-fated mission.* I always want to say *ill-fated mission.* Anyway.) I was on ART pacing the corridor between Medical and the engineering pod while most of the humans were on a rest period. I was watching a show with ART, but I couldn't stand still. (Probably because of—it's not redacted anymore, right, so you know, the thing that happened.) Then my drone that was stationed in the galley area picked up raised human voices. Short duration, but long enough to pick up actual agitation, not excited agitation.

I paused the episode and asked ART, *What's that?*

You don't want to know, it said.

Yes, I do fucking want to know. I pinged Three, who reported that its situation was normal, i.e., boring. (It was in the lab module watching student educational vids.) (I know.) (It didn't get fiction yet, it was a whole big thing.) Though after you hack your governor module, boring was probably a great option. It just hadn't worked for me.

If the humans were having a fight . . . The percentage was low, let's put it that way. There had been some argucussions, but that was all. For a long time I had been stuck with humans who hated each other, hated me, hated where we were, and all for absolutely rational reasons. Now I had gotten used to humans who liked things, and were mostly nice, even to humans they didn't know well, and who could have a disagreement about what to do next without knifing each other and/or poisoning half the mess hall. So it bothered me.

You're upset, ART said. I had already started for the quarters section.

I was supposed to "check in regularly with my emotions," which I pretended was a thing I had any intention of doing. *Yes, this is upsetting,* I told it. *I am upset. Are you happy now?*

Delirious, ART said.

ART's cameras showed nothing in the corridors, and any visual surveillance it had in its crew cabins was locked down where I didn't have access. I found Kaede, standing in the galley and eating food pieces out of a container, with the abstract expression of a human reading in their feed. That was encouraging. I didn't have much experience working with Kaede, but I knew if it was something life-threatening she would have made an effort to intervene or get help and not just turn up the volume on her interface. She saw me and pointed down toward the quarters corridor without otherwise reacting.

Midway down the corridor, Tarik slammed out of a doorway. He stopped abruptly, just short of running into me. He looked startled. I said, "Is there a problem."

"What? No!" He stared at me. I stared back, just above his sightline. He winced and ran a hand through his hair. "Not that kind of problem."

"What kind of problem." There's no question mark there because I didn't really want to know and was hoping he would refuse to tell me.

Ratthi stuck his head out of the doorway. "Oh, hello, SecUnit. I'm sorry we bothered you. We were just having a discussion."

I didn't move. I figured I only had maybe four seconds at most before they broke down and told me anyway.

It was barely two seconds before Tarik said, "I know what it looks like—"

Ratthi interrupted, "It doesn't look like anything." It's odd for Ratthi to interrupt when it's not the excited-yelling kind of conversation when the humans all feel the need to talk at the same time. He turned to me. "It was a sexual discussion."

ART said in our private feed, *I told you that you didn't want to know.*

Oh, for fuck's sake. I had an expression (I couldn't help it) and involuntarily retreated two meters back down the corridor. Ratthi waved both hands, trying to reassure me. "It's all right, it's over."

I left. I passed Kaede still standing in the galley. She said, "I'm not getting involved in that, either.")

Now Tarik said, "Matteo and I aren't together that way."

Tarik and Matteo weren't listed as marital partners in ART's crew records. Seth and Martyn were, and Karime was listed as having marital partners back at the University's primary site. I could share that information with Ratthi, but I don't think he'd appreciate it right now. And at least if Barish-Estranza (a) knew our location and (b) had managed to get a listening device within range, this was a useless conversation to overhear, though I doubted they would be as simultaneously bored and appalled as I was. I looped my audio so I could filter their voices out (except for a keyword search in case one of them screamed for help) and then resumed wall-staring.

The humans managed to get some sleep and eventually ART-drone got me to watch an episode of *World Hoppers*. According to AdaCol2, the weather destabilization would peak in 3.2 hours and then subside. I had fifty-seven unique sources of concern/anxiety, speaking of checking in with my emotions, but nothing I could do anything about right now.

Then our comm activated: it was Trinh, to tell Iris that Barish-Estranza wanted an in-person meeting with one of us.

Make that fifty-eight.

Chapter Seven

THAT WOKE THE HUMANS up fast, and Iris had a polite conversation with Trinh about the fact that we came in here for an in-person meeting with the colonists, not Barish-Estranza who we had and could talk to all the time, whether we wanted to or not.

(The timing was also suspicious, and the humans thought so, too. Basically they had been allowed enough time to get into REM, before being abruptly interrupted, which is not an ideal scenario for most humans and augmented humans.)

This resulted in Trinh admitting that Barish-Estranza had explained it wanted to "relocate" the colonists due to the alien contamination. Trinh didn't reveal any hint as to how she felt about that. Which could be a good sign or a bad sign. ART-drone did a voice analysis that agreed with the humans' emotional assessment; it didn't sound like Trinh trusted Iris, but hopefully that meant she didn't trust the B-E team, either. If she trusted them but not us, we might as well all sit here and watch *Cruel Romance Personage* until the storm was over.

When the comm call ended, ART-drone tapped our private connection and said, *SecUnit*. It didn't need to tell me what it wanted, I could hear the "fucking do something" tone.

Iris had an expression like she had a headache, and Ratthi was up and pacing. Tarik watched Iris, his brow wrinkled in a worried way. I said, *Absolutely not.*

ART-drone added, *As security consultant, SecUnit has the final authority.*

I could tell from Ratthi's guilty face he had planned to volunteer to go. Iris just looked more determined. She said, *We can't refuse this meeting, it might give us intel on how B-E is planning to get these people out of here. Whether they're going to trick them into leaving, or use force.* She did something with her mouth that was not a smile. *Or worse.*

I could have asked what "or worse" meant in this context but there was only so much I could take and I thought I'd hit my limit about, I don't know, four years ago.

Tarik shook his head. *I'm with SecUnit. It may not be a deliberate murder attempt, but they don't want to get you out there to just chat. They're going to try to get something out of you, that's what they think negotiation is.*

Tarik didn't sound like an asshole, though I distrust new humans who agree with me too quickly, especially about security. (I know it doesn't sound rational but I have data and charts to verify my assessment, okay. Good charts, too, not like for the thing with the round hatches.) But he wasn't wrong about the different concepts of negotiation.

It was a problem with humans from Preservation, who thought of negotiation as "let's figure out how to solve this problem in a way everyone is happy or at least okay with," and there was a 96 percent chance that literally nobody else in the Corporation Rim, even across all the different human cultures that the different corporations operated under, thought of it like that. But Iris was also right that we couldn't just sit here and watch *Cruel Romance Personage*. On the team feed, I said, *I'll go. You can tell me what to say.*

There was 3.7 seconds of unflattering silence. Ratthi frowned worriedly at me. *Are you sure, SecUnit?*

Nobody liked the idea, but it turned out Iris was right: as security consultant, it was my call. I just wished I knew what the fuck I was doing.

AdaCol2 picked the spot for the meeting. It was in an adjacent underground development, currently unused, which had apparently been storage for big things that the Pre-CR colony had needed, which weren't there anymore. The Adamantine colonists used it for large building projects and recreational activities, anything that needed extra space. (If they were like other humans, recreational activities probably = throwing balls or sticks at each other really hard.) Because of that, in addition to being able to activate temporary life support inside the room, AdaCol2 had a couple of camera points in there (for collecting video of the recreational activities/ball throwing). It was actually a great spot, because if the B-E negotiator shot me, AdaCol2 would have video evidence of it, and it would hopefully

make them look bad. As long as no one realized I was a
SecUnit.

(Okay, that sounds way worse than I mean it. It would
take a special kind of weapon to shoot me in a way that
would kill me immediately, in a way that a MedSystem
couldn't repair. The SecUnit with B-E Sub-Supervisor
Dellcourt had one, but the two I had seen here had not carried any extra weapons, though both probably had an onboard projectile weapon like Three. Barish-Estranza hadn't
come here expecting to fight SecUnits or CombatBots or
CombatUnits or anything else on that level, so it was unlikely the negotiator (or "negotiator" since we're taking
about a corporation) would walk in armed with something
that was capable of delivering that kind of impact. If it actually turned out to be a trap, I guess they could have sent in
one of their SecUnits, which would have been interesting
because surprise, me too, and I honestly had no idea what
would happen next.)

(I told ART-drone that I suspected the separatist colonists would think both us and Barish-Estranza were pretty
shitty, if the negotiation turned into a big SecUnit fight, re-
gardless of who won.)

(*You'd win,* ART-drone said.)

(Yeah, well, normally, sure. It was basing that on my past
performance stats. Right now I wasn't angry enough for a
good SecUnit fight. Mostly I was just tired.)

The hatch at the corridor's end was big and square, and
had a sign and an old-fashioned feed marker in one of the
languages the main site Adamantine colonists used, read-

able via Thiago's translation module. It was a safety warning about checking the room to make sure it had good atmosphere before entering. There was a little monitoring readout beside it. Not as important for me, as I don't have the same kind of breathing restrictions as a human or augmented human and would have plenty of time to walk out (stroll out, even) if the life support were cut off.

Also, AdaCol2 was in control of the life support, and I kind of trusted it? Or was indifferent enough to what happened that it amounted to trust? (Yeah, I know, that doesn't sound right.)

As AdaCol2 opened the safety seal on the door for me, the overhead lights started to blink on. I sent ScoutDrone2 ahead to station itself up on the ceiling. Its video wove between the bands of shadow until it halted to focus on the entrance at the opposite end of the chamber.

The hatch slid open and a human in a B-E environmental suit stepped through. ART-drone said, *This is unfortunate. It's Supervisor Leonide.*

You're kidding me, I said, and at the same time Iris said, *Who?*

ART-drone pulled my drone camera view and zoomed in for the humans. The chamber had already pressurized and the filtered air had a high quality rating. The approaching figure let the helmet of their suit fold down into a broad collar around their shoulders. I could see ART-drone was right, it was Leonide.

When Supervisor Leonide had first spoken to Arada on the comm and then in person, I thought she looked as perfect as one of the humans who acted in the shows and serials, the ones that were made in the Corporation Rim, where nobody had any skin issues and their hair looked good even if it was messy. She still looked like that, though my drone video picked up subtle cosmetic enhancements to her brown skin, and her dark hair was coiled more to the back of her head now. She was still wearing the metallic chips and gems around her right ear; I didn't even think any were feed interfaces, they were just for show.

Back in the room, on ScoutDrone1's video, Ratthi sat up straight, his eyes going wide. On the feed, he said, *Oh shit.*

Alert to the fact that shit had just gone wrong but not how wrong, Iris asked, *You've met this person before?*

Arada spoke with her, when we first encountered the B-E supply vessel, Ratthi replied. ScoutDrone1 watched him draw a hand down his face. In despair? Probably despair. *An in-person meeting. SecUnit went with her.*

Tarik grimaced. *Maybe she won't recognize it.*

Leonide walked forward confidently, so I did, too. Just without the confidence. The floor was smooth with some kind of sealant over the stone, a little grit from dust grating under my boots. I folded my hood and faceplate back because it would be extremely suspicious at this point if I didn't. I had engaged all my walk/stand-like-a-human code so maybe she wouldn't recognize me. When she had seen me before I was wearing ART's crew uniform, and my hair was flat, and she had been expecting to see a SecUnit. I was in an environmental suit now and Amena had made my hair fluffy (she was trying to make me feel better) and

Leonide expected to see some random human. Risk assessment suggested I had a 63 percent chance of pulling this off.

At 3.4 meters away, Leonide halted. I halted, too. Her forehead crinkled and she said, "I recognize you." Her expression turned incredulous. "You're the SecUnit."

Well, fuck risk assessment.

In the room, the humans made various expressions and gestures but I didn't think they were surprised.

I could stand here and argue with Leonide about whether I was a SecUnit or not but I knew she was smart enough to see it as a stalling tactic. Also, I had nothing to stall for, this was pretty much it. I said, "I'm the SecUnit."

Her gaze flicked around, checking for the human supervisor who should be here. I don't think she thought I was a rogue; if she had, I think she would have called for backup or tried to retreat. Her jaw set in a grim line. "Is this a threat?"

I said, "Have you done something that you feel you should be threatened for?"

Yes, I knew it was a mistake, I knew it instantly, just not instantly enough to shut my fucking mouth. Seriously, I'm coding at least a two-second delay right now. I pulled a secure feed connection with Iris and said, *I fucked it up. What do I do?*

It was a mistake because the tension went out of Leonide's shoulders and neck, her eyes narrowed, and my threat assessment spiked. Because, while she was afraid of a mindless killing machine, she wasn't afraid of sarcasm. And if I was talking and being sarcastic, I wasn't a mindless killing machine.

Her voice dry, Leonide said, "This venture continues to be full of surprises."

Shitty, shitty surprises.

Iris replied, *You did not fuck up. You have a connection with her now, she thinks she knows you. Our goal is to find out what she's going to do to get these people to leave here and hand themselves over to a corporation. Just keep her talking, see what she reveals.*

What Iris meant was that Leonide wouldn't consider me a threat, not in the talking part, so she might let down her guard. Which, what the hell, maybe, anything's possible.

To Leonide, I said, "You could leave." This would be easier if I was angry at her, but she was just a typical corporate supervisor. I could be angry at her, I guess, since she tried to take Arada prisoner. But since the thing that happened I don't think I've had an emotion that wasn't the visual equivalent of a wet blanket crumpled on a floor.

Leonide didn't appear to consider that suggestion seriously. "Why is the Preservation ship here? Has Mihira-Tideland offered Preservation a claim on the resources of this planet?"

I didn't know if she really thought that because I was a SecUnit I would be compelled to answer a question from a human, or if she just wanted to give it a try to make sure it wouldn't be that easy. I said, "Preservation already has all the alien contamination it needs."

Via ScoutDrone1 in our rooms, I was watching Iris tell

the others to not contact me directly now if they had a suggestion; she wanted all communication with me going through her feed connection because she didn't want me distracted. I can't be distracted with multiple inputs like a human (okay, I absolutely can, but I wasn't going to be right now), but I appreciated the gesture.

Leonide's whole affect was skeptical. "Then what are you doing here? Why send a tool to what was supposed to be a negotiation between equal parties?"

So her plan was also to get me to talk so I'd reveal our plans unintentionally. I had a feeling it wasn't going to work out for either of us. Also on *Sanctuary Moon*, the Colony Solicitor will act skeptical when she questions people, because it makes the humans talk more, trying to convince her. I'd seen feed journalists do the same thing in interviews, so it was a real thing, not just for the show. It doesn't work if you'd really rather not be talking at all. I said, "The University has a contract for sustainability evaluation and mapping with the Pan-Rim Licensing Agency and this system was listed as a priority." It was the exact same answer Arada had given her, the last time she had asked that question.

One of Leonide's eyebrows tilted. Arada had done kind of a shit job with that whole negotiation, so maybe a callback to that wasn't my best move. "And why is a SecUnit part of that evaluation? Aren't your kind used only for enforcement and imprisonment and attack?"

Unfair, considering she was exactly the kind of human who had made sure there was a market for us to be doing those things, and was actually here with two of her own SecUnits right now.

I could have said I was a member of the Preservation Survey team on the responder or that I was part of Mensah's staff, but that contradicted the other lies we had already told or implied to Leonide. The only thing that was keeping the stalemate between us and the B-E task group in balance was the University's legitimacy and recognized authority with the other corporates that were signed up with the various licensing agencies the University did evaluations and testing for. If the B-E task group found out we were big liar-heads, then they could claim we were raiders or that they thought we were raiders or whatever, and they might attack us. And they wouldn't win.

ART had run the numbers. Killing a whole bunch of humans and augmented humans, some of whom you had rescued previously, most of whom were just doing jobs they or their families had been indentured into, was not a great solution.

From the rapid eye movement and grimaces going on in our room, the humans were trying to come up with an answer, too, just slower, because of organic brains.

I said, "That's proprietary information." Not great, but all I could come up with before I ran out of time. Then I made it worse by attempting a counterattack. "You have two SecUnits with you. Why did you bring them here?"

She did a sad smile thing with her mouth, like she gave a shit about SecUnits. It seemed out of character. "The only thing that can stop a SecUnit is another SecUnit." Not true, actually, but it was like a rhetorical question, but not a question. Also a logic fallacy, or a logic something, since she hadn't known there was another SecUnit here until just now. Before I could think of something else pointless, she added, "And what will that evaluation be? Is this planet still viable for a colony?"

I was relieved by the change of subject for .05 seconds. In the room, Ratthi mouthed the word *shit*. Tarik was squeezing the bridge of his nose like he was trying to will something to happen. ART-drone hadn't reacted but I could tell it was on a private feed with Iris. On our secure connection, Iris said, *When the report is ready, it will be released to the colonists.* Which was a good call, I had been about to lie and say it was great.

Because it wasn't great, that had been increasingly obvious. Ag-bots were vital to the survival of the colony and they kept turning up infected with the remnant contamination. It was still a possibility that there were other sites on this planet with possible contaminants.

I said, "When the report is ready, it will be released to the colonists."

"Hmm." Leonide folded her arms and looked down, paced a step to the side, like she was deep in thought. It looked performative. (I'd watched enough performances in my shows to know one when I saw one.) Performative like the sad smile. I thought it was meant for me, since her opinion of SecUnits' intelligence could not be that high, let's be real.

(Since the thing happened, I had been relying a lot on

threat assessment, which has a high success rate. But Leonide's body language here was not threatening.)

(I should have paid more attention to Iris's body language, her increasingly worried expression, and the way she had folded her arms tightly. All three humans were alerting to something, some unconventional evidence of hostile behavior, that threat assessment was not set to pick up on.)

(I'm going to have to code a patch for threat assessment.)

Still playacting thoughtful, Leonide said, "Barish-Estranza's evaluation has already concluded that this planet is not viable for continued inhabitation by any kind of colony. It could be a research center for the effects of alien contamination, certainly."

Uh. Yeah, I didn't like that she'd mentioned that. The research center in the drop box station was one of the more feasible ideas for keeping corporates off the planet and giving the colonists more time to decide what they wanted to do. The colonists hadn't been approached about it yet because without more muscle from the University, there was no way to make B-E agree to it.

The humans didn't like it, either. ART-drone said, *Our comm and feeds are always secure. Barish-Estranza could have employed audio surveillance while our teams were in the field.* It was pissed off.

They could just be good guessers, Iris said. *It's a good idea, that's why we thought of it. SecUnit, ask her if that's Barish-Estranza's intention.*

Yeah, I should have thought of that. "Is that Barish-Estranza's intention?"

"I think we both know that isn't the case," Leonide said. "It's been clear to us since arriving here that the University, an institution that researches alien contamination and makes a great deal of profit off its evaluations, is planning to turn this planet into a testing laboratory—"

Uh? "No. The University doesn't own this planet. The colonists own it. That was in the Adamantine charter." Probably not, we had no idea, because we didn't have a copy of that charter. It was in the charter we were in the process of forging, to get the colony listed as an independent entity under the ownership of its inhabitants. Iris passed me an answer on the feed and I said, "The University submits evaluations for multimember licensing agencies for set fees. There's no bonus for finding alien contamination. For any kind of ongoing research here, there would have to be a leasing and licensing agreement with the colonists."

But Leonide was talking over me, ignoring the smart answers Iris was giving me and saying, "Yes, the colonists own this useless, dangerous place. The University wants them to stay here, where they will be trapped, turned into laboratory subjects during the next outbreak. That's the plan, isn't it?"

Threat assessment wasn't spiking, but it should have been. I said, "No, that's not the plan. That's a stupid wrong plan." The only response I could think of was that the evaluation and testing thing was also a cover for the University's side business in freeing lost colonies from permanent indenture and exploitation by predatory corporations. Yeah, even I wasn't stupid enough to say that out loud. "You're the one with the plans."

Iris said grimly, *I don't know where she's going with this.*

Leonide demanded, "Then why were you repairing the routers?"

"Because humans need routers." I mean, obviously. Also to fool Barish-Estranza into thinking we weren't hoping to convince the colonists to evacuate as soon as ART's backup ships arrived. I couldn't say that, either.

In background I was running Leonide's body language through an analysis and it finally threw out some results: indications suggested she was talking to someone else, someone who wasn't me. It wasn't just a cultural bias: I'd watched her talk to Arada, this wasn't the way she normally communicated with other humans. Was she acting this way because I was a SecUnit?

Forcefully, emotion in her voice, she said, "The University needs the routers, to safely record the effects of alien contamination on the trapped population!"

"We don't need routers for that." We could do that with pathfinders, if we— Oh shit. "That's not true. You want to take the population away to indenture them in a mining colony."

"We've offered to transport these people to a viable living situation," she corrected, making her voice do some emotional throbbing thing like she was upset.

Despite the performance, that was contract language.

The Corporation Rim's legal definition of "viable" covers a lot of horrible territory, I had seen it over and over again in surveys and living conditions in work habitats.

I didn't know what to say. The research lab thing was true but it would help put the colonists in charge of the planet, to leave or stay however they wanted.

I had the sick feeling that wasn't going to happen.

Performative emotions, my analysis said. With increasing intensity. Leonide had been performing, all along, but. But I wasn't the audience. Shit. Oh, shit. AdaCol2's cameras were active and she was performing to the one ten meters away, giving it her best angle.

Okay, my brain works much faster than a human's, right? It handles multiple inputs at one time. Especially under emergency conditions, it can be like the humans are moving in slow motion. That was still happening, Leonide was moving in slow motion, but I couldn't fucking do anything about it. It was like a transport was slow-motion falling on me and no matter how fast I was I couldn't get out from under it.

ART-drone had access to my results and had come to the same conclusion I had, at about the same second. It said, *Iris, SecUnit, I just deployed a targeted burst of interference to disrupt the camera feeds.*

Distracted, Iris said, *I'm seeing one view from SecUnit's drone. Is there—*

ART-drone said, *The cameras installed by the colonists for viewing events in this space. They were watching this.*

Iris's mouth opened but she didn't say anything, aloud or on the feed.

Ratthi said, *But they wouldn't believe it. Even the most na-ive corporate would realize Barish-Estranza's motive—*

They aren't corporates, Tarik said. He leaned back on the bed, like he was exhausted. *Their parents and grandparents were corporates.*

That media that AdaCol2 had was either Pre-CR or from forty years ago. Their last contact with a corporation was from forty years ago. The adults who were in charge here now had no real idea what the Corporation Rim was like. There were probably older humans here who could tell them, maybe, depending on what that first contamination event at the main colony had done to the group's general health and life expectancy. But would they listen? Did humans ever fucking listen to anybody—human, augmented human, bot, SecUnit—who was trying to tell them that they were in danger, that their world was about to fall apart?

Leonide had paused, frowning as she listened to her feed. Someone must be telling her the cameras had been cut. She turned and started to walk out.

Okay, now I hated her.

Iris looked furious. *SecUnit, I'm sorry, that was my fault. I should have realized what she was doing. I'm going off feed now, I'm going to try to contact Trinh.*

This was what Barish-Estranza wanted, this was why they wanted a negotiation. The colony leaders wouldn't let them make their pitch so they made it this way. They had told the colonists here that the University meant to turn their colonies into a lab experiment and now everything we did and said was suspect. Trying to convince them to go away on

ART and other University ships? We could be taking them off someplace to experiment on. B-E would offer an employment contract that would get them off the planet and look great right up until they got to the mines, or were dumped on a barely survivable planet to park it for more development later, or were subcontracted out to something worse.

I walked out of the big chamber into the corridor, and just stood there.

I wanted to kill every Barish-Estranza human here. I could do it.

It wouldn't help. They would just send more.

We would have to give up, get on the shuttle, go back to the humans we still might be able to save at the main colony. I didn't want to do that. I wanted to save these fucking humans, who hid underground and watched all this media with their kids and had no idea of the kind of danger they were in.

I told ART-drone, *We have to make them leave. We can't let this happen to them.*

ART-drone said, *We can't force them. It's against the University's charter.* It added, *It is immoral.*

I said, *It would be kinder to kill them.*

It would not. Not unless they were in physical extremity with no hope of medical intervention, and even then, they would have to agree to it. Would it have been kinder to kill you, before you disabled your governor module?

I said, *Yes.*

ART-drone said, *You know I am not kind.*

In the room, Ratthi said, *SecUnit, are you all right?*

I was so furious, and ART-drone was being stupid, and unfair, and right, and I wanted to smash something, mostly myself. *You'd kill them if they tried to hurt your humans.* Even having an emotional collapse, I knew saying that meant I'd lost the argument. Once we'd entered "this increasingly unlikely scenario which is not actually occurring in any way makes me right" territory, it was all over.

Of course, ART-drone said. It poked me in the threat assessment module. *And what is the probability of that, again, exactly?*

It's such an asshole when it knows it's winning. *Fuck off,* I told it. Okay, killing them to save them was the worst idea, I got that, I just wanted to say it, to have some kind of release for the buildup of rage and regret and this . . . despair at the fucking waste of it. And ART-drone had even ruined that for me.

I wouldn't give up, I couldn't. We had to persuade them, I had no idea how. I wish Me 2.0 had survived for a lot of reasons, but specifically right now I wished it had survived because I suspected it would be really good at this. It had persuaded Three to disable its governor module and help it rescue a bunch of humans from the Targets. On Tran-RollinHyfa, I'd offered to hack a CombatUnit's governor module and it had just tried to kill me even harder. On RaviHyral I'd hacked a ComfortUnit and turned it loose, and for all I knew it might be out rampaging around wiping out whole stations, but okay, the chances were against that. I'm just saying, this is not something where you can guarantee a result, with humans or constructs.

Me 2.0 had used my private files, something I had never tried before. But Three had made the decision to read the files and to use my code to disable its governor module. It could have made a different decision after that, and killed all the humans the Targets were holding prisoner, instead of retrieving them to take to ART.

Me 2.0 had persuaded Three to make a decision that was difficult and dangerous for it and that changed Three's whole . . . everything, all of its existence. It had made the difference between survival and death for ART's crew and the other captured humans. How the fuck had it done that? Just with my files?

Dr. Bharadwaj was making a documentary about Sec-Units and constructs, trying to convince humans to not be shitty to us. I had the sections that were completed so far in my archive, but that wasn't what we needed. We needed something to show the humans what Barish-Estranza was like, what it would be like for them, signing a contract that took their lives away. That made them as much prisoners as SecUnits were, but more disposable, and without any bond companies to get mad because you destroyed their property.

I started searching my archive, looking for everything I had on what corporations did to humans. I had a lot of clips from Preservation media, both documentary news and fiction, but I knew it wasn't persuasive by itself, not unless you already knew what the Corporation Rim was like.

I dug deep, looking for my oldest vids. Everything before I'd disabled my governor module had been deleted in memory wipes, so what I had was fairly recent. Again, I had clips of work camps, mining installations, groups of contract workers, excerpts from reports, segments from newsfeeds, the time the worker had almost fallen into the collector, but most of it didn't have context, there was nothing to pull it together. It was just a lot of random data and video.

ART-drone could probably come up with exactly what we needed; there had to be anti-corporate documentaries in ART's archives. But ART-drone couldn't access ART's archives here in the blackout zone. Did we have time to leave and come back? I didn't even know.

This was so fucking frustrating.

I looked again at what Me 2.0 had done, hoping for a clue. It hadn't shown Three just raw data, it had shown it my curated logs. I could probably reproduce what it had done, if I wanted to convince the humans to disable the governor modules they didn't have. Though really, parts of this were sort of relevant . . .

It's the format. No, not really. It's what you do with the format.

(While this was happening, weird shit was going on in my organic parts. Like, a sweat broke out on my organic skin. I would think I was heading for another emotional breakdown, but my performance reliability had started a slow, steady climb. It would have been more frightening, but my performance stats were close to what they looked like when something unexpected but interesting and exciting happened in some really good media. I had taken snapshots of my internal diagnostic processes during my first time through watching *Sanctuary Moon,* and a brief comparison showed this didn't match exactly, but it was very close.)

(In the room, Iris tried to get Trinh to talk to her on the comm while Ratthi and Tarik tried to get me to respond. AdaCol2 tried to ping me. ART-drone told them all to wait.)

I pulled my archive of conversations with Dr. Bharadwaj, how she and Mensah had talked about the fact that they knew how constructs were made and used before they met me, but it wasn't until they interacted directly with me that they had really understood what it meant. That's why Bharadwaj thought it was so important for me to be in the documentary. She said I had to tell my story. Which I knew, already, sort of. It's not just the data that has to be correct, but the way that you present it has to feel right, be right. I'd learned that the hard way, trying to convince humans to not do stupid things and get themselves killed.

It was obvious that media could change emotions, change opinions. Visual, audio, or text media could actually rewrite organic neural processes. Bharadwaj had said that was what I'd done with *Sanctuary Moon*: I'd used it to reconfigure the organic part of my brain. That it could and did have similar effects on humans.

I had to make media to tell a story to these humans. Not my story, and not just me talking. I had to tell their story, the story of what would happen to them if they said yes to Barish-Estranza. It would technically be fiction, but the kind of fiction that was true in all the ways that mattered.

I realized I was sitting in a huddle on the floor, my face buried in my hands. When I looked up, ART-drone said, *What happened? I didn't want to interrupt while your stats indicated a positive development.*

I said, *I had an idea,* and put together a brief synopsis of my conclusion and how I'd gotten there, and sent it into our shared processing space. *We need media, visual, audio—we'll need music—and text.* We had to hit them with everything.

I wasn't sure it would understand; ART doesn't experience media the way I do.

But ART-drone said, *Interesting. We need to consult the humans.*

Chapter Eight

BACK IN OUR ROOMS, I was stitching together a preliminary set of clips and writing the first draft of the narration. I was basing the story around the human contract workers I had met on the way to Milu, like a fictional version of what I knew had probably happened to them after they arrived at the work camp they were being shipped to, framed with a lot of corroborating documentary data.

It was taking up 94 percent of my processing space to do both at once, so ART-drone had to do all the explaining. Tarik looked dubious. Iris, who was still on the comm with Trinh, looked stressed. Ratthi looked blank and preoccupied because I'd already sent him the first draft of the outline to revise. I wanted him to revise the narration, too; I'd read a lot of his reports, he was really good at explaining things and making them interesting. It was obvious that we could have used more humans; I wasn't sure we had enough with us to pull this off.

I'd partitioned a large segment of ART-drone's and my processing space into a general feed work area for the whole group. The documentary clips I'd assembled to start with included the interviews with the corporate labor refugees who had been rescued from the bounty hunters on Preservation Station, segments from Dr. Bharadwaj's documentary where she talked about indenture and slavery in the Corporation Rim, articles, newsfeed segments, clips from incidents I had seen in mining and work colonies. Times when I had been ordered to kill or hurt a worker for violating a rule. Times when humans had killed or hurt each other because they just couldn't stand it anymore.

But it had to be personal to work, so the story I was making up/extrapolating from data was the most important part. I was using the recordings of my conversations with and interactions between the contract laborers on the ship who had thought I was an augmented human security consultant. The clips would show their personalities, show what kind of humans they were (mostly good, trapped in a terrible situation, knowing their future sucked but trying to pretend it didn't) to make it personal, to make other humans care about them the way I cared about the fictional humans in my shows.

It was hard. I never liked watching helpless humans because I knew what happened to them, now I was having to not just watch it but create a story out of it and explain why and how it was happening.

I needed human opinions of the story and the documentary clips to make sure I was emphasizing the right things, and for them to make suggestions and to add any clips or research from their private feed storage. We had to get that done fast so ART-drone could put in the subtitles and citations. We also needed to start mixing the music and I was going to need a lot of human input for that.

SecUnit, Ratthi said in the work feed, *I've been working on a history of corporate colony abandonment and I have a lot of sound clips and transcripts saved in my archive. I think we can use some of it.*

This wasn't a surprise; I knew that was one of Ratthi's side research topics. The humans who lived in the Preservation system now originally came from an abandoned colony, and would have all starved to death except for an almost decommissioned colony transport with a crew who had decided to rescue everybody or die trying.

Die trying. It's not the worst thing that could happen.

I sent him an acknowledgment and a quick guide to our input tagging system.

Then he sent me a note back: *So, you may not know this, but I read your letter to Dr. Mensah, the one you sent when you left Port FreeCommerce. I think you're absolutely the right person to write this.*

I can't handle that right now so I'm just going to archive it for later.

Some of the better newsfeed material I was turning up in my onboard archive search came as text descriptions of events and transcripts. ART-drone could translate them, turn them into dramatic readings, and run the text on a black background while the audio played. I know it's not the most original technique, but it's fucking effective. Also it would save a lot of time and our graphics-building queue was already too long with all the research data ART-drone had just dumped on me from its onboard archive.

ART-drone was also helping me organize our growing list of persuasive, emotional scenes from the fictional and nonfictional media we had in our archives. These were clips that weren't relevant to the subject, but that we needed to compare and analyze to see how they did what they did. I know, this was why we needed the humans. Just copying the technical aspects was not going to get us what we needed, but it sort of helped to have them for comparison. Inspiration? Maybe it was inspiration. Anyway, looking at them made me feel weirdly encouraged.

ART-drone had also put up a list of guidelines, including: *Think of this as a persuasive piece, like a presentation seeking funding for a research proposal. It does not have to compete with the commercial media composed by humans who know what they are doing.*

Tarik, with an air of *they can't be serious,* asked ART-drone, "How many human voices can you do?"

Since Barish-Estranza wasn't pretending to play fair anymore, ART-drone had set up a listening device countermeasure around our area so the humans could relax and communicate without worrying about being recorded. My drones hadn't detected any incursions; it was possibly an indication that B-E didn't see us as any kind of a threat. Which, fine, do that, do whatever, B-E could go set themselves on fire for all I cared.

ART-drone said, *Functionally, not an infinite amount, but as many as could be realistically needed.*

"Any voices?" Tarik persisted.

"Of course any voices," ART-drone said, aloud, in Seth's voice.

"Holy shitting deity," Tarik said.

I will be taking no more questions because our time is limited, ART-drone told him. *You will be in charge of music since you have the most experience of those here.*

Wide-eyed, Tarik put up his hands not unlike the way he had when he said he didn't want to fight me. "I played traditional oud and bouzouki and danced a little when I was in school, I certainly don't—"

Iris put the comm on mute, pointed emphatically at us, and said, "You need to interview him!" Then unmuted the comm again.

Interview him? Oh. Because Tarik had been in a corporate death squad. Maybe we could just steal the music from another show; it wasn't like the colonists would recognize it.

Ratthi came out of his feed trance and said, "I'll do it, but I have no idea what to ask."

"Ah. That's— Uh." Tarik was thinking rapidly. ART-drone's threat to put him in charge of the music had worked. "I think I know what we're going for. We can figure it out together."

Ratthi sent me an updated outline and I got to work assembling clips for ART-drone to start editing. The narration was going to be the hardest part. I started paging through the inspiration clips again. ART-drone caught me at it and said, *Don't worry about being persuasive. Just tell the story. We still have time for the humans to give their input.*

You can't slam down a comm, but Iris pulled the comm interface off her ear and made an aborted gesture like she wanted to throw it against a wall. (Been there, threw my whole body against a wall once.) My drones watched her set her jaw, frustration giving way to determination. She stomped over and dropped down onto the bed next to Ratthi. "The colonists agreed to watch our presentation, but they insist we leave by morning, when the weather is supposed to let up. That's five hours. Where's this music you need someone to work on?"

———

It took us four hours and twenty-seven minutes. We didn't let Iris work on the music, because she was better at organizing and editing, and she had a huge supply of relevant text stored in her archive augment. She took over evaluating clips when Ratthi and Tarik were doing the interview. Also, she ended up reading the narration, though she didn't think we should use her voice. ("I think they're as sick of listening to me as I am of talking to them," she told us.) So ART-drone converted her voice into Dr. Bharadwaj's, which it had a good sample of from her documentary segments. ("This is absolutely not ethical, it's the opposite of ethical and is explicitly against Preservation law, but I think she'll forgive us under these specific circumstances," Ratthi said.)

By the time we finished, we didn't have time for the humans to watch the whole thing through, because it was 47.23 minutes total. So we divided it up into three separate segments and each watched one simultaneously. ART-drone

System Collapse

processed the tweaks and corrections, and then we had
almost no time left.

But when Iris called Trinh and asked to deliver it, someone else answered. They said only Trinh could speak to us
and she was "unavailable until later."

Iris closed the call very politely, and then sat there on
the bunk squeezing her fists while we stared at her. She said
finally, "Trinh didn't trust me, but she didn't trust Barish-
Estranza, either. If she's not part of the discussion anymore,
that's not good."

I was sweating out of my organic parts again, we were
so close. There had to be something we could do. Then
Iris said, very quietly, "I will not give up." She looked up at
ART-drone. "Peri, how do we make them watch it?"

I don't think force will be necessary, ART-drone said, and
displayed the media directory AdaCol2 had shown us. *I
think we just need to make it available.*

I should have thought of that, but after all that processing,
my performance reliability was down. I needed a restart like
nobody's business. I called AdaCol2 and said, *query: file upload permissions?*

I didn't know if AdaCol2 knew or understood what we
had been doing. It had a connection to our feed but it would
have had to get past ART-drone's walls to see how high our
activity levels had been. It said, *query: file type?*

I answered: *video tag: entertainment, educational.* It was
really important that the entertainment tag go in first.

AdaCol2: *query?* It was asking me why.

343

We want your humans to see it, I said. *Information, assistance.*

It gave me an address and I sent the upload. ART-drone had a real-time view of the media list, but it hadn't updated yet. *It's reviewing it,* I told ART-drone.

It's far more sophisticated than it's pretending to be, ART-drone said.

"But will they watch it in time?" Ratthi asked. He was rubbing his eyes; all three humans had been tired before but now they were beyond exhausted, hyped up on stimulants and every food item we had with simple carbohydrates in it.

"It's new," Tarik said, waving his arms. "How long has it been since they got something new to watch?"

"And it's good, it's really good." Iris paced. I wanted to think she wasn't just trying to convince herself. "This was a good idea, SecUnit. Even if . . . It'll be useful to a lot of people."

Then AdaCol2 said, *query: accuracy.*

ART-drone had already bundled our annotated data and was shoving it at me. That was something the humans had come up with that I wouldn't have thought of. We had our emotionally engaging story, and a presentation of the facts behind it with references, but we also had all the interviews, transcripts, videos, academic papers, newsfeed articles, etc., we had used to make it, like the data package part of a survey report. Including the original, longer version of Tarik's interview done by Ratthi, though in the finished product we had given it the backdrop of ART's crew lounge, which ART-drone thought was aesthetically better than the bare blue wall of this room, and we used the technique of cutting out Ratthi's voice, so it was just Tarik giving the answers that complemented that section of the story.

AdaCol2 said, *File uploaded* just as it appeared in the colonists' download menu. It was tagged *entertainment* and *educational* and most important, *new,* with a note that it was a gift from the visitors from the University of Mihira and New Tideland. I wished AdaCol2 hadn't put that last part in. I didn't think any visitors were super popular in this underground installation at the moment, but we, the uncaring academics who wanted to turn them all into lab experiments, were definitely coming in last. "It's uploaded," I said.

Iris stopped pacing and all three humans stared at me. I stared at them with my drones until ART-drone said, *Even if they download it immediately, it will take approximately forty-eight minutes for a human to view it.*

"Right, of course." Iris pressed her hands to her face. "We should probably try to get some rest."

"Or," Ratthi said, perking up, "we could watch the whole thing together, the way they'll be watching it."

Tarik groaned. "You think that will be less stressful?"

At least no one had said *if they watch it.* Except I thought it, so. Whatever, I need to watch *Sanctuary Moon* now.

———————

I couldn't sit on the entertainment menu and watch the download counter because ART-drone cut off all our access to it until at least forty-eight minutes were up. The humans thought watching our video was a good idea and not a painful exercise in self-flagellation, but what do I know. Iris and Ratthi sprawled on the bunk while Tarik sat on the floor with his legs stretched out. ART-drone put up a display surface in front of them. With the editing, I'd already seen the video about 273 times so far, so I sat on the other bunk and watched *Sanctuary Moon*.

It was comforting, right, but I was really in the mood for something new. I hadn't wanted to watch anything new since my stupid memory incident. ART had been keeping a list. When we got back, I'd have to let it pick the next show to make up for me being useless. I had new downloads off AdaCol2's archive, but the humans were starting to distract me by not doing anything distracting.

I'd watched a lot of humans watch or read all kinds of media, so I knew that when they didn't talk and didn't move much except to eat crunchy things out of bags, it was a good sign. But then these humans had seen the Corporation Rim for themselves, they weren't at all like the ones we were trying to convince.

And I was having a moment. The humans and ART-drone had tried so hard to make my stupid idea work. Tarik had clearly not wanted to talk about his past any more than I wanted to talk about my emotions, but he had done it anyway, because it might help. And Ratthi had been supportive and asked good questions no matter how pissed off he was with Tarik about the sex thing. Iris had trusted me to know what I was doing, despite all the evidence to the contrary that I had already given her. ART-drone had created graphics and voices and used our shared media storage to give itself a crash module in dramatic documentary production.

I gained interesting insights, ART-drone said. *You should stop worrying.*

Yeah, I'll just code a patch to stop feeling anxiety, wow, why didn't I think of that earlier. (That was sarcasm, I have too much organic neural tissue for that to work.) (Of course I've already tried it.)

The video finished. We had the list of sources appended, but hadn't done credits, just a statement that it was a joint production of the University of Mihira and New Tideland and the Preservation Independent System Survey Auxiliary Team. (Credits listing three humans, a SecUnit, two intel drones, and a drone iteration of a transport just looked weird.) Iris sighed and said, "That was excellent, SecUnit."

Ratthi said, "If they don't like it, fuck them."

Tarik snorted a crunchy thing and had to be pounded on the back by Iris. "I'm serious," Ratthi said, doing an exasperated hand-wave thing. "If they can't recognize the truth in an attempt to save their lives, I don't know what else to do."

Tarik drank from a container and croaked, "So how are we doing? Come on, Peri, I know you're keeping track."

ART-drone said, *Three hundred and sixty-two downloads, two hundred and eighty-seven views still in progress, seventy-five views completed within the past 2.3 minutes. And counting.*

We were all staring at each other again: the humans, my drones, ART-drone's unresponsive carapace. It gave me access to AdaCol2's media menu again so I could check for myself. It wasn't lying to make us feel better. Two more completed views popped up while I watched.

"What does that mean?" Tarik was obviously trying not to be too hopeful. "How many people are here?"

"Four hundred and twenty-one." Ratthi did look hopeful. "Almost everyone downloaded it. Except the young children. And some people would watch in groups."

ART-drone picked up a static message to Iris's comm. She started to accept, and ART-drone stopped her before she got too excited. It wasn't from the colonists. *It's Supervisor Leonide,* ART-drone said.

Iris's expectant look turned disgruntled. She accepted the message and frowned as she listened to it. "Barish-Estranza wants to meet again. They're leaving, apparently."

The colonists had told us to leave by morning; they must have told Barish-Estranza, too. That had to be a good sign? I checked AdaCol2's updated weather report and the disturbance was starting to die down, though later than predicted. I didn't know whether we should leave or not, or pretend to leave and hang out somewhere nearby. Maybe the colonists just needed time to think and talk it over. Ugh, having hope that it might have worked was almost worse than knowing for sure it hadn't. (I know, I'm never satisfied.)

Iris had made up her mind. "SecUnit and I will go talk to them. Tarik, you and Ratthi and Peri go get the shuttle ready."

ART-drone said, *Iris.*

348

Iris shook her head. "We've done our best with the col-onists. I've told them how they can contact us. But I want to know what else Leonide has to say. At best, maybe it'll give us some idea of what they might try next, or if they're writing these people off as a loss."

It wasn't a bad plan, as plans go. I could still object and say I'd go alone, like before. Iris had already said as security consultant that kind of thing was my decision. But consid-ering how that had worked out, I didn't want to get set up by Leonide to say something stupid again, not when we might be close to succeeding.

Chapter Nine

THE MEETING PLACE WAS a different room, still spacious but smaller, only a third the size of the ball-throwing space. It was obviously meant more for humans to gather in and it looked like the colonists used it that way. The silver-gray side walls were slanted in to meet a curved ceiling with little blue tiles, and there was decorative trim framing the two big hatchways, one on either end. Padded chairs and curved benches were pushed back against the walls, with bright patterned fabrics that matched the colors in the room but must have been added later by the colonists because I don't think Pre-CR furniture would have survived that long, at least not the soft parts. (Humans of every era are hard on their stuff.) The other obvious difference was that this room didn't have any cameras.

As Iris and I walked in, I put ScoutDrone1 on the ceiling where it slipped in between two tiles and had ScoutDrone2 sit on my shoulder where it looked like part of the enviro suit. I started a video feed and offered it to AdaCol2. The earlier conversation had been broadcast, so why not. It picked up the channel and an instant later a new live viewing feed appeared on its media menu.

I showed Iris what I'd done and she lifted her brows in a way that suggested she approved.

(ART-drone was in the small hangar with Ratthi and Tarik. The shuttle was ready to lift off and they had the hatch open, pacing around outside it waiting. Someone, probably AdaCol2, had turned on the hangar's lights for them, since the outside light was still so dim. Past the open hangar entrance the world was dark gray, heavy dust swirling in the harsh wind.)

Then the B-E group walked in. Leonide, with three other humans. Feed IDs said Adelsen, Beatrix, and Huang. Leonide stopped three long steps away from us, the rest of the group spread out behind her. Iris smiled tightly and said, "You wanted to see us."

Leonide tilted her head thoughtfully, then she smiled. "You're casting this."

Iris was still smiling, but it was a fuck-you smile. She said, "We just thought the colonists might want a record of this meeting, too."

"You can attach it to your sales pitch," Leonide said, casual and amused, as if there was nothing riding on this, as if the colonists' lives didn't depend on it. "Good work with that, by the way."

All the corporate assholishness aside, I thought this might be a good sign. Leonide wasn't conceding, but it seemed like she was regrouping. Which should give us time to get out of the blackout zone and communicate with the rest of the humans and ART-prime, so we could strategize a

351

next move that hopefully someone else would be in charge of. (Because I didn't know about the humans and ART-drone, but I was tapped out. My organic neural tissue hurt and I really needed a shutdown and restart.)

Threat assessment pinged. Ugh, not now.

I checked its report and ugh, yes now. It had caught abnormalities in body language in two, no, all three of Leonide's coworkers. Mostly changes in muscle tension out of sync to the conversation and reactions of Iris and Leonide. Tension for humans was normal in this situation, but this wasn't tracking. Were they nervous of me, since by this point they all had to know I was a SecUnit? But they worked with SecUnits, and all they knew was that I was a weird SecUnit; they had no idea I was a rogue. I hope they had no idea I was a rogue.

There had been no stipulations about coming unarmed (if there had been, Iris wouldn't have been able to bring me and we wouldn't be having the meeting at all), so I still had the projectile weapon clamped to my harness. The B-E humans were wearing sidearms, all projectile weapons, but small ones, meant to threaten other humans and annoy the crap out of SecUnits and large fauna.

I'd missed Leonide's anomaly until it was too late; I wasn't going to let this go. I sent ART-drone an alert.

(I planned to query my archive later about a situation where an anomaly did mean something good, but I wouldn't get excited about the potential results.)

Iris was saying, "The documentary explained the reality of the situation. I think that's the opposite of a sales pitch."

If I reacted to a false alarm, it would be a major fuckup on my part. We would look like the aggressors, just the way Leonide had tried to depict us. So it could be a trap, a trick to get me/us to react . . . Yeah, that's really subtle, isn't it. It's not that Leonide wasn't subtle, but I couldn't see how she could possibly get the information she would need to give my threat assessment a false positive. Or how she would even know I had a threat assessment module to begin with. Corporates may use SecUnits, but very few clients have a clue how we actually work.

(At the landing area, ART-drone reviewed my analysis of the anomaly and said, *Ratthi, Tarik, get in the shuttle.*

Tarik turned to face the hatchway that led back into the installation, frowning. Ratthi, who had been making notes in his feed, said, "What?")

Leonide made a graceful shrug. "Ah, well. These colonists have asked us to leave." If she was planning an ambush, she was really good at hiding her intention, even to muscle tension and pupil dilation. She was relaxed, amused. It wasn't like I hadn't encountered humans before who could fool my threat assessment, and something about this scenario was still pinging all the "shit is going down" stats. "We have so many colonists at the original site to speak to."

Iris's jaw did something like she was thinking about biting someone, but her smile stayed the same. "We'll see you there."

ScoutDrone2 picked up motion from Adelsen's arm and all observable data said it was a contraction indicating that he was about to reach for his sidearm. Same problem: my projectile weapon would blow a large hole through him. But I could disable him with the energy weapon in my left arm (it had the best angle, right would have taken another tenth of a second), but if I was wrong, he'd be, you know, shot, and we'd look like the overreactive assholes. So I lunged instead.

(If I was wrong, I'd still look like an overreactive asshole, but at least nobody would be shot.)

But I wasn't the asshole. As my arm went around Iris, Adelsen gripped and halfway drew his sidearm. And that was the moment I realized my assumption about the trajectory was wrong. He wasn't going to aim at Iris.

The margin of error was not small, but better safe than sorry or whatever. As I swung Iris around and threw both of us into the air, I gave Leonide a light tap in the shoulder with my right boot. It would push her into a sideways stumble.

As we hit the ground, I twisted to take the landing on my side to keep from crushing Iris. As I rolled with her to get upright again, I checked ScoutDrone1's video. I was right; Adelsen had fired at Leonide.

Because my tap had shifted her position, the projectile had clipped Leonide's shoulder instead of hitting her in the middle of her back. She cried out in shock. I should have shoved harder so the shot would have missed her entirely, though she would have hit the paved floor and maybe broken some important arm and shoulder parts. But I hadn't really believed she was the target, despite what my data was saying. (Note to self: always listen to the data.)

I was on my feet with Iris. She gripped the sleeve of my environmental suit and she'd lost her scarf. She seemed really surprised. Leonide pressed a hand to her wounded shoulder, also really surprised. Adelsen and Beatrix and Huang (who were now displaying weapons but not pointing them at Iris or me yet) were also, you guessed it, really surprised. I had a very limited number of seconds before the humans recovered from the surprise and the shooting restarted.

Humans are horrible with weapons, in every sense of the word. I lifted Iris's hand off my sleeve because I was planning to take out all three hostiles. (Energy pulse from my left arm to Adelsen's left shoulder, then right arm to Beatrix's right shoulder and Huang's forearm, all disabling hits.) But then ScoutDrone2 alerted. Behind me the hatch was opening, the hatch we needed to use to take the quickest route to the shuttle.

And the Barish-Estranza SecUnit ran in.

(ART-drone said, *Ratthi, get in the fucking shuttle. Tarik, if you have to be stupid, don't run toward the hostile SecUnit.*

Running through the hatch back into the installation, Tarik sent back, *Then give me the motherless map!*)

I swung Iris away from me and pushed her toward the hatch in the opposite wall. It went deeper into the installation, but it wasn't the colonists we needed to worry about right now. I told her, "Run." *ART, get Iris out.*

Leonide yelled out, "Unit, stop! Command code—"

It didn't stop. Because when you want to murder your supervisor (it's not uncommon) one of the first things you do is revoke her security codes.

This changed the whole strategic whatever of our situation from "somewhat tricky" to "oh shit." If they were just trying to take out Leonide, that would be one thing. (I had mixed feelings about it, frankly.) (I wouldn't kill her myself unless I had to, to protect another human from her, but I wouldn't have to watch a lot of *Sanctuary Moon* episodes to cope with it if it happened in front of me, let's put it that way.) But Iris was a witness and they had their SecUnit ready to take me out, so obviously my humans were next on the list.

This also meant Barish-Estranza, or at least this faction of this task group, planned to just take the colonists, whether they signed the contract or not. Indentured employees can't testify against the corporation that holds their contract. (I hadn't known that; it was in the documentary, we'd gotten it from Iris's research archive.) There were no statistics on how common forcible indenture was, but it did happen a lot, apparently. (That was also in the documentary.)

The SecUnit was lifting one arm, pointing it toward me. Three had an onboard projectile weapon, and this one's armor configuration looked similar. The B-E hostiles were starting to lift their weapons. I had a SecUnit and three armed humans in play and I needed to not have them anymore.

With the SecUnit coming at me I needed my projectile weapon but I couldn't use it on the humans. (Even at this point, kill shots would kick this up to a whole other level of "oh shit." The plan was still to keep anybody from ending up dead.) I needed the drones too much and they couldn't get past the SecUnit's armor anyway. But I couldn't leave Iris vulnerable during her retreat.

So I pivoted and shot Adelsen with my left arm, then used my right for two quick pulses to Huang and Beatrix. (I went for disabling shots, aiming for the muscley part in the side they were using to hold their weapons. It caused more physical damage than my original plan, but was just as survivable. If Mensah or Karime or anyone else could salvage this situation, they would have to be like space wizards from one of my shows, but I had to give them the chance. If it was going to be a bloodbath, it couldn't be my bloodbath.)

Before I could pivot again, I took the SecUnit's projectile in my upper right back which, yeah, I had been expecting. I tuned down my pain sensors because it hurt, but I finished the pivot in time to pull my projectile weapon off my back—

That fucker had shot me through my projectile weapon, right through the casing, smashing the trigger mechanism.

Yeah, very clever, and you're going to fucking regret it.

I dropped my broken weapon and flung myself at the Sec-Unit. I slammed into it, wrapped myself around its helmet and upper body, and threw us both down.

I used every bit of force I had and we hit the artificial stone floor hard. It wasn't expecting to suddenly have me wrapped around its face and hadn't been able to brace itself. Because this is not how SecUnits fight. (We shoot at each other and take hits until we can't anymore.) But it was how this SecUnit fights when it doesn't have armor, so get used to it, asshole.

Unlike suits that have life-support functions for humans, there aren't a lot of ways to get into armor from the outside. On one channel I was running my list of control codes on the off chance I had one that would let me take over the armor, but I knew that was unlikely. (SecUnit armor isn't usually vulnerable to hacking because it's so cheap and doesn't have a lot of higher-level functions. I was only giving it a shot because the armor looked newer and fancier than Three's.) I was also trying the more direct solution, trying to fire my energy weapon directly into the weakest junction in its neck, but it had grabbed my wrist and was holding me away from my target.

ART-drone was (1) yelling at Iris on their private channel; (2) lifting the shuttle off the landing pad with Ratthi in it while Ratthi was yelling at it; (3) guiding Tarik through the installation. Tarik had just run into a confused and understandably upset group of colonists who had been watching the live feed, and he was talking to them via (4) ART-drone's translation. And (5) ART-drone had managed to pull an unencrypted B-E comm transmission originating from the B-E shuttle and—oh shit they just deployed the second SecUnit.

Then the SecUnit under me froze in a way that meant an order from a human had triggered the governor module. I checked ScoutDrone2's channel and ran the video back a few seconds.

Adelsen was on his knees, where he had collapsed after

I shot him. Iris stood behind him, gripping his shoulder, pointing his weapon at his head. She had just said, "Tell it to stop or I'll blow his head off." The other two humans were half sprawled on the ground. Watching her warily, Huang put down the weapon she had managed to still lift despite her wound. (Note to self: next time two disabling shots per hostile.)

On the team feed, ART-drone said, *Iris, I am both proud of you and greatly disappointed.*

She was breathing hard. *Thanks, Peri.*

Leonide was still on her feet, blood dripping from the tear in the shoulder of her environmental suit. She had her weapon out, though was carefully not pointing it anywhere near Iris. She collected the dropped weapons from the other two humans and said, "They've called the second SecUnit." Her voice sounded strained, as if her throat was dry.

ART-drone said, *Confirmed, ETA 2.32 minutes.* It put a partial map in our team feed, with a moving dot. The map was partial because AdaCol2 hadn't given us a complete map yet and I was really fucking hoping it had done the same to Barish-Estranza.

I climbed off the B-E unit. Its helmet turned to track me. It didn't have any drones, which was unfortunate. I really wanted more drones. "Iris, tell Adelsen to say, 'Manual operation engage: shutdown delay restart' and to add his command initiate. Leonide can tell us if he uses the wrong code."

"I will, if you take me with you," Leonide said. She was still calm, though the pinched look on her face said she did not actually feel great right now.

359

Grimly determined, Iris said, "We'll take you." She gave Adelsen a shake. "Say it."

Sweating and trembling, he ignored her, saying to Leonide, "You brought this on yourself. You knew what would happen to us if we go back without this contract. You don't need a promotion, you don't care—"

Iris looked murderous and Leonide impatient. ART-drone had started a running countdown to Hostile!Sec-Unit o'clock in our feed, which I absolutely didn't need. I said, "Adelsen. Say it or I'll tear your head off."

He stopped abruptly and looked up at Iris. She grated out, "Say. It."

He said it. Leonide gave me a tight nod to confirm it was the correct code. The SecUnit's body went limp as it collapsed onto the floor. I waited the extra three seconds I couldn't spare to make sure it wasn't faking (the shutdown makes a distinctive sound, if you're close enough and have augmented hearing), then I started toward the hatch that led to our original escape route.

Iris dropped Adelsen and followed me. Leonide lifted her weapon, but not toward Iris. Striding past, Iris told her, "If you shoot them you can't come with us. And we're still casting this to the colonists." Because of course this was a perfect chance for Leonide to eliminate her dissatisfied co-workers and blame us. And no, we were recording, but not still broadcasting to the colony's channel. (There weren't a lot of routes we could take to the shuttle, but I didn't want to make it extra easy by giving everyone who wanted to look for it a live video of our progress.)

Leonide looked sour like she had really wanted to shoot them, but lowered the weapon and followed Iris.

I took point with ScoutDrone1 as rearguard. Iris said, *Tarik, try to warn the colonists that Barish-Estranza is armed and has attacked us. Tell them not to intervene, we don't want them hurt.*

I already have, Tarik said. *They said they were trying some kind of defensive measure, but it didn't work. I didn't get what it was, something about the power supply.*

Iris was relieved and dubious. *They're listening to you?*

Yeah, they said they recognized me from the video.

Iris made a combination laugh-groan noise.

You know, if Barish-Estranza had thought of the idea of a persuasive documentary first, we would have been really fucked. I mean, ours was all based on documented research and events we had actually witnessed, and even with the extrapolation about what could have happened to the contract workers I had met, it was as true as we could make it. But Barish-Estranza could have lied and faked their documentation and come up with a story about how great indenture was, and that would have been it.

Tarik should meet us in the next seven minutes if he could stop talking to other humans and get moving. At least he would come in handy because Leonide was stumbling a little and if she collapsed she was too big for Iris to carry, and I needed my arms free.

Our shuttle was still in the hangar, ART-drone keeping it in a hover position about four meters off the ground. It had also called in pathfinders for a defensive perimeter to protect the shuttle once it left the hangar, but with the lingering storm it was taking the pathfinders longer to get here. I wanted the shuttle in the air; ART-drone (and Ratthi, though he couldn't do anything at the moment but pace the shuttle cabin in frustration) wouldn't leave without us. ART-drone had run a risk assessment showing it was just as dangerous for the shuttle to leave the hangar and return to pick us up as it was to hover there and wait for us to arrive and board inside the hangar. I thought it might be faking its results, but this really wasn't the time to have that argument.

The big bright corridor made me jumpy; I had ART's projected map but that wasn't real intel, just estimates based on the earlier marked positions of HostileSecUnit2 and the potentially armed B-E humans moving either from their quarters or their shuttle hangar, and that sucked. I wanted cameras, I wanted real-time intel. The openness of the corridor felt like anything could come at us from any direction, even though we were reasonably certain that our escape route was currently clear. (I would never admit I was glad Tarik had run in here; at least I had recent good intel and mapping from his current position.) I needed more drones, I needed more eyes.

I tapped AdaCol2 and said, *query: assistance.*

ART-drone caught it when Leonide tried to access her feed and failed, and passed the info to the team feed. Iris asked her, "Did they cut your comm, too?"

"Yes." Leonide's face was frustrated and tight, like she was holding in emotion. Like it was weird to be upset when your coworkers shot you. Even before I hacked my governor module, I was upset when my coworkers shot me. I wasn't surprised, but I was upset. She added, "I was trying to warn my assistant." The glance she threw at Iris was calculating. (That didn't mean much, I was pretty sure everything Leonide did was calculating.) "If I could get a message out, we might be able to resolve this."

Really, could we? Do you think? ART-drone said. It had created a new channel to include her: teamFeed+Leonide.

"Peri," Iris said in her "not now" voice. "As soon as we get out of the blackout zone, I'm open to discussing resolutions."

No answer from AdaCol2. I sent, *query: assistance* again.

Behind me, Iris said, "SecUnit, were you hit?" She must have noticed the hole in the back of my environmental suit.

"No," I lied. *Query: assistance.*

Yes, it was hit, ART-drone told her. *But it has the situation under control.*

Even when you're a bot, there's things you say because you believe them and things you say to keep the humans going in the right direction.

On the feed, Tarik said, *Any possibility we can get the other SecUnit to shut down? Or will they change the command code immediately?*

No, I sent. *Shutting down HostileSecUnit1 with a manual command will generate a warning to any other SecUnits on their feed, to whatever system is acting as their security hub and the human supervisor. HostileSecUnit2 will advise a command rollover.* I mean, maybe they wouldn't do it? But the B-E humans had been smart enough to lock Leonide out of access to the SecUnits before trying to kill her, so they had to be smart enough to do the same to Adelsen and anyone else we'd had access to. It was why it wasn't worth taking a hostage. Also I hate the whole hostage thing, there's just too many ways around it.

ART-drone said, *And without access to Barish-Estranza's feed and comm, the command shutdown attempt—which currently has a 96 percent chance of failure due to standard security protocols involving SecUnits—would have to be done in person. Ideally, we wish to avoid that.*

AdaCol2 hadn't answered me. It was possibly reevaluating who it wanted to be friends with. Yeah, right back at you, AdaCol2.

I still didn't know if the combo of me and ART-drone could hack a central system. We still had no idea of its capabilities. But getting into a code fight with what was basically an unknown right this second while hostiles were closing in on us and our escape window was depressingly narrow was not a good idea.

We came to a junction and I took the right turn into a curving corridor. Iris kept up easily, but Leonide's breathing was getting shaky. We were close, though. Tarik was two turns ahead and in two minutes and thirty-four seconds we should be at our hangar.

Then ART-drone said, *We have a problem* at the same time Ratthi said, *Everyone, the pathfinders are reporting that there's another shuttle coming in. You think it's one of ours?*

I still had ScoutDrone3 inside the shuttle's cockpit, and all I could see was Ratthi's anxious face and ART-drone hovering in the background. I checked the channel for the shuttle's exterior cameras.

The shuttle was still about four meters above the landing platform, a good height for making it clear to potential boarders that they weren't welcome. (A SecUnit could jump that. With ART-drone on the controls, a SecUnit would regret that.) The forward view showed the landing platform's ramp in the foreground and then farther away, the large shuttle-sized hangar doorway into the installation's interior. Side views showed empty platforms and shadows; rear showed the wide open outside entrance, dust still swirling in the dim gray light. Dust and something else. A shadow, the shadow of another shuttle lowering into entry position. On our private channel, I asked ART-drone, *Is it one of ours?*

There's a 66 percent chance, ART-drone replied. *If after our first message they decided to send assistance, they could have met the second pathfinder en route and received the map coordinates that would allow them to locate our exact position.*

Uh-huh, and fly into an enclosed space controlled by humans with unknown motives and intentions, with zero current intel. ART-prime, whose drone iteration wouldn't let the shuttle land without checking the bedrock with a ground sensor, would be fine with this.

Sometimes the thing where it's like ART reads my mind goes both ways. I said, *But you don't think it is.*

No.

Are they trying to call us? Iris asked on teamFeed+ Leonide.

They are in range now despite the interference and there is still no attempt at contact, ART-drone said. *It's not us, Iris.*

ScoutDrone2 caught Iris's wince, the one that said she knew this was bad. Leonide glanced at her, her lips pressed into a thin line. Pain made her look older. We couldn't slow down, the timing was too tight, and we had to get somewhere, anywhere that HostileSecUnit2 wouldn't know to look for us. Unless AdaCol2 was letting it use its cameras.

Iris said, *Peri, get the shuttle out of here.*

It's too late, both ART-drone and I said at the same time. ART-drone added, *Just get here. I can get us out.*

On our private feed, I asked, *You can?* ART lies a lot.

I can. ART-drone sent me eleven different scenario/ flight path projections for outflying a pursuing shuttle that was less than 270 meters away, which, fine, why not. Crashing and dying is better than watching the humans be murdered, I guess.

Then two things happened at once.

(1) Tarik hissed on the team feed, *They're ahead of me. Barish-Estranza, coming up on your position.* Tarik's helmet camera indicated that he was backed up against a wall, two anxious colonists still with him.
(2) An explosion hit the side of the hangar entrance. The outcrop protecting it came loose with an abrupt crack and collapsed down into a pile of rubble, partially blocking our shuttle's only way out.

I stopped, held up a hand. Iris and Leonide stumbled to a halt. I could hear footsteps ahead now, whispers of movement, humans trying to be quiet.

We were in a corridor, not moving. We needed to not be here. Time was running out and HostileSecUnit2 would find us at any moment. I needed a defensible position. I hadn't seen that the Barish-Estranza shuttle was armed, and I should have noticed that when I went to look at it in the north-side hangar. To AdaCol2 I sent, *assistance: are you going to let them kill my humans you piece of shit.* I turned and grabbed Iris's arm, backtracking down the corridor. Leonide struggled to keep up. I took the next turn to the left. From what the partial map was telling me it might work, but I wouldn't be able to tell until I saw it.

In the shuttle, Ratthi asked ART-drone, "What should we do?" He sounded mostly calm, but he had flinched and fallen back against the seat at the explosion, and now he was gripping the chair arms like they were the only thing keeping him upright. It was being alone; if he had another human there to worry about, it would have been easier for him.

Can you get him out overland? I asked ART-drone. How good was Ratthi at hiding? I had no idea, but the environmental suits weren't designed for stealth. If Tarik could make it out to him, they might have a better chance together. I was juggling different scenarios, like sending Iris and Leonide away to hide separately in the installation, but nothing was giving me even decent survival numbers. I would be panicking more, but I didn't have time.

In the input from Tarik's helmet camera, he parted from

the two colonists, who ran away down one corridor. He was now running down another corridor back toward the hangar. He was saying, *Ratthi, can you get inside the installation? Peri—*

The lights fluctuated, and that was all we fucking needed; if AdaCol2 started actively opposing us we were going to be even more in the shit than we already were.

Tarik, no time. I have an alternative, ART-drone said. *Ratthi, strap in.*

As Ratthi grabbed for the safety restraints, the shuttle moved forward in hover mode. The rear camera caught a glimpse of the hostile shuttle angling for a better firing position outside the partially blocked hangar entrance. "Uh, where are we going?" Ratthi asked.

I took another turn into a smaller passage. I wanted to use it to get to a large corridor maybe thirty meters ahead, part of the system that extended out from the larger disused hangar that we had first encountered on the way in from the terraforming excavation. AdaCol2 had directed me through it when it was still fucking talking to me.

Behind us, ScoutDrone1 went dark. I had run out of time.

I shoved Iris into the first open door on our right and tossed Leonide in after her. Just as HostileSecUnit2 rounded the corner, I stepped in and hit the release for the hatch. The good part: the hatch was working and started to slide closed immediately. The bad part: it was not a heavy outer hatch but a flimsy inside one, designed for privacy and to keep humans out of places they didn't need to be.

HostileSecUnit2 caught it before it could close.

Its fingers wrapped around the hatch lip and it tried to pull it open while angling its arm to fire projectiles through the widening gap. In armor made for humans, its fingers would have been encased in a powered metal glove. Since our fingers are metal anyway, the gloves for most SecUnit armor were only a thick deflective fabric. Hopefully not too deflective in this model. I braced myself against the door and fired three narrow pinpoint pulses from my left arm energy weapon at its three main finger joints.

Three fingers hit the floor and the door snapped shut.

We can't get out through this hangar, so we're going to another one, ART-drone told Ratthi. The shuttle powered forward in hover mode, accelerated through the interior hatch into the installation, and whipped through the turn to slot itself down the dark tunnel. Ratthi made a strangled noise. ART-drone flicked on the shuttle's outer lights, though at least inside the tunnel, protected from the terraforming interference by the rock, the shuttle's proximity and obstruction sensors would function better. ART-drone added, *Tarik, find a place to hide and wait for SecUnit.*

Tarik might be waiting a long time, depending on what happened in this stupid room I had trapped us in. Iris stepped up beside me, looking down at the fingers, her furrowed brow indicating that she was appalled but relieved. She said, "How long will—"

The first thump against the door interrupted her. Yeah, it was going to smash its way through. The next blow dented the metal into a fist shape.

Iris finished, "Shit." She pushed at her hair and looked

around. The room was probably meant for storage. It was four by five meters. The ceiling a full meter above my head was bare of any exit except a ventilation access the size of Iris's tiny palm. The walls were covered with cabinets like the kind of lockers you might have for tools. Leonide was methodically opening them but they were empty so far.

ART-drone, flying a shuttle through a poorly mapped dark corridor that had originally been meant for slightly smaller aircraft and hadn't been used in probably a century at least and held who knew what kind of obstruction now, said, *Was it a good idea to go in there?*

We were on teamFeed+Leonide, but you know what, who cared. I said, *Fuck you, ART.*

You haven't spoken to me that way in weeks. I've missed it. ART-drone rocked the shuttle sideways to miss a mass of cabling hanging from the ceiling. Ratthi made an eek noise.

I'd definitely told ART to fuck off since the thing that happened. I'd told it to fuck off a lot. But I knew what it meant. This was the first time in weeks when I wasn't using it to mean *leave me alone.*

Leonide threw Iris a glare and said, "Tell your employees to shut up and get us out of here." I think she thought ART-drone was a weird human who liked SecUnits.

Distracted, thinking hard, Iris said, "You can fuck yourself. They are getting us out of here." She pressed her lips together and asked me, "What if I call them and try to arrange a surrender? It would buy us some time."

The door dented again. Scan indicated we had two minutes left before the seals gave way. "Try it," I said. It was a good idea, corporates liked to talk and gloat, generally (internal screaming). Surrender was not good, surrender meant ART would never get Iris back.

Ratthi, still with a white-knuckle grip on the chair, said, *You can beat it, SecUnit, we know you can.*

On the team feed, Tarik was whisper-swearing a lot. He said, *I'm going to find the colonists, they must have weapons.*

They probably had a bunch, considering how the rest of the humans on the planet had been using them on each other. *Hold your position,* I told him. Tarik made a frustrated noise but stopped where he was. From his helmet cam view, it was a cubby where some machinery had been removed, next to a tube lift with the door welded shut. He was too close to us now, and I didn't want HostileSecUnit2 to hear him. It would report to its supervisor and the B-E assholes would be coming toward us, plus any that might have been held in reserve on the shuttle that had been about to land outside the now-blocked hangar.

Iris and Leonide both had small sidearms, suitable for intimidating other humans and murdering supervisors, and unlikely to injure a SecUnit in any important places. HostileSecUnit2 wouldn't notice the projectiles until it went in for repairs. And if they tried to shoot while I was fighting it, the chances of accidentally hitting me were high.

I would have liked to have an "oh shit" moment but I literally couldn't let myself or I was terrified I'd go into involuntary shutdown again. (I'm more afraid of that than anything else right now. Of restarting to find all the humans and ART-drone dead.)

Then the lights blinked three times, the hiss of the air exchange above us made a burp noise. Then it surged, like the power had cut in and out. Oh, wait. *That was a restart,* ART-drone said conversationally. It was slowing the shuttle down as the cameras picked up a patch of light ahead. It was in the oblong shape of the large entrance to the north-side hangar, the one the Barish-Estranza shuttle had originally been docked in.

If AdaCol2 had been down, it made terrible sense. Barish-Estranza had decided they might as well forcibly take the colonists as long as they were killing their own supervisor, so taking down the local system was a great first step.

In late-breaking Tarik news, he had just jumped two Barish-Estranza employees who had been approaching his position, knocking one unconscious and choking the other out, and now he also had two tiny sidearms that wouldn't take out a SecUnit plus the sidearm from our shuttle's supplies that he had started out with. He obviously knew his new guns were pointless because he was snarling to himself in a language I didn't have a good translation module for. It sounded sweary with religious overtones.

In the shuttle, as Ratthi saw the light, he gasped in relief. "Oh, thank—" He stopped as ART-drone slowed the shuttle to a halt. It focused the forward camera on the hangar ahead. There was still a shuttle docked on the landing platform.

Wow, you don't think it can get any worse, and it always does.

"What? That's—" As realization hit, Ratthi groaned.

"There's two Barish-Estranza shuttles! The armed one is new!"

Tarik said, *That explains why there's so many of these <untranslatable>.*

Yeah, as the humans had realized, it was a second shuttle that had arrived, probably in response to a message drone the first group had sent to their baseship. So we were dealing with possibly at least twice as many B-E humans. And potentially more SecUnits.

Iris was in the corner talking to someone on the comm, her voice calm and her face set in a grimace. From Leonide's expression of despair, it was not going well. There were a lot of fist shapes in the door now and the seals were strained. Gaps showed with every hit.

Ratthi is correct, ART-drone told the humans. In private, it added to me, *You did not make a mistake in identifying the shuttle as unarmed.*

Technically I had made a mistake, I had assumed the second shuttle was the first one. But I knew what it was trying to say.

The lights and air pressure had stabilized. Because I am a stupid optimist, I sent to AdaCol2, *query: assistance.*

AdaCol2 replied, *assistance,* and suddenly I had cameras, so many cameras, it actually made me dizzy. Or maybe that was relief.

I asked, *query: attempted breach?*

Detected weapons activation. Lockdown initiated. Breach attempted via network bridge. Failover: secondary processors. Lockdown failure. Breach confined, primary down.

It had tried to lock down the installation when it detected the weapon fire, which would have wrecked Barish-Estranza's plan and rendered the two hostile SecUnits useless for intimidation and murdering purposes. But B-E had been ready with an attempted hack. AdaCol2 had stopped it by shutting down its breached primary unit and shifting to a secondary. Not bad, and confirmation that it was packing a substantial amount of processing heat.

I said, *query: network bridge location.*

Humans forget these things work both ways.

Network bridge active at 82734202q345.222.

I hadn't been able to get to Barish-Estranza's systems before with AdaCol2 keeping its network locked down. Now it had given me access. *Give me a minute,* I said.

AdaCol2 said, *clock set. Mark.*

Their SecSystem was a proprietary brand but not different enough to slow me down. I made sure it thought I was just another component and started to search around for what I needed. It was resident on their original shuttle, the one that had just noticed our shuttle hovering in the interior hatch corridor. I checked for links to the security system that would be on the second shuttle, the armed one, but there was nothing, just some empty addresses. That didn't make sense. Oh wait, the stupid B-E humans hadn't synced their feeds yet. Well, that's great.

I gave up on that and pulled their original shuttle's exterior camera feed. The B-E humans on watch in their cockpit and Ratthi in our cockpit were currently staring at each other in consternation.

I found a view from one of their interior security cameras. (Yes, one of. This was a shuttle from a corporate ship, everybody had to be on camera all the time because they might steal a paper napkin.) A B-E employee, an augmented human with multiple interfaces embedded into their temples, forehead, and the back of their skull, sat in an acceleration chair behind the pilot's seat, their head wreathed in a visual feed display. They were monitoring via the feed and with their eyes at the same time. So they were like an augmented human HubSystem? Weird, and fucking inconvenient. It was a system I'd never seen before, I wasn't sure how to handle it, what the augmented human would be able to do, and I didn't have time to figure it out. I could just burn their interfaces and probably destroy part of their brain, but that seemed mean . . . ugh, there had to be another way.

There were two other humans in the cockpit, one in the pilot seat and one in the copilot seat, monitoring systems. *I need you to distract them,* I told ART-drone.

It hailed them on comm. The human pilot picked up immediately, which was his first mistake. He said, "We have your group locked down and are negotiating surrender. Set your shuttle down—"

"I'm not with them," ART-drone replied. It was using a human voice, the same vaguely menacing one it used to speak on the feed. "You'll have to negotiate your surrender to me separately."

"We're not surrendering to you—" The pilot blurted, while the copilot glared at him. The augmented human HubSystem winced in either sympathy or disgust.

The copilot interrupted, "Stand down or we will engage."

This shuttle wasn't armed, and a quick look through their security archive said nobody had planted any explosives or anything. She was bluffing.

ART-drone said, "I wouldn't recommend it. I lack a sense of proportional response. I don't advise engaging with me on any level."

The pilot gave the copilot an "it's not so easy, is it" look. But the augmented human was ignoring them again.

In our little storage room, the next punch broke the seal along the top of the hatch. I said, *ART, you need to distract them right the fuck now.*

ART-drone pushed the shuttle forward in one abrupt surge of power. It stopped just short of ramming the B-E shuttle; the cockpits were less than a meter apart. All the humans, Barish-Estranza and Ratthi, screamed.

And the augmented human dropped all their inputs, jerking back in their seat. I picked up the one to HostileSecUnit2 and sent a "stand down, cancel all current orders" command through the governor module.

In our room, on the other side of the hatch, it went silent. Iris and Leonide stared at each other, not sure what I had done. ART-drone accessed Iris's comm and cut off the B-E supervisor who was dicking around with the surrender discussion.

I could have destroyed HostileSecUnit2's governor module. Also HostileSecUnit1's governor module; it had restarted back in the meeting room and was stuck in standby mode waiting for new orders. (I told it to render assistance to the wounded B-E employees still there, which nobody had thought to do yet, then shut down again.)

In the two spare seconds I had before the humans would start reacting, I thought about it.

But at best it would be leaving two SecUnits to fend for themselves, who might not be smart or aware enough yet to hide what had happened. They could be killed. They could be recaptured and memory-wiped, or broken down for parts. At worst, or the other worst, they could become typical rogues just like in the media and attack the Barish-Estranza personnel and the colonists. It did happen. And if we survived this situation long enough to have to justify what we had done here, it would look like that had been my plan all along, to let the other two SecUnits murder the humans. The colonists would lose their chance to escape; Preservation and the University would be in the shit. ART and all my humans would be blamed for my actions.

I'm not spiraling, this is all accurate. But whatever.

But I couldn't just leave them like this. I should, but I couldn't.

ART-drone was no fucking help, sitting there waiting for me to make the decision, and we were running out of time.

I took the file bundle 2.0 had given Three, and the code to hack the governor module, and buried it in both SecUnits' archives.

Then I wiped their shuttle's comm and feed code and sent their bot pilot into a forced shutdown and restart diagnostic that would take an hour.

Take that proportional response and like it.

AdaCol2 sent: *mark: time,* and I let the connection go. I lost the B-E shuttle cameras, but I had our shuttle's exterior cameras and my drone in the cockpit, so I had a clear view when ART-drone rocked the shuttle sideways. It looked horrifically like it was about to roll. (You can't roll on hover, I don't have a shuttle piloting module and I know that.) But ART-drone used the motion to dip around the B-E shuttle. It clipped something I hoped was not important, and shot out through the hangar exit into the darkness and the dust-filled wind.

In the storage room, Iris and Leonide stared at me. Leonide was wary and confused, Iris was hopeful and beginning to be relieved. I thought ART-drone was updating her on their private channel. Tarik was still braced in his cubby, too busy keeping visual watch to check the feed.

With the new permissions to view AdaCol2's cameras, I finally had accurate video intel and maps. Five armed Barish-Estranza from Leonide's original group were stalking us and Tarik through the corridors, but AdaCol2 had sealed two strategic doors and they were heading in the wrong direction now. Nine B-E humans had come in on the second shuttle, three remaining with it where it had landed outside the east hangar while the others made their way inside. The two humans Tarik had taken out were from that group. This group did not apparently have SecUnits. (Huh. That bothered me. I'd rather see the SecUnits I'd expected to see than not see them, if that makes sense.) They could have landed somewhere near the installation and dropped off the SecUnits as backup and reserve, especially if they thought they were going to be rounding up colonists to be taken away as contract labor, and they didn't want anybody making a break for it across the surface.

So it was a really good thing ART-drone got Ratthi out in the shuttle. If I had sent him and Tarik overland and they had run into— Yeah, let's not.

The colonists had managed to lock themselves down in various places, mostly the other side of the installation, and hopefully they would stay out of our way and out of danger, thinking hard about their choices regarding signing any kind of contract with fucking Barish-Estranza.

The door was broken so I shoved it open. I slipped past the stationary HostileSecUnit2. I could feel it watching me through its opaque visor. I wondered if it had found the files yet. Whatever, I didn't come here to make friends.

I held my hand out to Iris and she took it, let me guide her behind me so I could stay between her and the SecUnit while she got past and out the door. Leonide followed her without a protest. I started down the corridor; I still needed to put as much distance between us and the SecUnit as possible.

It occurred to me belatedly (the way most important things occur to me) that if the SecUnit found the code I put in its archive immediately, it could take out its governor module, go rogue, and attack us anyway. Well, it's a little late to worry about that, Murderbot.

Are we clear? Tarik asked on the feed.

Good question. I sent to AdaCol2: *second B-E shuttle query: network bridge?*

Will you give me access to the other B-E shuttle? I could

find out if there were new SecUnits in play and wipe out their comm and feed and ground them. Then we'd be clear. Except for the armed humans, but with AdaCol2's camera access we could avoid those now.

AdaCol2: *Negative. Risk of secondary breach.*

It wouldn't chance being hacked again.

I could argue with it, that now it knew how they got in the first time, it could fix any vulnerabilities. But I couldn't risk it getting pissed off and taking away my camera access. On the feed, I said, *We're not clear. I couldn't take out the second shuttle.* I sent Tarik a map of a safe (currently, relatively) route to a rendezvous point. From the shuttle, ScoutDrone3 watched Ratthi watching us worriedly via ScoutDrone2's camera feed. (I was down to four drones now, two of which were back on ART-prime.) Ratthi said, *Where can we pick you up? Can you get outside?*

The nearest exit was the east-side hangar, which was blocked. But there was still that long corridor heading back to the unused hangar and then the tunnel to the terraforming construction access. There had been no indication that Barish-Estranza knew that hangar or its connection to the terraforming excavations existed at all. And it would be well outside the radius where they might have dropped off SecUnits to catch escaping colonists. I said, *I think I have a place in mind.*

Chapter Ten

TARIK CAUGHT UP WITH us in the junction to the corridor, and we headed toward the lock leading into the powered-down section of the installation. Past that lock was the passage that led into the giant dark cargo receiving area that had scared the hell out of me, and then the hatchway out into the giant hangar that had also scared the hell out of me.

As we reached the lock, Tarik asked Leonide if she needed help. Leonide gave him a wary look, but politely said no. Iris had given her some medication tabs that were painkillers and stimulants and she was walking better now, so we were moving faster.

There was no filtered air past this lock, so we stopped so the humans could secure their environmental suits again. Mine was leaking because of me being shot, which I was going to ignore. We didn't have that far to go, and I'm not as affected by the lousy air as a human. But Iris said, "Wait, SecUnit," and pulled out the little suit-repair kit she had attached to her belt. She patched the projectile hole in the back, and ScoutDrone2 watched Leonide, who had a slight confused crease between her brows, watch Iris be nice to the SecUnit. Leonide's suit was expensive enough that she had been able to turn on a self-repair function to close up the hole the projectile had torn through the shoulder.

Once we were through the lock into the corridor with no power we had (1) complete darkness; (2) a large space that ScoutDrone2 couldn't adequately scout (again); (3) the humans needing to use at least one of their hand-lights so they didn't trip on the intermittently buckled floor plates.

I positioned ScoutDrone2 as rearguard because as far as our intel went, nobody but AdaCol2 knew we had come in this way. Barish-Estranza could still find us, but it would depend on (a) what information they had managed to download before AdaCol2 stopped their hack; and (b) how good they were at guessing our intentions from what they knew about our previous position. It was the first one I was more worried about.

I had been across the cargo chamber once with AdaCol2 guiding me, but I knew it was busy right now. It had been curtailing my camera access and mapping data since we entered the corridor, so I could see the area immediately around us but that was it. I knew why: its humans would be preparing defenses or escape routes or both, and it didn't want to risk that intel becoming available to Barish-Estranza if there was another hacking attempt.

The cargo foyer was so big the hand-light didn't help, and I had told Tarik to keep it on the lowest setting, pointed at the floor. Even without full scan function, I still had my dark vision filters and my own mapping data, so with the fixed point of the corridor hatch, I could retrace my steps to the ramp. It just looked awkward and stupid because for the first part I had to navigate like a floor-cleaning bot.

While we walked in the dark, on teamFeed+Leonide, Iris said, *How extensive is this rebellion in your task force? Is it just you they hate, or is it all the upper management?*

That . . . was a really good question. I had a private channel open with Ratthi in the shuttle, in case he was nervous and wanted to talk without tying up the feed. He said, *Ahh, I hadn't thought about that.*

Iris understood corporate backstabbing better than Ratthi.

Leonide said, *I don't know.*

There was a skeptical pause, then ART-drone said, *How terribly imperceptive of you.*

Leonide's voice was clearly irritated. *You can fuck off into the abyss.*

Tarik tried, *Is it a schism in the upper management? Come on, you owe us that much.*

Iris added, *If we come out of the blackout zone with no idea what the situation is, how exactly do you think that's going to work in your favor?*

All right, Leonide snapped. *It is a schism. There was a small management faction that was angry at the prospect of losing bonuses because of failure to deliver on all the operational goals. I had no idea . . . they were this serious about it.*

By "operational goal" do you mean signing up the colonists for your slave labor pool? Ratthi asked.

She ignored him. Humans never want to hear about that part.

Iris switched to the regular team feed, cutting Leonide out of the conversation. Her voice was grim. *So do we think the fighting will be confined to the two Barish-Estranza factions or will taking us out be part of their business plan?*

ART-drone said, *The only thing preventing Barish-Estranza from seizing the colonists is our presence. The dissenting faction may believe that eliminating us is their next logical step.*

Which meant ART-prime and the Preservation responder could be under fire right now. They would be defending themselves, and ART would start with disabling strikes on the B-E ships but if that didn't work, it had probably calculated what the point would be where it had no choice but to start slaughtering B-E humans in order to keep our humans alive. I said, *Barish-Estranza could have intercepted our two messenger pathfinders.* If the let's-get-those-bonuses faction had already started an attack, there was no reason to pretend to be respectful of each other's surveillance equipment anymore.

Ratthi made an unhappy noise. Tarik said something religious and sweary again. Iris was quiet for a couple of steps. Then she said, *We need to hurry.*

You can take them, I said, privately, to ART-drone. I was talking about ART-prime, but it knew that.

I can, it agreed. *But they may decide to hold the colonists hostage.*

That was what I was afraid of, too. The mission priority of our humans was to save the colonists. With everything that had happened, I had been up in ART's business almost as much as it was up in mine. I knew that its mission priority was to save our humans.

I was so tired of dead humans. *You won't let hostages stop you.*

I will not.

———————

I was able to see a difference in the darkness of the wall and partially closed hatch at the top of the ramp and the darkness that was the opening into the hangar. I sent ScoutDrone2 ahead to check our route. The separatists could have told Barish-Estranza about the tunnel to the terraforming engines, but what we had seen of them made it hard for even threat assessment to imagine them sitting around chatting to visitors about all the obscure exits and entrances to their secret cave hideout, so the chances were negligible.

As we climbed the ramp, ScoutDrone2 entered the hangar twenty meters ahead of us. I told it to accelerate into a quick scout run. From its camera, the hangar was another giant shadowy cavern, but the very faint gray storm-light from where the opening had been cut into the jammed overhead hatch let the drone make out a lot more visual detail. The humans would still need the hand-light.

ScoutDrone2 was sending video of the tall landing platforms, the one occupied by the aging and half-assed hopper possibly built by amateurs, the stacks of supplies and salvaged materials. Nothing looked disturbed, except there were more drifts of windblown dust.

It would have been nice to go up through the opening in that overhead hatch and have the shuttle meet us there like the humans had done before, but (a) the armed shuttle was still in play somewhere and there was an unknown chance it would be out looking for our shuttle; and (b) we didn't have ART-drone with us so it could carry the humans up to the unresponsive hatch. (That was such a big "but" it should probably have been (a) instead of (b).) Our shuttle could land or hover to let ART-drone out, but it would have to come all the way down here to get the humans and that was more time on the ground, more time for the B-E shuttle to find us.

There was a lot of equipment here and Iris and Tarik were smart, there might be something they could use to get up to the hatch. But that didn't help the problem of the shuttle landing and being a static target.

No, even risk assessment thought my original plan was better. We'll take the tunnel back to the terraforming construction access.

As I led the humans into the hangar, the contact with AdaCol2 started to drop. I sent, *End session, acknowledge.*

It sent back, *End session.* There was a pause, then: *Be safe.*

I can't deal with that right now.

The lack of visibility in the hangar was not great for the humans but it had less of an air of "Pre-CR site with monsters" than it had initially. On the feed, Leonide said, *What is this place?*

It's an unused part of the old Pre–Corporation Rim site, Iris told her. *As far as we know.*

The humans started talking on the feed about the feasibility of waiting until dark again to land our shuttle near the construction access. With the blackout conditions, the armed B-E shuttle wouldn't have any short-range much less long-range scanners to pick us up at night. Iris pointed out that we wouldn't have any scans to assist with a night landing, either, and we couldn't afford the chance of even a minor accident that might strand us. Tarik said the shuttle could land farther away and we could walk to it. Ratthi said the visibility was still shit out here and started going through the last weather reports that AdaCol2 had issued. I had the conversation mostly backburnered. For once we had time to figure out the best strategy, and they were doing a good job of going through all the relevant issues—

The vehicle was gone.

I stopped. The humans jostled to a halt behind me.

ScoutDrone2 had gotten far enough to get a view of the tunnel entrance, and under the stark emergency lighting, it was empty. The vehicle from the terraforming access was gone. Ugh, organic neural tissue, whatever the hell you're doing with the secretions and neuron firing, it's not helping. Okay, okay. Maybe a colonist found it and moved it, let's check threat assessment—

ScoutDrone2 winked out, gone between one tenth of a second and the next.

Iris drew breath to ask what was wrong. On team-Feed+Leonide I said, *Kill the light.*

Fortunately, Tarik was the one holding the hand-light. He clicked it off instantly, corporate death-squad training making him comply while any of the others would have needed a second or two to figure out if I was talking to them or which light. I said, *We have to move. Hold hands, stay tight behind me.*

Tarik grabbed Leonide's good arm and stepped close to put a hand on my shoulder. Iris grabbed him and the back of my suit utility belt. Leonide was squished in the middle but did not protest. I walked as fast as I could while still letting them keep up and stay in position. Their boots shuffled a little and on the comm I could hear them trying not to breathe loudly. Their suits would muffle a lot of that. Hopefully enough of it to keep the hostiles from audio tracking us. I took us in a zigzag pattern through some stacks of metal salvage and past two looming broken stalks for missing landing platforms.

The hostiles could have marked our position from the hand-light; the hangar was big but if there were two of them there was a 96 percent chance one had taken a position high up somewhere to watch for us. The other had to be where ScoutDrone2 had gone offline.

And quiet and fast enough to take it out with no warning.

It had to be SecUnits. Something in my organic neural tissue said it was SecUnits.

On the feed, I said, *One, possibly more, hostile SecUnits in immediate range.* I was falling back on company protocol to talk, the rest of me running terrifying potential sequences of events and trying to figure out where to send the humans. This was a fucking worst-case scenario. In the shuttle, Ratthi gasped in dismay.

These SecUnits must have come from the second Barish-Estranza shuttle, the armed one. It might be still on the ground where Ratthi and ART-drone had seen it last, it might be hunting for our shuttle, but at some point it had dropped its SecUnits outside the installation, to watch for escape attempts by colonists. I knew their SecUnits had the same 100-meter limit . . . No, I didn't know that. They had the same kind of kill switch if they were too far from their human supervisors, but I had no idea what the limit was, or if this proprietary brand allowed a human supervisor to waive the limit for emergencies.

I was 98 percent certain that they would be using that same weird HubSystem setup with an augmented human controller. I couldn't get to it to hack it; there were no signals in here that I could detect, which meant their communications were locked down as tight as ours were. AdaCol2 was out of range this far into the hangar.

The Barish-Estranza shuttle would have to stay in contact with their SecUnits. I asked ART-drone, *Are you close enough to jam their comm?*

Not yet, it replied. *The interference has shortened my range. Their HubSystem may be operating inside the shelter of the installation.*

Which meant the rest of their task group was closing in on us.

I had been in worse situations with humans to protect,

but I couldn't pull any from my archive right now. I had never been in a worse situation with humans to protect when I was this likely to panic and shut down from a stupid memory of something that hadn't fucking happened. (Okay, it had happened, but nobody ate my leg.)

The fear that a hostile SecUnit would snatch one of my humans away in the dark was almost incapacitating.

ART-drone said, *We're six minutes out. We'll land and I'll go in for you.*

On our private channel, I said, *You can't risk the shuttle.* And Ratthi, I didn't say. If it went like it looked like it was going to go, he was the only one we still had a high chance of saving.

The purpose of the shuttle is to retrieve the team, ART-drone replied, deliberately misunderstanding. Or not misunderstanding. It wasn't going to listen to me about this, was the point. Back on the team feed, it said, *Prepare for evac.*

Iris let out a breath, probably about the risk to the shuttle, but she must have remembered I was supposed to be in charge of security and this was definitely security. On the feed, she asked, *Do you want this?*

I held out a hand and she put the tiny Barish-Estranza sidearm into it.

Despite faster pulse rates the humans were moving quietly, but we were pressing our luck; somebody was going to step on something loud or fall at some point. I stopped behind a blocky obstruction that was big enough to cover us, then told them, *Crouch down.*

Everybody did. Leonide made a little mostly-suppressed

gasp of relief. ART-drone had started a time-to-arrival countdown in the feed. We had to be in a good position. So I needed to find one. On the feed, Tarik said, *If we were higher up, it would be easier for Peri to get us out.*

Iris agreed. *They won't be watching for that. They don't know what Peri can do, they don't know that we have a way up there.*

That was a really good point. But I didn't like this plan, it would leave them vulnerable throughout the process. But the only other option that was coming up in my procedure module (I called it the panic module because that was the only time I looked at it) was to find a secure area to shelter in place until retrieval, which was just unbelievably stupid in our current situation. Who wrote this fucking module, for fuck's sake, it's not factoring in the exceptions. No wonder taking advice from *Sanctuary Moon* was better.

Put the fucking panic module away, you know what to do.

Ratthi hadn't said anything because he was in the feed tearing through the shuttle's equipment inventory listing looking for anything to help us. ("SecUnit isn't in armor and they are," he said feverishly to ART-drone. "We can exploit that, yes? Is there something that would disrupt the armor but not SecUnit's onboard systems—"

A number of things, ART-drone said, *none of which we currently have aboard.*)

I had led them at an angle, toward the side of the hangar that was closer to the dim shaft of light from the gap in the hatch. The SecUnits would expect us to avoid the place where it was easier to spot us, so I'd done the opposite. (I know, believe me, I know. This is an illustration of the phrase "grasp at straws.") The landing platform with the pseudo-hopper on it was the closest high spot, and a quick review of the video the drones had taken on the way in here showed the access stairs were intact. Also it would give them something to take cover behind. I sent Iris and Tarik an image of it, with more detail than they could see with unaugmented vision. *We're going to this one, with the aircraft,* I told them. *When we get there, start climbing. I'll cover you.*

With no drones and no cameras I had to look at them to make sure they were listening and just to see what they were doing. They didn't move immediately, and it stretched .04 seconds past the point where even a human would have reacted by now. ART-drone said, *There is no time to waste, move now.* And I think it added something to Iris on her private feed.

Iris said, *Right, let's go. SecUnit, we'll wait for you up top.*

I know they will, which is why I'm willing to die to get them up there.

We were twenty meters from the target platform access and it was mostly under cover, except the last approximately thirteen meters. I eased upright and led the way toward the platform, watching for moving patches of darkness that might be SecUnits.

Two minutes out, ART-drone said, and added privately to me, *Prioritize escape. You can't kill more than one in your current circumstances.*

It meant without armor or a larger projectile weapon

and with no feed for hacking. It was giving me a lot of credit to think I could do even one right now.

We were just crossing into the area without cover, low visibility for humans but not bad at all for SecUnits. And suddenly I knew the second one was about to hit us.

I said on the feed, *Run now.*

They ran, blundering a little in the dark, and it made its first mistake. It bolted toward them and its boot scraped on the gritty floor and I had its position. A quick speed/direction analysis and I ran forward, jumped to the top of a crate, and leapt off.

It might have been prepared for me to run up on it, but it was not prepared for me to come from that angle. It flung an arm up and managed to fire three projectiles before I grabbed the arm and swung my weight and momentum and whatever it's called and flipped us both onto the ground.

I said before, most SecUnit armor isn't powered like armor for humans, it's just giving our squishy bits extra protection and protecting the manufacturer's investment. So it's not like this SecUnit was stronger than me, it was just a lot easier for it to tear bits off me if I wasn't careful. Also it had that stupid projectile weapon arm, which it immediately started trying to shoot me with again.

We scrambled around on the pavement, it tried to keep me off its helmet and I fired energy pulses into the joints I could reach, and it shot me three more times. My advantages were that it didn't know how to fight this way, at least not with another construct (governor modules aren't helpful for learning and dealing with new experiences, you may have noticed) and that I knew how its armor worked, where all the vulnerable points were likely to be, even though it wasn't the same as company armor. But I had no cameras, no intel, no idea what else was happening except heavy breathing as the humans ran and Ratthi cursing quietly in the shuttle. You'd think it would be nice not to have distractions and you would be so, so wrong. I am not meant to function without multiple simultaneous inputs. If this was what being a human was like, it sucked massively.

HostileSecUnit managed to clamp a leg around my knee and flip me over. It got a hand on my environmental suit helmet (which was not meant for this kind of pressure and was already creaking) and tried to smash my skull into the floor. It had my left arm pinned in its armpit, which was a bad move because I fired my energy weapon in a sustained stream and that was a weak point in its armor.

Suddenly I had a camera view on the humans. It was disorienting for a second, it was such a relief. Then I realized the shuttle had arrived and ART-drone and Ratthi had let my last drone, ScoutDrone3 = FinalDrone, out. Fuck yes.

It had gone into a standard surveillance mode, focusing on movement, and I immediately saw two things: (1) the humans had reached the access stair for the landing platform and started up; and (2) a second SecUnit ran across the open stretch of paving toward them.

(3) ART-drone dropped through the gap in the overhead hatch.

I sent the drone's camera feed to ART-drone with

HostileSecUnit2's approach tagged *acck,* which was a typo but ART-drone got what I meant. It jammed the comm that Barish-Estranza was using to connect their SecUnits with the weird augmented human HubSystem setup. At the same time it changed direction and swooped down on the approaching HostileSecUnit2.

HostileSecUnit1 twisted desperately to get away from my energy stream as I drilled through the weak patch in its armpit. I twisted with it, got an arm free and a finger under its helmet's release.

HostileSecUnit2 spun and fired projectiles up at ART-drone. It should have dodged, but it didn't. ART-drone took the impacts to the right of its carapace. One of the four limbs on that side fell off.

HostileSecUnit2 spun back around, barely breaking stride as it ran toward the tower. Tarik and Iris were on the stairs, Leonide behind them. The central stalk of the landing platform gave them temporary cover from Hostile-SecUnit2's projectile fire until it reached a better position on the other side of the platform access.

HostileSecUnit1's helmet came loose under my hand and I reached in and gripped the back of its neck. My angle was bad but I didn't have a choice; I fired an energy pulse right into its spine and through my palm and fingers. (I've had to do this before and it's never fun.)

HostileSecUnit2 assumed that ART-drone was just a drone under the control of me or the humans, which, mistake. HostileSecUnit2 circled the platform at a run and reached the angle it needed to fire at the humans. But

ART-drone had controlled its near freefall, pretended to limp like a wounded drone. Now it accelerated at the last second and slammed into HostileSecUnit2 from behind.

I knew ART-drone had at least two drill attachments and a cutting tool that could get through the armor, but it had some other things, too. HostileSecUnit2 had a moment when, if it had an actual separate projectile weapon instead of a built-in, it could have angled it back and blown ART-drone to pieces. But it didn't. Instead the fucker tried to empty its onboard weapon into the humans, but ART-drone snaked a limb around and knocked its arm upright. Projectiles knocked fragments out of the platform's stalk but no fragile bodies tumbled down the stairs.

I felt HostileSecUnit1 go into shutdown mode. It wasn't dead, it was just catastrophically damaged. (I know, who isn't?) Shutdown would conserve resources until it was retrieved. (If it was.) I wanted to shove it off me, but I had to pry what was left of my hand out of its neck first.

HostileSecUnit2 didn't have a chance to shut down. When ART-drone let go, it fell into pieces.

I got my hand free and struggled upright, stepped away from HostileSecUnit1. ART-drone had shut down the comm so Barish-Estranza didn't know what had happened here, but we had an unknown number of minutes before they caught up—

I caught simultaneous alerts from FinalDrone and ART-drone. I turned.

There was another SecUnit ten meters away, just standing there. That's not good. With my pain sensors tuned so far down I wasn't sure where I'd been shot. I was leaking through the holes in my suit, and I'd used so much power for my energy weapons that I was going to need to go down for a recharge cycle soon or I would risk involuntary shutdown. Immediately, if I had to use my weapons again. Oh, and my right hand was missing three fingers and had a hole in the palm. Performance reliability 68 percent and dropping. ART-drone was right, I couldn't do two.

ART-drone hadn't moved. It had sunk to slump on the pavement, like it had lost control of some vital systems, including the ability to hover. The humans had reached the top of the platform and taken cover behind the pseudo-hopper. Iris was talking to Ratthi on our feed, trying to figure out a rescue plan with the soft-drops, and Tarik and Leonide wanted me to lure the SecUnit toward the platform so they could push the aircraft off to land on it, what the hell, that won't work.

Then the SecUnit said, "They're coming. You have to go."

This is one of the two you gave the code to, ART-drone said. *It's disabled its governor module.* The SecUnit's voice was different from Three's. A different tissue batch, maybe. It didn't trust me enough for a feed connection. That was mutual. Then I surprised the shit out of myself and said, "Come with us."

It stepped back. "They don't know."

They didn't know about it. It was going to do what I had done, pretend to keep doing its job.

It added, "You need to go. They're two minutes out."

We had to go. I stepped back, then turned and ran toward the landing platform. ART-drone hadn't moved.

On the feed, Iris said, *Are you all right? Can I come down and help you?*

No, stay there, we have to go, we have two minutes, I said, and then realized our way to get to the overhead hatch and reach our shuttle was out of commission and needed to be rescued just as much as the rest of us, and that was why they were talking about the soft-drops. That would take way too long; they were too slow, it would take more than two minutes for Ratthi to send them down here, he'd have to get out of the shuttle to drop them through the gap and it would take more minutes of work to get them to go up again. Wait, why had Tarik and Leonide thought they could push the pseudohopper off the platform? *Can that thing up there fly?*

Tarik thinks so, Iris said. *It's not as old as it looks. Tarik thinks they can fly it out of here.*

Get it started. I called in FinalDrone, set it to hover over my head, and leaned down to put an arm around ART-drone. It wrapped a couple of limbs around me, and I lifted it, grabbed the handrail, and started up. On our private channel, it said, *I apologize. I can download this iteration to the surplus storage in the shuttle, but the tech in this drone cannot be allowed to be closely examined by corporate—*

Shut up, I told it. On the team feed, I said, *Ratthi, you need to get that shuttle in the air, now, they're almost here. Meet us at the terraforming construction access.*

ART-drone told me, *Fuck off.*

From the noise Ratthi made, I could tell he didn't want to leave us. But he said, *Right, going now. Just be careful!* I heard the thumps on the comm as he dropped the armful of soft-drops and hurried for the pilot's seat. The bot pilot sent an acknowledgment to ART-drone that it was beginning liftoff.

Near the top of the stairs, I looked back to see the SecUnit was gone. It would loop back around and pretend to be searching the other half of the hangar. At least that's what I'd do. The augmented human controller I'd disrupted on the other shuttle had been relatively easy to fool from the inside. It must have been the first thing this SecUnit learned how to do when it hacked its governor module.

Focus, Murderbot.

Tarik and Leonide were in the pseudohopper and the engine was making cranky humming noises. I was climbing the last section of steps when Iris came down to meet me, her body language broadcasting anxious human. On the feed she said, *Are you all right? Do you need help with Peri?*

Barish-Estranza would be in the hangar by now and the pseudohopper was not quiet. "We need to go," I said aloud. And I needed to stop just repeating that or they were going to think I was losing function, which I was, but. "They're here."

ART-drone reached out a limb to Iris. *My function is impaired, Iris. So is SecUnit's.*

Will you shut the hell up? I said.

You shut up, it replied.

"Let's everybody shut up and get in the flyer," Iris said, and shouldered ART-drone's limb, taking part of its weight.

ART-drone's size was awkward and Iris had to help me heave it into the pseudohopper's cabin. She shoved me in after it, climbed in, and pulled the hatch shut. There was a hiss of badly filtered artificial air. Tarik and Leonide were in the copilot's and pilot's seats, arguing about who knew more about flying semi-derelict aircraft jury-rigged from parts left behind by terraformers, but they were both working over the controls in the piloting interface. I have a module for piloting hoppers, which this seemed similar to, but I also had a low performance reliability and a yellow warning on my power reserve, so. I sent FinalDrone to take a position in front of the control board anyway. If we slammed into a wall, I'd get a good view, I guess.

"There's no bot pilot," Iris told me, helping me wrestle ART-drone into a seat so we could strap it in. The passenger compartment was small, with only four seats and a webbed cubby for supplies. Most of the cabin was meant for cargo. Somebody had left an old mask filter on the floor.

ART-drone said, *This is unnecessary. I am capable of—*

"People who get shot don't get to argue about safety protocol," Iris told it. I could see her face through her helmet plate and she was sweating though she was making her voice sound normal. "They said it looks like the colonists did maintenance on this thing at some point in the past forty years, so it's not as bad as— Ah! Your hand!"

"It's fine," I said. While the upholstery was worn and cracked, the interior looked better than the outside. (It was going to look a lot worse the way I was leaking.) You could tell there had been repairs and even some updates. I leaned

System Collapse

over to make sure ART-drone's strap was secure and a couple of projectiles fell out of my suit. I could feel a few more rattling around in there. (Sometimes they pop out on their own.)

With no drones in the shuttle, I was relying on the bot pilot's data feed and Ratthi's verbal reports, but he was pretty good at those. They were in the air now, navigating back the way we originally came in, staying low to the ground and using the dust as cover. The shuttle had mapped the terrain along the way, so by retracing its path it was unlikely to run into anything, even in low visibility with impaired scan. Our remaining pathfinders had formed up around it, though without me or ART-drone to manage their inputs, I didn't know how much that was going to help. Bot pilot could do it to a limited extent, but that was it. Ratthi said, "See you soon," and I got a last ping from bot pilot as it vanished out of our feed range.

The bot pilot is also me, ART-drone said, testy.

Also sounding testy, Leonide said, "You said there's an opening up there—"

"Your friends know where we are. By the time we get in the air, their shuttle will be out there and it's faster than this jury-rigged bag of spare parts," Tarik told her. "We're taking the tunnel."

"You're out of your mind." Leonide calmly brought up a terrain interface. It floated above the control board, parts of it blinking red. It was an old-fashioned layout and style that I'd only seen in retro dramas. "You people astound me."

"Says the person whose fault this all is." Tarik made some

401

rapid adjustments and the engine humming got louder. "How do you think this thing has been getting in and out of here? Does it walk? Iris, strap in, we're ready."

Somehow Iris had shoved me into the seat next to ART-drone and strapped me in, too. She shifted over to a seat to strap herself in. "Let's go."

I couldn't hear shouting but I did hear weapon fire as the pseudohopper slid forward and fell off the landing platform. It dipped down, pressing us forward against the acceleration straps, and shot into the tunnel.

Chapter Eleven

I DIDN'T FEEL GREAT but just sitting down helped me recover some power reserve. I couldn't do a full recharge until we were clear. Not that I could do much to protect the humans now because the primary danger at the moment was one of them slamming the pseudohopper into a wall.

We were moving a lot faster than we had in the tunnel vehicle. (Yeah, I had thought the open compartment was unsafe but compared to this, not so much.) The pseudohopper didn't have a bot pilot or anything like what we were used to with a modern aircraft, just a rudimentary self-navigator that helped keep it on course in the middle of the tunnel. Tarik and Leonide kept their hands on the controls, gazes locked on the interface.

In the team feed, I put up the map we had made on the way in and did a calculation of our current speed and projected time of arrival. Any navigation aids or warning systems this tunnel might have had were long offline. We were lucky to have the emergency lighting.

If we were right and Barish-Estranza didn't know about the construction access, they would have no idea where we were going. They would have to follow us in the tunnel vehicle, if they could find where the two hostile SecUnits had moved it. Up top, their shuttle would be searching for our shuttle or looking for where the pseudohopper would come up to the surface. Or both. Probably both.

Iris rustled around in her bag and pulled out a medical kit. She said, "I know you don't like physical contact, but that much bleeding can't be good."

"It'll stop in a minute," I told her. The reserve energy drain was worse, and moving around trying to get my suit off so she could patch leaks would use up more energy and be stressful, and I wasn't up for stressful. What I wanted to do was sit here and watch *Sanctuary Moon* with ART-drone. Or, actually, ART-drone was in worse shape than I was. In our shared processing space, I started up its favorite episode of *World Hoppers*. I couldn't tell if that helped, but I could tell it was watching.

"One question," Leonide said, keeping her attention on the control interface. "Is that actually a SecUnit?"

"You know," Iris said conversationally, taking a pad out of the medical kit and wiping bloodstains off ART-drone's carapace. "You can mind your own damn business."

"Oversensitive," Leonide said, but she must have been too tired to hide the frustration in her voice. She was quiet for 5.3 seconds, then burst out, "Is someone actually watching entertainment in the feed right now?"

Oops, I guess there was a little bleedover, probably from ART-drone's end. Deadpan, Tarik said, "I always watch entertainment when I fly."

Leonide let out her breath in an exasperated hiss. "Fuck you all."

"Right back at you," I said.

We didn't crash, but as Tarik and Leonide slowed for the end of the tunnel, they saw we couldn't land in the bay. There was some kind of large obstruction in it.

It was an "oh shit" moment for all of us. Then as we got closer, we saw it was our shuttle. We just hadn't recognized it because of the bad light and because it looked like it was wearing a hat.

Sounding amused and also exhausted, Iris said, "Ratthi, what did you do?"

"It's the survival tent." His voice came over the comm, normal and reassuring and wow, that's a little spike in my performance reliability, I must have been more worried than I thought. "I was looking for something to help hide us. I didn't want to close the big construction hatch and then not be able to get it open again. Dust collects fast here and from the pathfinders' view it looks like the bay is a sand drift."

"That's just a little brilliant," Tarik admitted, setting us down in the mouth of the tunnel. The pseudohopper thumped when it landed and some interfaces flashed red, but that seemed to be part of its normal operation. "I guess that's why you're a scientist."

The shuttle's hatch opened and Ratthi jumped out, waving at us. "We need to hurry. One of the pathfinders got an image of a B-E shuttle a little to the west about twenty minutes ago."

Ratthi used the tent's feed interface to collapse it down

and he and Tarik shoved it back into the cargo hatch. Iris and I loaded ART-drone into the shuttle. Leonide climbed in first and moved the seat for us and pulled down the safety restraints so Iris could get them on its carapace. (Yeah, she went into the shuttle first. She didn't make any attempt to leave without us. Which was good for her, since ART–bot pilot, while not vocal, is still an ART iteration and I could feel it watching her in the feed like a thoughtful predator.) (I think she was just impatient to get the show on the road and knew the only way to speed us up was to help.)

Ratthi and Tarik piled in and bot pilot shut the hatch and lifted off while they were still strapping down in the cockpit. In the team feed, Iris pulled up a navigation screen that showed what should be ART-prime's current position, based on where it was when we entered the blackout zone. She said, "There's no point in being stealthy. Let's go straight home."

She was right. We had come here from the other end of the inhabited continent, across the planet. Now the faster we could get out of the blackout zone, the better.

The bot pilot engaged thrusters and we lifted straight up out of the bay. The pathfinders pinged in, pulling back into a scouting formation around us. But I could tell ART-drone was losing function; it was taking in their data from the bot pilot but not sending back instructions. I took over, gently slipping the connections away from it across our shared processing space and sorting them into the same inputs I used for drones. It changed the positioning a little, but bot pilot thought it would work.

Even with the bot pilot assisting, I couldn't fly the pathfinders all simultaneously like they were little miniature shuttles like ART-drone or ART-prime could. They were too different from intel drones and also, I didn't know shit about flying into space.

The shuttle's scan was still limited, but the dust was providing some visual cover. The navigation interface showed where the projected edge of the blackout zone was and our time to exit. It was somewhere in the upper atmosphere, that part where it stops being atmosphere and starts being space, I don't know what it's called and ART-drone was drifting, watching *World Hoppers*, and I didn't want to disturb it by asking.

Minutes passed and the humans were starting to relax, folding down environmental suit helmets and hoods. Tarik and Ratthi were monitoring controls but had started a conversation in their private feed. Iris was still watching the navigation interface but absently patting ART-drone. Leonide sank back in her seat and let out a long breath of relief. I was almost relaxed, too; ART has nice shuttles and I liked this one. The upholstery was in good shape and it didn't smell like human feet. We were minutes from ART-prime and safety.

We came out of the dust cloud and the pathfinder in the lead pinged me a warning right before its input went dead. I sat up and said, "Incoming."

Leonide threw a startled look at me. Tarik flicked through interfaces, pulling up the exterior cameras. His voice tense and controlled, he said, "There it is."

"Oh no," Ratthi whispered.

I already knew from the pathfinders' visual data. Yeah, there it was. The armed Barish-Estranza shuttle, coming up at us from below at an angle, closing in.

Her face grim, Iris said, "SecUnit, if you need me to authorize deadly force—"

I didn't, but it's always nice when they do.

I'd put the pathfinders in a variation of drone formation that can be used for both scouting and defense. Anticipating the pulse attack and trajectory, bot pilot did something that made the shuttle jerk and dip. With bot pilot assisting with the navigation, I sent one pathfinder into the path of the estimated trajectory and the B-E shuttle's pulse struck it instead. The pathfinder exploded.

The B-E shuttle prepared to fire again, but its blackout-limited scan would be full of noise from that explosion. It didn't see the second pathfinder I'd already put into motion. It finished its dive with an impact directly on the B-E shuttle's nose.

The shuttle fell away, still intact but probably dealing with damage, a disoriented bot pilot, and a terrified human crew.

Our shuttle powered upward, back on course and widening the distance between us.

———

The humans were tense and quiet, waiting as the wind dropped away and it started to get dark. We were up there now in space or still in some sort of transition zone, but there was no sign of the B-E shuttle following us.

I picked up whispers in the feed and comm, and it freaked me out until I realized I was stupid. "We're coming out of the blackout zone," I said. Bot pilot was reaching for ART-prime, sorting all the communication signals for us.

Tarik studied the interface. "Iris, there's another ship. It's a big—" He let out his breath and made a hooting noise of relief. "We're picking up a University ID beacon. It's one of ours."

Ratthi slumped in his seat. "Oh, finally. What a ride."

Iris got on the comm and called Seth to tell him we were alive. I backburnered her conversation and found ART-prime's comm signal. I sent, *We're coming in with possible pursuit* and sent it a vid of the B-E shuttle getting booped by the pathfinder.

Acknowledge, it said.

Bot pilot picked up a B-E comm signal. I notified Iris (we'd broken their comm codes two days after they arrived) and told bot pilot to decode. Iris added Seth to our team feed so he could hear and said, "Can you play it, please?"

I put it on the feed and we listened to several Barish-Estranza employees having a collective fight/panic attack:

"There's another ship, it must have arrived via wormhole but we didn't pick it up on approach—"

"You lame-skulled pieces of excrement—"

"Stand down! You heard me! What do you think is going to happen—"

"It's armed and powering weapons, oh high one, oh deity—"
"You stupid—"
"Stand down—"

Leonide said, "Please, give me access to comm." She was urgent, as agitated as someone like her could be. "That's my command staff, talking to the mutineers."

Tarik turned to look at Iris and she nodded. He gave Leonide access to the comm channel.

Leonide took a breath, her expression hardening back into a cool sardonic mask, and said, "You heard her. Stand down. That's an order from your supervisor."

The channel got so quiet, Tarik tapped it to make sure it hadn't gone dead.

We were close enough now that I felt ART-prime—ART—in my feed again. It took over the pathfinders I'd clumped around us, and they split away and turned back toward the planet. It was going to redeploy them now that they weren't needed to protect us.

ART slid into the shared processing space with ART-drone. For a brief moment, there was two of it.

ART-drone: *Which baseship?*

ART: *Guess.*

ART-drone: *It's* Holism, *isn't it? Oh, joy.*

I was monitoring ART-drone's systems and it was dropping toward catastrophic failure. I said, *You need to hurry.*

ART: *handoff initiated.*

ART-drone: *handoff.*

And ART-drone shut down. Suddenly, it was just a chunk of metal. Iris made a half-sob noise that startled me so badly I flinched. She threw a wary look at Leonide and said on our private channel, *Did they have time for the upload?*

Yes, I said.

She nodded and wiped her eyes. *I know they're the same, it's all just Peri. That the drone will be repaired and the next time we need it, it'll be the same. But still, when something happens like this, it scares me. I just don't want to lose any piece of Peri, you know?*

I know, I said. And I did know, and now I was having an emotion. Like a big overwhelming emotion. It felt bad but good, a weird combination of happy and sad and relieved, like something had been stuck and it wasn't stuck anymore. Cathartic, okay. This fits the definition of cathartic. It was like the way I'd felt when I killed the Target who threatened Amena and laughed at me because I was upset when I thought ART was dead. Except without the violence, and that only lasted a minute or so, and this seemed like it would go on a while. Nobody was dead and I hadn't had a relapse of my stupid memory thing. And if I did have a relapse, at least I knew what it was now.

Don't just sit there, ART said to me and Iris as it brought the shuttle into its docking module. *Console each other.*

I said, *You fuck off* at the same time as Iris said, *Oh, shut it, Peri,* and that felt even better.

Chapter Twelve

"**WHY DO YOU HATE** *Holism*?" I asked ART.

I was on the bridge, in the most comfortable station chair, surrounded by floating display surfaces. ART's interior was quiet; on the planet it was night over the main colony site, so half of our humans were taking a rest break. The ones who were still active were on either *Holism* or the Preservation responder.

It had been seven planetary days since the mission and we were finally working on getting colonists off the planet. *Holism*'s backup ship *Sum Total* was coordinating the evacuation of two shuttles full of Bellagaia's faction, and the Preservation responder was acting as escort and making sure that Barish-Estranza didn't get any ideas.

ART said, *I don't hate anything. I am discerning in my company. My judgment in this area is impeccable.*

It keeps pinging me, I said.

Don't answer it, ART said. *It's doing it to annoy me.*

With *Holism* and its crew and its two support ships and their crews as our backup and witnesses, Barish-Estranza had been forced to grudgingly acknowledge the documents Pin-Lee and Karime had prepared and admit that under Adamantine's original charter (or what they thought was Adamantine's original charter), the colonists were now the sole proprietors of the planet and could stay or go at will. We knew B-E still wanted to get at least some of the colonists to sign up as contract labor, but since the task force's implosion, they were mostly too busy dealing with their own shit to try that hard. The last situation update had said that the colony's main factions were getting ready to formally ask B-E to leave.

(Martyn had said he wasn't surprised that the Barish-Estranza task force had tried to eat itself. He said there were indications that intra-corporate violence was increasing, that it had always been an unsustainable system.)

(I really hoped he was right, but it sounded like something that would happen a long time from now, and I was mainly worried about now.)

The other factions of colonists had been continuing to negotiate with the tag team of Mensah, Thiago, and Karime. Like Bellagaia's group, they were looking at resettlement options in newly independent colonies outside the Corporation Rim that needed to increase their populations to be viable. Basically, they would be doing the same things they were doing here, but on a better planet with no alien contamination, and no corporate control or ownership. And the option to pick up and leave on the next transport if they felt like it. (I had taken that option once, so I could relate to how important that one was.)

A second team led by Iris with Kaede and Martyn was also now in negotiation with the separatists. They still weren't big on leaving or rejoining the other colonists, but they had committed to going forward with the idea of managing the planet as a place for studying alien remnant contamination. In four hours Mensah and Pin-Lee (Preservation was acting as an independent third-party arbiter) would be going to a meeting between the separatists and the University representatives from *Holism* to start working out the contract.

Part of the lab plan was getting the separatists access to a planetary feed and comm via hard cable connections to points outside the blackout zone. For now, we were communicating with them through pathfinder-delivered message packets. (AdaCol2 had requested copies of all ART's entertainment files.)

Holism pinged me again, this time with a message packet. I checked, and the packet was tagged *infrastructure proposals*. Also as part of the alien contamination lab deal, the University was going to repair or establish the infrastructure that Adamantine hadn't had time to install. This would be stuff like fixing the rest of the routers, rebuilding the satellite network, establishing transport to the drop box station, introductions to an independent polity trade network, hunting down the rest of the contaminated ag-bots, etc. All normal planet stuff that I didn't know anything about. I sent back a message packet that said, basically, that I was a security consultant and that wasn't my job. (Except for the batshit ag-bots, that was clearly my job. I needed to get on that.)

A message came back: *I could help you learn about it, if you're interested.*

ART said, *Stop talking to it.*

I think it's just bored, I said.

I don't give a shit, ART said.

Holism was like ART. (An enormous asshole who thought it was omniscient.)

(Yes, ART was not the only one. I was still processing whether this was a surprise, not a surprise, or a horrible shock. So were my humans. My Preservation humans.)

(It was weird to have so many humans I had to give them group names.)

I thought at first ART fucking hated *Holism* because it was bigger and potentially smarter. But after further observation it might be because *Holism* was doing such a good job of acting genuinely indifferent to ART's hatred. This was mostly reflected in a passive-aggressive competition to see who could use the most annoyingly correct comm protocol. The only fallout from it so far was collateral damage to me and Seth, because it was irritating the shit out of both of us.

I sent, *ETA on shuttle arrivals. Sum Total* only had two big enough for bringing up large groups of colonists and was offloading to both *Holism* and its own module dock to save time. They could have brought more ships, but *Holism* had already been en route here—too late to find out that preserving the main colony site was impractical at best and negligent homicide at worst.

ART said, *7.32 minutes* at the same time as *Holism* said, *7.3247 minutes.* The resulting silence on the feed was stony, except for Seth's exasperated sigh. (He was on the Preservation responder, sitting with the captain on the bridge.)

I pinged Three, who was in its assigned cabin watching educational videos, and asked it, *Do you want to listen to* Holism *explain planetary infrastructure to you? You don't have to if you don't want to.*

Three indicated that it did want that. It was still tricky trying to tell if it was actually interested instead of just saying yes to everything you asked it, but it did have that weird thing for nonfiction and educational entertainment. I connected it with *Holism* on the feed.

It wouldn't be too long now before ART could leave.

One of the first things *Holism* had done on arrival was deploy one of its modules designed to operate as a temporary station. Docked to ART, its crew and bots had started to help with decontaminating and repairing ART's wormhole drive. Once they were done, and the contract stuff was finished and the colonists were situated, ART would be ready to leave the system, with *Holism* staying here to work on infrastructure with the separatists. Mensah and the rest of my Preservation humans would be going back home on the responder. Amena had decided to apply to the University, but she had education modules to finish up at FirstLanding on Preservation.

We were going to have to figure out what Three wanted to do, or how to get Three to tell us what it wanted to do. Ratthi and Arada had been talking about putting together a team to work on a trauma recovery program for free SecUnits. They wanted me to work on it, too, which I think they knew wasn't going to happen.

I had given them a bunch of the data about my memory

incident, and they were going to get Dr. Bharadwaj to work on it with them. They thought they had enough information for a good starting point.

They also would have liked Three's help with it, but they were afraid to ask it, since they didn't want it to think it was being conscripted or something. Yeah, that was going to be an ongoing problem for a while.

So was my whole memory incident/thing. But at least I knew I could still do my job.

(I know I needed trauma recovery, I just didn't want to help figure it out for anybody else when I was still figuring it out for myself. But at least I knew now that was what I needed. I wanted to send a message to Dr. Bharadwaj about it—I don't know why, but just telling her stuff made it easier for me to figure out what I wanted to do. I had asked ART for a detailed description of what its trauma recovery treatment entailed and it had sent me the file, I just hadn't been able to make myself open it yet.)

(I'm getting there, okay.)

I was ready to get out of this system. I was never going to like planets, and nothing had happened here to change that.

And I had decided, for real this time, which ship I would be on when I left.

Do you know where we're going next? I asked ART.

Acknowledgments

It takes a team to make a book happen, and this book would not be here without the entire Tordotcom team, especially editor Lee Harris, Irene Gallo, jacket designer Christine Foltzer, Matt Rusin, Desirae Friesen, Michael Dudding, and jacket artist Jaime Jones. And thanks also to my agent Jennifer Jackson, Michael Curry, and Troyce Wilson.

About the Author

MARTHA WELLS has written many novels, including the *New York Times* and *USA Today* bestselling Murderbot Diaries series, which has won multiple Hugo, Nebula, Locus, and Alex Awards. Other titles include *Witch King, City of Bones, The Wizard Hunters, Wheel of the Infinite,* the Books of the Raksura series (beginning with *The Cloud Roads* and ending with *The Harbors of the Sun*), and the Nebula Award–nominated *The Death of the Necromancer,* as well as YA fantasy novels, short stories, and nonfiction.

Printed in Great Britain
by Amazon